Bluebird in Bodrum Bay

A blast from the past.

x x

03. 07. x y

Bluebird in Bodrum Bay

A Dan Sylvester Adventure

H. Allen Mann

iUniverse, Inc.

New York Lincoln Shanghai

Bluebird in Bodrum Bay
A Dan Sylvester Adventure

iUniverse, Inc.

For information address:
iUniverse
2021 Pine Lake Road, Suite 100
Lincoln, NE 68512
www.iuniverse.com

ISBN: 0-595-27877-9

Printed in the United States of America

To my four children, Larry, Christi, Chris and especially Sheri who asked for a third adventure. I like to think Bob would have wanted another one too.

.

The Wisdom of Nasreddin Hadja, born 1208 in Horto, Turkey, died 1284 in Akşehir:

A pupil asks: "Which is more important, Teacher, the sun or the moon?"

Hadja replies: "Surely, the moon. We hardly need light during the day now, do we?"

Acknowledgements

Again I thank the 62nd Street Writers for patiently listening to and editing this novel. I'd also like to thank Charlie St. Sauver, a long-time military and commercial airline pilot whose enthusiasm for Dan's adventures never wanes, for answering my many questions about planes, piloting and aerial combat.

The characters in this novel are entirely fictional but the places are not. Bodrum Bay is a true delight to visit. In fact, I met my wife there. Capadocia is a marvel to behold, Pamukale should be the eight wonder of the world, and Disko Hit is as fearsome—and loathsome—as I described it. As an Intelligence Officer, I spent many days in there during NATO excercises, and I'm sure military staffers assigned there still are.

Prologue

May, 1993, Southwestern Turkey

A cold dank fog, muffling all sound, hangs silently over Bodrum Bay obscuring all but the highest ramparts of stodgy Saint Peter's Castle anchored firmly in the center of the watery crescent. Like a creeping fungus, the fog slithers through crooked cobblestone streets shrouding whitewashed homes and faded apartments, even the ruins of King Mausolus' grandiose tomb, one of the Seven Wonders of the Ancient World.

It is nine thirty at night. Soon, the ethereal miasma will creep over dun-colored foothills ringing the city.

A weary but winsome fifteen-year-old steps from a tiny restaurant, her ten-hour shift over. She looks about furtively in hopes her father or brother is there to walk her home. Seeing no one, she edges along the narrow lane, walking so close to one side her arm brushes aging buildings fronting the street. Drawing her sweater tighter around her shoulders, she wishes she didn't have to work so late on weekends.

Suddenly, a dark furry creature darts in front of her. The girl stumbles, and nearly falls.

"*Ovmek Allah!*" she gasps, hurrying on.

Black cats are bad omens.

At the corner she pauses for a passing car. Few are out that night; most are near the castle; tourists making a night of it in fancy restaurants and garish nightclubs, unaware of swirling fog, chilled night air, and evil omens lurking in darkened alleys.

Continuing, she passes one such alley, awash with litter and fetid odors. She doesn't see the man hiding in wait for her there.

He grabs her from behind, one coarse hand covering her mouth, the other encircling her waist. The girl gasps for a breath as his powerful

1

arm squeezes her stomach and lifts her off the ground. She kicks wildly, frightened beyond belief, as another man grabs her legs.

Both men smell of cigarettes and beer.

Struggling to free herself, the girl is carried to the next corner where an aging car is waiting, the back door open. She cries out as she is thrown into the rear seat, but her voice is instantly stilled when a third man flashes a four-inch blade of steel at her.

The girl recoils, pressing herself against the car door as far from the man as possible, her mind paralyzed with fright.

Grabbing her wrist with a gloved hand and waving the knife at her with the other, the man barks at her to sit back and be quiet and she won't be hurt. The girl complies, too addled to do otherwise, her mind a void.

His tight grip causes her hand to grow numb. *"Lutfen…!"* she pleads, vainly trying to pull her hand away.

He releases her when one of her two captors slides into the front seat with the driver. The other man, standing on the driver's side of the car, pockets a few Turkish lire the driver has been given and disappears into the swirling fog.

The car pulls away and the girl's heart stops. Grasping her mouth, she prays her ordeal will end soon and begins to cry.

"Sakin!" the man with the knife barks, cutting her cheek with the back of his free hand.

The girl is stunned. Blood trickles from her mouth. She holds her breath but is unable to stifle her tears.

Again the man tells her to be quiet and lays the knife blade across her throat.

The girl cowers like a whipped puppy, thinking, this has got to be the devil or a messenger from hell. But what does he want with me and where are we going?

The man glares at her with dark sullen eyes, his face pockmarked. A thin scar brands his cheek. She has never seen him before, but the man next to the driver looks vaguely familiar. A fisherman like father, perhaps, but where are they taking me…and why?

As the car heads north out of the city, the girl gazes into a featureless night and wonders if she'll ever see Bodrum again, wishing she'd waited until someone had walked her home.

The man with the knife says nothing more to her. At least, he isn't going to rape me. Not yet, anyway, the girl worries.

The driver mutters something to the man next to him, followed by crude laughter. The man with the knife tells them to be quite. He seems to be in charge.

The driver says nothing more for ten or fifteen minutes, then speaks again but receives the same rebuke. He doesn't try a third time, nor does the other man.

Two hours later they enter Izmir. The girl strains to see a familiar object, a building, something she recognizes from visits to a favored aunt and uncle. But she sees only blackness, broken occasionally by a passing lamp post or faded restaurant sign.

Eventually the vintage car pulls into a brightly lit, circular drive of a palatial hotel. The driver stops. The man sitting next to him climbs out and opens the door for the girl.

She glances at his face. She is sure she has seen him before but can't remember his name. Frozen with indecision, she turns and glares at the man with the scar.

"Gidin! Acelem!" he growls, pushing her out, the knife no longer visible.

The girl scrambles to the sidewalk, followed quickly by scar face who throws his arm over her shoulder as if she is his evening's entertainment. When the other man climbs back into the car, the driver roars off; their chore finished.

Holding her close, scar face steers the girl up broad steps and through plate glass doors, tended by a man in a gaudy uniform who greets them warmly. The girl tries to protest but her cry is stifled by the knife pricking her side under her sweater.

The lobby is crowded with people but no one notices them. Passing the front desk, the girl again starts to cry out but scar face squeezes her arm until it hurts, stilling her last hope of rescue.

They stand before an elevator marked *Penthouse Only*, oddly enough in English. Withdrawing a key from his pocket, the man inserts it into a lock and turns it. When the elevator opens, he pushes the girl inside, holding her tightly until the door closes.

As the elevator rises the girl stops breathing, her body trembling with fear. She begins to feel faint, but the man keeps a firm grip on her arm as if afraid she might escape. But escape is impossible now, and she knows it.

Her body sags in defeat.

Facing them when the door opens is a tall, gaunt, Asian wearing a brocaded ankle-length gown with matching slippers and cap. He bows and leads her away without speaking a word. Scar face returns to the elevator and descends.

The girl shudders. Is this why I'm here…for this old man?

Traversing a short hallway the man bids her to stop with a knurled hand then touches three coded buttons inside a metal box mounted on a heavy oaken door—a formidable obstacle.

The girl's heart sinks, thinking, this is surely the end. No one will ever find me here, or even know where to look for me.

As the door swings open, he asks her name. "Sultana," she says, cowed in terror.

They enter a vestibule lined on two sides with wall lockers similar to those found in schools. He tells her in broken Turkish—more pantomime than voice—to remove her sweater, blouse and skirt and place them in an empty locker. Choosing one for her, he leaves through the door they have just entered.

As the door closes the girl hears the distinct sound of a bolt clicking shut, sealing her fate. She begins to panic, scans the room for another door, but only sees draped walls and metal wall lockers.

Torn with indecision and weary with despair, she slumps to the floor and bursts into uncontrollable tears, sobbing, "My life is over; I'll never see my family again."

✳   ✳   ✳   ✳

The giggles are sharp and distinctive.

Looking up, the girl sees two Asian women standing before her. She is startled because they've appeared out of nowhere. Only a few years older than her with round cherubic faces, they're skin is translucent and pale, as if they've never been outdoors.

Wearing only white panties and bras, they smile and reach for her. But the befuddled girl slithers away, which induces more giggling, followed by singsong chattering not wholly unpleasant.

Again the scantily clad girls offer their help.

Disarmed by their friendly smiles and engaging ways, the fifteen-year-old rises to their coaxing. But when they try to disrobe her, she backs away and again cringes in fear.

The two chatter softly to each other and try again.

Speaking in low, soothing tones, they slowly remove the girl's sweater. Then, indicating in pantomime that they want to bathe her, they remove her blouse and skirt.

The girl looks bewildered—frightened beyond caring, but in awe of the two maids with their soft smiles and lilting language.

In her underclothes she is led through a door, hidden behind a drape, into a steam-filled spa. Two naked women are talking quietly while soaking in a Jacuzzi. One is Caucasian, the other East Indian and both are beautiful. In adjacent cubicles, an olive-skinned teenager is having her hair styled, another, blond and voluptuous, a body massage. Both are tended by scantily clad Asians. An empty cubicle is obviously for manicures.

Two hours later the fifteen-year-old is transformed into a nubile beauty. Wearing a gossamer gown of white silk and lace with matching slippers, her long black hair loosely braided into a French twist, she is led down a long hall by a stunning woman who welcomes her, says she is from Thailand. With a face of a porcelain doll, the woman has rosebud lips, thinly arched brows and shiny black hair. Her finely sculptured body is sheathed in pale lavender satin, her walk fluid and graceful as if a queen.

They enter a room with high windows draped in ice blue, the carpet lush and soft. A circular bed, reflected in overhead mirrors, dominates the room. The girl feels oddly detached. Like she is another person, primped and shaved, and terribly vulnerable in such a diaphanous gown, her immature breasts taut and quivering underneath.

Fidgeting nervously but resigned to her fate, she prays her nightmare will be over soon and she will be allowed to leave this place of perversion and promiscuity.

A recessed lamp in the ceiling bathes the off-white carpet with a circle of rose-colored light. The woman leads the girl into the light and gazes appreciatively at her trim figure and full lips, brushing a strand of hair from her comely face. The girl's eyes are lined in black and shaded in pale blue, her lips cherry pink, her cheeks touched with coral blush.

Tears form but the girl fights them off by clenching her fists. Her freshly manicured nails, the same color as her lips, bite into her flesh as she cried inwardly, "Give me strength and let me return to Bodrum and my loving family."

Moments later the same Asian man appears. Standing in darkness just outside the circle of light, his angular face is expressionless, his skin pale. The woman responds to his nod by opening the girl's gown and letting it fall to the floor.

The girl tries to cover herself, but pressure on her wrist freezes her hands to her sides. "*Lütfen, Allah—*" she begins in a whisper, her cry stilled by pressure on her elbow as well.

The man touches her breasts, her extended nipples. His hands are soft, not unpleasant. He smells of lavender.

As the woman speaks to him in the same singsong language, the girl holds herself immobile, praying the man will be displeased with her.

He gently slides his hand down her flat belly and over her freshly shaven pubes, then forces his finger inside her. The girl flinches but feels the woman's fingernail dig into her back. Enduring the pain and the man's touch, she now knows for sure why she is there.

With an almost imperceptibly nod and a half smile, he withdraws his finger and disappears as quickly as he arrived.

Vallahi! It isn't him. But who then? Someone even more despicable?

When the rose-colored light goes out, the women picks up the fallen gown and slips it on the girl, then guides her to a Queen Anne settee illuminated only by moonlight sifting through highly arched windows. There they sit, and in a low modulating voice she tells the girl in stilted Turkish how extremely fortunate she is to have just been chosen as mistress-in-training for her fabulously wealthy *Hakim* because of her beauty, poise and innocence.

And that, if she learns her lessons well, cooperates fully, without reservation, and is found pleasing by the Master; she can enjoy a life of luxury beyond her wildest dreams. A life devoid of hardship and strife. A life of such opulence her every need will be met instantly by maids and eunuchs.

The girl nods numbly, understanding little.

As if to test her submissiveness, the woman caresses her body and kisses her lips.

The girl pulls away and begins to whimper. The woman frowns and says crying will spoil everything. When the girl stops, the woman tries again.

Stonily at first, the girl gives in to the woman's gentle hands, soft lips and probing tongue. The women smiles and pats the girl's cheek like a mother might a child. The girl warms to her grace and regal elegance. They stand and kiss again, their bodies touching.

At once, a bearded giant with a long ponytail and slits for eyes emerges from the shadows. Wearing only bloused pants, his bulging chest gleaming bronze, he is massive and unsmiling. A shimmering scimitar is jammed into a sash which girds his waist.

"Ovmek Allah!" the girl cries, shaken by his bulk, his fearsome height. Is this the *Hakim?* Do I have to submit to him? Oh, please, dear *Allah*, not him.

Paralyzed with loathing, her mind vacant, she almost faints. But the Thai woman quickly drops to her knees, pulling the girl down with her, and bows in total submission.

The girl follows suit. But the man makes no move toward her, only the ivory-skinned women, stroking her head gently.

Raising her eyes, she says four questioning words in yet another strange-sounding language—more guttural and harsh like Turkish, yet not Turkish at all.

The man smiles and pulls her face into his crotch. The woman doesn't resist. Instead, she kisses his bulging pantaloons, muttering what sound like words of affection and praise.

The girl gasps in resignation, sensing she will be next and knowing she could never do that.

"Allah, teslim beni!" She prays for deliverance and the end of her ordeal.

Chapter One

Late May, 1993

From ten thousand feet Chios looked like an iridescent jewel. An opal in the tranquil Aegean Sea—a wash of azure, teal and emerald. I banked the Bluebird, my eight-passenger Grumman Mallard, so Noli could see the Greek isle from the copilot's seat.

The eyes of the gangling seventeen-year-old lit up like a video game. "Is big, Señor Dan...like...like, my *ilha, Terceira*," he stammered.

Everything Noli said or did was fast—too fast sometimes. Born in the Azores, an autonomous region of Portugal, he served as my valet on São Miguel, the largest of the nine mid-Atlantic islands. Back then, I was flying for a man who owned two vineyards, and later for his son. Noli was only fifteen when he was hired, after loosing both parents.

So why was he with me, a thirty-four-year-old pilot with little savings and no income—save the remnants of my last job? Easy. With my love of flying, plus being gone so much, I figure I might never wed again. I tried it once—too much hassle, too much uncertainty. Never knew what to expect, or even if she'd be there when I came home.

And since I've got no kids and Noli's a good one—eager to please, full of life and wonder—I brought him along when my last job ended. Who knows, with my penchant for finding trouble, he might haul my fanny out of a jam, someday.

Besides, he begged me to come along.

I've only known him six months, but we've been through a lot together. One thing's for sure, I trust him more than my last girlfriend—perky Penny, the private nurse. Still don't know how she could have betrayed me like that. And maybe she didn't, not really.

Tightening the bank, the Bluebird responded easily. It's a sweet plane built in the fifties, so it's a bit long in the tooth like me but still reliable. In the eighties Frakes Aviation completely refurbished eleven of the original fifty-nine planes, converting them to turboprops, so the Bluebird is really not that old…nor am I.

"Chios looks like a fat comma, doesn't it?" I said to Noli with a chuckle.

He laughed. Noli laughs a lot and learns more English everyday. He should. I teach him new words and phrases every night.

"Where's the airport?" I asked Alexis, standing by my elbow in the keyhole-shaped cockpit entry. A former Miss World runner-up, she still looked good at forty.

When her millionaire husband died, after a five-year loveless marriage, I agreed to fly her home, stopping in Lisbon, Majorca then Palermo, where we finally slept together. We both needed companionship—someone to touch and kiss. You know, someone to make love to but not to love. She understood completely; said it was a Greek thing.

Agreeing to fly Alexis to Chios wasn't a difficult decision. I had nothing else to do and flying is my second passion. The first is what Alexis and I did on Palermo.

Besides that, I looked forward to soaking up some warm Mediterranean sun, seeing her beautiful island and trying out some good Greek wine. I'd learn to enjoy wine in the Azores and Alexis had promised that on Chios the wine barrels never emptied.

From Sicily, it had taken just over four hours to reach Chios, cruising at 180 knots. Alexis had invited us to stay with her family for a while—even permanently, the last said with a coy smile. Since the Bluebird isn't pressurized, I flew at nine thousand feet to avoid having to use oxygen, although it's available in overhead bins.

We could have made it from the Azores in three days, but we weren't in a hurry and I had a pocketful of traveler checks. My bonus for what I'd done for the Briaga family—what remained of it. A tragic affair.

Since Alexis inherited a bundle—splitting her husband's fortune with his sister, she paid for the plane, the fuel and hotels. I paid for food.

"Do you want to land at the airport or in the bay?" she asked, her hand resting on my shoulder. "The bay is much prettier."

I checked the fuel; still enough to land then fly to the airport tomorrow and refuel. "In the bay, I guess." One advantage of flying an amphibian, the landing choice was mine.

"Just don't lower the wheels!" she replied with a tease, although, it sounded more serious than it should have.

"Don't worry. I won't." I hadn't done it yet, but I suppose I could. Maybe I should teach Noli to check the gear each time before we land. Better yet, teach him to fly the plane, himself, make him my copilot.

The thought made me chuckle. Hell, I could even adopt him. Think of it: Dan Sylvester, proud parent.

It sounded crazy, but I sort of liked the idea.

✳   ✳   ✳   ✳

Lining up Chios Bay in the windshield, I reduced power and lowered flaps ten percent. The Bluebird entered into a slow descent.

The pristine island shimmered in the warm afternoon sun, the beaches glistening white yet almost deserted. According to Alexis there weren't as many tourists on Chios as there were on other Greek isles, making it a great place to spend time with a warm and vivacious woman like her.

"That's Asia Minor," she said, pointing to the rugged Turkish coastline on our right. She then returned to her seat.

I looked back and chuckled. Her fleshy front made it difficult for Alexis to fasten her seatbelt. "That's some gal," I muttered to myself. "Gorgeous *and* stacked. Make someone a mighty fine wife someday."

Continuing my descent, I scanned the sky for other planes. A six-deck cruise ship was crossing beneath us, probably headed for Athens, a city I hoped to visit someday.

Glancing toward Turkey, just ten miles away, the many historic battles between the two ancient rivals popped into my mind, starting with Alexander the Great. And even before that. Didn't the Greeks launch a thousand ships to rescue Helen from Troy, a Turkish city on the coast?

I searched my memory for what I'd learn in college about Homer's classic tale of the famous Trojan horse then yanked my mind back to the cockpit. "Stay focused, Dan," I murmured.

It had been a long four days...enjoyable, but long.

At one thousand feet the sea looked glassy smooth. It would be difficult to judge the distance between the water and the plane.

I lowered the flaps to fifty percent.

Pulling off power, the high-winged plane descended to the sea, careening across the surface like a flat skipping rock. To slow down more I pulled the throttles back, passed the detent and through the Beta Range, engaging the thrust reversers.

The engines roared mightily as the plane settled comfortably into the water.

As we did, I thought of Buster—the man who'd taught me to fly the Bluebird—what he'd said the first time I did that. *"Never do it in the air, Sonny, or you'll be in a heap o' trouble. She'll fall out of the sky on you like a stone!"* To emphasize the point, he'd slapped his hands on his thighs.

His warning had made such an impression on me; I never tried it in flight. But I always wanted to, just to see what would happen. Hell, I might need to lose a lot of altitude, someday…in a hurry.

The Bluebird mushed into the crystalline water, held steady by float tanks hanging from each wing. *"Òmorfo!"* Alexis shouted from her seat, clapping her hands like a child.

I nodded and smiled. As a former Continental Airline pilot, I still didn't feel comfortable landing on water, although I was getting more used to it in calm seas.

*   *   *   *

Chios Bay is guarded by a breakwater which juts out from both sides, extended on the right by an ancient stonewall, chipped badly and patched and nearly twelve feet high.

"That's Old Town," Alexis shouted from her seat. "I'll take you there sometime."

Following her directions, I entered the harbor and headed for an empty buoy on the left—well away from the colorful fishing boats, a small cruise liner and an oceangoing yacht—to a place Alexis had seen seaplanes tied up before. As I shut down the engines, I thought about having Noli slither between his rudder pedals into the nose of the plane and toss out the anchor from a hatch in front of the windshield but decided against it.

I'd wait to see if we could park there.

Twenty minutes later a man from customs pulled alongside in a motor launch and asked to see our passports. After showing them to him and answering a few questions, Alexis took his arm and drew it into her ample chest. Sporting the sweetest smile he'd probably seen in months, she asked him in Greek if I could leave the plane there and if he would take us to shore.

His scowl immediately changed to a grin. Nodding, he helped her from the plane, over the gunnels and into the launch. He even returned for her zipper bag and suitcase.

Alexis could charm a snake.

After Noli had secured the plane to a buoy with a rope, I passed the rest of our luggage across the gunnels to him, then locked the entry door and climbed aboard also. I never used to lock the plane; but this far east of Gibraltar, I decided I'd better from now on.

As the launch sped toward the wharf, I wondered why they built the harbor on this side of the island, away from Athens. Anticipating my question, one she said was asked by many visitors, Alexis explained. "The harbor was built to face east and the trade routes of Asia Minor."

Again she avoided saying Turkey, a hated enemy, and I was sure the feeling was mutual. After all, Turks are Shiite Moslems. Greeks are Orthodox Christians. Despite living only a few miles apart, the rival nations seemed to have very little in common.

The nearest large Turkish city I knew was Izmir, due east about one-hundred miles—thirty minutes in the Bluebird. An exotic place where rough-hewn men wore mammoth mustaches and fleshy belly dancer, draped in veils and spangles, writhed sensuously while clicking their castanets. Images from *National Geographic*, I suppose. Making me wonder what Alexis would look like in a filmy, see-through gown, or if Greece even has belly dancers?

Shaking the thought from my mind, I asked Alexis if her school chum, Sasha, was on Chios. We'd met on São Miguel—rail-thin, her model perfect face etched in stone.

Alexis gave a little chuckle. "Not here, in Athens...chasing a new boyfriend."

Ahead of us, a six-foot seawall buttressed weathered buildings—stores mostly with flat roofs. Crowded behind were more aging buildings, only with red-tile roofs. Apartments, I guessed. And behind them, a domed cathedral topped by an intricately carved steeple.

Beyond that, whitewashed villas dotted dry foothills, which rose to the crest of the island three thousand feet above the sea. To our left a wide sandy beach fronted a promenade where young people walked and old men sat on benches staring out to sea.

Crowding a patterned sidewalk, restaurants with faded awnings looked less than full. "Between seasons," Alexis remarked, again anticipating my question. "They will be crowded in summer, although, many more tourists will visit Aegina, Poros and Hydra, islands near Athens, or

Santorini, the volcanic isle. And, of course, Rhodes and Crete. Chios is farther north and off the beaten path."

"Or too close to Turkey," I added.

"That too," the Greek beauty replied as the launch pulled up to a battered wharf.

Stepping off the boat, her smile brightened. It was obvious Alexis was happy to be there. I was too. Glad I'd agreed to fly her home.

I liked Chios immediately—or Chora as she pronounced it—a bit run-down but friendly and laid back, out of the mainstream. Only Alexis' ominous hints about Asia Minor being so close and so unfriendly bothered me.

Looking back toward Turkey, a chill ran up my spine.

Chapter Two

The next few days were quiet and pleasant, a chance to rid my mind of perky Penny and the infamous Briaga brothers, filling it instead with scenes from an idyllic Greek isle, thoughts of Alexis, a lovely Greek woman, and a bit of Greek history.

Noli and I slept in a guest room in her parent's farmhouse a few miles from the city. When we arrived, her father, a short wiry man in his late sixties, effervesced at the sight of his only daughter, kissing her cheeks and hugging her affectionately. Looking rumpled in his coarse blue shirt and dark pants, his face deeply lined from a lifetime of farming, his greeting to Noli and I was more subdued but warmly received. His ruddy face made a sharp contrast to his stark white mustache and square-cut beard. A white tuft just below his lower lip added a striking accent to an already distinctive face.

Alexis' mother, on the other hand, was chunky and drab with no waist at all. But her welcome was pure Greek. Hugs for all of us, followed by a gush of excitement then more hugs. After that, she disappeared into the kitchen to prepare our meal.

Since neither parent spoke much English, I said little to them. But Alexis' older brother, Michael, who lived there with his family, made Noli and I feel equally welcome with a full smile and a firm handshake.

According to Alexis, Michael now ran the forty-acre farm, with help from his two teenage sons, although he looked more like a college professor—tall, angular face, wire-rimmed glasses and salt-and pepper beard. In broken English he told me that his cash crops were olives and tangerines, but he also raised goats, pigs and chickens, and his wife tended a large vegetable garden.

More Spanish looking than Greek, his wife had the sultry air of an actress but wore no makeup. Loose-fitting clothes covered what appeared to be a sparse figure. I only spoke with her briefly before she scurried into the kitchen, as well; but her sons took an immediate shine to Noli, hurrying him to their room to show him their most prized possession, an ancient clay pot they'd found while scuba diving in the Aegean.

Later, while thumbing through a family photo album in the living room, I heard Noli trying to explain his home island to them in stumbling English, which they were taking in school and anxious to practice. It felt good to be immersed in so much warmth and love, and I was sure Noli felt the same way, having no real family of his own.

When Demetri, Alexis' younger brother, and his family arrived, the greetings started anew. An accountant at a fish cannery just outside of town, Demetri had intense brown eyes and pursed lips. Guarded, at first, I wrote it off as being shy, although he spoke excellent English, having spent a few years in the states.

His wife, however, was a true delight. Pretty and full of energy, Martine laughed at everything. Her two daughters, a year or two younger than their boy cousins, were pretty also and obviously adored Alexis, rarely leaving her side. Especially, after she'd handed out gifts to everyone. It seems that Alexis had been gone for over a year and everyone was happy to see her again.

With the entire family inside an enclosed patio, each adult with a three-ounce glass of *ouzo*—a clear but potent anise-flavored liqueur that turns cloudy when diluted with water–Alexis' father proposed a toast to the return of his daughter. At least, that's what it sounded like to me.

The family followed with a resounding cry of "*oompa*," the Greek equivalent of "cheers."

Loud chatter among family members ensued, so I concentrated on a table full of appetizers, which Michael's wife had brought out: two kinds of sliced cheese—one white, one yellow; cooked grape leaves filled with rice, onions and dill, which were delicious, and a platter of smoked herring, stuffed green olives and cucumber pickles, all washed down with more *ouzo*.

Alexis cautioned me on my third. "Remember, it is half alcohol."

"But it's so good," I replied with a foolish grin, "and so smooth going down."

Ouzo does that to you and so does *raki,* the Turkish equivalent, but I'm getting ahead of myself.

Dinner started with Greek salad: layered lettuce scattered with crispy croutons, lively *feta* cheese, black olives, all drenched in tangy vinaigrette. With it, we had a hearty local wine which compared favorably with Portuguese wine, although, I'm no expert.

Next we had *moussaka*, baked eggplant and lamb with a tangy white sauce, also zucchini spears, cubed potatoes and freshly baked, hard-crusted bread served by Demetri's two daughters. We finished with *baklava*, a flaky filo pastry with nuts dredged in honey syrup, and *metaksa,* a decent Greek brandy—although, again, I'm no connoisseur.

Later, alone on the patio, the stars mere pinholes of light in black velvet, Alexis said she'd just learned that her favorite aunt on Kos, another Greek isle, was seriously ill and asked me to fly her there. "I'll pay for everything, of course."

"I'll be happy to," I replied. "Do we have time to see Chios first?"

Alexis' dark eyes twinkled like the stars above us. "Of course, we start tomorrow." Reaching around my neck, she then gave me a long lingering kiss.

Not trusting myself, I pulled away...eventually. Alexis had suggested earlier that we not share a bed at her parent's house but hinted that we might elsewhere. Despite being gun shy from my last two ill-fated romances, I was tempted, although I wondered what her family would think, her being wealthy now and seven years older than me. I knew we'd never marry and I doubted she would want to. We just enjoyed being together, sharing each other's lives for a brief moment. Nothing more, nothing less.

But then I could be wrong. When it comes to women, I often am.

       *   *   *   *

The following day Michael drove Alexis, Noli and I back to the wharf where she sweet-talked a fisherman into taking us out to the Bluebird. It was so easy, just a smile and a wiggle. I would have paid the customs man to do it, and he would have griped about it all the way out and back. Her way was faster and cheaper and made everyone happy.

With Noli again in the copilot's seat, I taxied out of the harbor and took off. But instead of flying directly to the airport, I let him steer the Bluebird on two laps around the island. He'd done it before and his beaming smile told me he hadn't tired of it.

"Maybe it's time you begin flying lessons," I said, taking the wheel after twenty minutes. "I started about your age."

Noli was still grinning when we landed.

       *   *   *   *

Alexis opened an account for me at the airport and made a generous advance deposit. I then ordered fuel. While we waited, I checked the wiring in the left engine. The generator light had been blinking lately and I wanted to know why. Poking around, I found a frayed wire leading to the igniter and showed it to Noli.

"Have to get it fixed. The plane won't start without it. And if it fails in flight—" I flipped my hand over in a diving motion.

Alexis found a mechanic and I showed him the wire, indicating that he should replace it then check the other engine as well. He told Alexis it would take him about an hour. *"Kalo!"* she exclaimed. "We'll go to Old Town. You'll like it, Dan...very historic."

Outside the terminal Alexis hailed a cab. Nothing coy about her; speaks her mind too and does what she wants. You either go along or get off the bus. I like that, as long as she didn't start thinking something more serious might develop between us.

The driver took us down a winding road to the city, then across to the north side of the bay where massive carved oaken doors stood open behind a grass-filled moat.

"Except for the moat, the town looks like it did in the old days," Alexis said as we walked along serpentine lanes crowded with fretted doorways that looked as old as the city wall themselves. Pausing in front of one such doorway, Alexis said, "This is where I was born, where I lived until I was nine. A family of six lives there now. In the old days, when the Ottoman's ruled, Christians were forced to live *outside* the city walls. Now the Turks, the mosques, the baths...they are all gone. The way it should be."

More hatred, I thought, wondering if Old Town was kept shabby looking and rundown to remind residence of those oppressive days, a little like Civil War monuments and carefully preserved battlefields in the States. A way to perpetuate the hate.

At the center square Alexis pointed out the stodgy Romanesque gymnasium, also the town library, then led us to a small museum filled with archaeological treasures. There, I learned that Chios had been inhabited since 3,000 B.C.E. First by Pelasgians who built the Temple of Zeus on Mount Pelon, the island's highest point, followed by the Aechaens, the Ionians, and the Persians, before becoming independent for a few year during Homer's time. After that the Romans held sway, followed by another few years of independence until the Ottomans took over in 1566.

No wonder the Greeks distrust their neighbors. And if that wasn't enough, the assistant curator of the museum related that, during a brief rebellion in 1821, Turkish troops under Admiral Kare Ali killed 30,000 islanders, including 600 monks, and enslaved 45,000 more. "The Greeks had their revenge, though," he continued proudly in near-perfect English. "They blew up the Admiral's ship, killing him and 2,000 Turkish soldiers."

He later admitted that Greece didn't gain its independence until the Ottomans sided with Germany in World War One and lost. A long time to hate…much too long.

I left the museum, with its grim reminders of past massacres, vowing to stay clear of Turkey. It couldn't be a pleasant place, not like Greece, anyway.

The thought persisted, even as a cab took Noli and me up a hill to the airport. Alexis would meet us at the wharf after visiting a few old friends.

Little did I know how short-lived my vow would be.

   *   *   *   *

Sunday, while Alexis and her family went to church, I took Noli up in the Bluebird and showed him what a stall felt like. Naturally, he wanted to try it, but I wouldn't let him.

"Not in this plane. We'll rent a Cessna 150 for that."

After explaining several of the instruments to him—his first official lesson—I gave in to a long time urge. Climbing to ten thousand feet, I scanned the sky for planes. Seeing none, I pulled the throttles back to the stops, passed the detent and into the Beta Range.

I could hardly believe what happened. The Bluebird fell out of the sky like an anvil.

Straining against our seat belts, as if I'd slammed on the brakes during a high-speed car chase, we dropped five thousand feet before I realized what had happened. The plane would have stalled, I'm sure, if I hadn't dropped the nose and regained airspeed.

Climbing out, I vowed never to do that again unless I needed to lose a lot of altitude in a hurry. Although, heaven only knows why I'd ever need to lose that much altitude in that big a hurry. I could have torn a wing off.

"Sorry about that," I mumbled to Noli, still frozen with fear in the copilot's seat. "I just wanted to see what would happen."

"What *did* happen?" he gasped, his face pale, his eyes filled with unshed tears.

"I actuated the thrust reversers...turned them on, which feathered the props and killed our forward momentum." I knew he didn't understand. I was just trying to ease his anxiety. "I shouldn't have done it with you on board. Don't worry. I won't do it again."

He just nodded and gave me a weak smile.

❊   ❊   ❊   ❊

That afternoon Alexis borrowed Demetri's ten-year old Porsche and drove me to Nea Moni, the most visited place on the island. Climbing into the foothills, the air smelled surprisingly sweet. Thyme and honeysuckle, she said.

With the windows down, Alexis' long black hair whipped wildly in the wind. The speedometer hovered near one hundred kilometers, too fast for a winding country road. But then that's Alexis, always in a hurry, living life to the fullest.

In the distance I heard the faint peal of church bells.

"That's where we're going," she said, shifting down to negotiate a tight turn. "A Byzantine church and convent built in the year of our Lord, 1042."

"It's hard to fathom anything that old," I replied. "Fourteen hundred and ninety two, when Columbus sailed the ocean blue, seems old to me."

Alexis drove as if in a Monaco road race, taking each turn to the limit, the Porsche edging much too close to one hundred foot drop-offs. She laughed. "That's funny because this is the *new* church, built on top the old one where three hermits once saw a vision of Virgin Mary."

I shook my head. "She was seen in many places, Portugal, France. Why not Chios?"

Again she laughed but kept her eyes glued to the road, despite the panoramic views afforded us at every other turn. In between, I saw herds of white goats grazing amidst groves of ancient olive trees.

Halfway up the mountain she pulled over for a view of Chios Bay and the Aegean beyond, sparkling like Cinderella's slipper. A newly arrived yacht, princely and sleek, was moored just inside the breakwater, making the Bluebird look like a tiny blue dot.

I asked if she recognized the boat. She shook her head. "Greek shipping tycoons come here occasionally but not like before. Ari Onassis used to stop here on his way from his villa in Izmir to his mansion in Athens."

"Why don't they stop now?" I asked.

"The bubble burst. On the south end of the island, there is a large stand of Terebinth trees only found on Chios. From the bark they collect resin used in paints, textiles, cosmetics, many things. There was much wealth here then but synthetics have replaced it, so most of the money is gone now."

She started the car moving again. "Only a few wealthy men remain. You'll meet one tonight. An old friend who lives in a marvelous manor house. Unlike others, he worries about the island's economy, thinks we depend too much on tourism. You'll like him. He's well-traveled like you, even owned an airplane once."

Alexis paused to make another tight turn then laughed. "I'll tell you a sad but true story about the widow of one of those wealthy landholders. She had a burial chapel built for her dearly departed husband then hired four priests to pray for *her* soul day and night in six-hour shifts to insure that she would enter paradise when she died. But when the city council asked her to build a road to the chapel so others could use it, she refused. She told them to build the road themselves, on an island filled with poor people and few jobs."

"What happened?"

"The road wasn't built for many years, yet four priests kept praying for her long after she died."

I shook my head, unable to fathom that kind of wealth or arrogance.

Cresting the top of a hill, Alexis pulled over at another vista point. "I love this spot," she said, patting my hand, a loving look in her deep brown eyes.

I pulled my hand away and looked at the view. Don't get me wrong. I'm not opposed to romance and Alexis looked exceptionally beautiful that day. I just didn't want to jump into anything right away. Anything serious, that is.

    *   *   *   *

Nea Moni is a massive structure, highlighted with salmon-colored floors decorated with intricate mosaics. One depicts Jesus saving Adam and Eve from eternal damnation, another, his betrayal in the Garden of Gethsemane. Also impressive is a glass-front cabinet filled with skulls from the 1821 massacre; and close by a grandfather clock set on Byzantine time which is based on sunrise and sunset.

We wandered through ancient convent galleries for nearly an hour, leaving me with a much deeper appreciation of the Greek Orthodox Church. And speeding back down the mountain, Alexis chatted gaily about Greek history and how much she adored Chios, giving me a deeper appreciation of who she was as well.

At the farm we were greeted by Noli and Michael's two sons, filled with stories about their afternoon of snorkeling and the pottery shards they'd found on the Aegean's sandy floor. All-in-all, a pleasant day but it wasn't over.

That evening, in a cab on the way to her wealthy friend's house, Alexis explained their relationship. "Mister Margoles was like a grandfather to me, although I never called him that, always *Keereeos* Margoles. Mister Margoles. He'll be seventy-six this year but he's still peppy and energetic, at least he was the last time I saw him. His wife has died since then and he may not be doing as well now. In fact, I'm a little worried about him."

"Any family?"

"Of course. Two sons and two daughters. Before they became wealthy, they lived next to us in Old Town. I played with their two daughters. And when I was fourteen, Mister Margoles paid for me to attend a fancy girl's school wth them in Athens. Hoping, I suppose, that his two girls would be less lonesome with me going there too. That's where I met Sasha. Remember the stories we told on São Miguel about our stay at a girl's school?"

"Yes. Those were some stories."

"The two daughters live in Athens now; but Simon, the oldest son, and his wife, Olympia, live with his father."

"How did Mister Margoles become so wealthy?"

"Hard work, mostly...and some luck. He started out harvesting bark on a Terebinth Tree farm on the south end of the island. He did well there and the owner liked him, so when the owner died, he willed him a few acres. Each year after that, Mister Margoles bought a few more acres, and when he had forty, he sold out—at top price, a year before the bubble burst—and bought an interest in the cannery where my brother works. Now the old man owns the whole thing, plus a half dozen other businesses. So many I've lost track.

"Simon runs the cannery—that's how Demetri got his job and eventually became head accountant—but Olympia runs the manor house. She's something else. A real tyrant. Don't let her big smile fool you. The other son lives in New York and runs that end of the family business. I haven't seen him in years."

The more I heard, the more Mister Margoles sounded like the man I'd just worked for—he had two sons also. Two sons I would have been better off not knowing, for all the trouble they caused me.

✳   ✳   ✳   ✳

The cab stopped in front of a ten-foot gated wall. A uniformed guard appeared from a cubicle. Shining a light into the back seat, he opened the stately wrought-iron gates by hand and waved us through.

At the end of a long curved driveway stood a magnificent house, columned in front with a wide porch. "A palace by Chios' standards," Alexis said before I could comment. "Built in the sixties. It has over twenty rooms...eight bedrooms, plus the servant's wing."

A starchly uniformed butler greeted us at the door and led us to the living room, where he said the family was waiting. Along the way, I saw vaulted ceilings capped with intricate crown molding, walls draped with tapestries, which deaden our footsteps on highly polished hardwood, and expensive looking furniture on Persian rugs. Antiques, I suspected. The real thing, of course, including the rugs.

Standing beside a rock fireplace, Simon greeted Alexis warmly but not expansively as did her own family. A short man in his fifties, I would hardly call him handsome, with receding hair and sagging jowls. But he wore an expensive suit and a black bow tie and had gold studs on his French cuff shirt. Along with a firm handshake, he gave me the contrived smile of a successful businessman as if tolerating our intrusion into his opulent and well-structured world but not fully enjoying it.

His wife, on the other hand, was more outgoing, with a hug for Alexis and a limp hand for me. Her eyes nearly closed when she smiled, which she did often, and she seldom stopped talking. Only mildly attractive, she had a clear but pale complexion, ruby lips, and was an inch taller than her husband was. Stylishly dressed in lavender with a coral scarf around her waist to disguise it, she looked every inch a duchess in her pretentious home, even to the diamond-studded combs keeping her dark hair tight against her head.

Compared to them, we must have looked like hayseeds, Alexis in a skirt and blouse, me in my only sport coat. That's about as dressed-up as

I get. I'm not big on fancy social gatherings and this was definitely one of them, at least it started out that way.

Moments later, the patriarch of the family arrived. His white hair almost gone, skin pale as if recently bed ridden, he limped into the room on a cane. Neither Simon nor his wife arose, but Alexis couldn't contain herself, rushing into our host's frail arms for an enormous hug and kisses on both cheeks, amid a flurry of Greek words of welcome and love.

It was obvious who we'd come to see.

With drinks in hand and seated beside Alexis on a beautifully uphol-stered sofa, the old man listened intently as she filled him in on her trou-bled marriage and how she'd lost her husband. When she finished, he hugged her for a long time then told her how sorry he was and how happy she'd come to visit.

This time, he spoke in English. To include me in his welcome, I sup-pose, which showed a lot of class. Sitting across from them in matching chairs, Simon and Olympia looked bored, although Alexis took little notice of them. I was glad she hadn't told them my part in her husband's death, only that I'd been supportive throughout her ordeal.

Further discussion was cut short when the same stiff-necked butler who'd greeted us at the door and served us our drinks announced that dinner was served.

✻   ✻   ✻   ✻

"…and please, Alexis, if I can be of any service to you, don't hesitate to call," Mister Margoles offered in English during dessert—sliced melon, mild feta cheese and rich Greek coffee. All three spoke excellent English, interspersing it with Greek throughout the meal. "Will you be living here permanently now?"

"It's too soon to say," Alexis replied, glancing at me as if I had some-thing to do with her decision. "First, I need time to forget, time to heal—inside."

"I understand perfectly," Olympia offered, holding rein over the con-versation as she had throughout dinner. "My sister lost a husband in a hunting accident and…."

I tuned her out and by the strained look that swept Alexis' face, she did too.

Later, in a room lined with books and mounted trophy fish, the three men sipped forty-year old brandy while Olympia showed Alexis some bone china she'd recently purchased. I know the age of the brandy because I filled my own glass the second time. It was so smooth it made the *ouzo* I'd had the night before seem tasteless.

"Do you fish?" Simon asked as my eyes swept the trophies.

"Nothing like this, although I did catch an eight-foot yellow tail off the coast of Mexico once. The last serious fishing I did was on the East Coast—the Outer Banks, we call it."

"What a coincidence," Simon said with surprise. "My brother fished there. North Carolina, isn't it?"

Before I could reply, Mister Margoles raised his glass for more brandy. "Most of these are mine," he said with contempt, waving his bony hand at the many mounted fish, adding as his son leaped to his bidding. "Simon isn't much on fishing; too busy, too much work."

"It pays for all this," Simon said testily, returning with his father's refill.

"How *is* the canning business?" I asked to defuse the awkwardness that followed.

"It has its ups and downs," Simon replied curtly, "a bit down, right now."

I was sitting opposite them in a straight-backed chair with curved legs and clawed feet. I was tempted to tilt back but didn't dare. "Do all your fish come from the Aegean?"

"Yes, but not all from Greek waters. There are several excellent Turkish sources. Until recently, that is. A man in Izmir has cornered the market and demands higher prices every month. He also controls most of the small-boat building. I tried to order a motor launch last month but his prices are—"

"Enough of the Turks!" the old man cried suddenly. "I don't know why you do business with them. There isn't an honest one in the bunch!"

Turning to me, he asked about my plane. Taken back by his reaction to the Turks, I described it to him, ending with, "...so you can land on water or at an airport."

"Interesting. Quite useful, I'd say." He then told me about the plane he'd once owned and the pilot who'd flown him all over Europe and the Middle East, adding to his son, "Maybe Dan could fly for you? Once you've had your own pilot, you'll wonder how you did business without one. Certainly more useful than a damn motor launch!"

"Perhaps I should," Simon said, rubbing his chin in thought while studying me carefully.

I said nothing, feeling like a sack of fish being judged for his cannery. Beside that, I wasn't sure I wanted to fly for him, especially to Asia Minor as Alexis was in the habit of calling Turkey.

Shortly after that Alexis and I left, again by cab, but on the way to her parent's farm, she seemed pensive. "I'm worried about Mister Margoles. He used to be…well, so much fun to be with…so full of life."

"He's seems feisty enough to me," I said, telling her about his reaction to the Turks.

"He's always been like that, most Greeks are. It's how he looks that worries me."

"It happens to all of us," I said, taking her hand. "That's why we can't waste any of it."

Kissing my hand, she pressed it into her breasts. Then, with a sigh, "You know, I should find a place of my own…soon, I think. Don't you, Dan?"

Chapter Three

Tuesday morning I awoke early. Looking out the window by my bed, a hazy dawn had just exposed the barn behind the house. Chickens pecked at bare spots in search of spilled grain. Demetri and his boys were herding four stubborn goats into the barn to be milked. The boys would be off to school soon, the oldest in his last year.

By then I'd seen enough of Chios and was itching to leave, to go somewhere new. Yesterday, Alexis and I had driven all over her picturesque isle, sat on a few crystalline beaches, saw some ancient churches and ate a savory fish supper. Now, it was time to go, and Noli felt the same. I could tell by the way that he'd greeted me after our daylong drive.

He was bored. He'd help Demetri around the farm but that wasn't enough to satisfy his love of adventure, or mine.

I would have taken him with us the day before, but the Porsche only had two seats. Besides, I sensed that Alexis had other thoughts on her mind. Her comment about finding a place of her own—presumably, so we could live together—still rattled through my brain. It was a tempting thought, but I had reservations about living with a female—any female.

It hadn't worked before. Why should it with Alexis?

Looking across at Noli, asleep in the other bed, I decided he was enough to worry about right now. But I did have to find work. My traveler's checks wouldn't last forever. Besides, I've always held that marriages work best if both spouses are close to the same age.

Alexis and I weren't, albeit she hardly looked forty.

It's also not good when one spouse has a lot more money than the other. Alexis was a millionaire, although you'd never know it the way she acted, strictly middleclass.

I suppose I *could* live with her for a while and fly a wealthy merchant like Simon Margoles to the Middle East and Europe. But that could become a problem, if Alexis started badgering me about marriage.

Admittedly, Greece would be a perfect place to fly a seaplane, plenty of islands to land on and isolated coves to land in. And with its range the Bluebird could reach all of North Africa, Southern Europe, even Saudi Arabia from there. And with three radios, IFF, VOR-Tacan, ILS, Doppler and four bed-seats, it would be safe *and* comfortable. I even had a collapsible liferaft stowed in an aft compartment.

But flying east from there still bothered me. Especially, into countries filled with Moslems, where Christians were called *infidels*.

Another reason to distrust and hate...even kill.

✻   ✻   ✻   ✻

By the time Alexis arose that morning, Noli and I had finished a bowl of Muselix and were enjoying a second cup of coffee on the patio, served by her mother. Alexis was anxious to fly to Kos, but she wanted to visit a friend first. "He will know if there is a cozy place in town that I can rent," she whispered, brushing my cheek with her lips.

I knew then I'd be in trouble if I remained in Greece for long. And making matters worse, she returned that afternoon with a bright smile and a sparkle in her eyes.

She'd found a place overlooking the sea which would be vacant in two weeks. "Isn't that great, Dan? I can't wait for you to see it. I'll show it to you when we return from Kos."

I smiled too, but my heart wasn't in it.

✻   ✻   ✻   ✻

I started my takeoff run well clear of the breakwater and at sixty-five knots pulled back the yoke. The Bluebird leaped into the air effortlessly, as if wanting to fly again too.

Turning toward Kos, I leveled off at five thousand feet. "No point in flying any higher on a thirty-minute run," I said to Noli in the copilot's seat. "Besides, we'll have a better view of the ships we pass over. See if you can spot the fancy yacht that was in the harbor the day you and Demetri's boys went snorkeling."

I wanted Noli to get used to looking all around the plane. Not just straight ahead.

Crossing Samos, an island even smaller than Chios, I dropped to three thousand. Kos was next. We would land on the south side of the island.

Thinking I might have drifted into Turkish waters, I banked right. At that moment, Alexis yelled from her seat. "Look, Dan! A fishing boat is in trouble down there. See the SOS sign on the deck?"

Leveling out, I glanced down but couldn't see it. Alexis came forward and stood in the cockpit entry, her perfume invading every corner of the cramped space. "It must be underneath us," she insisted, leaning over me to look, the full weight of her breasts pressing against my shoulder. "There it is. See? Maybe we can help them. Both my aunt's sons are fishermen...maybe it's their boat."

"Okay," I said, halfheartedly. "Get back in your seat and buckle up. I'll take her down and have a look." Alexis returned to her seat, her thick black hair brushing her shoulders. A handsome woman, I thought. Strong willed too...maybe a bit too strong.

A thirty-foot sailboat with slack sails lazed about a mile from the stricken boat, too far to be of any help and probably too preoccupied to care. It might not even have a radio. I wonder if the fishing boat has one. Maybe not, it looks pretty old and beat up.

Circling the boat, the SOS sign became clearer to me.

I started to descend, thinking, why would they paint a sign like that on the deck? Why not use a cloth or paper?

Turning, I yelled back at Alexis, "Don't Greek fishing boats have radios? Why don't they just call someone for help?"

She shook her head. "My cousins didn't when I visited them five years ago."

Surprised, I continued my descent, but second thoughts clouded my mind. It just didn't add up. The painted sign, the placement of the boat—in Turkish waters or Greek.

My heightened fear of Turks made my stomach begin to roil.

At five hundred feet I scanned the fifty-foot vessel from stem to stern. Wallowing in a glassy sea, it didn't seem out of place or suspicious, other than the painted SOS sign.

I decided to take the Bluebird down and have a look.

Descending to fifty feet, I eased off the power. Seconds later, the Mallard skipped along shimmering wavelets until I engaged the thrust reversers. The engines roared mightily, water spraying on the windshield as the plane slowed, coming to rest about two hundred yards from the ill-fated boat.

Two men were waving at us from a chipped and faded upper deck. No wonder they lost an engine. The boat looks older than Methuselah and in desperate need of repairs.

I taxied closer. A third man stood inside a cubicle enclosing the helm.

Why would he be in there, if the ship had no power? Again, something about this smelled fishy and it wasn't just the boat. We weren't even sure they were Greek? There was no flag on the stern. What if they turned out to be Turks?

Clenching the wheel tighter, a hard knot formed in my stomach. It was then I saw a fourth man, a boy really, his face in a porthole below deck, along with a glint of metal.

A gun? I wasn't sure, but a sick feeling turned my breakfast into bile.

I grabbed Noli's sleeve and pulled him down. "Stay out of sight, just in case."

He did what I said but looked at me with questioning eyes.

"I don't what the fishermen to know you are here, in case…" I paused then said no more, not wanting to scare him. Being overprotective, I suppose, treating him more like a son than someone who used to be my valet.

I started to steer away, not liking any of it; but Alexis cried out to stop, saying it *was* her cousins. "At least, I think it is…I haven't seen them in years."

Disarmed by her cry and against my better judgment, I turned back and slid open my cockpit window. Noli remained crunched down in his seat, hidden from view.

Alexis came forward. Leaning over me, she shouted out the window in Greek.

The man couldn't hear her over the roar of the engines, but he responded to her wave by pointing as if he wanted me to tie the plane to the boat then come aboard. He then pointed below deck and made several gestures I didn't understand.

"He needs help, Dan," Alexis said. "Someone below deck is hurt and his engine wouldn't start."

"Is he Greek?"

"I think so…he acts like it, but he's too old to be my cousin."

"Maybe he ran out of gas," I said half-jokingly. I wasn't comfortable tying the Bluebird to his boat, let alone boarding it. All three men looked like convicts, scruffy and unkempt. But then most fishermen do when they're at sea.

"Should I ask?" she replied in earnest. "Do you have some gas they can use?"

I shook my head. "Even if I siphoned off some fuel, I doubt it would work in that old tub. It looks like it's on its last legs."

"Do you have a first-aid kit?"

"Back there." Easing the plane forward, I jerked my fist, thumb extended, over my right shoulder. "On the wall in the latrine...you know, behind the curtain."

"*Kalo*. I will take it to them. Maybe I can help the man who is hurt."

"Not by yourself, you won't. I'll go with you. The one below may have a gun. He's only a boy, but I thought I saw a flash of metal. This might be a trick to steal the plane or hold us for ransom."

"Don't be silly. They're fishermen. We *must* help them...especially if it's just a boy who is hurt."

"Okay, but Noli stays here." I motioned to him to climb into the nose of the plane. "I don't like the looks of this, so don't come out until I tell you to. Okay?"

"I won't, Senior Dan," the frightened youth replied, as if he was still my valet.

I wished then that he still was, and that we were still back in the Azores.

*   *   *   *

With Noli well hidden, I taxied closer and shut down the engines. We'd have to use the liferaft to access the fishing boat, but first I had Noli throw the anchor rope out of the nose hatch, pretending to do it myself. I then went to the rear of the plane and launched the inflatable liferaft. Helping Alexis into it, I rowed the short distance to the disabled boat, dragging the anchor rope with me.

The Captain hailed us in Greek and thanked us for helping. Alexis called back then turned to me. "See...I told you they were Greek."

After we'd climbed aboard, the crewmember tied the Bluebird and the liferaft to the stern of the fishing boat and that's when our nightmare began.

Two crewmembers jumped me like jackals on a rotting carcass. While one wrestled me to the deck, the other slammed his fists into my face and stomach. I thrashed about wildly but the biggest held me down until the other had my hands and feet securely tied.

Alexis tried to help, pummeling their backs and heads, but the Captain pulled her off and threw her to the deck, causing her head to hit a turnbuckle. The sound was sickening, like a hammer slamming into wet cement. I feared she'd die and tried to wrest myself free, but it was too late.

The damage was done and I could do nothing. It was maddening.

I stared at Alexis from my prone position but she didn't move.

Suddenly, the boy appeared, brandishing a handgun, a Saturday night special. More sympathetic than the others, he knelt beside her and touched her bruised cheek.

Alexis flinched and drew away. At least she was alive, but she looked bewildered and made no sound.

The boy said something in a guttural language I didn't recognize. Alexis stiffened when she heard it and looked up, fear clouding her eyes.

It was then I realized they were all Turks. My worse fears realized. Only the Captain could even speak Greek. I should have gone with my instincts and landed in Kos.

*   *   *   *

We'd forgotten the first-aid kit and Alexis needed it badly. None of them were hurt at all. It had just been a ruse to get us on board. But how did they know that we'd be flying over them? Or had they baited a trap for anyone passing by—in a plane or a boat?

Now sitting against the stern bulkhead, thanks to the boy, I looked at Alexis huddled a few feet away. Her face had started to swell and her head was bleeding. They hadn't bothered to tie her, but she didn't seem coherent enough to do anything. Yet, moments later, she began cursing them for what they'd done.

The Captain yelled something at her in Greek. When she didn't stop, he came over and slapped her hard.

Straining at my bond, I swore at him too. What a jerk I'd been, sucked me right in. If only I hadn't listened to her and pressed on to Kos.

Undeterred, her face now bleeding as well, Alexis cursed him again.

With a nod from the Captain, the biggest cremember came over and strapped her mouth shut with duct tape. In the process, Alexis kicked at his groin and missed, receiving a crushing blow to the side of her face for her heroic, if not misguided, efforts.

Nearly insane with rage, I cursed him again. With hardly a glance, he slammed his huge fist into my jaw and then taped *my* mouth shut as well.

I felt blood running down my cheek and nearly passed out. In a way, I wished I had. I wouldn't have seen the grisly ordeal that followed.

With the Bluebird and rubber lifeboat in tow, the Captain started up the engines and cruised south. He looked pleased with himself; he'd captured an expensive prize. But what would he do with it—and us?

The boat reeked of fish, odors embedded in slimy decks and salt-encrusted bulkheads. Glancing beyond the Bluebird, the sailboat I'd seen before appeared to be trailing us but stayed well out of rifle range.

No doubt curious about what was going on. It wasn't everyday a seaplane landed near a fishing boat and was tied to it. Probably drunk as skunks by now, I mused grimly. It's well past the cocktail hour. I wonder how Noli is doing. Will he stay in the plane as I told him to, or risk trying to help?

There was no way he could, not really. The Bluebird trailed the boat by twenty feet or more. Still, I knew how impatient teenage boys can be. I just hoped he'd wait until help arrived, if it ever did.

In the meantime, all we could do was wait...and pray.

*   *   *   *

A bottle of *raki* suddenly appeared, the crew passing it among themselves until it was gone. During the second bottle, they began to sing and dance. In between, they listened to a battery-operated radio, which they had to coax to operate.

When the sky darkened, the Captain entered a sheltered cove. Two crewmen dropped the anchor. The boy, barely Noli's age, untapped my mouth and gave me a swallow of tepid bottled water then taped it shut again. He did the same for Alexis, who was more subdued now and obviously hurting. Her head had stopped bleeding, but her bruised cheek still oozed blood and was so badly swollen, her left eye remained closed. She again seemed dazed and incoherent and said nothing, just stared out to sea, darkening in fading sunlight.

No one seemed anxious to help her, which wasn't hard to understand. She was Greek, an *infidel,* a wild animal that *should* be left to die.

My heart went out to her. She looked terribly frightened.

I was too, knowing what would probably come next. Despite being Greek, she was also a woman and with a sensuous body.

Alexis didn't have to wait long.

The Captain was first. Even among scum, rank has it privileges. The two older crewmembers stood by to hold her down, if necessary. I didn't see the boy. The Captain must have thought he was too young to participate, or even watch, and sent him below.

Standing over Alexis, he smiled, as if relishing his mastery over her—over a Greek *infidel*. A simple nod caused one crewman to tear off her dress. The other cut off her panties and bra with a dirty fishing knife then squeezed her breasts crudely.

Both were laughing.

Alexis tried to cover herself with her hands but the two crewmen restrained her.

When the Captain started to kneel, Alexis lashed out with one foot, missing his groin by inches. Her eyes were wide with fear but the tape muffled her cries.

The Captain looked startled and stepped back. Surprised, I suppose, that she had the temerity to resist him.

Grinning, the man with the knife drew it lightly across her weighty breasts leaving a thin line of blood. Alexis whimpered. Fear streaked her once beautiful face...or was it rage?

A sick smile played on the Captain's cruel lips. With a nod, the two men grabbed her legs and held them immobile. Still smiling, the Captain then released his throbbing member and waved it in at her.

Alexis shook her head violently and looked at me. Then, her lush body slumped in defeat. She couldn't fight them anymore.

Grunting something foul, the Captain rammed himself into her.

Alexis winced in pain and I did too, berating myself for being here, for letting this happen. We should be in Kos with her ailing aunt. Or on a beach somewhere, relaxing, talking, even making love. Not like this. This is inhumane savagery, vile and disgusting.

Mercifully, it only took a minute.

As the Captain stood and zipped up his pants, Alexis lay still, her eyes seething.

Sick with rage, I wrenched in dry heaves. But each time I looked away, one of the men would punch me in the face or kick me in the side. They wanted me to watch. To witness how little they felt for an *infidel*, a non-believer.

One kick must have broken a rib, the pain was excruciating. It became difficult to breathe. I would have cried, but I was too angry, too repelled by what I'd seen.

The bigger of the two crewmembers was next and no more humane, grunting his pleasure in less than ten strokes. His partner followed, finishing equally fast and leaving Alexis even more dazed than before.

Then, more *raki* flowed, coupled with dancing and singing, their victim left horribly mutilated and barely breathing, breasts battered, thighs stained with blood, face swollen beyond recognition from slaps and bites.

Again I feared for her life—and mine. What would they do next? Did they just want her or the Bluebird? In which case, they might need to keep me alive.

Blessedly, Alexis slept—or passed out. I couldn't tell which, my mind in turmoil over the savagery I'd been forced to witness.

As the night deepened, the men grew louder but left us alone. They'd had their sport, ravishing a gorgeous Greek, watching her squirm, pretending she enjoyed it.

I dozed fitfully, praying they wouldn't do it again, not in her condition. She'd never survive another onslaught.

I was sickened by the whole ugly mess, so easily avoided if I'd only followed my instincts. Now look at us...at Alexis, an ex-beauty queen, horribly disfigured, barely alive and probably wishing she wasn't.

*   *   *   *

Alexis shook me awake when it was still dark, only gathering light glowed in the east. Almost incoherent and weak from lose of blood, she'd summoned the courage to pull off her gag then crawl to me. Pulling off mine, she tried to release my bonds but was too weak, dazed beyond belief, muttering, "Must get away, Dan...away from those horrible men."

Seconds later, she passed out.

Frustrated, my ribs aching, I could do nothing and feared Alexis would die without medical attention. I also worried that Noli might have seen all this and try something heroic.

*   *   *   *

Just before dawn, I awoke with a splitting headache, throbbing ribs and labored breathing. I knew my face must be badly bruised. It had to be after the beating I took.

Alexis lay across my legs, clutching her torn dress to her battered body. Her shoes, panties and bra scattered about the deck.

She sounded bad, gasping for air and coughing up blood.

When she saw that I was awake, she stuffed her Crucifix and St. Christopher medal into my shirt pocket. "Take them," she gasped, obviously in great pain, her face distorted, her body covered with purple and red bruises.

I knew she must be bleeding internally and wished I could help, make her feel like a human being again not a mutilated animal. I strained at my bonds but my hands wouldn't function, numbed beyond feeling from stopped blood circulation.

"Don't...tell...family," Alexis mumbled, her head on my chest, her naked body sprawled by my side."

I felt so helpless. "Maybe Noli will—"

"Promise, Dan." She kissed my cheek with swollen lips. "Too much hate..."

She couldn't finish. With a gasp, the Greek beauty was gone.

I cried, wishing I'd fallen in love with her, married her, and that we'd lived on Chios forever.

With tears streaking my cheeks, I stared into the brightening dawn and wondered what it all meant. What would happen next...to me...to my plane?

But when the sun arose, a perfect orange globe balanced on the blue-green horizon, my grief turned to rage. Someday, somehow, these men had to pay for what they'd done to Alexis. I'd see to that.

Chapter Four

When the Captain awoke and found Alexis dead, he had the two older crewmembers toss her naked body into the sea: no ceremony, no prayer, not even a sign of the cross. Only a muffled splash marked her departure from earth.

I shuddered with guilt for having brought her to such an unspeakable death.

The men obviously felt no remorse, as if they'd rid the world of something inhuman, an undesirable…a Greek. Struggling with my thoughts, I said a silent prayer and wondered if I'd be next. I felt so helpless. My mind seethed in anger, but all I could do was wait…and hope.

Shortly after the burial, such as it was, the boy appeared and untied my hands but not my feet. I relived myself over the railing while the big one held the gun on me.

When finished, I rubbed the circulation back into my wrists then touched my battered face. I had a large knob on my cheek and one eye was tender to my touch. I suspected it was black and blue. Besides that, my rib cage still ached, making it hard to stand erect, my breathing restricted.

Weak but alive, I hobbled back to my place and slumped to the deck. They must need me alive, I pondered, or I'd be in the briny deep too. Maybe the Captain thinks the Bluebird will be worth more if a pilot comes with it.

A crazy thought, I know, but this was Turkey, my worst nightmare. They'd already demonstrated their savagery, although, I doubted they planned to highjack a plane. Probably just rob the catch of another fishing boat and kill the crew—eliminate the competition, so to speak. I wondered if the Captain even knew what he'd do with the plane, or me, for that matter. He didn't look too bright.

Bushy eyebrows covered coal-pit eyes, deep-set and hard, his leathery face seared from the broiling Mediterranean sun. When he spoke, which was seldom, he grunted, mostly. But the men never questioned his right to make decisions for them—even life-threatening ones, like raping and beating a beautiful women to death—a Greek woman.

Heartened when the boy didn't retie my hands or replace the gag, I thought about Noli. Had he slept through the mayhem? Or had he seen it all and desperately wanted to free me somehow?

Glancing back at the Bluebird, I noticed the tiny trapdoor in the nose, put there by a previous owner—a gunner in World War II with dreams of reliving past glory. It wasn't tightly shut.

Noli *had* been watching, but what had he seen? More importantly, what would he do about it? What *could* he do about it?

I looked about furtively. No one else seemed to have noticed the trapdoor.

"Thank God for that," I muttered to myself.

*   *   *   *

The boat continued south through calm seas, swaying easily from side to side. A westerly breeze wasn't enough to keep flies away from fish-parts encrusted in the deck. To keep from becoming seasick, I focused on the horizon and kept my eyes open. I would have taken deeper breaths but my ribs ached each time I tried.

While at sea the Captain never left the helm, and only when the boat had been anchored had he spoken to me. Once, after the third crewmember had raped Alexis, he knelt down and asked in broken English if I was an American, pronouncing it, "A-mer-ri-can."

The question was so filled with contempt I hesitated answering.

It didn't matter. Straightening up, the Captain spit in my face then pissed on me.

*   *   *   *

At midday, my ankles throbbing from being bound so tightly, my ribs aching even with shallow breaths, we stopped at a crumbling Turkish village nestled between scorched, low-lying hills dotted with sparce vegetation and void of trees. The decrepit pier could barely accommodate the scruffy-looking fishingboat. A dirt road flanked by rundown buildings skirted the waterfront.

The Captain shouted several admonishments at the teenage boy—presumable to watch over me carefully—then left the boat with the two older men.

The boy waved at them then looked at me, his eyes brimming with suspicion.

I asked for water, faint from the rising heat and hours of shallow breathing.

"*Hayir su. Yasaktir!*" he shouted, shaking his head.

"Please," I returned, needing water for my cracked lips and bruised face as well.

"No talk!" he said in English, which surprised me. Then, suddenly, he became agitated and began waving his hands about wildly. "You GOD DAMN A-mer-i-can!"

Stepping closer, he spit in my direction, missing me by several yards. It was more a sigh of contempt than a desire to drench me as the Captain had the night before.

Taking another tack, I edged toward him a few feet and pointed to my mouth. I wanted him to realize that, although my ankles were tied, I might still be a threat to him.

For a moment I thought he might relent. Instead, he hurried below and returned with the handgun. The Captain had obviously left it for him, telling him not to use it unless he had to. He waved at me to return to where I was and threatened to shoot me if I didn't.

I doubted he would have but slid back anyway.

For the next hour we had a Mexican standoff. He did nothing more, except avoid looking at me, and I did nothing either. During that time no one came near the boat. Even if they had, they wouldn't have understood me if I'd called to them.

Once, when my youthful guard's attention was distracted by a pair of sea gulls flying overhead in search of scraps, I glanced back at the Bluebird bobbing gently behind us. The trapdoor remained tightly shut.

Had Noli given up trying to help me? He was so close—only a few feet away, yet so far...too far to jump onboard. Besides, my guard had a gun.

Suddenly, I remembered something. There was a rifle stowed in the luggage compartment, but would Noli remember it was there? Did he even *know* it was there?

Probably not. Besides, I warned him not to leave the nose of the plane until it was safe. Maybe he will later, when they take me off the boat...*if* they take me off the boat.

      *   *   *   *

The men returned, and my teenage guard seemed pleased with himself for controlling me so long without help. *"See! I can be trusted,"* I could almost hear him say in the rush of Turkish that spilled from his mouth as the men climbed over the starboard scuppers. Besides eating, they'd obviously had a few beers as well.

Taking the gun, the largest crew member handed the youth a hard roll, a brick of cheese and a Coke. The boy grinned, found a scrape of shade next to the port railing and sat down to eat.

After relieving himself over the side, the Captain entered the helm and started the engine. Heading south, I looked for other boats and saw only one, a sailboat west of us about a mile. But I couldn't be sure if it was the same one I'd seen before. My mind wasn't functioning too well at that point, sick with grief over what had happened to Alexis, aching from my beatings and lightheaded from lack of water.

I was also worried about Noli, thinking how hot it must be in that cramped cubbyhole. Like me, he had to be desperate for water.

Not desperate enough to try something foolish, I hoped, shifting to the left to ease the pain. My rib cage was too sore to touch and the throbbing never ceased, making me wonder if they'd damage a body organ. I also wondered if the boat that had followed us yesterday, or the one west of us today, had radioed for help, but quickly dismissed the notion. If they had, help would have been here by now.

Eventually, I began to feel dizzy and nauseous, hardly knowing which country we were in anymore. The Turkish shoreline was visible in the distant haze, but these could easily have been Greek waters. After all, there are no borders at sea.

Late that afternoon we approached a crescent-shaped bay dominated by a magnificent castle built on a spit of land jutting into the bay's center. With grey stone ramparts, square turrets, two guard towers and a moat, the mighty citadel looked as if it had come from a Prince Valiant comic strip.

A fitting end to my macabre journey to the outer reaches of civilization, I thought.

Turkey, a country steeped in religious persecution and violence. A country synonymous with mystery and intrigue. A chilling thought suddenly came to me: What if they chain me to a wall in the castle dungeon, never to see light of day again?

I glanced back at the Bluebird. The trapdoor was open just a crack, enough for Noli to see where the boat was headed. I shook my head and was relieved to see the door close, the only contact I'd had with the Portuguese youth in twenty-four hours.

I hoped it gave him as big a lift as it gave me.

*   *   *   *

The Captain eased the boat against a stone wharf, projecting into a marina crowded with magnificent yachts, sailing vessels and catamarans, alongside a colorful array of small skiffs and scruffy fishing boats like his. Compared to the tiny harbor the Captain had stopped at for lunch, this one was huge and looked first class.

I heard "Bodrum" mentioned by one of the crewmembers and remembered the name from my map. A city in the southwest corner of Turkey, a rectangular country about the size of France and Great Britain combined.

Rising from the harbor beyond the city, interspersed with whitewashed villas catching the last rays of a fading sun, dun-colored foothills with low trees and dark shrubs guarded the bay.

Darkness would soon be on us; the thought filled me with despair. Where would I be held until the Captain decided my fate? Could I survive another night with no medical attention, no food and no water?

Thinking of what I'd witnessed the night before, my eyes swelled but tears wouldn't come. Alexis—beautiful, vibrant Alexis—was gone. I'd never see her again, never kiss her again…or make love to her.

The thought nearly made me sick to my stomach.

*   *   *   *

With the Bluebird bobbing freely a few yards behind the foul-smelling fishing boat, the two older crew members untied my ankles, then lifted me by my arms, one on each side, and half-carry, half-dragged me off the boat, across the wharf, and onto a wide promenade. In searing pain from my badly bruised ribs and faint from lack of water, I nearly passed out. A backward glance at the Bluebird told me that Noli was watching through the trapdoor, but what could a seventeen-year-old do, even with a rifle? What could *anyone* do?

I was tempted to say something to a passing couple out for an evening stroll, but they wouldn't understand—or care. Just another drunken sailor, his face battered in a fight, being dragged home to sleep off his stupor. Besides, the Captain was right behind me with the gun in his pocket. I'd seen him put it there after taking it from one of his crew.

Suddenly a loud cry pierced the air—high-pitched and tinny, almost screechy. Pausing, my captures looked toward the minaret facing the bay. It was the evening call to prayer. One of five I would hear every day while in Turkey, a vivid reminder that, unlike Greece, this was a Moslem country.

Fighting the pain as we continued, I was surprised by how few people stopped to pray. One shopkeeper knelt on a prayer rug just outside his store. No one else bothered.

Once, I stumbled to my knees and cried out in pain. The Captain grunted and prodded me with his boot. Swaying as I stood, my two handlers dragged me on.

Several blocks from the pier, strident prayers still blaring, we turned down a narrow lane. The smell of spicy food turned my stomach. I almost threw up. Until then, I hadn't been concerned about food, only water—too revolted by what I'd witnessed to be hungry.

Still, I haven't eaten since yesterday morning, I thought, as hunger pangs twisted my stomach. Chios seemed like such a long time ago now—in another world and another time.

We stopped in front of a faded door, which the Captain opened with a key. The crewmembers then dragged me inside, down a flight of stairs to a room barely six feet square and threw me inside. A deadbolt slamming shut sounded like a death knell.

Partially underground, the room had no other doors. One high window, encrusted with grime and cobwebs shed a little light...very little. The walls were lined with shelves filled with canned fruit. Bags of potatoes and carrots were strewn about.

A root cellar.

Slumping to the dirt floor, my ribs on fire with pain, my heart became filled with dispair. I had no water, no food, and it was obvious they weren't going to call a doctor. My only glimmer of hope lay in Noli. Maybe he was able to follow us. If he wasn't, the chances of finding me were slim. And even if he did, how could he possibly get me out of here?

Footsteps creaked on the floor above me and I heard voices—shouting, angry voices. Is the crew arguing about what to do with me? Hardly. From what I'd seen, the Captain made all the decisions.

Disregarding the noise, I pushed aside two boxes so I could lean against the wall. Holding my side against the pain, the shouting continued, but I couldn't understand any of it. Maybe they are arguing about something else. It was hard to tell. Nothing made sense anymore.

Since landing in Turkish waters the whole world had turned upside down. My world and Alexis'—beautiful, vivacious, fun to be with Alexis—had abruptly ended.

I started to cry. I couldn't help myself. And when I stopped, I felt a little better.

At some point the house became quiet. It's hard to keep track of time when it's pitch dark. I wondered if everyone was asleep, and if this was a time I could escape. But how?

Forcing myself to my feet, I tried the door. It was still bolted.

Ignoring the pain, I gave it a shoulder.

Nothing.

Undeterred, I looked up at the window, thinking, maybe if I stood on something, I could break it. A quiet stillness enveloped the house. That would be too noisy; and what would I do if I did get out...go to the police? Not likely. Even if I found them and they spoke English, they wouldn't believe me. I hardly believe what happened myself.

Collapsing onto a pile of rags, depression overwhelmed me and fatigue kicked in. If only Alexis hadn't seen that fishing boat. If only I'd left her in the plane with Noli. If only....

*   *   *   *

I awoke to dull gray light filtering through the dirt-encrusted window. It was morning and I was still sore, as much from being dragged through Bodrum and thrown into the root cellar, as from my beating. Standing with difficulty, I found an empty pot and filled it with urine. Before returning to my rag pile, I tried the door again. It was still bolted shut.

Again I looked at the window. Seven feet off the ground and only a foot tall, there was no way I could climb through it. My rib cage throbbed from the slightest touch. Besides, where would I hide if I *did* get out? From what I'd seen, Bodrum was pretty small. A place where everyone knew everyone, where a fair-skinned stranger with a beat up face would stand out like sore thumb.

I sat down and held my side. The pain lessened but not the frustration. I had to get out of there and away from Bodrum. At least they hadn't taken my wallet, passport or traveler checks. Apparently, it wasn't money they were after. But what then?

It had to be the Bluebird.

Sometime later the dead bolt clicked and the door opened. The largest crewmember stood in the doorway snarling his discontent.

I looked up at him, wondering why he hated me so much. He didn't even know my name. I could understand Turkish hatred for Greeks and vice versa. I'd seen it...here and in Alexis' family. But why Americans, a Turkey ally, a member of NATO. Maybe it was a Moslem thing, hating Christians since the Crusades. Or maybe they just hated rich people? Or people with planes? Or maybe they just hated?

A frumpy-looking woman wearing a blouse and loose jacket over pajama-like pants and a skirt—all in mismatched colors and patterns— pushed aside the crewmember with grunt of contempt. From a wooden tray, she handed me a sardine sandwich on a hard roll and a cup of tea, only she called it *çay* (pronounced, chi) and repeated it several times.

Thinking she might be the Captain's wife, I thanked her, which caused a brief smile to hover on her lips. A smile that said she was concerned about my safety, making me wonder if that had been the cause of the argument the night before.

The smile quickly disappeared, however, and her face became clouded with fear. Fear of what they'd do if she helped me, I guessed.

She didn't linger long and the crewmember locked the door behind him as he left.

Later, when the other crewmember returned for the cup, I asked him for more çay. Snatching the cup from my hand, he growled something unintelligible and shook his head.

This time when I heard the deadbolt slam shut, I felt as if I'd been buried alive.

Thirsty, sore and worried about what they'd do to me, I thought about what they'd done to Alexis—her brutal rape and her callous burial. They're complete insensitivity, and all for what? Spite for ancient wrongs? Hardly. Lust? Hardly that either. Just pure evil, and so unwarranted.

Clutching Alexis' two medals, I took heart in what she'd made me promise. *"Don't tell family, Dan...too much hatred already."*

*　　　　*　　　　*　　　　*

I awoke when the deadbolt clicked open. By the pale light filtering through the grimy window, it appeared to be late afternoon.

The same woman emerged from behind the same burly crewmember. From her tray, she handed me a date cake sweetened with honey and another cup of tea. But this time she winked at me, as if I might have an ally.

I winked back and thanked her several times.

Turning to the crewmember, she muttered something in Turkish. He growled something back and pushed her toward the door.

I tried to rise but a severe pain shot through my side. Crumpling onto the rags, I cursed my side, my situation, Turkish men...all of it.

Later, I got to thinking about the boy and wondered if he was upstairs. I might be able to overpower him, if he came down with the woman. From the looks of it, she might even help me. But what would I do then? Run upstairs and confront the others? Not in my condition. Run outside and call for help?

No way. I was an infidel in a country filled with Moslem.

      *   *   *   *

That evening I received a third meal, if you could call it that, delivered by the same woman and the same burly crewmember. I was disappointed, they weren't taking any chances. I'd hoped it would be the boy. The throbbing in my side had diminished some but there was no chance of escape with the burly one blocking the door.

This time my tea came with a plate of sliced lamb—mutton probably, full of gristle and laced with garlic—along with a piece of aging goat cheese. It didn't matter. By then I was ravenous and it tasted like a banquet.

When the other crewmember retrieved my dishes and left, bolting the door as usual, I again tried to sleep. Not much else I could do in the dark.

I dosed for a while, although I thought I was awake. You know, kind of in and out...fitful, worried about my future and saddened by my past.

Anyway, a soft tapping began to enter my consciousness.

At first I ignored it then I awoke, thinking it was the wind rattling the window or rats scurrying around the room. I'd seen several earlier. When the sound persisted, I tried to sit up but the muscles in my back had stiffened and a sharp pain shot through my chest.

Seconds later I heard a muffled crack followed by the sound of tinkling glass raining on the earthen floor. The noise wasn't particularly loud but it startled me. If I'd known the window could have been broken that quietly using a cloth, I might have tried it myself.

Looking up, I was stunned to see Noli's face beaming at me through the opening. "We get you out, Señor Dan," he whispered, his finger pressed to his lips for silence.

With great effort I stood, my side aching. Noli was about a foot above my head. Moving aside, his face was replaced by a muscular arm extending into my earthen coffin.

"Grab hold," a voice whispered in a heavy Turkish accent. "I pull you up."

"I'm not sure I can," I replied, reaching up. "I think my rib is broken."

Weighing just over one hundred and eighty pounds, I also wasn't sure he could lift me, or that I wanted him too. At that moment, my opinion of Turkish men was pretty bleak.

The man grabbed my arm anyway and lifted. I stifled the pain, severe as it was, and felt myself rising, then being dragged through the narrow opening. The broken glass embedded in the window frame tore at my pants and scratched my leg, but the pain in my ribs blocked out all other thoughts.

With my head and shoulders clear, Noli lifted also.

Once outside, I muttered my thanks then curled into a fetal position, holding my ribs tightly until the throbbing diminished some. When it did, I tried to stand but my legs gave out and the insistent burning began again.

This was hardly a problem at all for the giant who'd pulled me from my clammy chamber. Lifting me like a child, he carried me through a back gate between two houses and laid me in the back of a banged-up pick-up on a pile of ropes and fishing nets. He then covered me with the same blanket he'd used to deaden the sound of breaking glass.

I expected him to climb into the truck and drive away, with Noli in the back with me. But he didn't. Instead, he lit a cigarette and offered one to me. He seemed to be in no hurry, yet my greatest fear was that someone would see us and tell the Captain.

I declined his offer, happy I'd never taken up the habit and relishing the clean, fresh air again. Turning to Noli, sitting beside me in the truck as the giant paced nervously alongside it, I asked him why we didn't leave.

Noli jerked his head toward the giant. "His brother talk to Captain." He pointed toward the house we'd just left, although we couldn't see it from the truck.

"About what?" None of this made sense in my addled state. We should be careening out of there before we were caught. Before *I* was caught.

Noli smiled nervously. He seemed anxious too. "Captain owe him money. Brother come soon...I hope."

"What about the Bluebird?" I asked, fighting off nausea and pain.

"Is okay. Ahmet drag away...behind boat. You see...we go there soon."

"Who's Ahmet?" I asked, even more confused. But before Noli could reply, another man appeared, shorter but with muscular shoulders and a barrel chest. Looking in on me, I thanked him for what he'd done and introduced myself.

"Is nothing," he said in broken English, as if in no hurry. "I am Nazif Kesfin. This my brother, Hasan." He waved his hand toward the giant. "We go now...to your plane. Okay?"

When I nodded, the brothers climbed into the front. Noli stayed in back with me. A few minutes later, we passed a sign announcing Gümbet Cove. The marina was only a short distance farther, Noli said. And suddenly, there she was, bathed in pale moonlight and bobbing gently behind a fishing boat, only not the same one it had been tied to before. The lifeboat was tied along side it.

Becoming emotional, not sure I'd even see the Bluebird again, I stemmed my tears and ask Noli whose fishing boat it was.

"Hasan...the big one. His bother, Ahmet, brought it here. They are fishermen."

For the second time that day I cried. I couldn't help myself, as tears of joy ran down my cheeks. Suddenly, I felt reborn. As if part of my body—my soul, perhaps—had been returned to me.

Now if the damn pain in my side would just go away.

From a rear bed-seat, I watched as Noli deflated the lifeboat and stored it in the aft cupboard of the plane. I was anxious to leave Turkey. I'd had enough of the place, but I knew that wasn't possible. Not in my present condition and not until I'd avenged Alexis' death. Meanwhile, I was in the hands of two Turkish brothers, both with barrel chests, powerful shoulders and large mustaches, which made me even more anxious.

Why were they doing this, and what would they expect in return?

Whatever it was, I'd gladly pay it as long as I had my revenge.

Chapter Five

Hasan carried me aboard the Bluebird and laid me on a bed seat. "You stay," he said stoically. "We leave soon...hide plane."

It sounded good to me, so I smiled and nodded.

Later, while eating a meat sandwich on a hard roll that Noli produced from somewhere—I didn't ask or care I was so hungry—along with water from a Thermos I always keep in the plane, I asked him how he'd found Nazif and how Nazif had found me.

Before he could answer, we heard the boat engine start, rumbling loudly in the still night. I hoped it wouldn't alert anyone.

As the boat pulled away, it felt odd lying in a moving plane without the twin turbos roaring. I strained to see out the windows but only a few boats were visible.

Turning back to Noli, I thought came to me. What had he seen from his hiding place in the nose of the Bluebird? A concern I'd had since Alexis' brutal rape. So I asked him.

"*Nada*. I hear men sing...and shout. I no sleep good. In morning, I come out and sit here." He pointed to the seat across the aisle from me. "I eat sandwich and Coke...from cool box back there." This time he pointed to the rear of the plane. "Then *dormo*—I sleep...then eat more...then sleep until next morning."

"Did you look out then?"

He nodded. "When I hear splash. I see you, no see Señora. I think, she still sleeping, so I come back here and wait. When boat slow down, I look again and see *castelo*. See you shake head. I glad you see me. I close door. No look until men take you away."

Thank God, I thought. He missed the worst part. "Did you follow us then?"

"I try. I find key…lock plane, then look and men gone!" The seventeen-year-old raised his hands like a puff of smoke. "I look more but no find. It almost dark and I no like Bodrum…no like *castelo*…dark and gloomy."

Noli shuddered. "I no like when people look at me. So I leave…walk down road toward sunset." Again Noli motioned with his hands. Without them, he couldn't tell his story. No Portuguese could, man or woman.

"I walk long time. Cars pass. I hide…afraid Captain find me. Then I see sign. Say Gümbet."

The same sign I'd see earlier. "Is that where Nazif found you?" In spite of my keen interest in Noli's story, the longer he spoke the harder it was to keep my eyes open. The low rumble of the engines, the sway of the Bluebird trailing behind kept wafting me into Lala land.

"*Nao.* I find *grande* building…see window open—um pouco." Noli held his fingers a few inches apart. "I climb in. Sleep long time. *Señor* Nazif and his daughter find me in morning…in his boat *fabrica.*"

"Factory?"

"Sim…his boat factory."

"Was he angry with you for being there?"

"*Nao!* He say it happen before. Boys run from home.

"Then what?"

"I tell him what happen. He get mad at Captain. Say he help. Ask many questions. Tell Leandra, his *filha*—ah, daughter, 'Take Noli home. I come later.' So I go with her. She nice…fix supper. I eat…sleep some more. Tonight, we find you. He know Captain. Know where he live. He guess you in root cellar."

"That's incredible," I said, relieved to know there were at least some good Turks, maybe a lot. "And Hasan, the giant, is Nazif's brother?"

Noli nodded.

Too tired to think about it anymore and too sore to care, I forgot to ask who dragged the Bluebird to Gümbet Bay. Later, I remembered it was Ahmet, the sneaky youngest brother, a man who bore watching. But I'm getting ahead of myself.

Just as I was dozing off, Noli ask what happened to Alexis. I was sure he knew—had guessed, but I needed to tell him. When I did he cried, which started me crying too.

I wasn't the only one who would miss her. Noli liked her too.

       *   *   *   *

The next morning I could barely sit up. Looking out the window I noticed the Bluebird was no longer moving, or even floating. We looked to be in a sheltered cove backed by a scraggy hill maybe three-hundred feet high and littered with dark shrubs and fist-size rocks. The Bluebird was parked on a narrow beach covered with black stones, dirty sea shells and stringy black seaweed.

The place looked deserted—no buildings, no roads, no people anywhere. Good, I thought, that must be why they brought the Bluebird here.

When Noli awoke, I told him to get the first-aid kit in the latrine. When he returned, I had him tape my chest as best he could to help diminish the pain, then I washed down four aspirin with water from the Thermos.

Shortly after that, thickset Nazif entered the cabin, his wiry eyebrows looking as if they'd never been trimmed or seen a comb. His hulking brother followed. Both were grinning like boys who'd played hooky from school and gotten away with it.

Nazif did all the talking and asked how I felt. He smiled when he talked, and even when he listened.

"Sore," I replied, "but better. Thanks again for helping me out of a jam. Your brother saved my life. No telling what they would have done with me. I guess Noli told you what happened—how I got in that crummy cellar in the first place."

"Captain Tokolu, *yabani*...savage!" Nazif growled, his thick brows twitching excitedly. "What he do *medeniyetsiz,* uncivilized. We good Moslems. Koran say, no treat women that way." Shaking his head in disgust, he sighed. "I sorry. I very angry and my English is poor." Grabbing his brother's stove pipe arm, he added, "Don't worry, we get Captain Tokolu, put him in *cezaevi*...ah, prison, you say."

I was touched by his fervor. "And I will help you. But right now, I can't even walk very well. Is it all right to leave my plane here?"

"*Evet!* No one touch it here. Hasan will carry you to his boat. You ready now?"

I told him I was but felt like a jerk when his square-jawed brother lifted me like a child. Before we left, however, I told Noli to open the left cowling and disconnect an igniter wire. "The one I had replaced in Chios, remember? I don't want anyone flying off with the plane."

As Hasan carried me aboard his boat, which looked and smelled like the one I'd been help captive on for two days, I noticed a man at the helm. With the same chubby face, heavy eyebrows and thick mustache, he had to be the youngest brother, but he neither spoke nor acknowledged my presence.

"Ahmet," Hasan said without my asking. Hasan's English was obviously limited but like Nazif, he smiled when he spoke. His little brother didn't. In fact, he looked unhappy, a deep frown nearly hiding his dark and brooding eyes.

Moments later, lying on a faded mattress below deck, watching through a porthole, I saw Nazif, Hasan and Noli push the Bluebird off the beach and into the water. The anchor would hold her steady enough in the sheltered cove, but I didn't want to leave her there for long. A day or two, at most. Eventually, someone was bound to begin nosing around, even try to steal it.

Just as Noli came below, I felt the boat begin to move. Closing my eyes, the previous day flooded over me like a depressing fog. Alexis was gone—viciously raped and murdered. I was banged up so bad I could hardly walk. What have we gotten ourselves in to? What kind of country is this?

I looked at Noli. At least we're both alive and the Bluebird is okay. But when will we be able to leave this God-forsaken place—never to return? I'd had enough of Turkey for a lifetime, and we'd only been there two days!

*   *   *   *

Skirting the island, to the side facing Bodrum, Nazif came below with coffee, a hard roll and a slab of goat cheese, the only kind I'd been offered since Sicily. Simple fare, but it tasted delicious. Even the coffee, after I diluted it with water.

As I ate, he pointed through a port hole. "Karaada...Black Island. A famous spa...*sicak su*—hot water. It come up from island."

Looking out I saw several people soaking in a pool of steaming water held back from the bay by a low tidal wall. "Tourist," he said. "They no bother plane. No spa on other side." Pointing to where we'd just come from, he laughed, as if he'd made a joke.

Wincing, I laughed too, knowing my life lay in his hands. As it turned out, I could not have found a man—two men, really—more willing or capable of coming to my aid.

Finishing the coffee, I asked Nazif how he knew it was Captain Tokolu who had captured me.

"Bodrum…Gümbet, small towns. Noli describe Captain good…also his boat. He owe me money for repairs I do. He try sell your plane to man in Izmir, Bai Simaphong, *vahşi…savage!*"

It sounded like a curse. Then he explained.

With several legitimate businesses—import-export, mostly—Bai Simaphong also had several illegal businesses—namely arms, drugs and prostitution. In addition, he'd cornered the fish market in Bodrum and was attempting take over small-boat building as well. Besides that, several young girls had been recently kidnapped off the streets by disreputable men and taken to Simaphong's headquarters, rumored to be trained as nannies in England, mistresses in France, or concubines in Saudi Arabia, depending on their aptitude and physical appearance. A few, it was said, were kept for his own personal use.

Besides a fabulous penthouse in Izmir, Simaphong had a fortress-like mountain stronghold just east of Izmir. Called Disko Hit when it was an underground NATO facility, Nazif assured me that it could withstand a hit by an atomic bomb. Simaphong had bought it at the close of the Cold War and had it remodeled into a near-impregnable headquarters guarded by an army of assassins.

"That's hard to believe," I gasped, stunned and not knowing what else to say.

"Only in Turkey, I think," Nazif replied with his usual smile.

He then told me the main reason he visited Captain Tokolu the night of my rescue was to divert attention away from what Noli and his brother were doing. "My plan work good, too. Tokolu even pay *lire* he owe me."

I congratulated him on his effort and thanked him again. But for some reason I worried about the youngest brother. Dour. Unsmiling. As if he didn't want me there. Or else he expected to be paid for helping me. Make a fast buck. The Ugly American thing.

Back in Gümbet Cove, Hasan helped me off the boat. Loaded with aspirin and wrapped with tape, the pain was tolerable. To assuage my concern about Ahmet, I offered to pay him for his help.

A smile spread across his roundish face. But as he took a step toward me, hand outstretched, Nazif berated him as if a child. The outburst surprised me and caused Ahmet to pull his hand back and turn away. He looked furious, making me wonder if he might be a problem someday.

That wasn't what I needed right then, another thorn in my side.

Chapter Six

With Noli helping on one side and Nazif on the other, I hobbled from the old truck though a wooden gate into the courtyard in front of Hasan's white stucco house just a few blocks from the marina. The patio was filled with greenery and enclosed by a seven-foot wall, shielding it from his neighbors and the cobbled lane in front.

Inside the modest house, faced with faded blue shutters, stood Hasan's skinny wife, Phidaleia. And huddled behind her were their two children—both girls, twelve and ten.

With her dark hair pulled back in a tight bun, Phidaleia smiled briefly when introduced to me, only to launch into a tirade of Turkish on her husband and Nazif about how upset she was over them being gone all night and not telling her beforehand. At least, that's what it sounded like to me.

Besides that, she seemed unperturbed by my sudden entry into her busy life. Making sounds like a clucking hen she made me comfortable on the living room couch, from which I could watch the family come and go or just doze, catching up on sleep I'd missed in the last three days.

That afternoon Noli introduced me to Leandra, Nazif's doe-eyed fourteen-year-old who wore her straight black hair on her shoulders and parted in the middle. Her mother, an American exchange teacher in Bodrum on a two-year visa, had fallen in love with Nazif and married him, which accounted for Leandra's fair skin and near-perfect English, also for the rest of the family's ability to speak it a little.

Unfortunately, Leandra's mother died when she was ten, a critical period in her life. A time when young girls begin to learn about becoming a woman. With a mother to teach her how to use make-up and create a more attractive hairstyle, she might have been beautiful. But she only had a carping aunt who used no beauty aids, and a doting father. The result was a precocious teenager, more cute than pretty, who was more comfortable with adults than children.

She'd come to Hasan's house after school that day to help Phidaleia prepare dinner for us. She was a joy to talk to and seemed delighted to see Noli again, her dark eyes shining with pent-up excitement. Since his discovery in the boat factory, they'd spent several hours together and I sensed they liked each other. Noli could hardly keep his eyes off her.

After recounting the highlights of my escape, I asked Leandra about Ahmet, her uncle. Why he seemed so angry all the time.

She sighed and rolled her eyes, as if she didn't understand him either. "He lives in a shed behind this house. He used to help *baba*...ah, father, build boats. Now he fishes with Hasan. He was married once, but he—"

She paused to see if any of the family was listening then lowered her voice. "He gambles and drinks, and was mean to his wife...even hit her. So she left him...a big disgrace in Turkey."

"I can imagine. Any children?"

"No...Praise, Allah."

"Are there any more brothers?" Noli asked, edging closer to the comely teen.

"*Hayir*. Only Regina. She lives here too. She will be home soon. She is nice...a schoolteacher...widow of a fourth brother."

"What happened to him?" I shifted to ease the pain building on one side.

"Two years ago he was fishing with Hasan and drowned. Bad storm. Hasan was very sad, told Regina she would live here. Phidaleia wasn't happy, but Hasan felt, ah—How you say, '*sorumlu*'?"

"Responsible?" I guessed.

"*Evet*, res-pon-si-ble. A long word. I forget. If you stay here long time my English will get better." Leandra laughed.

"It is excellent already. Don't worry about it."

Noli looked besotted. I wondered if I was ever like that at his age.

I chuckled. Probably worse.

✳　　　　✳　　　　✳　　　　✳

When Regina arrived the children rushed to her side like a favorite aunt, received warm hugs then scampered off. About thirty and not overly attractive, she had a finely sculpted figure and smiled a lot, just like the others. Only *her* smile nearly shut her eyes.

Less outgoing than Leandra, after welcoming me, Regina listened
intently as her niece described my rescue. I couldn't understand any of it,
of course, but it sounded more daring with each telling. Heard all at
once, I suppose it was a bit hair-raising, and certainly unusual. Leandra
knew nothing about *how* I was captured; only that I was a pilot with a
seaplane, and that I was in Captain Tokolu's custody for several days.

Regina also spoke excellent English—British English, having served as
a nanny in London for several years before returning to become a
schoolteacher. She seemed impressed with my rescue and asked me
about my health. I told her I was still sore but felt better than I had yesterday in the root cellar.

Regina wrinkled her face in disgust. "Captain Tokolu is evil man, not
like other Turkish men. No one likes him. He beat his wife. She died
many years ago. Gave up, I think. I don't know how his housekeeper
puts up with him, except that she comes from a very poor family. Needs
the money, I suppose." She shivered her revulsion.

"She was certainly nice to me," I commented. "She fed me regularly,
and I think she wanted to help me...maybe even tried. But Tokolu is
something else...his men too."

I liked Regina right away. She seemed to have a good head on her
shoulders and a body to match. By Western standards, only her aquiline
nose spoiled an otherwise pretty face, although the Turks probably
thought that was her best asset. All the rest was just fine—wide smile,
bright teeth, wavy, shoulder-length hair, and a shapely body.

But all that seemed academic, right then. I was too sore to be
impressed by any young women...even a schoolteacher with soft brown
eyes.

       *   *   *   *

Leandra served me supper on the couch, just as the rest of the family
was sitting at the dining room table. Then Ahmet showed up.
Unexpectedly, I guessed, as if he didn't normally eat there.

I could tell he'd been drinking by the way he slurred his words and
waved his arms about. Phidaleia invited him to eat with them, quickly
setting an eighth place beside a frowning Regina. Nodding his thanks,
Ahmet sat awkwardly, almost missing the chair, then loaded his plate
with tossed salad. Aside from his initial greeting, he said nothing to me,
but I noticed he finished off a bottle of table wine all by himself.

He obviously liked Regina, eyeing her and patting her hand. He even patted her knee once, which I could see but the others couldn't. She fended him off as best she could and tried to ignore him, but it looked like a battle that had been going on for some time. Since she'd become a widow, perhaps.

I admired Regina's patience—removing his hand time after time, but I couldn't say the same for him. Childish beyond belief, he seldom stopped talking. I guessed, about his part in my rescue, by the way pointed to me and pumped up his chest. What a jerk.

Regina looked unimpressed; but Phidaleia seemed to egg him on, asking him questions and offering him more wine. Making me wonder if she was taunting Regina; still upset because she was living under her roof. A way of getting Regina to move out, perhaps.

*   *   *   *

For the next few days I remained on the living room couch most of the time, cared for by Phidaleia. She even flirted with me, occasionally. I'm sure she thought of herself as attractive and she did have a pretty face—deep set eyes and smooth complexion. But she had no figure at all. Her collarbones even protruded from her neck, and her arms looked like toothpicks. I like women with meat on their bones, but that didn't deter Phidaleia, especially when no one was around.

Since it was late May and balmy at night, after spending one night on the couch, she decided I should sleep on a fold-up cot in the front patio, which I liked better, not being in the center of things all the time. Despite this, on Saturday morning, I heard Phidaleia shush her kids to be quiet then send them out to play via the back door. Moments later, she was fussing over me like a new lover. She even brushed my cheek with her lips—with Hasan in the kitchen!

That's when I decided I'd begin taking long walks to get out of the house for a few hours, although I still ached some.

Regina was a different case entirely. That delightful creature had plenty of meat on her bones. I grant you her nose was a bit large, and some would say her eyes were too close together, and maybe her mouth was a bit wide; but to my sore eyes, she looked just fine.

Talking in the courtyard after dinner one night, she expressed concerned about the recent happenings in Bodrum. "Just a few days ago a fourteen-year-old girl was taken away...whoosh!" Her hand swept up, as if the girl had vanished into thin air.

Like Portuguese and Greeks, Turks uses their hands a lot too, making their stories seem larger than life, which makes them more interesting.

"You mean, kidnapped?" I questioned.

"*Evet.* Kid-napped. That is a funny word." Regina beamed. "What does *napped* mean? Kid...*napped*. It should be *kid-taken*. No?"

I laughed and told her I didn't know.

Her frown returned. "Leandra is afraid now. She knew girl. And just before that, in Izmir, another girl was kid...napped. We read in newspaper. Same thing. Whoosh! Leandra stays close to home now. Is good Noli is helping Nazif in his *fabrika*...ah, factory."

I agreed. To give Noli something to do and to repay Nazif for his kindness, I'd suggested that Noli help him while I recuperated. Both jumped at the chance: Nazif for the help, Noli for the opportunity to spend more time with Leandra. After school, she posted accounts and did paperwork in the factory office, and her smile always seemed brighter when Noli was around.

Regina continued. "I sorry. I don't speak English so good anymore."

"Your English is fine—a lot better than my Turkish. What grade do you teach?"

Her smile broadened. "Level three and four. But I hope to teach Turkish history at the university someday."

"Maybe you could teach me some Turkish history. I would enjoy hearing about it...from you." Suddenly my left side began to throb. Phidaleia had insisted I keep my chest well-taped, and if Noli didn't do it right, she'd re-do it. The doctor, who came to the house—a friend, didn't do much. Just gave me pain pills and told me to rest. Said it would repair itself, eventually.

"I would be happy to," Regina responded. "There is much to tell." Her smile was coy but sincere. I really felt she wanted to. Not just saying it to make me feel better—although it did.

*　　　*　　　*　　　*

Sunday afternoon, I walked to the boat factory to get away from Phidaleia. It felt good to be outside and on my own for a while.

Busy working in the office while Noli helped Nazif build the two rowboats, Leandra gave me her most infectious smile. But I also detected fear lurking behind her pixie face. Particularly, when her father left for a few minutes to pick up some supplies.

When he returned, I asked him about the kidnappings.

"*Çok kötü*," he muttered with a heavy scowl, his bushy brows twitching as usual. "First Izmir…then here, friend of Leandra. Both gone and police do nothing. I *çok* worry. Leandra worry too."

Remembering what he'd said about the crime lord in Izmir, I thought of a movie I'd seen called *Turkish Express*. About an American teenager in Turkey caught with drugs and what happened to him in prison. It was brutal, inhuman.

"Do you think it was Bai Simaphong?" I asked sympathetically.

"*Evet*," Nazif hissed, his jaw clamped shut, his tightly focused eyes spewing hate, as if the crime lord was from another planet. "If he ever try on Leandra—"

Standing, he smashed his fists together then walked away, unable to continue.

Later, he told me more about Bai Simaphong, his stranglehold on the fishing industry in Bodrum, an important part of the economy along with tourism. As he spoke, I remembered Alex Margoles comment after dinner at his father's house on Chios. "*I used to have an excellent source of fish in Turkey, now the prices are higher every month.*"

"And he controls boat building too?" I asked with surprise.

"*Evet*…everything. He own *büyük fabrica* in Bodrum. Get best jobs. I get little jobs." He pointed to the two rowboats. "He also own *büyük buz dolaba.*" He raised his hands over his head to show the size then shivered as if very cold.

"A walk-in refrigerator?"

"*Evet*. All fishermen have to sell to him now. He pay low, sell high. Make *çok lire*."

I only understood a few Turkish works—*evet* for "yes", *hayir* for "no", *çok* (pronounced *chok)* for "much", "many" or "very", and *büyük* for "big", "large" or "grand". But I understood Nazif perfectly and felt I should help him. It was the least I could do after retrieving me from sure death in a cold, dark root cellar.

Thinking about it, however, I began to worry about the Bluebird, leaving it so close to a favorite tourist spot, despite Nazif's assurance that it would be safe there and Hasan's daily checks on it.

Mentioning it to Nazif, he grinned. "I know better place, if you can fly. I show you. Hasan bring us back in boat."

My rib cage was still tender but I was sure I could fly, with Noli's help.

When I nodded, he asked if Leandra could come.

When I nodded again, he said, "Regina too? They bring lunch."

"Sure, why not?" I replied, knowing Nazif wasn't likely to leave his daughter alone anyway. And having Regina along would add some zest to the outing.

*   *   *   *

On a nautical map mounted on the wall of his factory, Nazif pointed to an isolated cove about ten miles west of Bodrum, not far from the ruins of Myndos.

"Good place." He grinned. "No one see plane there. Is better...you see."

"Sounds good to me. Let's go."

I knew with the Bluebird better hidden, I'd feel more like helping the Kesfin brothers do battle with Bai Simaphong. But before we did that, I had a depressing chore to do. A chore I dreaded: telling Alexis' family what happened to her.

Motoring back to Black Island in Hasan's tired boat, this time with the whole family save Ahmet—Phidaleia and the children wanted to come too—I thought about what I'd say to Alexis' parents, or not say. If I told them the truth, a blood bath might start. Something I'm sure she feared would happen. But I had to tell them something.

In the meantime, what if Simaphong's men struck again? Kidnapped Leandra, this time? I didn't even want to think about it.

*   *   *   *

It was good to see the Bluebird again riding low in the water; like being away from your child for a few days. After Noli and Nazif dragged it ashore, I had Noli open the right cowling and reattach the igniter cable. Following the women and children on board and seeing that they were all buckled in, I considered taxiing to the new hideout but decided against it. Too bouncy on them and my sore body.

From the left pilot seat, I yelled at Noli and Nazif to push the Bluebird off shore and climb aboard. By the time Noli had closed and locked the entry door and joined me, I'd checked the instruments and radios. All was well, nothing had been tampered with.

Leaving the cockpit entry door open as I always did, I could hear the family chattering excitedly behind me. It was the first flight for all of them.

The engines started easily; and taxing out of the cove, I told Noli to help me pull back on the yoke during takeoff to ease the strain on my sore ribs.

Fortunately, the bay was calm and the Bluebird soared into the air like a graceful bird. Since none of the Kesfin family had seen their crescent-shaped harbor or Crusader Castle from the air, they all kept their noses pressed to the windows while I circled Bodrum twice. Two seaplanes were parked in the harbor now, which was good. If I ever had to park the Bluebird there, it would hardly be noticed, except by Captain Tokolu.

With him still around, I'd never park it there. Even the cove at Gumbet, four miles away, wasn't far enough.

*   *   *   *

My landing near the new hiding place was fair. Noli helped me hold the yoke steady until the plane settled in the water and the thrust reversers had slowed us down. I then let him taxied for a bit while I held my throbbing side.

Nazif directed me into the cove, although Leandra told me later it was Uncle Hasan who'd suggested it, not her father. I wasn't surprised, only a fisherman would know of a place this inaccessible. Facing the Aegean, sheer cliffs dropped to a narrow beach cluttered with gray, house-size boulders. A grotto, tucked behind two of them, was deep enough to shield the wings and high enough to cover the tail, even in mildly shifting tides.

We spent two hours there, eating, talking—Noli and Leandra walking on the rocks, all waiting for Hasan to arrive in his weathered scow. Again, Ahmet wasn't with him, which pleased me greatly. I didn't trust Ahmet and guessed the feeling was mutual by the way he glowered at me all the time. He never looked me straight in the eye and we'd only spoken once or twice—a few clipped words. I sensed something sinister about him—cunning and twisted, besides being a braggart.

Despite the small part he'd played in my rescue—dragging the Bluebird from Bodrum Bay to Gümbet Cove behind Hasan's boat—he acted as though he was the central player in the elaborate scheme. It didn't seem to bother his brothers—they were probably used to his conceit—but it bothered me. He was definitely someone to keep an eye on.

*   *   *   *

The return trip in Hasan's boat took almost two hour, arriving in dimming light, the Western sky streaked with burnished gold. It had been a good day and I was tired, but I felt better than I had since my rescue and would worry less about the Bluebird now.

After dinner I spent some time with Regina on the patio. She was beginning to get to me, in a nice way, which was odd, since I'd sworn off women after my last one.

We spoke of many things, but mostly she wanted to know about America and if it was like England.

"Some," I hedged, "but not the same. Like Greece and Turkey, but without the hate."

✻   ✻   ✻   ✻

Monday I felt even better—less sore, and awoke with an idea rattling around in my brain. A way of cracking Bai Simaphong's stranglehold on Bodrum fishing. It's funny how some of our best ideas occur to us when we're asleep, or nearly so.

Later, I told Nazif about it, knowing he'd have to agree or nothing would come of it. Not surprisingly, he liked the plan and heartily concurred. "You fly...I sell. Is good...we make *çok lire*."

My plan called for Noli and me to fly Hasan's latest catch of fish to a nearby Turkish city where Nazif would sell it. I figured, with his gift of gab, he could sell anything—igloos to Eskimos or Turkish rocks to Western gardeners, which wouldn't be a bad idea. Turkey had a ton of them.

Anyway, while he was selling fish, Nazif could also drum up a few boat orders as well. All without Bai Simaphong's knowledge, of course, which I knew would be difficult, Bodrum and Gümbet being such small towns. But I also had another idea, which was even more bizarre. A way of getting rid of Bai Simaphong for good.

But that I would save for another day...when I was more fit.

Chapter Seven

The banged up cooler that Nazif found and Hasan hauled to the Bluebird in his boat was not large—about five-foot square, but adequate. To make room for it, I removed the last two seats, which I then inverted and tied to the next two. Hasan, Nazif and Noli all wrestled it into the plane with me shouting instructions but unable to help. I tried once but was rewarded with a sharp pain in my side and decided better of it.

I was needed to fly, not load cargo.

After securing the cooler, Hasan and Nazif carried a four-inch slab of ice from his boat to the plane and placed it into the bottom of the double-walled box, followed by the fish, alive and squirming in perforated plastic bags. I watched for a while then climbed into the cockpit. Everything looked okay. Again, no one had tampered with anything.

When they finished loading, Nazif appeared in the cockpit entry. "Fifty kilos," he announced proudly. "Turbot and mackerel, mostly...and five kilos s*ardalya*, ah—sardines. Cooler only half full. Bring more next time. Hasan return Gümbet now."

I nodded, wondering how many times he expected me to do this. Strapping himself into the first passenger seat on the right, he asked if the plane would be too heavy to takeoff now. "No problem. I could takeoff with ten times that much." I grinned. I couldn't help myself. It felt good to be flying again...and away from Phidaleia. I really missed flying. It was my life. It had been for fifteen years.

I knew what I'd offered to do for Hasan was impractical, but I wanted to do something to reward him for saving my hide. Nazif too, for helping Noli. I'd carry fish once or twice, help them with Simaphong, maybe, then move on—find a job, or another wealthy patron. Although, the last part didn't appeal to me much, not after the last two patrons I'd flown for. But not flying for anyone didn't sound good either.

Oh, well, I'd come up with something. I always did...even with Noli along. Or should I say, especially with Noli along. Didn't I tell you he'd save my butt someday?

Securing the entry door, he climbed into his seat as if he belonged there. This time I checked the instruments *with* him, telling him a little more about them each time.

Our fuel was still good. We'd used only a little flying to the sheltered cove...and on our fateful flight with Alexis, which seemed like a long time ago but had only been one day shy of a week.

Again I thought of my stupidity, landing like that, trying to be a Good Samaritan. I'd never do it again. The vision of Alexis squirming under those three men brought tears to my eyes. Then seeing her tossed into the sea the next morning, like shark bait—a bag of trash. It was inhuman, ungodly and despicable.

"Somehow, I've got to stop thinking about it," I told myself. "But how?"

I started the left engine. I'd have to tell her family something. The engine spit and popped then settled into a droning roar. But what? That she drowned? How do I explain why I landed in the first place? "I'm sorry, sir, your lovely daughter drowned while helping four stranded fishermen—Turkish fishermen, but Noli and I survived."

As phony as it sounded, it was probably more believable that what actually happened.

Starting the left engine and trimming it to match the other, the image of Alexis' two nieces popped into my head—how they adored her. To keep from tearing up I gave Noli a thumbs up sign and eased the throttles forward, snaking passed huge rocks and into the Aegean.

After a run across a glassy sea, Noli and I then lifted the Bluebird into the air; the grim realities of the past left behind.

Nazif planned to sell the fish in Denizli, a city large enough to support several decent restaurants, he said, and only one hundred miles away. He had a friend there who would help. "I call him. He come to airport, pick up fish in truck." When I'd ask about inspectors and permits, not wanting to end up in a Turkish jail, he'd replied, "No inspectors...no permits. We in Turkey now...not America."

I hoped he was right.

        *   *   *   *

A city of seventy-five thousand, according to a guidebook Regina had lent me, Denizli was nestled in a wide river valley bounded by rolling foothills.

"The Menderes," Nazif said, pointing to a sluggish brown river as we searched for the airport from one thousand feet. "It go to sea...that way." He pointed west, toward Ephesus, also in the guidebook. An ancient city where Saint Paul had preached and been thrown in jail, according to legend.

When we found the airport, the runway was so covered with sand blown in from the north and east it looked like a dirt road. A windsock whipped in a stiff breeze atop the only building—a scruffy metal hanger.

I landed in a cloud of dust and sand and taxied toward it. No one seemed to be around, so I shut down the engines and followed Nazif inside the hanger. Noli would keep an eye on the plane.

At first we saw no one then a man appeared wearing bib overhauls. When he asked if we needed gas, I shook my head and thanked him, saying, *"Hayir, teşekkür ederim"*.

By then I'd learned a few more words, like "thank you" and, *güzel*, which meant beautiful. Noli had taught me that one. Said he called Leandra that a few days earlier, making me wonder if I'd ever say that to Regina.

When Nazif's friend arrived, he backed his truck up to the plane and the three of them unloaded the fish. I felt foolish just watching, but I was afraid I'd strain something if I helped. As it was, it only took a few minutes to fill five freezer chests his friend had in his truck. For ten percent of the profit, he'd found a restaurant willing to take all the fish at a much better price than Hasan had been offered in Bodrum.

Our first cut into Bai Simaphong's lucrative trade monopoly.

Noli and I waited in the plane while Nazif and his friend drove into town. I read Regina's guide book while Noli washed down a sandwich with a Coke, then slept. Two hours later, Nazif returned, saying the owner of the restaurant, the largest in town, had asked to see a picture of a sailboat he had recently built. "I bring next time."

"Why would anyone want a sailboat around here?" I asked. "It's nothing but desert for miles around."

Nazif beamed expansively. *"Büyük göl*...big lake...over there." He pointed toward the dusty brown foothills covered with rocks.

I laughed and shook my head. What an optimist.

*   *   *   *

No longer concerned about finding the airport, such as it was, after takeoff, I had time to scan the rugged terrain surrounding Denizli. From the air it reminded me of New Mexico, starkly beautiful but survival tough. According to the guidebook, the center of Turkey is a plateau. Starting about three thousand feet in the West it gradually climbs into the Eastern Mountains and the former Soviet Republics of Armenia, Georgia and ever cantankerous, oil-rich Azerbaijan, areas from where many Turks have migrated.

That I learned from Regina, the ever-pleasant schoolteacher.

Standing in the cockpit entry, Nazif directed me north to an astonishing sight he wanted us to see before heading south. From flat silvery pools shaped like giant platters crystalline water cascaded over chalky white cliffs into the valley below. It was incredible; and beyond the cliffs, ancient ruins dotted the countryside. One area was filled with rectangular blocks of darkly stained marble about six feet long and two feet across, as if toys left by careless giant children, perhaps.

"*Pamukkale*," Nazif announced proudly, pointing to the chalky cliffs. "You say, Cotton Castle. *Kale* mean "castle." Warm water flow there, filled with...how you say—*kireç*?"

"Lime?" I offered, astonished by the incredible beauty of the platter-shaped discs. Sculpted, perhaps, by the father of the careless giant children rather than Mother Nature.

"*Evet*...lime. Make cliffs white."

"And the marble blocks?" I asked, before turning toward Bodrum.

"Ancient coffins." Raising his hands in an upward motion, he added, "Büyük earthquakes...toss them up. Çok earthquakes in Turkey."

Nazif pointed toward scattered ruins nearby. "Hieropolis. Roman city. Sick people come for hot baths. Some live...some die." Pointing to a graveyard lined with Cypress trees, he added, "When people die, tree is planted...like arrow, point to heaven."

"They just leave the coffins there?" I gasped. "They don't re-bury them?"

"*Hayir*...bad luck bury coffin twice."

I glance at him to see if he was teasing. He wasn't.

*   *   *   *

That night in Gümbet, Nazif insisted we celebrate the family good fortune with a meal worth remembering. After a glass or two of *raki*, served with dried fruit, crackers and goat cheese, Phidaleia brought out a platter of roastbeef on a bed of rice. It surprised me. Until then I thought Turks preferred lamb—or could only afford lamb. But Phidaleia assured me that Turks eat beef on many special occasions. Along with it we had carrots, cabbage and freshly baked *ekmek*, hard-crusted bread. Also, a cucumber and tomato salad with yogurt sauce, which her daughters served us beautifully, considering their tender ages.

Truly a meal fit for a king—or a broken-down American pilot and a Portuguese orphan with a big grin.

✻   ✻   ✻   ✻

The next afternoon I walked to the boat factory where Noli was helping Nazif prepare boards for the hull of the second rowboat. When he wasn't bothering Leandra in the office, that is. Seeing how well they got along, I suggested to Noli that it might be better if he stayed with Leandra the next time we hauled fish somewhere. "You know, to keep an eye on her. With all the trouble around here, I'm sure Nazif would worry less if you did."

"You think so?" the rangy youth asked with a crooked smile. The idea obviously appealed to him. "Nazi showed me how to bend boards this morning. Should I ask him?"

"Sure. Tell him I suggested it."

✻   ✻   ✻   ✻

That evening, in the patio under a half moon, I received my first history lesson from Regina. About the Osmani Family who ruled the Ottoman Empire for six hundred years—a realm, at one point, greater than the Roman Empire. "But in the Great War Turkey side with Germany and lose!" she exclaimed, her built-in smile momentarily gone. "But after war, Kemal Ataturk, our top general, fight Greeks and British and win freedom. Like your George Washington, I think." Her smile returned. "Without him, we would be Greek in West, Russian in East, and I don't know what in center."

"Probably British," I teased.

Regina laughed outright. Something, I'd learned that Turkish women seldom do in male company. "Ataturk change many rules," she continued brightly. "Say, no more veils! Say women can work now, have jobs, make money, start a business, and even own land. No more slave to husband."

Being a widow in Turkey couldn't be easy, I reflected. Yet, Regina was as proud of her heritage as we were of ours. And rightly so, especially after the struggle the Turks had gone through just to gain back part of what they'd lost in World War One.

*   *   *   *

The second load of fish went to Istanbul, a more ambitious trip than to Denizli. This time, Noli would stay with Leandra. A chore he eagerly agreed to and this pleased Nazif, his ruddy face beaming with pride *and* relief. By then he'd found a second cooler—a smaller one but on wheels. It held one hundred pounds, the larger one almost two hundred. He also found two ice chests. One they would fill with sardines, the other anchovies. I still wasn't worried about weight. The Bluebird could carry much more than that with so few people on board.

The reason we had more fish was Hasan's doing. He'd convinced two other fishermen to join him, hopefully to break the stranglehold Bai Simaphong had on the community. Both Kesfin brothers were enthusiastic about it, although I guessed they'd be worried about what Bai Simaphong might do in retaliation to them or their families.

"He do nothing," Nazif replied with a sneer when I asked him about it. "We sell two hundred kilo, every week. He sell two thousand kilo— every day."

At the moment Ahmet was easing Hasan's boat into the isolated cove. In Noli's absence, he'd had agreed to help, although I didn't expect much work out of him unless he was paid. We would have loaded the Bluebird in Gümbet Cove, but Nasif was afraid Captain Tokolu would get wind of it and tell someone who might tip off Simaphong.

As it turned out, Hasan and Nazif wrestled the second cooler aboard the plane while Ahmet held the boat steady and I kibitzed. Then Nazif and Hasan started loading fish.

Again, it didn't take long; Hasan did most of the work. And when they finished, the gently giant seemed so pleased with himself, I asked him if he'd like to come along to help at the other end.

He agreed when Ahmet said he'd take the boat back to Gümbet Cove, but I could tell by his deep scowl that he wasn't happy about it. There was something strange about Ahmet...a darkside I couldn't explain. He just wasn't friendly like his brothers and I wondered why.

*   *   *   *

Flying north along the rugged Turkish coast, the Aegean shimmering on our left, barren mountains spread out for miles on our right, I spotted a fishing boat just north of Kos. A chill ran through me, remembering what had happened the last time I flew over this patch of water. Would I ever forget? It wasn't likely.

Moments later, from the copilot's seat where I'd let him sit, Nazif pointed to a Turkish harbor filled with cruise ships. "Kuşadasi," he said. "Tourists from Russia, America, Canada…they all come."

"What do they come to see?" I asked, glancing back at Hasan, his face plastered to his window, taking it all in.

"Ephesus!" Nazif cried, as if I should know. "Famous Bible city…also Sardis, Priene, Didyma…ancient Greek cities."

"This entire coastline was part of Greece once?" I was astonished by what he'd said.

"*Evet*. In old days *çok* Greeks live there."

No wonder they hate each other so much, I thought, and for two thousand years. It was hard to fathom two countries being enemies for that long; even two hundred years seemed like a long time.

"See…Ephesus there," Nazif said moments later, pointing to an amphitheater large enough to seat twenty thousand people. Next to it, marble columns bordered a wide street, some facades fully standing. One, Nazif identified as the library, adding, "Street is marble! You see?"

I dropped to one thousand feet to take a closer look. It was an impressive sight.

Near the library, Nazif pointed out the Roman baths and brothel, side-by-side.

"Is good idea, no?" Nazif laughed at his observation then told me how the Menderes River had filled in the mighty seaport and forced the people to move inland to Selçuk.

"See? Over there…by Saint John Cathedral…*çok* old…*çok kutsî*…ah, sacred for Christians."

Farther north I saw Izmir, the third largest city in Turkey, and the largest on the West Coast. To our left sat Chios, so close it could have been part of Turkey.

Seeing the idyllic Greek isle made me again wonder what I'd tell Alexis' family. A problem that had plagued me all week. I'd have to stop on the way back. I couldn't put it off any longer, although they surely know by now, since we never arrived in Kos. They probably think Noli and I are dead too. Her parents must be sick with grief over losing their precious daughter. I know I am.

Approaching the sprawling city, centered by a circular patch of green, Nazif pointed to it. "That is Kulture Park...spelled with a "K". Like your Central Park in New York, no?"

I nodded. "It looks like a nice place to get away from noisy traffic." Passing over it, my mind wandered. I began thinking about Ahmet, his petulance, his boastfulness.

"Has Ahmet always been grouchy and argumentative?" I asked Nazif.

"*Evet*...and lazy," he replied. "He no work much...mostly he gamble, drink *raki* and spend *çok lire*."

"Where does he get his *lire* to spend?"

"Big question...I ask many times but he no answer."

It was obvious Nazif didn't approve of Ahmet's lifestyle, making me wonder how they could all be so different. Hasan, the strong silent type. Nazif, the talkative, take charge guy, the schemer, making things happen. Ahmet, also a schemer but on the darker side, looking for easy money. He could be trouble someday. Big trouble, if Simaphong ever gets wind of our little scheme. And he might, if little brother boasts about it all over Bodrum.

The thought stayed with me as we flew over the ruins of Pergamun, an ancient city begun in 281 B.C.E., according to the guidebook. Its library rivaled the one in Alexandria.

Next we flew over Troy. From 5,000 feet the ruins were unimpressive. The Trojan horse—a replica twenty feet high, according to the guidebook—looked like an ant.

Moments later, at the Dardanelles—the straight separating the Black Sea from the Aegean—I turned toward Istanbul, one of the most fabled cities of the world. My pulse quickened as we approached the gateway to the Far East. Looking at my map, I realized that the part of Turkey on the left of the long waterway was in Europe, the rest in Asia. It made me feel pretty insignificant, like the equine ant I'd just seen at Troy.

           *   *   *   *

Fortunately, we didn't have to fly into the heart of the Golden Horn. It wasn't so much the air traffic—I only saw one airliner. It was river traffic on the Bosphorus, dividing European Istanbul from Asian Istanbul. Nazif had arranged to have a friend of a friend meet us in Kadiköy, a small, outlying city on the Asian side of Istanbul.

Landing on the Sea of Marmara, south of Istanbul, I taxied into a shallow bay at Nazif's directions and parked next to a pier. The man we were to meet was already there; and within and hour, the fish had been transferred to a waiting pick-up, *lire* had been exchanged and hands shook.

Taxiing away from the pier, I wished we could have visited Istanbul, a city of over two million people. A city, according to Regina who spent a year there studying, crowded with magnificent palaces and mosques, and markets filled with gold, frankincense and myrrh.

I did fly over the city, noting streets clogged with cars, busses and pedestrians. From the air it looked like a rat maze. Even the bridges were jammed, especially the double-deck Golata Bridge, which Nazif said was lined with shops on the lower level.

Winging back toward Chios, with Nazif again in the copilot's seat, Hasan joined us in the cockpit entry, stooping to conform to the six-foot bulkhead. With *lire* in their pockets—Nazif got ten percent too, the brothers seemed upbeat and talkative. Nazif did, that is. His hulking brother mostly just nodded and smiled. And by rights they should be happy. They'd just made the biggest sale of their lives.

"We do every week, okay?" Nazif said with a wide grin. "We make *çok lire.*"

I didn't discourage him, but I knew that wasn't possible. First, I didn't expect to hang around that long. I had to find work—hauling people or cargo for pay. Secondly, fuel would eat up the profits. Right then, we were flying courtesy of Alexis, but that wouldn't last much longer...one or two more refills, maybe, on her account at the airport on Chios.

I had no idea who would inherit her millions. Someone else would have to figure that out. All I knew was, I had to tell her parents what happened and then find another wealthy client...like Simon Margoles, the cannery owner. His father had put a bug in his ear about having a private pilot, maybe something would come of that. It wouldn't hurt to talk to him. Of course, that would mean living on Chios; and without Alexis, that wouldn't be the same as before.

Banking left to avoid a cloud buildup, I remembered something else the cannery owner had said. That he'd tried to order a motor launch in Bodrum but the price was too high, that someone was taking over many of the boatyards there.

Bai Simaphong, of course, the man I was beginning to hate.

Returning to course, I told Nazif about Simon Margoles and the trouble he'd had trying to buy a motor launch. "Did you bring photos of the boats you've built?"

"That *piç* Simaphong," he growled. Ignoring my question, he smashed his fist into his hand then made a choking motion. "I kill someday," he muttered, staring out the cockpit window, adding finally, "...*Evet*, I bring photo this time."

*   *   *   *

I asked for fuel at the airport on Chios, thinking Alexis would expect me to until her deposit ran out. I then asked Nazif and his brother if they would go see Alexis' family with me to corroborate my story. "I'll understand if you don't want to, the way Greeks and Turks hate each other so much, but I'd really like your help."

Nazif pondered my question for a moment then spoke to his brother. Turning to me, he said, "We go. Maybe I sell boat...Greeks and Turks—all same, in business."

*   *   *   *

The dreaded confrontation at the family farm was not what I expected. They already knew that Alexis had died and had spent the previous week mourning her loss and venting their rage at the men who'd killed her. They just didn't know the specifics and I didn't elaborate much, Alexis' dying request still ringing in my ear, *"Don't tell family...too much hate already."*

As Demetri explained, the boat trailing us that day had several Greek businessmen on board and a few female models—mixing business with pleasure. Two had come to the funeral and told the family what little they'd seen and heard. When they saw the Bluebird land on water, they became curious and hung around to see what else would happen. Two had never seen a plane land on water before. But when night came they backed away and didn't see what happened to Alexis, although they heard music and raucous laughter...mixed with theirs, I suspected.

The next morning they moved in closer and saw two men toss what looked like a body overboard. Later, they tried to retrieve it, but it was too late. The body had disappeared. They called the police on Kos, but they wouldn't do anything because the death was out of their jurisdiction and no one on Kos had reported a missing person.

A few days later Alexis' waterlogged body, her face disfigured but identifiable, had washed ashore on Kos and returned to the police. Because of this, she had already been interned in the family plot on Chios; and her family, still showing red-eyes from sleepless nights, greeted me with warm smiles and hugs, thinking Noli and I had suffered the same fate. Demetri's boys were particularly pleased to hear that Noli was okay, cherishing the time they'd spent together.

However, the family was less enthusiastic about meeting Nazif and Hasan, until I told them the part they'd played in my rescue. Then they welcomed them as if part of the family, even invited us to dinner so they could celebrate our return from the dead properly, which meant much food and many rounds of *ouzo*. For a few hours that evening, before Demetri took us to our hotel, there was little difference between Greeks and Turks, except language. That's why most of the talk was in English.

Watching them toast each other's good health, I noticed a surprising similarity among them—same dark olive skin, same coal black eyes, hair ranging from black to salt-and pepper depending upon their age. The Greek women could have easily passed for members of the Kesfin family. Even the food we ate was similar, ending with honey-drenched *Baklava*, called the samething in both countries.

It seemed such a giant waste of energy and emotion hating people akin in so many ways. But tell that to a Greek or a Turk.

*   *   *   *

The next morning Demetri drove Nazif and me to the cannery. Hasan remained at the hotel to enjoy a leisurely breakfast. His first ever in a hotel.

After showing us his office, Demetri took us to see Simon Margoles. He too was delighted to see me, thinking I'd died with Alexis. "Please, sit down. My secretary will bring coffee—or tea, if you prefer." Demetri excused himself and returned to his work.

Simon's office was quite large, lined with file cabinets on one side, straight chairs and settee on another. "We heard about Alexis. A terrible business. Such a beautiful lady."

"Yes...it was. We were lucky to escape." I then introduced Nazif. "He has a boat factory in Bodrum, and along with his two brothers, helped Noli and I out of a terrible jam over there."

"Tell me about it. From what I heard from Alexis' family, it sounded barbaric." Simon sat behind a large oak desk as his secretary passed out cups of strong black coffee served in demitasse glasses, the same way I'd seen it served in Turkey.

"Captain Tokolu, savage man!" Nazif exploded. "Good Turkish men not like that!"

I agreed with a nod then explained what had happened, praising the three brothers for what they'd done for Noli and me. "I'm just sorry we couldn't save Alexis as well."

"As are we. My father was devastated...still is. She was always his favorite."

"She was everyone's favorite," I replied.

An awkward silence followed, broken by Simon. "Yes, a truly remarkable woman. Now...what brings you here, business or pleasure?"

It seemed a bit curt...but then he was a busy man.

"Both, really. Hasan and Ahmet are fishermen. Nazif here builds very fine boats. They were hoping to do business with you—bypassing Bai Simaphong. The man with a stranglehold on Bodrum fishing and boat building and indirectly responsible for Alexis' death. Captain Tokolu lured me to his boat, hoping to sell my plane to Simaphong. Alexis was an afterthought...a reward for his success."

Simon looked shocked, his glass-encased world of impunity and wealth shaken.

"I didn't realize things had gotten so out of hand over there. I never liked the man from the start. He sat right there, on that settee. His oily smile looked painted on. Told me the increased price for fish was caused by higher petrol costs and taxes, along with a shortage of fish—even lazy fisherman. Everything but the truth—his greed. I agree that he is an evil man. What can I do to help?"

After hearing what Nazif and I had done to break Simaphong's stranglehold on fishing, both in Denizli and Istanbul, the heir to the Margoles fortune tapped his lips tentatively with two fingers and stared at the wall in deep thought.

"In that case," he said abruptly, "I'll buy two thousand kilos of fish per day from Bodrum fishermen—through you, Nazif, since you seem to know what you're doing. Is that agreed?"

"*Evet*, if price is right." Nazif beamed, looking me.

I winked to encourage him to continue. He seemed stunned by the offer. An offer made by a man dressed in a suit and tie, in a cannery half the length of a soccer field filled with odors he was more used to than I was. In fact, the quicker we left, the happier I'd be.

"I'm sure we can come to some kind of agreement." Simon smiled. "Maybe on a new motor launch, as well. Care for more tea...a cigar? I have a box of Havana Royales I haven't even opened yet."

Nazif smiled at the opening gambit to haggle, a skill enjoyed by all men with olive colored skin.

*   *   *   *

After a second night in the same hotel, we flew back to the secluded cove. Not totally surprising, Ahmet wasn't there as planned. Nazif had called the night before and told Phidaleia to tell Ahmet that we'd be there about ten that morning. It was now almost noon.

"Maybe he had trouble with the boat," I suggested, easing the Bluebird between house-size boulders.

"Maybe he drink too much and forget," Nazif growled, pacing the center aisle of the plane. Just over five-foot-eight, he didn't have to hunch over at all.

Hasan asked him something in Turkish then frowned as if worried too.

"*Hayir*," Nazif answered, shaking his head. "Phidaleia *hareket iyi, adil tuhaf.*" Looking at me, he clarified. "Phidaleia is okay...just—" He moved his fingers like a chirping bird and then laughed nervously. "Talk, talk, talk...always talk."

I felt the same way about Hasan's extroverted wife, caring and sweet but head-strong and gregarious. Too talkative for me.

Watching Nazif pace the aisle then stare out the side windows, I suggested we just fly to Gümbet Cove.

Nazif looked up in surprise, his bushy eyebrows bristling. He obviously hadn't thought of that. "Good," he replied. "Maybe something bad happen there...*çok kötü*...very bad."

I agreed. Ahmet wouldn't deliberately leave us stranded out here, or would he?

*   *   *   *

I taxied into Gümbet Cove at twelve-thirty. Hasan's boat was tied to the pier but Ahmet wasn't on board.

"We go factory," Nazif said, "Maybe Ahmet there."

About the size of a four-car garage, the factory had a lumber shed outside, along one wall. Nazif unlocked the front door and we followed him inside. The place was in shambles, pots of glue, cans of paint, boxes of nails scattered everywhere. The two skiffs he'd been working on were overturned and hammer-like holes bashed into their hulls. Someone had also tried to enter the wire-mesh tool crib along one wall but gave up after bending the grillwork in several places.

Nazif knew instantly what had happened and raced for the door. Hasan followed and I brought up the rear.

In Hasan's house, we heard the grim details from a distraught Phidaleia who did her best to stay calm but burst into tears after only a few sentences. The gist of it, I gleaned from Nazif as Hasan further questioned his stricken wife.

After Nazif's call from Chios the night before, Noli and Leandra had walked to the factory to make sure they'd locked it and turned off the lights. Also, I suspected, as an excuse to be alone. A few minutes later, Ahmet had come by and asked about Leandra then left. No one had seen her or Noli since...or Ahmet for that matter.

Later, someone on an evening stroll with his dog had told them he'd heard a terrible racket in the factory, then saw two men put a clawing and screaming boy into the back of a black sedan while a third did the same with a girl—clawing and screaming also. The man said the car drove off toward Bodrum. He didn't recognize the boy but was sure the girl was Leandra.

Captain Tokolu. It had his name written all over it. Vicious and evil. He must have ordered it done, even helped do it himself. It couldn't have been just a coincidence, not with the factory torn up as well. He must have discovered who'd rescued me and what we'd been doing. But how?

Ahmet, probably, but why?

Chapter Eight

The police came by shortly after we arrived to tell us they knew nothing more than they had the night before and then asked for any information we might have to help them find the kidnappers. I started to tell them to pick up Captain Tokolu but deferred to Nazif, doubting the police would listen or understand me.

Nazif was visibly upset and paced furiously. After a flurry of Turkish, during which I heard the name Tokolu mentioned twice, he said something that sounded like a curse, then something about the Büyük Hotel in Izmir.

When I looked at Regina, who'd taken off from school, the last day before summer vacation, she translated the rest, "…and you will find everything you want to know there—if you are brave enough to enter the lair of the lion itself."

With that, Nazif stormed out of the house in disgust.

My heart went out to him. Leandra was his only daughter. Then it hit me—and Noli was my only son. It hadn't occurred to me before, but he was as much a son as any I was ever likely to have. We had to get them back, before Simaphong could…

I didn't even want to think about the alternative. We had to find a way to enter the lion's lair.

Suddenly, a thought came to me. I could pose as a mercenary pilot…on the run from the police maybe. Offer my services to the crime lord. Once inside his lair, I could find Leandra and Noli, free them, and return to Bodrum.

It sounded so simple, but first I'd have to find a way to access the lion's lair.

Nazif helped with that. He called Mahoud Konuk, a longtime friend who ran a tour agency in Izmir, and told him the problem. We had to trust someone, although his friend could easily rat on us and tell Simaphong. People will do anything for money—even longtime friends.

Mahoud said he'd heard of the crime lord. Everyone in Izmir had, including the police, many of whom were on his payroll. He just hadn't met him, nor did he want too. He did agree, however, to take me to a favorite haunt of two men he thought worked for Simaphong, occasionally. Dockhands from the waterfront, who he'd asked on several occasion to do small jobs for him, like pick up stranded tourists.

When Nazif told his friend that I had a seaplane, he suggested I land on the water west of Izmir, near Karşiyaka, meaning "opposite shore", so no one in Izmir would see us. From there, we could take the ferry across the bay and meet him at his tour office.

*   *   *   *

The first part of the plan worked perfectly. Nazif paid the harbormaster in Karşiyaka a modest fee to let me tie the Bluebird to a buoy there, even offered us a rowboat to access it. Hasan agreed to remain in the plane, or keep an eye on it from a waterfront restaurant.

Nazif and I didn't have to wait long for a ferry, and the ride across the gently curving bay, faced with apartments, office buildings and retail shops, took just twenty minutes. We debarked at five o'clock. I remember the time distinctly. The call to prayer had just begun, even louder and tinnier than in Bodrum.

The tour office was a block away, in an office building on a colorful promenade bordering the waterfront. Once pristine and clear, according to Nazif, the bay was becoming polluted, despite repeated efforts to keep it clean.

Mahoud greeted us with a warm smile and a firm handshake. Medium height with a prominent nose and dark, narrowly-spaced eyes, it was obvious he was used to making strangers feel at ease. From his first floor office, we could see a Norwegian cruiseship tied to a wharf. His job, he said in near-perfect English, was to see that passengers were entertained during their brief stopover in Izmir.

"My last group will be returning from Ephesus soon," he continued, looking at his watch. "Their ship sails in one hour. I hope they are not late. I must wait for them to return before I can leave. Would you like *çay*...ah, tea?"

When we both nodded, Mahoud went to the door and yelled at a man across the street on the wide promenade. Moments later, I saw him darting across the busy street, dodging cars while holding a tray filled with tiny cups and a pot of freshly brewed tea. Where he'd made it, I never learned. It just magically appeared.

As we talked, sipping the strong black liquid, four buses pulled up and disgorged their tourists. Rather than board the ship, however, nearly half of them hurried into retail stores facing the promenade, bent on buying as much as they could in the remaining time.

I laughed, thinking, shopkeepers probably make as much in those few minutes as they do all day.

Just then, a loud horn bellowed from the cruiseship, rattling the tour office windows.

"First boarding call," Mahoud explained, continuing to talk to Nazif in Turkish, presumably about what we would do that night.

After a second persistent blast, tourists remaining in stores rushed to the gangplank and boarded, each showing a uniformed purser their pass. All were carrying bags of souvenirs, which they probably didn't need but bought anyway to prove they had, indeed, been in Turkey.

According to Mahoud, the Isle of Rhodes was their next stop. There, they would buy more trinkets—Greek trinkets, some of which might have been made in Turkey. It was a win-win situation, enjoyed by tourists and retailers the world over.

* * * *

At six thirty, after a final bellow from its mighty horn, the stately cruiseship backed away from the dock. Time for Mahoud to close his office and lead us along the wide promenade, now filled with evening strollers, to the large grassy area in the city center.

"Kulture Park," he said to me, "the largest in Turkey. We have an International Fair here every summer. Many countries have pavilions, including the U.S., sometimes."

I asked if he'd ever been to the States. "You're English is excellent."

"Two years. I studied there. I also speak Russian, German, Italian and a little Japanese. You have to in my business."

"No French?"

"*Petit mots*...some words. But few French tourists come here."

"I wonder why?" I mused out loud.

"They think they already live in paradise." He laughed. "Good weather, good food, good wine—*c'est magnific!*" Kissing two fingers, he raised them in an exaggerated gesture.

A real charmer, that one.

Exiting the immense park on the east side, far from the tourists shops and fancy hotels, the buildings became older and dirtier, and the streets narrower but no less crowded, as people fled to their homes after a long workday, some walking, some riding mopeds, others in old cars and small trucks. I saw no public transportation and very few traffic lights. Even more surprising, I saw no policemen, on foot or in patrol cars.

I ask Mahoud if this was due to a low crime rate or lack of public funds.

He shrugged and said both. "We have little street crime here but the government is full of it. That's why men like Simaphong thrive here. It is bad...very bad."

As the sun faded, I began to have doubts about what we were doing. It sounded easy on paper, but in person, with real people—not very nice people—I was less sure.

I started to say something to Nazif but stopped when Mahoud entered a dimly lit bistro. A teak bar filled one wall, backed by shelves of glasses. A dozen small tables crowded the center of the room, booths lined three walls. The windows facing the street were heavily draped, allowing no light and little street noise to penetrate the smoke-filled room.

Discordant music—strings and reeds, mostly—sounded Oriental but more strident. From a tape player, I guessed, it muted all but the loudest conversations, which I suspected was the purpose in a place frequented almost entirely by unshaven men wearing disheveled clothing.

Close to a dozen of them were hunched over the bar tended by a large man with an apron and a fleshy woman wearing a low-cut peasant blouse. Several patrons were eating. Two women in tight dresses sat in one booth. It was difficult to guess their age through their heavy eye make-up and brightly painted lips, anywhere from fifteen to forty.

They tried to look uninterested but covertly watched as we sat in a nearby booth.

"Prostitutes," Mahoud whispered. "No decent women would be in here without an escort."

Looking at the dirty walls, the shabby drapes and inhaling the greasy smells, I couldn't imagine *any* women being in there, even *with* an escort.

Mahoud hadn't elaborated on how I'd meet the men who he thought knew Simaphong. Only that he knew a place where they came, making me wonder how he'd know that, and if he knew more than he was saying. I also worried that Nazif would loose his cool and blow everything if we meet someone who knew Simaphong. He looked angry enough to strangle a man barehanded to get Leandra back.

I was angry too but somehow knew I'd find Noli and that he'd be all right. It wasn't the same with a daughter. All kinds of bad things could happen to her. In a way I wished Nasif hadn't come. For my plan to work, I had to approach the men alone, not with two pals. I just hoped Nazif would leave with his friend. I was sure Mahoud would, not wanting any part of this. I'd do the rest myself, although I didn't know how or even what I'd say.

The busty barmaid came to our table and asked something. When each of them ordered a *beri*, a universal word understood in every country I'd visited, I did too.

Returning, she displayed her prodigious front to us when she placed the three chilled mugs on cork coasters then asked something else.

"*Evet*," Mahoud replied, turning to me. "She asked if we wanted menus. I told her, yes. We might as well eat. We may have to wait a while."

After asking her a question and receiving an answer, he told me they would have a belly dancer later. "Men stuff *lire* into her bra and panties," he added with a grin.

Nazif never cracked a smile, smoking one cigarette after another, his mind brooding on the enormity of his loss, his brightest star, and Noli's first love. I just hoped they were still together, worried they'd dump him somewhere and keep her. I was sure they only wanted Leandra but had to take them both.

Mahoud ordered *sacuk sandvic ve kizartmasi,* so I did too. Nazif didn't want anything. Said he was too upset to eat. When our order arrived, it turned out to be a spicy salami sandwich on a hard roll with French fries. A little greasy but not bad.

A few minutes later, while eating my sandwich, I caught one of the prostitutes looking at us. Smiling, she asked in Turkish if we were tourists—hoping, I suppose, for an early client. Mahoud quickly said we weren't and invited them to join us.

I was appalled until I realized what Mahoud was up to...acting naturally. At least, I hoped that was what he was up to. We hardly needed two women to complicate the evening. We had enough problems already.

Up close, they looked younger but their heavy make-up and stringy hair made them look flinty and used. One wore three studded earrings on each ear plus a nose ring. Sporting a butterfly tattoo on her forearm, she told us she was from a village east of Izmir. The other came from Naples and spoke better English. Emaciated, as if she hadn't eaten in days, she had bottle-blond hair and wore a single dangling earring.

I wondered if she'd lost the other one or preferred it that way. Neither wore a bra, hardly needing one.

❊   ❊   ❊   ❊

Working through a second beer, I realized the music had changed to Western rock. The girl from Naples suddenly asked me to dance. When I said no, she pouted and moved to a table with three other men.

Moments later, she called her friend over.

Nazif looked relieved, but Mahoud insisted we should act normal. "Do what men do sometimes, sit with prostitutes. We just don't take them home," he added with a leering grin, then asked if I were married.

"Divorced. My-ex wanted kids but I couldn't give her any so she married another guy and had one the following year. Such is life," I added with a shrug. "Allah's Will."

Nazif smiled for the first time since we'd entered the bistro. "Then who is Noli?" he asked. "You treat him like son."

"I guess I do, in a way...probably won't have one of my own. So he's—"

"There they are!" Mahoud suddenly interrupted. "The two men who just sat at the bar...there, at the end. I saw them talking to Simaphong once, who I recognized from a photo I'd seen in the newspaper. Kind of a creepy looking guy—short and roundish, with his hair pulled back in a pigtail. So what do we do now?"

"You two leave. I'll take it from here," I said with more conviction than I felt. "Can Nazif stay at your place tonight?" Mahoud nodded. "Good, Hasan will sleep in my plane. If I need a place, I'll find a cheap hotel. But if everything works out, I may not need one."

"You sure?" Nazif asked. "I could—"

I cut him off. "It won't work with you along; you're Turkish. I'm an itinerant pilot with a seaplane looking for work." I chuckled. "Captain Tokolu thought he had to kidnap me to fly for Simaphong. All he really had to do was ask."

"You fly for Simaphong?" Mahoud gasped in dismay.

"No, but I'll try my best to make him think that I will—if the price is right."

"Well, you sure had me fooled." Mahoud grinned. He seldom spoke without one. "Maybe it *will* work."

"I hope so. Now go. I'll see you two at your tour office—hopefully, tomorrow morning. Check with Hasan, if I'm not there by noon. I don't know how this will play out."

"What if you don't come back at all?" Nazif asked, balling his fist in anger. "What if you can't find—"

"I'll find her—Noli too. Give me two days—'til noon Saturday. Then contact the police—for whatever good that will do."

"Okay," Nazif said with a deep sigh. "I hope this works."

"I do too. See you tomorrow or Saturday."

As I watch them leave, my stomach began to churn. Could I do what I said—enter the lion's lair, find Leandra and Noli, and escape? It sounded a lot more dangerous now than it did before, especially alone.

*   *   *   *

I sat in an empty stool next to the two men Mahoud had identified and ordered a beer. For a moment, I wished I smoked. I could have offered them an American cigarette. Instead, I asked the one next to me—the one with cold black eyes—where the bathroom was, using the Turkish word *tuvalet*.

He pointed to the rear of the bistro. "You American?" When I nodded, he said, "Is good...my aunt live there."

It wasn't much, but it was a start. Returning from the *tuvalet*, I offered to buy them a beer. Both accepted eagerly.

"Why you Izmir?" the same man asked when the beers arrived. I told him I flew a seaplane and was looking for work. "Why you come here...this place?" he persisted, his dark eyes menacing and cold.

"I'm staying at a crummy hotel nearby and stopped for a beer. You know someone named Bai Simaphong? Been trying to meet him all day." I began to worry that he was on to me. "I hear he has *çok lire*." I waved my arms expansively. "*Büyük bay*, very powerful."

"Yeah? What else you hear?"

"That he doesn't ask about a man's past...only what he can do." I had no idea how much he understood or whether he would buy it. I could only hope. Both looked mean as snakes. One had a deep scar on his chin and the other was missing half of his middle finger.

"Why? You have past?" the other man asked, leaning closer, as if I might share a secret. It was the first time he'd spoken. I was surprised they both spoke English as well as they did. Maybe most people do, if they work near the waterfront where the tourists go.

"No worse than yours," I returned, hoping to sound cocky and bluff my way through, knowing I'd have to repeat the performance for Bai Simaphong, if I got that far.

"How much you pay...find Simaphong?" The first one asked, pointing to the pile of Turkish *lire* I'd left on the bar in front of me. A half smile quivered on his gaunt face, his intimidating eyes staring right through me.

"You know him?" I asked with feigned astonishment. Not an Oscar performance but the best I could do.

"Maybe...for *çok lire*."

I pulled a twenty from my wallet and laid it in front of him, hoping he'd think that was a lot.

"And *başka bira*?" he said, pointing to their half empty glasses.

"Sure," I replied, slapping a ten spot on top of the twenty.

"*Iyi*...is good," he said, taking the ten and raising three fingers at the bartender.

I didn't want or need another beer. I still had half of my third. Three is normally my limit, if I want to keep my wits about me. Which I definitely did that night.

Before the beers arrived, I again went to the men's room. This time I took my beer with me and flushed it down the toilet.

Returning, another beer was sitting at my place. Both men were smiling and talking, as if unconcerned about me, so I asked if they'd take me to see Bai Simaphong sometime soon. I pointed to my watch; it was nearly nine. We needed to get started or it might be too late. I had no idea what happened to the girls he kidnapped, but it wasn't hard to guess.

It had been twenty-four hours since Leandra and Noli disappeared; enough time for a lot to happen. All bad.

Chapter Nine

When all of us had finished our beers, the man next to me slapped me on the back and said, "We go now...it not far."

Actually, it was farther than we'd walked to get to the dingy bistro in the first place. Back through the park, still brightly lit, to the bay, then south past Mahoud's tour office to the Büyük Hotel. Five star, according to the man with the missing finger.

A curving drive led to a wall of glass doors. A resplendent coachmen helped an elegantly gowned women emerge from an aged Mercedes while her escort paid another man to park it. Something must be happening tonight, I thought, a benefit? A fashion show?

My two bar buddies didn't seem to care. Nor did they act surprised when a uniformed doorman opened the door for us with only a glance, although I suspected he knew by our clothing that we weren't paying guests.

The lobby was elaborately decorated—marble floors, high vaulted ceilings, with a magnificent crystal chandelier hanging at the base of a wide spiral staircase leading to a mezzanine. The main desk, fronted with polished mahogany, seemed to go on forever.

I followed the two men as if I belonged there, stopping behind them at an elevator marked *Penthouse Only*. I was surprised it was in English.

Scar-face pushed the button.

Seconds later, a voice answered from a tiny speaker above a key-operated elevator button. Scar face spoke a few words in Turkish into the speaker, including, *deniz uçaği*, which I knew meant seaplane. Nazif had said it a few times.

Looking around nervously, I had another sinking spell, fearing I might not be able to pull this off and wondering what I would say to Simaphong, if I actually met with him.

Will he believe me? Even if he does, how will I ever get Leandra and Noli out of here? This hotel is huge; Simaphong must rent the entire top floor.

Suddenly the elevator door opened.

Gritting my teeth, I shuffled forward into a plush, red satin-lined space big enough for a bed. It was too late to worry about it now, my fate was sealed.

*　　　*　　　*　　　*

The elevator opened to reveal a tall expressionless Asian wearing a brocaded floor-length gown and matching slippers. Indeterminate in age, with receding gray hair, he looked as if he'd come from a distant land and a time long forgotten.

Frowning, he seemed displeased, until scar face explained more fully in Turkish who I was and why they brought me there. At least, I hoped that's what he said. I did hear the words *deniz uçaği* again, also *kilavuz*—Turkish for pilot.

Suddenly, the stone-faced Asian turned to me and bowed. "I am called Wong Fung," he said in clipped British English, his hands crossed, hidden in his voluminous sleeves. "I am head of the Simaphong household. Welcome to Izmir. Have you seen much of this magnificent country? Istanbul, perhaps? Ankara? There is so much to see here."

At loss for words, not knowing exactly what scar face had told him, I greeted him with an awkward bow and told him my name, adding, "I've only seen Bodrum. I just arrived in Izmir a few hours ago."

"And you seek employment? For whom did you fly previously?"

Again, his face was inscrutable. I almost laughed. If it hadn't been so damn serious I probably would have. But despite his almost comical get up and superior demeanor, I got the impression that I'd never see his boss unless he thought it was important. And unless I met Simaphong, it was unlikely I'd see Noli and Leandra again.

What worried me was how much Simaphong knew about what I'd been doing for the Kesfin brothers. Maybe a lot, many a little. In any case, I decided to stick to the truth as much as possible, and to act belligerent, like a real mercenary pilot might act.

"My copilot and I were flying for a wealthy Greek lady. A very attractive Greek lady, I might add, if you know what I mean?" I raised my eyebrow and winked, wanting him to think we'd done more than just fly together, which we had. "Anyway, we were flying from Chios to Kos last week to visit her favorite aunt when suddenly she spotted a fishingboat in distress and insisted I land on the water to help. Thought it might be her two cousins. Boy, was that a mistake."

As I spoke, the robed man led me down a long hallway. Behind me, I heard the elevator doors open and close. The men who'd led me there had left, probably returned to the same bar and spent the money I'd given them on more beer and the two prostitutes. Some of it, I guessed, would end up in the bra and panties of the belly dancer.

Without mentioning any names, I told Wong what happened on the boat, still difficult for me to do, about my imprisonment in a root cellar and my subsequent escape, which I implied I'd accomplished alone, then about Noli's sudden disappearance. I decided not to say anything about Leandra; thinking, if Simaphong had anything to do with her, it might make things more difficult.

Only when I described Alexis' callous burial at sea did Wong's brows furrow, but real concern never creased his immutable face. "I heard there was some trouble in Bodrum recently, but I had no idea it was so deplorable and so unnecessary. It must have been terrifying. How did you escaped?"

"My captures weren't very bright, or attentive. In my line of work, I have to get out of tight spots all the time. It's part of the job...comes with the turf, as they say."

After a few more word, Wong seemed to buy my story and left me in a small anteroom, hopefully to tell his boss the same thing. The room was small but sumptuous, draped in crimson and pale blue. I sat impatiently on a brocaded settee and wondered if I was being watched. I felt like I was, so I did nothing to cast suspicion on myself.

I'd purposely dressed down that night—jeans, dark cotton shirt and jacket—so I wouldn't look out of place in a seedy bar. Now I wished I'd worn something nicer.

✻   ✻   ✻   ✻

Moments later, Wong ushered me into a much larger room lined with books. A massive desk dominated one side. A computer sat at one end of the desk, glowing with soft green light. "Please, be seated," he said, motioning to another embroidered settee. "Would you care for a drink? Something to eat, perhaps? My master will be with you shortly."

"Thanks, I've already eaten, but I'll take some çay, if you have it."

He seemed surprised by my request, raising one eyebrow, then left.

"That was stupid!" I said to myself. "I should have asked for something stronger—a beer, maybe, or a shot of whiskey, even rum—more in keeping with my new persona."

The cryptic Asian puzzled me, his British accent and elaborate gown. What time and place did someone come from to call their boss "my master?" And where did "his master" come from? What kind of place is this, anyway?

Simaphong sounded like a Chinese warlord, yet Wong didn't strike me as Chinese. His skin was too dark, like a South East Asian's, although I'm sure that Eastern skin color varies as much as Western skin does.

Wong returned quickly, followed by a shapely, fair-skinned beauty about Leandra's age. She looked more European than Turkish. Dressed in a French maid's uniform—white eyelet blouse, short black skirt trimmed in lace, legs encased in black mesh panty hose, she had green eyes and short brown hair and carried a silver tray loaded with goodies.

When she rested the tray on the low table in front me, her blouse billowed open, partially exposing her ample breasts. A waist-cinching half-apron and a white doily hat completed her ensemble.

She curtsied before serving me; but her eyes, clouded with fear, remained on Wong. When he nodded, more with his eyes than his head, she knelt on both knees and poured me a cup of tea. *"Seker?"* she then asked in accented Turkish. *"Kerma?"*

As she reached for a spoon, I touched her hand and shook my head. *"Hayir teşekkür ederim."*

I'd learned "No thank you" fending off Phidaleia all week.

The girl seemed confused, as if expecting me to want sugar *and* cream. The first time I had Turkish tea, I used both. It was strong enough to stand a spoon in and had a real jolt. But by then I'd grown accustomed to the dark, rich flavor and preferred it straight.

I started to relent just as the girl looked to Wong for guidance. "Try some *börek* or *baklava*," he said, pointing to a plate of honey-covered sweets. "Both are delicious."

When I nodded to the girl, she smiled, serving me one of each on a tiny plate, then handed me a fork wrapped in a linen napkin. She remained on her knees—anxious, poised to help—until I took a bite and smiled.

"Çok iyi," I said, hoping to relieve her obvious distress.

It appeared to. Wong even gave her a half-smile. The first I'd seen from the stoic man.

The girl stood...a bit taller then before, with her shoulders thrown back. Happy to have her chore over with, I suppose.

When she left, Wong commented on how difficult it was to find good help. "And when we have one trained—taught to dress and use make-up properly, they so often leave and become servants or nannies in England or France, even America."

I was about to comment when a heavily muscled Cossack giant with a handlebar mustache entered the room, looked about quickly and left. His costume was peculiar: bloused pantaloons, tightly cuffed at the ankles, and turned-up slippers, his oiled chest rippling like a professional wrestler. Even more bizarre, the curved saber jammed into his brightly colored waistband. He made Hasan look like a wimp, a man who'd pulled me from a darkened cellar with one arm and carried me to his truck like a baby.

Suddenly, another man entered the room, followed by the giant, who I now noticed had spirals of silver wrapped around his bulging biceps. Fearsome and unsmiling, he stood by the door, as if daring me to make a move toward his master, which was the last thought I had at the moment. Just leaving that place alive would have pleased me at that point.

I stood, wondering if I should bow.

"I am sorry to have kept you waiting," the rotund Asian said in perfect English.

Like Wong Fung, he didn't look Chinese, more Malaysian or Indonesian. Medium height with a double chin, he wore a red-satin dinner jacket and dark trousers. Four fingers on each hand were marked by jeweled rings—sapphires, emeralds and rubies. A huge diamond, at least ten carats, hung from his neck on a thin gold chain.

"Has Wong been treating you well, Mister...ah...Sylvester? He tells me your first impression of Turkey was not good, that a terrible thing happened to you and your former client. Also your copilot. I am truly sorry. The Turks and Greeks have hated each other for so long it is inbred; there is no stopping it. The Greeks are more sophisticated, perhaps, but no less brutal. I am Bai Simaphong," he added, finally taking a breath. "Welcome to Izmir. It is obvious you have heard of me. I'm curious to know how."

"You are widely known in Bodrum. It wasn't difficult to find you."

I started to bow but didn't. Instead, I reached for his hand, which unsettled him—caught him off balance. His Cossack guard even jerked his hand toward his sword.

Simaphong ignored my hand and invited me to sit. "Yes...I suppose it was."

Walking behind his massive desk, he sat on a black leather chair which swiveled and tilted. "Tell me again what happened to you and your copilot—describe the men and their boat. Do you have their names? Perhaps I can help. And what of your plane? Did you retrieve it? Where is it now?"

Again I was caught in a dilemma. How much did he know and how much was he responsible for? Maybe none of what happened to Alexis and me, but surely he ordered the kidnapping of Leandra and Noli. Or did he? Maybe Captain Tokolu did that just to spite Nazif, or to settle an earlier wrong. Didn't Nazif say the Captain owed him money? Maybe there was a question as to whether he did or not, or how much. Enough to piss-off Tokolu that much? Maybe.

By then Wong Fung had left the room but the giant Cossack remained at the door, his heavily muscled arms folded across an enormous chest. Feeling like I was treading on the edge of a fiery inferno, I proceeded cautiously, my *baklava* uneaten.

For the next few minutes I explained about Noli, his age, how he hid in the plane, what happened to Alexis and me on Captain Tokolu's boat and my imprisonment in Bodrum—again not mentioning the Kesfin Brothers or Leandra being kidnapped—ending with this whopper, "...but when I escaped, I couldn't find Noli. He'd disappeared. I thought he might be in Izmir. We'd planned to look for work here when we finished with the Greek lady. We'd only agreed to fly her from the Azores to Chios. Flying her to Kos was a bonus flight...if you know what I mean?"

Again I tried to make it sound like I was a lech who hopped into bed with anyone, thinking it might come in handy later...if there was a later. I knew I was taking a chance. A big chance. But I hoped if he had Noli he might release him. Why would he want a gangling teenage boy? Leandra was something else—pretty *and* nubile. I'd have to figure a way of getting her out myself. But at that point I didn't want Simaphong to know that I even knew her. If he did, I'd have to tell him about Nazif and his brothers and I didn't want to do that.

I'd have to find Leandra without revealing anything about them. But could I? Looking across the desk at Simaphong I was beginning to have my doubts.

  ✳   ✳   ✳   ✳

"That is truly a remarkable story, Mr. Sylvester, although, I have heard similar ones recently—desperate men with no scruples, grabbing children off the streets. I will make a few inquiries. Perhaps I can find your copilot, even bring the fishingboat Captain you described to justice, along with his crew. They certainly deserve to be punished. It is inexcusable what they did to your client. Your copilot's name is…Noli?"

When I nodded, he scribbled it on a paper then looked up. "I am still a bit confused, however, as to why you came to me? Please understand, I had nothing to do with any of this, and I'm hardly in a position to—"

"I know," I interrupted, "and my client is gone, if not forgotten. She was very beautiful. Runner-up in a Miss World contest a few years back. I just thought a man of your means and influence might be able to help me find Noli…and well, do something about the men who did all this to us."

"Perhaps I can." Simaphong paused and stared at me—through me, really. From where I was sitting, he looked almost bald, his hair pulled tightly against his head.

I wondered what he was thinking and if he believed me. Finding Leandra might take more skill than I had…besides a good bit of luck.

"It's a pity about your client," he continued. "Such a waste. I admire female beauty—all kinds."

I'll bet you do, I thought, wondering if he had a harem. My ire began to rise and my face became flush, but I held myself in check. I had to. The next step was crucial to my plan.

"Was there anything else you wish to see me about?" he asked distractedly. "Would you like more tea, another sweet cake?"

"No thanks." I tried to remain pleasant and control my temper. But everything this man stood for—wealth, influence, his power over people, to say nothing of the lives he'd ruined through his illicit dope trade—made me want to puke. "But since you asked, the men who brought me here tonight thought a successful man like you might be interested in hiring a private pilot and plane for his personal use. If you are, I'm available. And remember, the Bluebird—that's what I call my plane—can land on water or on a runway. Very useful to a man on the go and considerably more private than an airliner."

"They said that about me?" His frown faded, replaced by a sick smile.

"Also that you're a man of influence in Bodrum, as well."

I started to say more but stopped, letting the corpulent crime lord absorb what I'd already said. Let it feed his ego, which I suspected was enormous. It had to be to live the way he did—beautiful maids—slaves, really—a major domo who called him "master". I wondered if he also had eunuchs to keep his women beautiful...and willing.

God, what a creep!

My stomach suddenly turned sour, maybe from the greasy sandwich I'd eaten in the bistro or maybe from sitting there in front of "my master". In either case, it didn't seem possible in this day in age that anyone could live like that...and treat people like that.

I had to find Leandra. Just thinking of her in his sick hands strengthened my resolve.

Looking up, Simaphong was staring at me. "My own pilot and plane...hmmm, an appealing idea. What is the range and how well appointed is it? The Bluebird, you say?"

I recited the Mallard's speed, range and cruising altitude then told him about the plush seats and the extras added by the previous owner. Feeling more confident, I also told him that I flew for Continental Airlines for eight years and mentioned my last two clients before Alexis. Both, I guessed, were as wealthy as him, but I didn't mention that.

"Interesting," he replied, bringing his hands together in front of his round face. "Is it possible to extend the range? Fly to England, say, non-stop?"

The way he looked at me—so intently, his mind probably going a mile-a-minute, made me wonder what he was thinking. I also wondered if he might be telling the truth about not knowing about the kidnapping, and that all of this might come to naught.

So why am I here? I thought. I'll never fly for him.

"It's possible," I answered evasively, becoming irritated by his one-track mind.

He must know something about the kidnappings. If not him, who? Captain Tokolu? Probably, but he wouldn't keep Leandra, not in Bodrum. It would be too dangerous. The neighbor said he saw the men who snatched her and Noli drive out of town...toward Izmir, I suppose. Besides, Simaphong is the only person who would pay for a kidnapped girl.

"Control youself, Dan," I simmered. "Getting mad won't help, not now, anyway."

Simaphong didn't respond right away, rubbing his smoothly shaven chin in deep thought. "Perhaps we can talk more tomorrow. You *will* be my guest tonight, won't you? Do you have a hotel? Wong could have your luggage brought here."

"That isn't necessary. My clothes are in my plane and that's well guarded. After my encounter with Captain Tokolu, I don't trust any Turk...not anymore."

"Pity...some are quite good men. Loyal, dedicated."

I thought of Nazif and Hasan, more dedicated friends I couldn't have. But could Nazif be wrong about Bai Simaphong? Maybe he wasn't behind the kidnappings.

Shrugging off the thought, I was glad I'd been invited to stay over, giving me a chance to look around, maybe. I was also glad that Hasan was guarding the Bluebird.

I didn't trust the smiling man sitting before me. Not one little bit.

*   *   *   *

Wong Fong appeared suddenly, alerted by a buzzer under the desk, I suppose.

While they spoke, in a strange singsong language I didn't recognize, I wondered what would come next. A meal? Entertainment? A barred cell? I could only guess.

When they finished speaking, my host turned to me. "Wong will escort you to your room, Mr. Sylvester. I hope you will be comfortable there. If you wish for anything, toiletries, something to eat or drink, female companionship, do not hesitate to ask. Someone will be outside your room most of the night to serve you."

To guard me, I thought, wondering if I should ask for someone—a terrified fifteen-year-old girl, for example. "Thanks," I said, shuttering at the thought. "You've been most kind. A toothbrush, perhaps, and a razor. I expected to return to my plane tonight."

"Of course." He gave Wong a quick nod then, "We will talk more at breakfast...say nine o'clock on the patio? Wong will help you find it. No need to wander about. It is easy to become lost in this place."

"I'm sure it is," I replied, following Wong out the door, "and thanks for the tea."

"Don't mention it. I think you and I could form in profitable partner-ship. Oh, I almost forgot. What is the last name of your copilot?"

"Cordeiro...Noli Cordeiro," I said.

"And he is only seventeen?"

"Yes...a very wise seventeen."

"I suppose so...and a good friend, I would guess."

"A *very* good friend...more like a son."

"Yes...Well, I will see what I can do about locating him."

Following Wong, a crazy thought hit me. Maybe I *should* ask for a girl. I might just get lucky and get Leandra. But if I do, how would get her out of my room...out of this hotel? And what about Noli?

I'd better concentrate on him first. I'll work on Leandra tomorrow. I don't even know if she is here. But, at least, I've made it this far.

*   *   *   *

My room was Spartan but comfortable—bed, dresser, nightstand, overstuffed chair and a shared bathroom with the room next door. I suspected they saved the fancier rooms for more important guests, not possible employees.

"I will return with a toilet kit shortly," Wong said, turning to leave. "Will you require female companionship tonight? I could bring several to choose from."

Again I wondered if I should, in case Leandra was here, then I declined. The odds of him bringing her were slim to none. And even if she was here, she wouldn't be expected to entertain guest already. It had only been twenty-four hours. And from what I'd seen of Leandra, she was pretty headstrong and had a fiery temper.

An only child, some would call her spoiled, used to manipulating her father to get her way. I chuckled. They'd have a devil of a time subduing her.

Wong returned with a cloth bag containing soap, razor and shave cream, a comb and brush, and toothpaste.

After a shower, I checked the door to the next bedroom. It was locked and it didn't sound as if anyone was in there. Later, however, I heard feet shuffling in the hallway, followed by muffled whispers. Changing of the guard, I suspected.

Lying in bed, I reviewed what had transpired since my ignominious arrival in Bodrum. It seemed like a month had passed, not just ten days. So much had happened since then it was incredible. But so far my plan was working. If I can just get Noli back, then retrieve Leandra. But how? Where would I look?

Simple questions with tough answers. Maybe no answers at all.

Chapter Ten

Wong Fung appeared at my door the next morning wearing an ice-blue gown trimmed in silver. Winding through a maze of hallways, he led me to the penthouse deck. The air was clean, the sun bright, and the view of Izmir Bay magnificent. On a distant spit of land stretching toward Greece stood an ancient fortress, complete with turrets and embattlements.

"Çeşme," Wong Fung said mechanically, "a sixteenth century Genoese fortress."

"Impressive," I replied. "I'd like to wander through it someday. Check out the ancient weapons." I assumed that mercenary pilots would be interested in weapons of all kinds.

"That can be arranged." It was all the head of the household could muster.

He seemed disturbed or else was just grouchy in the morning, making me wonder if he had access to the harem as well…or if he even liked women. A chilling thought.

Bai Simaphong was seated at a round table drinking coffee and talking on a cell phone in Turkish. With a wave of his bejeweled hand he offered me a chair opposite him. "I have good news," he said, holding his hand over the mouthpiece. "I'll tell you in a moment. Would you like breakfast?" He nodded at Wong Fung, hovering nearby, then continued his phone call.

My heart leaped…he'd found Noli. Thank God, now to find Leandra.

Wong motioned to another teenage beauty standing just inside the patio door. I must have walked right by her, or else she took up her post after I sat down. Not as shapely as the one the night before, but pretty: skin golden clear, eyes sparkling bright, and hair cut almost as short as a man's. Holding two pots, she offered to pour coffee or tea into a glass demitasse cup sitting on an equally small saucer, both on the table in front of me. Why Turks didn't use mugs had puzzled me for days. I suppose because it's so strong they don't want much.

I selected coffee but asked for a larger cup—and with cream.

The girl frowned and looked at Wong. After hearing a few stern Turkish words, she left, her head bowed in rebuked. I felt sorry for her and wished I'd settled for a smaller cup.

She returned with a larger one, filling it half with coffee, half cream then left. Moments later she returned with a platter of sausages, fried potatoes, a half dozen eggs—all sunny side up—and two kinds of cheese, white and yellow. A second server, younger and less pretty, carried a bowl of fruit—figs, pomegranates and dates, and a basket of hard rolls. She placed them both on the table in front of me.

As she left, the shorthaired one served me what I chose. I thanked her with a smile, hoping to put her at ease. But she seemed so anxious, to the point of becoming unstrung, I looked down and began to eat. The eggs were undercooked, the potatoes overcooked, but the sausage was good. Also the bread and yellow cheese, so I made a meal of them, along with a second cup of coffee from a third server—plumper, but far less nervous. She even smiled when she offered me more food. I declined, hoping this wouldn't become Leandra's fate.

The thought fisted my stomach.

*   *   *   *

"Good news!" my host shouted, interrupting my reverie. "Your friend Noli will be released within the hour."

"That *is* good news," I cried. "Who had him and where did they keep him?"

"Despicable men, in a crime-infested neighborhood. It would be an intimidating adventure for a foreigner to go there, especially an American. I suggested they take him to Kulture Park and leave him by the monkey cages. While he is waiting, he will enjoy the marmosets—they have faces like old men, chin whiskers and all."

"Wonderful," I replied, guessing all this was a bunch of crap, but pleased that Noli would be released soon. "I'm anxious to see him. How did you manage it?" I guessed he didn't want Noli in the first place. He was just there when they grabbed Leandra, so they had to take him. But why grab her? Just a coincidence? I doubt it...it was probably the Captain to spite Nazif...and to make a pile of *lire* off her by selling her to Simaphong.

My host smiled. "As you suggested last night…I have my ways, and a few influential friends…"

He left the thought hanging. What a jerk, I thought. Thank God, he doesn't know what I know about Leandra. Or does he?

Hardly, not and invite me to stay over and have breakfast with him.

Suddenly, another thought struck me. Simaphong must think that I don't know what happened to Noli, but he knows that I will when I talk to him. So maybe Simaphong *wasn't* involved in the kidnapping. If he was, of course, he'd deny everything. He had to. The important thing is that Noli is back and safe. Now if I can just find Leandra.

Maybe Noli will know something? God, I hope so.

"My driver will take you to the park shortly," Simaphong continued. "Later, I want to inspect your plane. Could you have it at the Izmir marina at noon? I will make arrangements so you can park it there."

When I didn't answer right away, digesting the implications of what that might mean, he continued. "It will be quite safe, I assure you. And if I am satisfied, and I suspect I will be, we will drive to my mountain retreat. You will find it most interesting. It is my headquarters, where I do most of my business. There is a flat area up there—where sheep and goats graze. I'd like you to examine it for a possible landing strip. What is the takeoff and landing distance of your plane? There might be times I'd rather land up there than at the airport or on Izmir Bay."

I decided to go along with him. "Forty-five hundred feet for landing, slightly less for takeoff."

"I am sure there are two kilometers up there, maybe more. What does it cost to fly your plane? Be truthful, now, I am a pilot myself. I fly a Piper Arrow Four. Are you familiar with it?"

I nodded. "Four-place with a single Lycoming. Cruises about one-fifty."

"I see you know your planes. If I have a longer trip, I rent a Caravan One and a pilot."

"I know that one too: ten-place with a single turbo, cruises about one-eighty."

"Close. One-seventy-five and nine passengers. Thirteen hundred mile range. It's the best plane available around here. I often fly with clients, wealthy Germans, Arabs. Other planes are either too large or too small, or don't have enough range. With as much flying as I have done lately, it might be worth having my own plane…and pilot."

"I won't sell the Bluebird but I might fly it for you—exclusively, that is."

Simaphong laughed. "I hardly need to buy it. But out of curiosity, how much would one sell for...approximately, and what does it cost to fly it?"

I felt like saying, "If you have to ask, you can't afford it," but I didn't. Besides, what difference did it make? I wasn't going to sell it, anyway.

"Four or five million, if you can find one. Only fifty-nine were built. In the eighties, Frakes Aviation converted twelve of them to turbos, but they seldom come on the market. I got lucky. My first employer gave it to me for saving his life a couple of times just before he retired."

"How commendable," the crime lord responded, as if impressed.

Fat chance he'd buy it anyway, I mused. He'd just steal it. Have his Cossack giant crack my skull and dump me into the sea. Except, he'd have to find another pilot or learn to fly it himself. I chuckled at the silliness of it all, until it occurred to me that it could happen that way. Look what had already happened.

Becoming more serious, I told him the cost of flying varied between one-hundred and one-hundred and fifty dollars an hour—at current oil prices.

As he pondered that—converting dollars into lire—my mind turned to Noli, hoping he hadn't been abused. I was anxious to see him and then tell Nazif and Hasan.

I wonder if the chauffeur will tag along. Maybe I can lose him somewhere.

In a macabre sort of way, I was looking forward to seeing Simaphong's command post, an isolated citadel where kidnapped girls could be trained.

It must be a formidable place, I reflected. Leandra might be there right now, or soon will be. God, I hope not. An underground fortress would be a bitch to escape from. Maybe he'll keep her here. After all, I was offered female companionship last night.

Damn, I should have asked for one—several even, in case Leandra was one of them. But what if she screamed when she saw me...and tried to hug me?

So many questions. So few answers.

＊　　　＊　　　＊　　　＊

Noli turned from watching the marmosets as soon as I called his name, his eyes clouded with anxiety. Closing the distance between us in three giant steps, he hugged me like a father. "Señor Dan," he sobbed, "I so glad you come. I-I…so frightened. Leandra too. You find her?"

"Not yet, but I will. Are you all right? Did they hurt you? Come on. A driver will take us to the ferry. Nazif will be worried. Do you know where Leandra is?"

"No…they take her away this morning. I'm okay…they only hit me once."

My heart sank. How would we find her now? We don't even know where she is. Unless…

Walking to the car, Noli explained that three men had taken them from Bodrum to an abandoned house in a rundown neighborhood of Izmir and tied them to a radiator. Then two of the men left. The house had broken windows, no furniture and was filthy.

"Did he bother Leandra?" I asked expectantly. "You know…"

"No."

"Thank God for that," I replied, thinking, they must have known that damaged goods would be worth a lot less.

Continuing his gruesome tale, Noli said the man gave them bread the next morning and a glass of water. Later, when the two other men returned, Leandra was taken away. Thinking they might have all left, Noli then broke a window and tried to escape but the remaining man stopped him and hit him.

"Here and here," Noli said, pointing to bruises above his eye and on his left arm. "I spend two nights there. Bad place…many rats—" Noli shuddered. "Then they bring me here and tell me wait, then leave. I afraid but *muito felix*…ah, very happy to see you."

Approaching the black Mercedes, the driver jumped out and opened the rear door. He was dressed like an East Indian, flowing gown, turban and all.

Noli suddenly stopped, his face streaked with fear.

Before he could speak I asked if he'd seen the man before, or the car. He shook his head, his eyes fixed on the driver. "It's okay then. Climb in."

I told the driver to take us to the ferry. He nodded, adding, "Very good, sir," as if it was a wise choice. Kind of weird. Along the way he called someone on his cell phone—probably Wong Fung or Simaphong, himself.

*   *   *   *

At the ferry I told the driver I didn't need him anymore and would return with my plane at noon. I hoped he'd leave. I didn't want him to know where we were going.

Thankfully, he did, after watching me buy Noli a Coke and two salami sandwiches at a booth on the wide, patterned sidewalk. A man fried them for him on fresh hard rolls.

Just to make sure, I waited until Noli ate one.

Then, with the other one in hand and the Mercedes nowhere in sight, he followed me across the street to Mahoud's tour office.

Nazif greeted me with a shout and hug. *"Fevkalade!* You find him...but where Leandra?"

"One step at a time," I said, returning his hug. "We'll find her too. Soon, I hope."

While Noli ate his sandwich, I told Nazif and Mahoud what Noli had related to me about being driven to Izmir, kept overnight but not abused, and about Leandra being taken away yesterday morning. Then I explained what happened after they left the bar the night before: meeting Simaphong, my two chats with him, his interest in my plane, and his desire to build an air strip at his mountain headquarters. "So my guess is that Leandra is up there, where she will start her training to become a maid or a nanny."

I said nothing about being offered a female companion for the night. Nazif looked upset enough as it was.

"You think Leandra there?" he asked, beginning to pace the tour office.

"Or soon will be. The tricky part is getting her out."

By then Noli had wolfed down his second sandwich and looked as if he could eat two more. Anxious to leave myself, I thanked Mahoud for all he'd done and told him that I planned to park the Bluebird at the marina while visiting Simaphong's underground headquarters. He agreed to keep an on eye it while I was gone and wished us good luck.

We'd need it after we freed Leandra from the lion's lair...if she was there.

*   *   *   *

After purchasing three ferry tickets, I gave Noli the change so he could buy a couple of candy bars and a bag of pretzels.

Just as the boatman cast off the last rope, we scurried aboard, sitting in an inside lounge lined with seats. During our crossing, I told Nazif an idea I had: a way to get Leandra out of the mountain stronghold.

"While Noli and I taxi the Bluebird to the marina, you and Hasan take the ferry back and rent a car...no, two cars...or one could be Mahoud's, if he's willing to let you use it. Use some of the *lire* you received for the fish you sold. Okay?" When Nazif nodded his agreement, I continued. "After Simaphong inspects my plane, you and Hasan follow his car to his command post. It's a black, late model Mercedes."

"Why we need two cars?" Nazif asked, his eyebrows twitching as usual.

"More confusing. His driver will be less likely to know someone is following him."

"Maybe we get cab," Nazif suggested with a shrug. "I have friend—"

I shook my head. "You may be on the mountain a long time, even overnight. Unless your friend is willing to do that." When Nazif said nothing, I continued. "Okay. So you both follow the Mercedes until you know where the commandpost is—which mountain road it is on. But don't follow too close and don't follow us all the way. Ask someone in a village. They will know about the command post. It's been there for years. It used to be a NATO facility."

"Mahoud will know which road, then what? We go in and get Leandra?"

"No! No! Noli and I will have to look around first. Spend the night, maybe. Ask questions. But we'll find her...and get her out too."

"I worry...*çok üzüntü*"

"I know you do. I'm sorry I got you into this mess. But we'll find her, and we'll get Bai Simaphong too—one way or another."

"What next?" Noli asked, becoming excited. Until then, he'd been subdued and uninterested. I figured he was just tired. Later, he told me it was when he knew that he'd be in the Mercedes with me. I nearly chocked up.

"I told Simaphong that you and I had become separated after we escaped and that you might go to Izmir because we planned to look for work there. Did you happen to see a short, fat oriental man with his hair pulled back?"

Noli shook his head.

"Good, then I'll tell him that someone grabbed you and a girl you'd just met, and drove you to a house in Izmir. The next morning, yesterday, the girl was taken away. Does that sound okay? Except for the part about you just meeting Leandra, it's the truth."

"Sure…You say man hit me when I try to escape?"

"I might as well. He'll see your bruises. I just don't want him to know that we knew Leandra before you two were captured. Do you think you can keep from saying anything that will make Simaphong suspicious? It will spoil my plan if you do. In fact, we could end up prisoners ourselves."

"I say nothing," Noli said with resolve. "Okay?"

"Good. The less you say the better." I didn't tell them how I planned to find Leandra…by asking Wong for girls until he brought her.

Nazif frowned darkly. "You think you find Leandra?"

"I hope so," thinking, if we aren't too late.

Continuing, I told them the second part…the hardest part. "When you know where the command post is, park a few miles down the road from it and wait…in a village, maybe. Remember, don't follow too closely or it will be obvious."

Nazif nodded his understanding, but I wasn't sure if he really did. It was a lot to grapple with in a foreign language, especially when your daughter's life was at stake or about to become a love slave for oil-rich Arab.

Looking at him, I wondered if he knew that. Hopefully not…at least, not yet. I wonder how long it takes to train a girl—days, weeks?

I continued. "If there is no village, just stay in your cars. But make sure it's easy for Noli and me to find you in the dark. Maybe we should have a signal."

"I know… I'll whistle like this." With two fingers in my mouth, I blew a loud wolf whistle. "That means we're looking for you."

An elderly couple on the other side of the ferry lounge looked at us oddly. Ignoring them, I turned to Noli and asked if he could whistle like that.

He could…even louder.

"*Dur!*" Nazif shouted, holding his ears. "That too loud!"

The couple left the lounge with a scowl. But a young man near the lounge entrance whistled also, then waved.

Waving back, I continued. "My plan is to sneak out of our rooms, find Leandra and escape—even bring out a few other girls, if I can. Another reason for having two cars is to carry them all, which means that you and Hasan should be ready to drive back down the mountain in a hurry. By the way, take my rifle. You'll find it in the Bluebird."

                    *   *   *   *

Hasan was as glad to see Noli as I'd been and lifted him off his feet with a hug. To save time so they could catch the same ferry back to Izmir, I told Nazif to tell his brother my plan later. "And keep a sharp eye on the marina. When you see the Mercedes leave, you two follow it, but not—"

"Too close," Nazif interrupted, "I know. And stop at last village and wait. First part easy. Waiting hard."

"It will be for us too. But we must be patient. And remember, no heroics. We'll find Leandra, somehow, and bring her home, late tonight, if possible."

The harbormaster's assistant rowed Noli and me out to the Bluebird. Having him back gave me a warm feeling, like he was in his rightful place again. But moments later, while taxiing across the two-mile stretch of water between Karşiyaka and the marina, my mind clouded with doubts over what we were about to do.

Could Nazif and Hasan follow the black Mercedes in traffic then into the mountains without being spotted by the chauffer or one of Simaphong's guards? And once inside the mountain stronghold, could Noli and I find Leandra?

The first seemed possible, the second...unlikely. We'd probably have a guard at our door all night, like we did at the hotel. And what if Wong Fung *did* bring Leandra to my room? Wouldn't she scream out something when she saw me? And even if she didn't, how would I get her out of a fortress that is buried inside a mountain?

Down the street from the ferry I'd seen a bronze statute of a soldier on horseback: Kemal Attaturk, the George Washington of Turkey, who Regina had mentioned. I wondered what he'd think of his country, in light of what had happened to Alexis and Leandra.

✻   ✻   ✻   ✻

Taxiing into the marina an elderly man wearing a felt beret and baggy pants waved from a boardwalk just few inches above the water. I eased the plane toward him, able to straddle the low walkway between the fuselage and the left tip tank. He then tossed a coiled rope over the tail like a lasso and cinched it to a metal cleat on the pier, tying another rope to the left tip tank. It was obvious he'd done this before.

I shut down the engines and reset all the switches for a fast takeoff, just in case.

As we exited the plane, the ferry arrived. I spotted Hasan easily, head and shoulders above the others. Nazif, shorter but equally muscular, followed.

My plan had been set in motion.

While we waited, Noli and I sat on a wooden bench near the marina office and watched a small bear dance on its hind feet to music pumped by a gypsy from a battered music box balanced on a pole. A capuchin monkey, dressed in a red cap and vest, sat on the music box holding a tin cup. When the bear finished twirling, the monkey scurried among the milling crowd and collected donations.

The monkey was cute but I felt sorry for the bear, also wearing a faded red vest, tethered by a nose-ring attacked to a chain held by the gypsy. The bear would only twirl once or twice then beg for food from its owner, who quickly retrieved the coins from the cup and jammed them into his pocket each time the monkey returned. It was all pretty pathetic, but the crowd enjoyed it and the gypsy made a few *lire* before moving on.

I spotted Simaphong and his turbaned driver as soon as the crowd dispersed. It was twelve fifteen. I was glad he was late, more time for Nazif and Hasan to find cars.

Introducing Noli, I briefly told his story as if the crime lord didn't already know it. Simaphong acted concerned, made a vague comment about Noli's bruises, but it was obvious that he was more interested in inspecting the Bluebird than anything else.

Climbing aboard, I stretched out the tour as long as possible, first showing him the aft storage bin where the ten-man, inflatable lifeboat was stored and also the latrine. In the passenger cabin I suggested he try one of the plush seats, demonstrating how to make it into a bed. Encouraged by his grin, I opened the locker where I kept coffee and ice water, then offered him the copilot's seat while I reviewed the instruments: the Doppler, the IFF, even the tracking radios.

"Do you have GPS?" he asked, absently touching but not moving the five over-head levers on the copilot's side.

I was surprised he knew of the Global Positioning System, the latest innovation in satellite navigation, and wondered if he *did* covet the Bluebird—after I taught him to fly it, of course, which I'd never do. I'd done that with my last boss. Worked myself right out of a job. I wasn't about to do it again.

"It's a little pricey," I replied, "Maybe later. It would certainly help on long over-water flights. I flew a client from the Azores to Bermuda once—against the wind. I sure could have used it then...I lost the Doppler."

"How *did* you navigate?"

"Old fashioned Dead Reckoning, mostly."

"And considerable skill, I suspect."

"That too." I was beginning to like his tone and wondered how much he'd pay to have a private pilot. Men who earn wealth in a hurry often become miserly in the process. It's the second and third generations who spend more freely, even give it away. It's easier to do when you didn't earn it yourself.

"Have you flown over water much in this plane?"

"Many times—ten hours on that flight. Had to carry extra fuel, of course."

"And you only had Doppler and tracking radios?"

"That's all you need, really." I tried to sound cocky, adding, "It was no big deal."

Bai Simaphong smiled and said something to his driver, bending to stand in the cockpit entry. More of that singsong stuff that I couldn't understand. He looked like a swami in his baggy pants and turban. We hadn't been introduced, nor did I care to be.

"Very interesting," Simaphong said, rubbing his bejeweled hand under his flabby chin. "I'm impressed. How much flying time did you say you had?"

"Close to five thousand hours."

"Are you an instructor pilot?"

I nodded. "Taught my last boss to fly from scratch. He'd never flown before."

"Would you teach me to fly this plane?"

"I might...if the price is right. You thinking of buying one? Remember, this one isn't for sale and Mallards are hard to find on the open market."

"I'm sure I could find one somewhere. Come, I want to show you my mountain command post."

"I'd like to see it," I said, hoping Nazif and Hasan had had enough time to find two cars...and could keep up with us.

Approaching the Mercedes, Simaphong explained that when the underground command post belonged to NATO it was called Disko Hit. Why, he didn't know. It was just a code name and discos were popular back then.

I was barely listening, more intent on spotting Nazif and Hasan without being obvious. When I didn't, I hoped they were at least watching us.

✳ ✳ ✳ ✳

Izmir is a crowded city and Turks, I decided, are the world's most impatient drivers—also the least experienced. Once, a car passed us on our right and drove on the sidewalk for a half-block—pedestrians jumping aside to keep from being hit. Only to find himself mired in an impenetrable jam of cars trying to negotiate a traffic circle. Horns blaring, fists waving, curses being exchanged.

Fortunately, our driver had the radio on, the windows up, and was running the air-conditioning so traffic noise was more subdued.

Noli sat in front. I sat in back with Simaphong. His Cossack giant hadn't been invited. Simaphong hardly need a bodyguard when he was with his turbaned driver.

Commenting on the traffic Simaphong asked how long Noli and I had been together. When I told him only a few months, he seemed surprised, as if expecting it to be longer. After that he asked no more questions about Noli or me, nor did he comment on what had happened to us. I still wasn't sure he was involved but guessed he was, at least indirectly. His men might not kidnap girls but other men did. Men like Captain Tokolu, knowing Simaphong would pay well if the girl was trainable, pretty and still a virgin.

What worried me was, if he knew about the flights I'd made for Hasan. Probably not, otherwise, he wouldn't be taking me to his underground command post and acting as if he wanted me to work for him. Unless that's all it was—an act, before he did away with both of us…in a place no one was likely to find us.

A chilling thought, and there were more questions. Why was Nazif's boat factory vandalized? An attempt by Simaphong to eliminate competition? Or did Tokolu order it done to spite Nazif for helping me? In which case, Simaphong probably had nothing to do with any of this. After all, didn't he call the men who did it despicable?

Looking out the window but seeing nothing, I tried to remain focused. Whether Simaphong knows what I've done or not, or whether he had anything to do with the kidnappings or not, it's for sure he wants the Bluebird. And when he knows how to fly it, he won't need me anymore. So either way, I'll be toast…either tossed into the sea like Alexis or buried underground in a former NATO facility.

Glancing behind us, in hopes of spotting Nazif or Hasan, I commented on the traffic. Simaphong merely nodded his mind somewhere
else. Seeing no one I recognized, my heart sank. Maybe they didn't have
time to rent a car, or maybe…

My mind suddenly went blank with doubt.

*   *   *   *

Beyond the last traffic circle, the traffic thinned considerably and we
began to climb. According to my guidebook, Izmir is located just west of
a plateau that stretched clear across Turkey, rising to over 15,000 feet on
the border of the old Soviet Union.

Reading on, I discovered that Mount Ararat, of Noah's Ark fame, is
in that range, and that they'd discovered wood beams up there carbon-
dated to the third or fourth century B.C.E. Hoping, I suppose, that bible
believers would be interested enough to hike up there for a look see.
Spending money in tourist shops for replicas of Noah's ark. Supposedly,
made from the same wood, but more likely made in China..

Being late in May, the low foothills were verdant and lush. In summer,
they'd be tinder dry and dull brown, since much of Turkey is a desert.

Turning off the four-lane highway onto a narrow two lane, a sign
announced we were entering Kemalpasa. It was there, at a BP gas
station, that I saw Nazif in a nearly new Ford—a rental car. He was
parked at the last pump waiting for us to turn in there. Mahoud must
have known where Disko Hit was and told him.

I was so pleased, my heart nearly jumped into my throat. Glancing
behind us, I saw Hasan in a battered truck, guessing it to be Mahoud's.
Just as Hasan pulled into the gas station Nazif pulled out. They were
doing exactly as I said, following as a team.

The two-lane road steepened as it climbed into the mountains. In several places our driver had to slow to negotiate sharp, switch-back turns
before speeding up again. It was obvious he'd made the trip many times.
His boss also.

After twenty minutes of this, we slowed for a small village—just a
store, a school, a tiny mosque, and a dozen whitewashed shanties people
called home. No restaurant, no gas station, but plenty of outside biffies.
It was then Simaphong began asking about my personal life: my parents,
my marriage, whether I'd ever been arrested or spent time in jail.

It irked me that in his line of work he'd even care, especially since I
knew so little about *him*. All I knew for sure was that I'd never fly for

him, so I kept my answers brief or made them up...with sincerity, of course, as if my life depended on it.

To my great relief, he seemed to buy it all...hook, line and sinker. And glancing back occasionally, I was also relieved that Nazif wasn't following us closely. It would be much too obvious. Besides, how difficult could it be to find a former NATO facility, knowing which road it was on? We were bound to come to a deadend somewhere.

Soon, I hoped. The longer we drove the farther away we'd be from the Bluebird, our only lifeline to safety. Our link to the real world...the sane world.

*   *   *   *

A few minutes later we passed through a second village smaller than the first, then a third, hardly a village at all. We'd been driving for nearly an hour. Six or eight bedraggled children waved at us as we went by, obviously recognizing the car. Their homes, a dozen mud huts hardly fit for pigs let alone children. No store, no school, no mosque.

"We're almost there," Simaphong said a few miles farther.

Looking out, I saw four goats munching thistles and tended by a goatherd. He was sitting under a knurled olive tree so old its truck was split wide enough for him to climb through it. I guessed him to be six-teen. And when he waved at me, his smile was a big as Noli's.

I wondered if Noli saw him and what he was thinking. But for the grace of God, there go I? Leaning forward, I patted his shoulder. At the same time I checked the mileage from the marina, in case I needed it for our return trip. If we had a return trip.

Noli was asleep and awoke with a start, jerking his head as if con-fused about where he was. I was glad he'd had a short nap, a chance to catch up on the sleep he'd missed in that battered house in Izmir. It must have been terrifying for him.

"We're almost there," I said. "Time to wake up." I wanted him to help me locate checkpoints we might recognize, in case we had to leave in a hurry and find the Kesfin brothers in the dark—with or without Leandra.

Unfortunately, all I could see were untended olive trees, dusty thistles and acres of dried weeds and rocks. That's when I began questioning my sanity.

This is crazy. Noli and I will never get Leandra out of here. And even if we do, we'll have to find Nazif and Hasan in the dark, then race down the mountain to the marina, hoping the Bluebird isn't surrounded by an army of Simaphong's thugs. Men like those I'd met in that seedy bistro last night. All it would take was a call from the command post.

Unless, somehow, he didn't know that we'd escaped?

Chapter Eleven

The Mercedes stopped in a dirt parking lot carved into the side of a mountain. Stepping out of the back seat, a soft breeze washed over me, cooling the desert-like air.

I wasn't sure what I expected Disko Hit to be but certainly more than this. At first glance, I saw nothing—no guards, no fences, no weapon emplacements, nothing that would lead one to believe this was a formidable, underground command post. Only a few cars huddled together at one end of the parking area.

Then it occurred to me: NATO must have wanted Disko Hit to look like this in case a family stumbled upon it in search of a picnic site. Although, I couldn't imagine why anyone would come to this desolate place for a picnic. There was no mountain lake, no panoramic vistas, not even a stream running through a grove of trees.

From the parking lot, Simaphong led us toward a cave opening cut into the side of the mountain. Until then I hadn't noticed it, although it was at least fifteen feet high and just as wide. Walking beside our host, I towered over him—barely five foot six, I guessed. His turbaned driver followed closely behind.

Noli seemed in awe of the place, staying close to me and saying nothing. I was sure he was frightened…and so was I.

Inside the cave, a long tunnel with asphalt floors and plaster walls aimed directly into the heart of the mountain. When my eyes grew more accustomed to the dimming light, I realized the tunnel was illuminated by fluorescent fixtures hanging from a twenty-foot curved ceiling. Air blowing in my face smelled flat and stale, as if generated by a huge fan.

A thought suddenly occurred to me: an underground facility has to be heated in winter and cooled in summer. Would it be possible to escape from this deathtrap by climbing through ventilation ducts?

A hundred yards or so into the tunnel, as wide as two lanes of traffic, Simaphong stopped at an open vault door, although the tunnel continued on. How far, it was difficult to tell. Another hundred yards? A second entry for deliverymen and servants?

The vault door was like those found in banks, with dials on the front and levers and wheels on the back. A uniformed guard, as implacable as our turbaned driver, stood rigidly at attention until Simaphong greeted him in Turkish. He then relaxed and let us enter a small, ante-room. There, another guard—no less ferocious-looking with a red mustache, waved me through a metal detector like those found in airports.

I'd thought about bringing a pocketknife—even a pen light, anything to facilitate our escape, but had decided against it. That's why it surprised me when the buzzer went off.

Thinking it was my Turkish coins, I emptied my pockets into a basket the guard held out to me, along with the key to Bluebird entry door, which I kept on a steel ring. When the buzzer sounded a second time, the guard motioned for me to remove my windbreaker.

When I did, he waved a metal detecting wand between my legs, behind my back and under my arms. No buzzer. But waving it across my chest, it chattered loudly.

The guard glared at me menacingly, until I showed him Alexis' crucifix and Saint Christopher's medal hung around my neck. I'd forgotten to give them to her parents in Chios.

Sheepishly, I pulled both from my shirt. The guard's frown quickly relaxed.

"Catholic, I see," Simaphong said with a tight grin. "For a moment, I thought you might be foolish enough to try to smuggle a gun or knife in here. Neither of which is allowed, of course, for obvious reasons."

Noli passed through the metal detector without comment. Simaphong then spun the combination on a second vault door, which swung open to reveal a hatch similar to those seen aboard ships. The kind you have to step over and duck under at the same time to keep from tripping or bashing your head.

Following our host through the hatch and into a narrow, steel-lined corridor cluttered with overhead pipes, I felt like we were entering a submarine.

Our host explained. "Disko Hit was designed to withstand all but a direct hit by an atomic bomb. Having the entry at right angles to the entry tunnel and encasing it with metal was meant to dissipate the heat and fire, even if a bomb fell on the parking lot. Ingenious, don't you think?"

"In a morbid sort of way. Did any bombs ever fall on it?"

"No, but the Cold War was played quite seriously, I understand, by NATO *and* the Warsaw Pact."

I couldn't argue with that. This place was incredible.

*   *   *   *

The steel-clad corridor emptied into a typical office hallway, again at right angles. Another safeguard, I surmised, in case both vault doors were open during a surprise attack.

A most unlikely occurrence, I thought. I couldn't even imagine being inside this mountain during an attack...even in a war game. And NATO must have had thousands of them, run from this command post, probably lasting a week or more.

I shuddered at the thought.

From there Disko Hit looked pretty much like any government office complex with drab walls and few frills. I toured the Pentagon once on a layover in D.C. On the inside, Disko Hit looked a little like that five-sided wonder, only smaller and with no windows.

Every dozen yards, office-lined hallways branched off from the main corridor. Opened office doors revealed desks, computers and file cabinets, all quite conventional.

An Asian man seeing us approaching looked startled, even afraid. Bowing quickly, he scurried off in another direction.

Simaphong ignored him. "Each corridor is a separate business. As you can see, I am into many things, imports and exports, commercial fishing, boat-building, petrochemicals, pharmaceuticals, investment banking...many things, and growing rapidly."

Not to mention, trafficking in young women, drug smuggling and illicit arms sales, I added to myself.

"Many years ago, when my father died, I took over his store," Simaphong continued with ease, obviously not feeling the increased tension as I was the deeper we penetrated the mountain. "He imported inexpensive jewelry from Thailand. That's where I am from, originally. My parents moved to Izmir when I was six...and died when I was eighteen. I now have three retail outlets: a fine jewelry and accessory store, a furniture store, and a store for silk and ladies apparel."

Discounting his many illegal enterprises, I was impressed by what he'd accomplished in such a short time...and without family backing. He must be a shrewd and ruthless businessman, but I still wouldn't fly for him.

We continued walking. Never thrilled about being underground, I began to sweat. I also wondered where he kept his harem, the girls not sold to oil-rich Arabs as concubines or wealthy English families as nannies.

I'd have to find Leandra soon. Time was running out...for me and for her.

*   *   *   *

Turning into another corridor, Simaphong showed us a large dining room divided by folding walls and devoid of any decorations or homey accoutrements—no paintings, drapes, table clothes, anything. Like a school cafeteria or army mess hall.

"We also have a reading room, lounge, and a game room with pool tables," he explained. "Most of my employees spend a month up here then have a week off. It saves driving up and down the mountain so much."

I nodded, thinking, but why here...underground? To keep his business secret...away from prying eyes? The police? He *must* train girls here. It's a perfect spot. But where? This place is huge. There must be a hundred rooms, maybe more.

Passing two more corridors, we stopped at what Simaphong called his nerve center. A bank of computer screens covered one wall. Three rows of PCs faced them but only half were occupied.

Turning away from me, Simaphong spoke harshly to a man in a business suit. The man's softly slanted eyes darted nervously from the screens on the wall, back to his PC. His responses were brief and in the same language I'd heard before.

I decided he must be Thai also. Maybe they all are. Several other men monitoring PCs had the same softly slanted eyes and skin coloring. Maybe he doesn't trust Turks to run his businesses. I'm not sure I would either. So far, I'd only met a few I even liked.

As Simaphong turned to leave, relief flooded the man's face. He'd apparently said the right things and his boss left with a half smile on his chubby face.

From there, with the turbaned driver still hovering behind us, Simaphong led Noli and me down a long hall that had fewer doors than the others did. Soft music filled the air, piped in from the nerve center, he said, "This is the guest wing, where you two will be staying. Do you think you can find your way back to the dining room?"

Pausing, I turned around. "Down this hall, turn right, then left, passed the nerve center, then turn...ah—"

"Left again." Simaphong laughed. "Very good. Most people I bring in here are totally lost by now. If you turned right, you will be in *my* wing...a private wing."

"It would be easy to get lost in here," I said, trying to remember what he'd said in case I had to find Leandra the hard way—by searching each room. An unlikely scenario but I was desperate, not knowing how I would find her in this rat maze.

"I feel like I'm aboard ship," I said, finally. "An aircraft carrier, maybe. I spent a couple of nights on one once."

"It is a bit like that. We are so isolated here. But on an aircraft carrier you can, at least, climb upstairs and look out. Here...well, there is only one way out. The same way we came in. The parking lot is nearly a mile from here."

The way he said it sent chills up my spine, reminding me how far we were from help and how difficult it would be to get out without him knowing it. Without anyone knowing it...or not meeting us at the marina with guns drawn.

He stopped in front of a door marked *Guest Room #3*. "This is your room, Mister Sylvester. Noli had been assigned the one next door."

"When do you want to look at the possible landing area?" I asked.

"After you two are settled." He looked at his watch—a gold Rolex, naturally. "Let's see...it is three now. Say about four? I will send someone to guide you to the entrance. This is not a good place to be caught wandering about. My people are told to keep an eye on guests and treat them with respect. But if you were to find yourself in a room where you are not welcome, most would take offense and...well, maybe forget their manners."

"Don't worry. We'll stay put. It looks to me like Noli needs a nap...a long one. He probably won't wake up until tomorrow morning. His last two days were pretty hard on him and he lost a lot of sleep."

"And so unnecessary," Simaphong replied with sincerity as he opened the door to our two-room suite. "I'm glad we found him. I can see that he means a lot to you. Do you have children of your own? I forgot to ask."

"None that I'm aware of," I said with a grin, remembering I was supposed to be a foot-loose mercenary pilot, although, I doubted he thought that. Not with Noli there.

                ⁜   ⁜   ⁜   ⁜

Left alone, Noli and I looked around the room. With no window or even drapes to make it look like there was a window, the room was stark; also small, smaller than my hotel room the night before. A double bed with night stands filled one wall. A four-drawer dresser and a small desk with a straight chair completed the furnishings. With no wall decorations, prints or paintings, it looked like a monk's cell, and the lamp clamped to a bedpost gave it a cheesy 1930's look.

For a moment I felt dizzy and a little nauseous, my face flushed. A touch of claustrophobia. I needed to be outside, breathing fresh air, being warmed by the sun.

The feeling passed and I noticed four recessed lights in the ceiling which mimicked the effect of daylight. Curious, I flipped them off, enveloping the room in ebony blackness. With only a sliver of light filtering under the door I could see my hand directly in front of my eyes but nothing else. I quickly turned the lights on again.

"Dark wasn't it?" I said to Noli not expecting an answer.

He nodded and went through our shared bathroom to his room. I followed. Smaller yet, it only had a single bed, one nightstand, a dresser, and a straight chair with a padded seat. But it did have a picture—an island seascape.

"I like better," he said, pointing to the picture. "It look like Azores."

"I guess we should have brought clothes and our toilet kits," I commented, looking into the room from the bathroom. "Our host never said we'd be staying over. I expected to drive back tonight."

Turning, I noticed two clear plastic bags on the counter, each containing a toothbrush, toothpaste, disposable razor, shave cream and a few Band Aids.

Nice touch. Like a five-star hotel.

Pausing, it suddenly dawned on me that the room might be bugged. With my finger to my lips, I began searching for a microphone, first in Noli's room then mine. I found none, but I did notice an air vent grill on the wall just above and to the right of the double bed in my room. Walking into the bathroom, I turned on the shower to drown out our voices, then asked Noli if he felt rested enough for some dangerous work.

His eyes widened in delight. "Sure! What I do?"

"The way I see it," I started, working out a plan as I spoke, "the best way out of here is through an air duct that leads outside. Some probably do, some might not. We need to determine which one does, then find Leandra and crawl through it."

"I can do," he replied with the confidence of youth, looking at the grill. "How I get in? You no have *faca*...ah—knife."

Without answering, I went to the door of my room to see if it was locked. It wasn't. A quick check confirmed there was no guard yet either, although I was sure there would be soon.

Returning, I slid the desk chair under the grill and climbed up. Using the edge of Alexis' St Christopher's medal, I unscrewed the fasteners on the bottom and sides, leaving the top screws in place, then eased the bottom of the screen away from the wall.

"Can you make it through there if I give you a boost?" I asked, not sure I could make it though the grill, even *with* a boost.

"Sim, Señor—" He started before I cut him off.

"Please...call me Dan. We're family now. Okay?"

Noli's face lit up like a kid who'd just seen Santa Claus, his grin so broad I thought his face might crack. "Ah...sure, Dan, I do. Should I go now?"

"No, first you need something to mark your way with. Look in your room for a pencil. I'll look in here."

Noli returned with a stubby, chewed up one. I found a pack of matches in my desk and gave it to him. From our toilet kits, I also gave him the Band-Aids.

"When you come to another vent—hopefully a larger one, turn into the wind. I'm guessing air is drawn in from outside."

"Turn into wind," he repeated, closing his eyes, as if locking that bit of information into his mind.

"Right. And mark which way you go with the pencil or a Band-Aid. Only use the matches if it gets too dark to see; and be quiet—someone might hear you. I'll shine the bed lamp in there so you'll have some light at first, but eventually it'll get very dark. If you get confused, follow your markers back here."

I handed him the St. Christopher Medal. "If you find an outside vent, open it with this. Don't come back here and don't screw it back on.

When I've located Leandra, we'll follower your marks and crawl out the same way."

I paused. "Oh...and before you leave that place, mark it with something so you can find it later, just in case. I don't know where you'll be when you get out, so look for the parking lot but watch out for guards. Then follow the road to Nazif and Hasan. They should be waiting by their cars. Whistle for them like we said. Remember?"

"I remember." Noli nodded, starting to do it.

"Not now...on the road...and only if you have to. Wait there with them until it's dark—after nine o'clock—then have them drive up the road just short of the parking lot and wait."

"Then I come back to vent...wait for you and Leandra?"

"Okay, but it may take a while to find her then follow your markers through the air ducts. So don't get impatient and don't let anyone see you. If I'm not there by dawn, return to Nazif and Hasan. They'll know what to do." I hoped.

"You want I go now?" Noli asked, optimism written all over his trusting face.

"Yes...I just wish you had a flashlight...and a bottle of water. It'll be dark and stuffy in there. Even hard to breathe, sometimes. So take you time and don't panic!"

"Is easy," Noli said without hesitation, as if I'd just told him to go buy a loaf of bread at a convenience store. "I climb through vent, find Nazif, wait until dark, come back to vent and wait for you and Leandra."

I shook my head, thinking, to be that young again, so willing, so oblivious to danger. Was I ever that that young? "Okay...but don't forget to mark the way for us."

"I do...find Nazif and Hasan too."

"Great. But it may be harder than you think. There must be miles of air vents in this place. So take your time, and always turn—"

"I know," he interrupted. "Into wind. I get out okay. You see."

Somehow I guessed he would, but could I? I was twice his size. My stomach balled into a knot. And how will I know he even made it out?

Easy, he won't come back.

But what if he gets caught in a vent and can't *get* back?

I erased that possibility from my mind. I had enough problems, finding Leandra, then squirming through those miles of air vents. "At least you won't be missed at dinner. I'll tell Simaphong that you fell asleep and won't wake up until morning. I just wish you had something to eat...something to carry with you. This could be a long night for you."

"I have," Noli said with his perpetual grin, pulling a candy bar from his pocket. "I save from marina."

"Good boy...you'll need it. Drink some water before you leave. You'll get thirsty later. Oh...and go to the bathroom."

Grave doubts swarmed through my head while Noli tended to his needs. Can he find an exit, then find Nazif and Hasan without getting caught? Will Wong bring Leandra to my room...and if so, will we be able to get though the vents as well?

We had to, it was the only way, and it had to be tonight. Tomorrow, we'd be back in Izmir—or dead, depending on whether Simaphong believed my story or not. But what if Leandra isn't here?

She has to be. Why would he have this underground hellhole if not to hide his harem of kidnapped girls?

Hoisting Noli into the vent, I could only hope that soon we'd be safely back in Bodrum and Noli and I would be leaving Turkey forever.

Or would we be buried in Disko Hit forever?

Chapter Twelve

"Don't forget to mark the ducts," I cautioned Noli for the third time. "I'll get a light up there right away."

He muttered something and slid in easily. It would be a much tighter fit for me.

When Noli's feet disappeared from view, I clamped the bed lamp on the grill, which lit up the air duct a lot.

"Better," he call softly. "I see bigger duct now. Wind come from *direita*."

"Then turn into it—go *direita*." I called back "But mark the way as you go." I could tell that Noli was excited; he'd used the Portugue word for "right."

"*Sim*, I do."

After that, I heard nothing from Noli. No whispered voice calling for help. No whistle for me to come and find him; or worse, recover him from an impossible situation.

With a sigh, I returned to the bathroom and turned off the shower. All I could do now was wait, which I knew I'd have trouble doing. I always do when I'm nervous and have nothing to occupy my mind.

*   *   *   *

At four-thirty I heard a sharp knock at my door. By then I'd pushed the air vent back into place, returned the bed lamp to my bed and stuffed extra pillows into Noli's bed to make it look as if he were sleeping, in case someone checked.

The giant I'd seen at the penthouse stood at the door—sash, saber and all. He motioned me to follow him, showing no concern that Noli wasn't with me. For that, I breathed a sigh of relief.

As we walked, I counted the corridors and memorized the turns in case I had to do it again in the middle of the night—a prospect I didn't look forward to. I was also worried about Noli, whether he was doing all right, or hopelessly lost by now in a maze of air ducts.

God, what a mess. How did we ever get caught up in this in the first place?

Turning into a vaguely familiar corridor an image of Alexis' bruised and tear-stained face suddenly popped into my beleaguered brain and I knew why—for her and for Leandra. And for all the others young girls caught in Simaphong's sinister web of evil.

*   *   *   *

The crime lord met us at the vault-doors. After the dining room, we'd taken two lefts, one right, then a left to reach the entry tunnel. Would I remember that? Would I need too?

God, I hope not.

"Did you find everything satisfactory, Mister Sylvester?" Simaphong's voice dripped with honey. "Is your young friend still sleeping?"

"Out like a gravestone," I said, immediately sorry I'd used such an inappropriate simile as doubt further plagued my mind. Maybe I shouldn't have sent Noli so soon…waited until he'd rested, even eaten?

A vision of his emaciated body coiled in a fetal position in a cramped airduct flashed through my mind. My God, what if I get Leandra into that rat maze only to discover Noli's lifeless body in there?

No way. He'd come back first. Besides, she might not even be here.

"Are you all right, Sylvester?" Simaphong asked. "You look pale. Being underground can do that to you, at first."

"Just a bit queasy. It comes and goes. I'll be all right."

By then we'd passed through both vault doors and were heading out the entry tunnel. Just seeing sunlight in the distance—a few bushes, a bird—lifted my spirits. Maybe Noli will make it out okay. God, I hope so. It's been over an hour. Any longer inside that ductwork and he'll be a basketcase. Maybe I can spot him from the parking lot.

But if I can, so can Simaphong and his Cossack bodyguard.

More worry…more agitation. A headache began to build in the back of my neck. Without two Tylenols I'd have a beaut real soon.

*   *   *   *

Exiting the tunnel, I sucked in warm mountain air and reveled in the bright sunlight. I just wasn't cut out to live underground.

Seconds later, my headache disappeared.

"Feel better?" my host asked at the edge of the parking lot. "Usually a couple of quick breaths are all you need. It happens to a lot of people. When I hire a new man, we let him come out every couple of hours during the first week. After that, they are fine—or they quit. Some people can't handle working underground at all."

"I must be one of them," I said wryly. "I'd rather work up there." I pointed to the sky—clear and pale blue.

"Not surprising, in your line of work. How long have you been flying?"

"I soloed when I was seventeen. My uncle was an instructor pilot."

Following Simaphong, we started up a low rise beyond the parking lot. "I soloed five years ago," he commented. "But lately, I've been chartering planes and having someone else do the flying."

"It's probably best. It doesn't pay to fly when you only fly occasionally. You forget things. It's not like driving a car; your life is on the line every time you take off."

"I agree completely. That's why…I hire…professionals." The corpulent crime lord was beginning to pant from the steep climb.

Feeling more confident above ground and having more room to run, although, with his giant stalking us, I wouldn't have gotten far, I ask Simaphong if he ever married.

"Too much trouble, too demanding. Not so, the young women I train to serve my guests." Pausing to catch his breath, a leering grin split his flat round face. "Those, I like, a different one every night. You should select one tonight."

I felt like punching his lights out; but I could feel the Cossack's breath on my neck, he was following us that closely. "Perhaps I will," I replied with feigned enthusiasm. "As many as it takes to get Leandra into my room," I added to myself.

By then I was convinced that asking for several girls was the only way I'd get Leandra out of there, if she was even there yet. If not, then all this was a waste of time.

❋   ❋   ❋   ❋

Thirty feet above the parking lot, Simaphong pointed toward a flat area covered with stubble grass and low bushes. A line of trees along one side marked a stream.

I took a deep breath, again relishing the clear air and warm sunshine. I hadn't known before how much being underground would bother me; the thought of crawling through a ventilation duct almost made me sick to my stomach.

"What do you think?" he asked with child-like anticipation.

I could see his mind was already made up; he would have a runway up here despite the cost. And who was I to dissuade him? I'd never land on it anyway. "There's plenty of open space up here," I said with as much interest as I could muster, "but you'll need several Bobcats to flatten it."

"Or fifty men with shovels and hoes," he snapped. "Americans always think technology will solve everything. In my country, as in Turkey, people solve everything. That is why I like it here. It is easy to find men willing to work hard for a decent wage."

Girls too, if you kidnap them and hold them against their will, I thought. "It's up to you," I replied, "people or machines. I was just thinking of the time it would save."

"Do you think it is long enough?" he asked, his anger dissipating quickly.

"Certainly. With enough money you could build anything you want up here."

Ignoring my sarcasm, he asked if it would be long enough to land the Bluebird.

"Easy. Prevailing wind is from that way, isn't it?" I pointed toward the sun, a great red orb low in the western sky. "So the runway would run parallel to those trees over there."

It was then I spotted the goatherd who I'd seen near the village and wondered what *he'd* think if a runway crossed his pasture. "Do you own all this land?" I asked Simaphong with sudden concern.

"Yes…beyond where that boy is tending his animals. I let him graze his goats up here and for that, he keeps an eye on things. Let's me know if anyone is snooping around up here."

I immediately thought of Noli. He wouldn't expect that the boy worked for Simaphong. He might even ask him directions to the parking lot.

One more thing to worry about.

"The runway wouldn't have to be *that* long for the Bluebird," I continued, "…or the other planes you fly."

I started to suggest that Simaphong hire a surveyor to measure the exact distance but didn't. Instead, I repeated what I'd said before, that it looked okay. But nagging doubt caused me to wonder why he was asking all this.

He's a pilot. Why wouldn't he know already? Is he testing my knowl-edge of aircraft? My ability as a pilot? Or is he suspicious of my motives and questions my sincerity?

"I thought so," he said, triumphantly. "I will get someone on it right away. In the meantime, consider yourself hired. I will have a contract drawn up tomorrow for you to sign. What were you making in the Azores?"

I told him, but with less fervor than I might have; finding it harder and harder to be civil to the pompous potentate. The quicker I found Leandra and got shed of this place—and that man, the better I'd like it; whether I had to climb through a rat maze or not.

               *   *   *   *

"Is your plane ready to fly now?" Simaphong asked on the way down to the parking lot, his trusty Cossack following behind.

"Primed and fueled."

"Good. We will leave here at nine in the morning and drive to the marina. From there, we will fly to the Izmir airport where I will open an account for you—fuel, oil, minor maintenance, that sort of thing."

I responded with a vacant nod, dreading the thought of going under-ground again, especially with the sun still shining. Without thinking, I stretched my arms, embracing the warmth, and sucked in a few last gulps of unfiltered air. As I did, a movement on the hill beyond the tun-nel caught my eye.

A rabbit?

It moved again.

A rabbit with sandy brown hair?

It was Noli. He'd made it out. My plan was working. Now all I had to do was find Leandra and get her out, as well.

God, I hope Noli doesn't see me and wave.

Increasing my pace toward the tunnel entrance, I heard the feint cry of a muezzin, calling the faithful to prayer from a distant minaret. Out of Noli's sight but still not eager to re-enter the tunnel, I asked my host how his underground workers knew when to pray.

"Soft bells ring throughout the command post. You might have heard them but didn't notice. Did you know the faithful always pray facing Mecca?"

"I've heard that. How do they know which way that is when underground?"

The rotund Asian laughed. "The door of every room is marked. Mecca is southeast of here. That way." He pointed toward a range of mountains beyond the next valley.

"Then Izmir must be over there," I said, facing the setting sun.

"Correct," Simaphong replied, becoming distracted. For a moment I thought he'd seen Noli...or the Cossack had. But seconds later, we entered the tunnel, Simaphong first.

From behind, he looked like a bowling ball. Actually, two bowling balls, one on top of another. "Dinner will be served at eight," he said, "followed by some amusement. Mohamed will guide you back to your room."

I thanked him and followed the Cossack past the dining room, remembering Simaphong's warning about wandering about on my own. Little chance of that, I mused, but I'm sure I could have found the way on my own.

First a right, then two lefts...

   *   *   *   *

The first thing I did was check Noli's bed. It was still as I'd left it. Breathing more easily, I checked the back of my door. Sure enough, next to an escape route showing the entry tunnel clearly was the direction to Mecca.

I turned toward it, knowing that if I crawled through the ductwork in that general direction I would eventually come to the same outside vent that Noli had found. It would be a daunting task, slithering through a labyrinth of airducts, yet comforting to know the direction I should follow. It was also comforting to know that Noli had made his way out.

I just hoped the goatherd hadn't seen him.

Suddenly, I thought of a compass and wished I had one. It would make escaping a little easier. Searching the furniture in both rooms more carefully, I did discover two more books of matches, both with Simaphong Import-Export Company logos on them. I put them in my pocket: one for me and, hopefully, one for Leandra, if I found her.

With two hours to kill, and thinking I was too nervous to sleep, I lay on the bed and leafed through a Turkish magazine. If I smoked, I would have gone through a half pack. As it was, I dozed off rather quickly. My last thought: concern that Noli might reenter the outside vent and worm his way back to the room.

A concern that would pester me all evening.

Chapter Thirteen

A few minutes before eight, Mohamed knocked at my door. Following him down the hallway, I wished I'd brought a change of clothes and hoped it wasn't formal. I felt a little tacky wearing the same clothes I'd worn all day.

The main dining room was large enough for two hundred people, sitting at round tables set for eight. But at that hour only twenty or thirty men were still in there. Most were scattered about in twos and threes, talking quietly and drinking coffee or tea served by teenage girls wearing white eyelet blouses and flared gray skirts.

Nothing improper about what the maids were wearing or the way they were acting, but how many of them wanted to be here...or were brought here by force?

The dining room still had a military look about it, as if nothing had changed since NATO pulled out. Antiseptic and sterile, like the cafeterias I'd seen in the Pentagon. The only wall decoration was innocuous wallpaper, which hinted at what the eaters were missing above ground but like no place I'd ever seen before. A made-up garden found only in the mind of an artist, with stiffly dressed people supposedly having a picnic.

It seemed so out of place I had to smile.

As we approached the first occupied table, talking ceased. Three men—obviously Turkish—ruddy skin, thick black hair and heavily mustached—looked at me as if joy had left their lives. One registered fear, another surprise. When the third nodded, I nodded back.

I wondered who the one man was afraid of, a sandy-haired American or the giant Cossack beside me.

At another table, three Asian men were wearing finely brocaded robes and speaking the same singsong language I'd heard before, which I now realized was Thai. They *also* became silent as we approached. And as we passed, they bowed their heads, which surprised me. They not only acted afraid but were subservient.

Again I assumed it was my guide who induced the fear, doubting they even knew who I was. By their fancy outfits, I guessed they might have something to do with Simaphong's harem. Eunuchs, perhaps? I bizarre idea, I know, but then everything about this place was bizarre.

The thought occurred to me that I could follow them and maybe locate the...

My mind quickly became diverted as we reached a third table, where eight Asians in business suits were drinking tea or sipping iced drinks. They didn't bow *or* cease talking. In fact, one jerked his head toward me and whispered something, which caused a flurry of whispers and chuckling among the others.

A joke at my expense, I suspected. God, I hate this!

              *   *   *   *

A small stage strewn with amplifiers, microphones and musical instrument cases crowded the far end of the room. Mohammed opened a folding panel on the side of the dining room and revealed a smaller room—more intimate and elaborately decorated.

Floor cushions surrounded a low, circular table set for six. Serving tables flanked the only door. A fusion of spicy aromas wafted though the room. I'd forgotten how hungry I was. Breakfast in the penthouse seemed like such a long time ago.

This room was draped with red satin and papered in romantic scenes. Wood nymphs, stylized fawns and scantily clad women trying to avoid muscular satyrs—half-men, half-horses. With the folding doors open, the stage was visible but diners in either room could not view each other, although, the rooms could have been made into one, if the occasion demanded it.

Wong suddenly appeared, greeting me with a low bow. Again he was wearing a brocaded gown, this one forest green with gold thread.

After I returned his greeting, he offered me a cushion next to a sallow-faced man with heavily rimmed glasses and wearing an expensive-looking pinstripe. "May I present Herr Brockner," Wong cited, "a business man from Munich, Germany."

"Dan Sylvester," I said, reaching down to shake his hand before Wong could complete the introduction. "From Atlanta, Georgia."

"Ah…an American," the man replied without a smile. He seemed disappointed, as if expecting someone else. His accent was slight, his grip firm, but it was difficult to see his eyes, sunken behind thick lens and capped with spiky brows. "For a moment, I feared I would be eating alone," he continued in flawless English. "I'm having *raki*—smooth going down but it will do you in, if you don't eat."

"Sometimes, even if you *do* eat," I added, sitting awkwardly beside him. "Thanks, I prefer beer."

Wong immediately asked which kind, "German or American?"

In deference to Herr Brockner, I chose German, then asked if our host would be joining us. I felt foolish sitting on a pillow. When you're over six feet tall it's awkward, unless you can sit cross-legged, which I have difficulty doing for long periods.

I dreaded spending an evening like that; knowing the longer I sat, the stiffer I'd become. More trouble, I thought, as if squirming through a rat maze wasn't enough.

"It appears Herr Simaphong has been delayed," the German replied. "Not unusual for a man with as many…how you Americans say—irons in the fire?"

I smiled at his attempted humor, wondering if it was the best he could do. He didn't strike me as the humorous type. It was hard to tell how tall he was, sprawled on pillows as he was, but his hands were large and his facial skin rough as sandpaper. Not scarred from chicken pox but pitted and grainy.

In his fifties, his hair was nearly white, tinged with pale blue highlights. A striking effect, easily remembered. I wondered if it was natural or dyed. There was something artificial about him, especially his hair. Almost too perfect.

"What line of work are you in?" I asked as Wong nodded to an attractive server standing nervously at the door. She wore an off-the shoulder peasant blouse and a short black skirt. Before Herr Brockner could reply, she knelt by my side with a silver tray.

Smiling, she offered me a warm washcloth and a bowl of scented lemon water.

Having just washed my hands and face, I shook my head but was instantly sorry. Her delicate features—exquisite, yet child-like—paled noticeably. Tears filled her deep expressive eyes, hazel and touched with green. Seeing her discomfort, I reached for the cloth, dampened it and wiped my hands. Her smile returned but the tears remained, making her eyes appear glassy and unnatural.

In her late teens she was striking—flawless olive skin, thick black hair, breasts bulging over her low cut blouse. But she should have been at home with her family, not serving two men in an underground dining room draped in red and papered with wood nymphs and scantily clad women.

"Lovely, isn't she?" my dinner partner said, stroking her bare thighs. She made no attempt to hinder the progress of his hand as it slid under her flared skirt. In fact, she encouraged him, leaning closer for a kiss. When Herr Brockner drew her to him, Wong stepped forward quickly, took the silver tray from her and left the room.

I couldn't believe what followed. As they kissed, Herr Brockner slid his hand inside the girl's blouse and squeezed. Again she didn't resist. Instead, she stroked his crotch. I'm sure she would have unzipped his pants and done whatever he asked, she seemed so eager to please him, but he pushed her away.

"Nice," he said with a catch in his voice, wiping his mouth with the back of his hand. "Nadja was my dinner companion last time I was here." The way he said it, with a leer at me, it was obvious she was much more than just a dinner companion, this time *or* last time.

Hearing her name, the server smiled, kissed him lightly, then stood and readjusted her blouse. "You should try her," the German continued, patting her leg. "She nearly wore me out."

"Maybe I will. Do you come here often?" I drained half my water glass to settle my stomach. Being underground, in an enclosed room, witnessing a wanton young woman so willing to please, it was making me queasy again.

"Several times a years. I'm in the arms business. How about you?"

Gritting my teeth I answered as civilly as I could, but felt no better for it. "I'm a pilot...fly a Grumman Mallard, a twin turbo amphibian."

"I've heard of them. Sweet plane. You fly for Simaphong now?" He seemed more than casually interested.

"Maybe. Should know tomorrow, when I see his contract offer."

For reasons I couldn't define, I didn't like him. His eyes were always in shadows, like talking to someone with dark glasses. I didn't trust him and felt uneasy talking to him, thinking he might be here to pump me for information...at Simaphong's request, of course.

I'd better watch what I say; a slip could cost me my life...and Leandra's.

*   *   *   *

Nadja removed the damp cloth and finger bowl with a warm smile, again exposing her ample chest, which looked freshly oiled. But when Herr Brockner asked her something in Turkish, she responded with a shrug, biting her lower lip to keep from crying.

She seemed so sensitive, first with me then with him. I wondered why. She looked as if she'd entertained men for several years.

"I just asked for Kaya," Brockner said, "but Nadja wants to be my dinner companion again."

Bending low she hunched her shoulders, displaying even more of herself than before; hoping, I suppose, to change his mind. If it hadn't been so pathetic, I might have found it humorous. As it was, it made my stomach roil. Suddenly, I wished I had some Tums.

"*Değil bu akşam*," he said with an off-handed wave. His dark frown gave him a satanic look. Reaching into her blouse, he squeezed her breast hard. "Now go find Kaya!"

"She come, Herr Brockner!" the girl cried in stilted English. "Please, she come."

With a sick smile—close to a sneer, but with no teeth showing—the German patted her arm. The girl looked flustered, her eyes brimming with tears.

Standing, she glanced hurriedly at the door just as it opened. It was Wong, followed by another pretty server, carrying a silver tray with our drinks on it.

Herr Brockner turned to me. "I gave Nadja a huge tip last time, so naturally she wants me again." His sick smile reappeared. "You have to show them who is boss or they'll walk all over you. You watch, for the rest of the night she'll do anything I ask now. That's Kaya with our drinks. She's English. Isn't she a beauty? I wanted her last time, but Simaphong gave her to a Russian...or maybe he was a Pole. I forget. I got pretty drunk."

"Your drinks, gentlemen," Wong said as Kaya half-filled Herr Bruckner's six-ounce glass with *raki*, adding water to turn it cloudy. She poured my beer into a pilsner glass ringed in gold. Crystal, I suspected. Nothing but the best for a crime lord.

"Thanks," I said, looking into the girl's vacant blue eyes. She was stunning, no question, with a trim waist, oversized top, clear skin and dazzling white teeth, yet her smile seemed forced, her movements mechanical, not as sensuous as Nadja. She also looked bored, even stifled a yawn once, making me think she was on drugs.

She didn't seem as frightened as the others. Probably an old timer, although she hardly looked twenty. Of course, in this place that could mean years of service. After all, Leandra was only fifteen.

Herr Brockner raised his glass. "Cheers...or, *şerefe*, as they say in Turkey."

"*Şerefe!*" I repeated.

Drinking half his *raki* in one gulp, he shuddered as he swallowed, as if a man bent on getting drunk in a hurry.

At once, two more servers appeared, each with a tray of nibble food. Both seemed a bit plain, quite common, really. Clean and healthy but straight from the farm, or perhaps a Turkish village, although neither looked cowed or frightened.

I wondered if it was possible that some were here by choice, their training paid for by their families. I'd have to ask Simaphong, when he arrives...if he arrives.

Following the two servers, a barefoot woman entered the room. Heavily made-up with dark blue eye shadow, she wore only lavender panties and a bra, her body draped in long gossamer veils of white, pink and pale blue. Without my realizing it, musicians had assembled on the stage at the end of the larger dining room.

As soon as the fleshy woman clicked her castanets, they began to play. At first, she just swayed, as if to feel the pulsing music—dissonant, yet throbbing—played on strings and reeds, and backed by the steady beat of Congo drums. She then descended to the floor, remained there for a moment then rose slowly like a coiled snake, every movement a marvel to witness that closely.

Clicking her castanets, she looked at me, her body swaying to the beat of the drums; then her carnal dance began, slowly, rhythmically, every step graceful yet measured, always under control. She twirled about the table several times, dipping and swaying, tantalizing us with her beauty and poise.

She continued this way for several minutes, her hips undulating sensuously, her breasts giggling. Staring vacantly, Kaya sat on one side of Herr Brockner, Nadja on the other nibbling his ear.

The tempo increased, the dancer began waving her arms over her head, letting each veil flutter down upon us, then pulling it back slowly, erotically. One caressed my cheek, hightening my excitement.

This was belly dancing as I envisioned it. Not in a seedy bistro where men stuffed money into the dancer's bra. This was an art form, seductive, fluid and polished, and with extraordinary muscle control.

I became entranced as she slithered closer, teasing, smiling, alluring, her breasts brimming, her castanets flashing. Forward then back, dropping one veil each time, until all were on the floor, then folding her body into a mound at our feet, as if in total submission, her dance ended.

Herr Brockner and I clapped heartily as she rose and smiled. Then, with a shy bow, she picked up her veils and hurried out.

Moments later, the band started up again and three younger women did a similar dance in the main dining room. We could only see them from the side but compared to our dancer, these were rank amateurs. Although, you'd never guess it from the raucous shouts and whistles we heard when they finished. I guessed from the applause there were now over a hundred men watching the dancers.

A virtual army, if Simaphong turned them on me, or if I got caught snooping around where I wasn't supposed to be.

*   *   *   *

The remainder of the evening is less clear to me, despite my efforts not to drink too much, knowing what I had to do later. The big question still plaguing me: would Wong bring raw recruits to me, if I kept refusing the others he brought? And if he did, and Leandra was one of them, would she blow everything by rushing into my arms?

A second question: could we escape though the ductwork, find the others, and make it to the marina without being caught?

A lot of ifs, I know, but it was our only chance. There was no way I could locate Leandra; I had to get Wong to bring her to me. The immediate problem was staying sober—difficult to do when drinks were being offered repeatedly by two rather plain looking servers who Wong had brought as *my* dinner companions but seldom smiled.

I was surprised Wong hadn't brought me prettier ones—not that it would have mattered. Whoever he brought, I had to act as if I was enjoying myself, yet stay focused.

Which was exactly what I told myself as I started on my second beer. Stay focused. This could be a long night.

Compounding matters, I was drinking with a man distracted by two lovely ladies, which was almost like drinking alone. Herr Brockner *did* say his first name was Heinz, but he seemed to have no other interest than to get drunk and get laid, no longer caring which of his dark-haired beauties he chose. Nadja, who was now tonguing his ear and rubbing his crotch, or Kaya, feeding him calamari and cheese balls from the platter on the table.

Granted, Kaya still looked bored, but Nadja seemed to be enjoying herself. Unlike the two with me, who kept glancing at each other as if unsure of themselves or at Wong when he was looking in on us. Twice, he nodded to them to offer me food from the platter or another beer. He never said anything outright, a nod was sufficient for their paired response, but they spoke no English and each only tried Turkish once. When I didn't respond, not knowing what they'd said, they didn't try again.

As the entertainment continued—two jugglers, followed by a singer in a slinky gown—the two girls loosed up some, coyly smiling at me or patting my arm. But neither had the charm or looks of Herr Brockner's two stunning companions, which was okay with me. I was more interested in enjoying the entertainers than being entertained by them.

I probably could have kiss and fondled my two companions, but the whole idea turned me off so much it was difficult to do more than just smile. Besides, it was obvious that neither had their heart in it anyway.

*   *   *   *

Our host arrived just as the main entrée was served—flaming beef kebob on a bed of rice with mixed vegetable, sliced tomatoes, cucumbers and yellow onions in a yogurt sauce, and two baskets of freshly made bread. Simaphong was full of apologies, especially to Herr Brockner; but my senses were so filled with the aroma of spicy food, I hardly heard him until I saw *his* female companion, the most exquisite Asian women I'd ever seen.

Her age eluded me, although she definitely wasn't a teenager. Her complexion, bone white and silky, set off a perfectly proportioned body for her height. Not busty but beautifully shaped, she wore a pale brocaded gown, similar to but lighter in weight than Wong's. Her rich black hair hung loosely around her shoulders as she knelt beside our host, geisha style, and carefully selected food she obviously knew he liked, then filled his glass with champagne from a bottle Wong had opened himself and offered to no one else.

Stunned by her beauty, I asked where she was from.

"Bangkok, as I am," our host replied.

He seemed pleased with himself, as if his latest business transaction had been prosperous, or else satisfied that I was who I said I was—an itinerant pilot with a plushy plane. Or maybe he'd just received a new supply of young women.

Hopefully, Leandra was one of them.

Embolden by two beers, I ask where the servers came from, including the two with me.

"Pretty, aren't they?" Simaphong said evasively. "Mostly from Turkey."

My senses heightened, I pressed further. "Do they come on their own or do people bring them here to be trained?"

"Most are brought by their family…or guardians. Many are orphans like those two with you. I take them in, train them and then pass them along to others, who give them a home and a good life. A life of opulence, as you can see. These two don't interest you? I have others."

"They're okay, but I like 'em a little more spicy, and with lighter skin. You know, feisty and with fire in their eyes, yet young and tender. These don't even speak English and they're way too shy."

In a way I was describing Leandra, but hoped Wong wouldn't bring her out now, if she was even here. It was too soon. Later in my room, maybe…as a last resort, if I kept refusing them. My greatest fear still, that she'd scream out my name when she saw me.

Simaphong nodded to Wong, standing by the doorway. "See who you can find."

One clap from the expressionless man was all it took to disperse the two girls sitting beside me. Following them out the door, Wong wore a frown of disgust.

During his absence, as Herr Brockner continued kissing and fondling his two beauties, Simaphong explained that he was doing the girls a service by training them in the ways of men. "It's a program run by Lai Ling." Turning to the Thai beauty beside him, he patted her thigh. She lowered her head, dutifully, and blushed.

Without removing his hand, Simaphong continued. "If not for her remarkable talents, these girls would spend their lives in squalor, or working long hours at a cigarette factory or on a farm, having one baby after another until their bodies gave out. Most welcome the opportunity to serve in expensive homes as maids and nanny's, even mistresses occasionally. Remember, in this part of the world, we are less bothered by Western morés than you people are."

I didn't respond. I couldn't, my mind filled with revulsion for this despicable man…and this place we were encased in, separated from the real world by steel doors and thick walls of stone.

"You don't believe me?" Simaphong asked, nodding toward the two women with Herr Brockner. "Ask them. Do they look abused or frightened? They are enjoying themselves as much as Herr Brockner. And isn't that the best way, the natural way? Although, better understood by Asians than Westerners, perhaps. Such talent those two have. Loving *and* beautiful. Lai Ling trains them to do many things."

Again he patted her thigh. "Some might call the things they do 'erotic'; but I assure you, each act is extremely satisfying...often, for both partners. Right, Heinz?"

Grinning from ear-to-ear, the German nodded drunkenly.

As we ate, I thought about the outrageous things Simaphong had said; rationalizing them so simply even a fool would agree...or an ignorant and desperately poor farm girl.

Maybe he *did* raise a few from the gutter of life. I suppose they eat better than they did before. But what about their rights...their free will? Do they ever have a say about who they are with or what they are expected to do? Of course not, they're never even asked.

Then again, maybe they don't care. Or, maybe it's better than anything else they could ever aspire to.

While I pondered this, I watched the door with anticipation and dread, wondering if Leandra would be next. "God, I hope not," I muttered in silence, fearing the worse.

❖   ❖   ❖   ❖

The two new girls Wong brought to me were indeed younger, lighter in color and thin—one looked anorexic, her collar bones protruding awkwardly—but neither was sexy or particularly pretty. Both wore heavy make-up and diaphanous gowns, more suitable for a bedroom than entertaining guests at dinner. I guessed them to be East European, but they said so little—even in broken Turkish, I couldn't tell for sure.

One kissed me, while the other half-heartedly rubbed my crotch; but neither seemed interested, responding to Wong's orders rather than their true feelings. I pushed both away and threw down the rest of my beer. The idea of paid hostesses had always turned me off. I preferred the hunt, the struggle to be loved, that exquisite relief that comes when you know you *are* in love, especially the first time.

Halfway through my third beer, Simaphong said something to Wong, who again hurried the women away, returning with two more. One was Asia. Barely fifteen, I guessed, a tiny slip of a thing. The other could have been any age, it was hard to tell. One thing was for sure. She looked like she'd come straight off the street and was hard as nails.

Most surprisingly, she was British. "Hi, Guv," she said, sitting in my lap, her short skirt riding high on her thighs. "Wong says you're a Yank and hard to please. Ever been to Cleveland? My brother lives there. Near Lake Erie, I think. Isn't it?" Before I could answer, she kissed me with her tongue and pushed my hand into her tiny breasts. "They're not much, but they love to be squeezed. Go ahead, you're kinda cute."

Pulling away, I looked at the other one, wearing a long kimono. She smiled and bowed, then knelt on my other side. "You like more beer...more food?" she coaxed.

She seemed to have no fear of me, suggesting that Simaphong was right, that he *was* doing them a favor. But he still had no right—

"It looks as if you have chosen your partners for the evening, Heinz," our host said expansively, interrpting my thoughts. "Are you leaving so soon?"

Simaphong's comment startled me. I hadn't even seen the arms dealer stand up...barely, wobbling drunkenly and leaning on Kaya *and* Nadja.

Muttering something in Turkish, he nodded, then staggered toward the main dining room, each girl trying to keep him from falling.

I doubted that anyone in *that* pathetic threesome would feel erotic, satisfied, or fulfilled when the night was over. It seemed so ludicrous...and so wrong, no matter what country we were in. Don't get me wrong, I'm no prude. If a gal wants to be a prostitute—or mistress, let her have at it. But if she has no choice in the matter, then it isn't right.

"One of my better clients," Simaphong said, as the threesome left. "So I indulge him. How about you? Do you not find these two attractive? They are so different from the others, and from each other. Surely one would—"

"I like 'em all right. They're both okay...in they're own way," I said, slurring my words to sound more drunk than I was. "But this one's way too prissy." I hugged the Oriental, much to her surprise. "And this one's too flinty. Somewhere in between would be better...if you have any like that. You know, young and nubile...but spirited."

I tweaked the Brits breasts for effect. With chewed-off nails, she reminded me of a Dickens's character in Oliver Twist—slovenly but streetwise and poor as a post.

Simaphong smiled—leered, really. "I think I know what you mean. We have several new girls who are quite young, hardly broken in yet. Would you care to see a few of them?"

"Sure," I said, standing unsteadily. Not surprising, I felt dizzy. It wasn't the beer—I'd only had three in two hours. From sitting on the floor so long. I could hardly walk and looked decidedly drunk. "But send 'em to my room. I'll check 'em out there. Got to go pee, now. Thanks for the meal...the entertainment was first class."

"You are quite welcome. Enjoy the rest of your evening. I'll have Wong bring the girls right away. Mohammed will see you to your room. Wouldn't want you to get lost between here and there."

"Thanks...I probably would. I've had a snoot full. Just make sure the girls are young and pretty. Fresh off the farm, as we American's say."

The Cossack giant suddenly appeared out of no where. I reeled off behind him, through the folding door and across the empty dining room. The stage was bare and the second part of my plan, baiting the hook, was over. Reeling Leandra in, if she showed up, and escaping would be considerably more dangerous.

If only I can keep my wits about me, I thought, hoping Noli hadn't come back. He'll go crazy if Leandra is one of the girls that Wong brings to my room. To say nothing of what he'll think of me for asking for a girl in the first place.

Chapter Fourteen

Alone in my room, I checked to see if Noli was next door. He wasn't; nor had the blankets on his bed been moved. They hadn't found him missing, and he hadn't returned.

"Thank god," I muttered. At least I don't have *him* to worry about. Although, it probably would be easier to find my way through the maze of ductwork, if he *had* come back. But that would be too much to ask of him. Once through there was enough.

Satisfied but nervous, I doused my face with water, hoping to reduce the buzzing in my ears. I never should have had that third beer. Two was plenty, especially tonight. What I needed was some strong coffee. But there was no pot in my room to make instant. After all, this wasn't a Holiday Inn, or even a Motel Six.

I lay on my bed to clear my head and ponder. If Wong would just bring Leandra—and anyone else who wanted to get out of here, we'd be set. And maybe he would. Didn't Simaphong say he'd just received some new girls? Maybe Leandra was one of them; but what if the others don't want to leave? All the girls I've seen tonight seem willing to live here, or at least, acted like it. Oscar performances, all of them.

As if on cue, I heard a soft tapping at my door. Closing the connecting door between the two rooms, I squared my shoulders and opened it. Facing me stood three teenagers in flimsy nightgowns, their eyes downcast as if ashamed to be there. It was difficult to see their faces in the dim hallway light, but two might have been sisters and were downright chunky. The other was lovely, her breasts taut and her waist tiny. She looked younger than the other two but no less ashamed.

"Perhaps you will find one of these to your liking," Wong said with an edge and the barest grin, mostly in his narrowly slanted eyes. No "Mister Sylvester", this time. No preamble at all. Obviously, he wasn't happy.

I lifted the face of the youngest. She *was* striking—deep olive skin, delicate features, but hardly sixteen.

"From Tunisia," Wong offered flatly. "Pretty, don't you think?"

He sounded like a salesman offering me a special deal on a Persian rug, and in a way he was. They were *all* special. Only I wasn't buying, only pretending; also wondering if I should try again. Would Wong put up with it, or become suspicious and tell his master?

The eyes of the youngest were coal black—vacant and staring, as if I wasn't there. As if *she* wasn't there. I wondered where her mind was, or if she was on drugs. She looked as though she'd been though this before.

"None with more pep?" I asked drunkenly, pinching her breast. She responded with a blink, nothing more. Not even a grimace. And she never looked at me once.

None of them did.

"Hell, all the fights gone outta 'em." I tilted up the heads of the other two. They looked drained and filled with fear, ashen and trembling. "Haven't you got a feisty one...but still a virgin? One with fire between her legs?"

"There are three others..." Wong paused, as if not sure if he should offer them to me. "All are virgins. I checked them myself. One came in last week, I believe, the others even more recently. One, I'd say, is quite feisty. But I am not sure, my master would—"

"Hell, send 'em over," I slurred, wavering a bit for effect. "Might be fun to try 'em all. You know, together...more fun than these...or the three losers you brought me before."

"Very good, *sir*," Wong said stiffly, as if barely able to control his anger. "I'll bring them right away."

As Wong turned, I again lifted the face of the youngest, noting her pale cheeks and blank expression. She had to be on drugs. Maybe they inject the new ones to subdue them. Or maybe she's just terrified...even beyond terrified, not caring anymore. God, I hope Leandra isn't like this already.

Looking at the other two, I wanted to help them all, but knew I couldn't. Not yet anyway. Maybe later. Then a thought came to me. "You do that, Wong," I said unsteadily, "...just shoo 'em in and leave 'em. I'll be in the shower." That way, if Leandra was in the next batch, she wouldn't react to me in front of Wong and blow the whole caper.

Watching them shuffle dejectedly down the hall in their revealing gowns made me wonder again why they were here. Because their parents wanted them to be as Simaphong had said, to be trained for a job elsewhere? Or were they kidnapped and brought here by force? More likely the latter. Yet in some countries, the life of a concubine was envied and revered by attractive, young women—a short life, perhaps, but luxurious.

Returning to the bathroom, I thought about the women who'd entertained us tonight—some with talent, some with charm and some with neither. Surprisingly, they all seemed content with an opulent life without care. A fair reward, perhaps, for their loss of freedom, especially those who came from a life of grinding poverty—willingly or not.

It was the idea of the thing that galled me. Women learning to submit to men with no love, no respect and no tenderness. Just sexual gratification for him and little for her. Call them what you will—geishas of Japan, courtesans of France, concubines of Arabia—they all served men in male dominated countries. And for this, they have what—a life? Hardly. An existence. They were allowed to exist.

Chinese parents sold unwanted females, or had them killed. Only males were revered, so they could support their aging parents and carrying on the family name.

"God, I hope he brings Leandra this time," I muttered, turning on the shower. "I doubt Wong will bring me anymore. I can't believe I asked for a virgin."

I hope Leandra is…for her sake, and for Noli's.

✳   ✳   ✳   ✳

I waited impatiently in the bathroom with the shower running until I heard Wong return. After a soft knock, the door opened.

The first voice I heard was unmistakably Leandra's. *"Duru!"* she cried, followed by a loud smack.

I cringed, knowing Wong didn't think I could hear the slap while in the shower.

"Sakin!" he hissed. "And speak English. He is American."

"Who cares? You have no right bringing me here. I'm a virg—"

Leandra stopped.

I visualized Wong threatening to hit her again, but I didn't dare go in there until he left for fear Leandra would blurt out my name.

"That is precisely why you are here," Wong snarled under his breath. "You are *all* virgins. I checked you myself, remember? Although, why you are being offered to an employee, I'll never understand. Such a dreadful waste for a man so undeserving."

It was the first time I'd heard Wong criticize his master—or me, for that matter. I'd always thought he'd rather liked me, or at least respected me.

Peeking through the door hinge just as he turned to leave, I saw two other teenage girls huddled together, their faces marred with fear. Leandra looked flushed, as much from anger as from Wong's slap.

"Remain here," he barked from the door, "and stop crying. Do what he says and you will be all right—you might even enjoy it. Tomorrow, it won't seem nearly as frightening."

"Will we be allowed to leave then?" Leandra asked brazenly, her shoulders squared, not yet resigned to her fate; subduing the fear I knew was deep inside her.

One girl was less pretty than Leandra, having darker skin and thick, unplucked eyebrows. The third looked older and a bit heavier. All wore jeans and blouses, which would be better for traveling than nightgowns; but the older one had on expensive designer jeans with a silk scarf that matched her blouse tied around her waist. She looked more sophisticated than Leandra and the other one, but no less frightened.

"Perhaps," Wong responded vaguely. "If you cooperate fully and don't cry. I doubt he will want all of you. He won't last that long."

With that, he closed and locked the door. I heard a key turn. My heart went out to the three girls, knowing it probably sounded like a death knell to them. The end of their childhood, as they once knew it.

✳   ✳   ✳   ✳

When I no longer heard Wong's footsteps retreating down the hallway, I entered the room and embraced Leandra, holding my hand over her mouth so she wouldn't cry out. She recognized me immediately and began to cry.

The two other girls looked stunned.

Still holding Leandra, I put my finger to their lips, admonishing them not to speak. The smaller of the two was visibly shaken and almost in tears. The older one stood with her mouth agape, her hands across her ample chest.

"Whisper," I said into Leandra's ear, "someone might be listening."

When she nodded, I released my grip and stepped away.

"Where did you come from, Dan? I am so happy to see you," she said, just above the noise of the shower. "We are so frightened. How did you get in here? This is Sultana, a school friend from Bodrum. She was

kidnapped just before I was." Leandra put her arm around her slim
friend, her hair in a loose braid, her lips cherry red. Turning to the other
one she continued, "And this is Carmen. She is Turkish but she lives in
Athens. She came to Izmir on a cruiseship with her parents and was kidnapped in Kulture Park. Neither speak much English. I will tell them
who you are and that you will help us."

When Leandra finished, the girls smiled tentatively but still looked
confused. Her schoolfriend seemed more immature than Leandra, her
breasts not fully developed. By eighteen, she'd be striking, while Leandra
would still just be cute. The other one was already striking, albeit a bit
chunky.

I smiled, hoping they would trust me and not panic. "Is okay...we go
now." I said slowly but with emphasis, pointing to the air vent near my
bed. "Through there."

When neither responded, Leandra translated. A half smile crept
across the older one's face, as if she understood. The other one still look
terrified.

"Noli has escaped already," I said to Leandra. "He is outside waiting
for us...I hope."

Leandra gasped. "How is that possible? We are underground...guards
are—"

I touched her lip with my fingers. "He crawled through the air ducts,
and we will too. Your father and Hasan are waiting outside with cars to
take us to Izmir. Tell Sultana and Carmen. We will start right away."

While I loosened the air vent, Leandra explained what I'd said.
Carmen grinned, her delight obvious, but Sultana clearly had reservations and began to shake. Leandra held her while I turned off the
shower.

Returning, I put my finger to my lips as a cautioned not to speak.
Carmen and Leandra nodded, but Sultana did nothing, now clinging to
Leandra and whimpering.

I knew she was a basketcase and would probably get worse inside the
rat maze, but we had to do it. There was no other way, and it had to be
now, before Wong returned.

Attaching the bedlamp to the vent, I decided it would be best if I went
last, with Leandra first, followed by Carmen and Sultana. That way, I
could boost all three into the vent and keep an eye on Sultana, who I
guessed could easily freak out.

                *   *   *   *

After telling Leandra about Noli's markers, I held her button-cute face between my hands for added emphasis and said, "Now, listen carefully. I told Noli to always keep the wind in his face; and if there wasn't any wind, to choose the largest duct. If you have any doubts, ask me. I'll tell you if I think you are going the wrong way."

With a peck on the lips, I gave her a book of matches. "Use them to find Noli's marks," adding as I boosted her onto the chair under the vent, "If it's any help, the parking lot is *that* way." I pointed southeast. "I saw Noli near there this afternoon just after he found his way out. And we will too, but it may take a while...over an hour."

"I will try," Leandra said, sliding her slim torso into the duct as I pushed from below, "but you stay close. Okay?"

Giving her one last shove, I told her I would and that the first turn Noli made was to the right.

As Leandra disappeared into the vent, I offered to help Carmen.

Pausing a moment, she whispered a few hurried words to Sultana, gave her a big hug and climbed up on the chair. "Okay!" she said with a grin.

I laughed, thinking, "Okay" is even more of a universal word than "beer".

Being chunky, it was a tighter fit for Carmen. It would be *very* tight for me.

By then, Sultana had stopped shaking, but I wasn't sure if she would follow her friends or not. As Carmen's feet disappeared, I looked back at the terrified girl and made a hoisting motion. She tried to smile but tears came, so I lifted her, myself, and pushed her inside.

When Sultana's feet had cleared the grating, I slid in behind her. Metal brushed my body on all sides and I began to feel claustrophobic immediately. My only comfort was knowing the ducts were more likely to get larger than smaller.

Still, I was unable to extend my elbows and had to propel myself with my feet, just a few inches at a time. It was tiring work, and I soon began to sweat and feel lightheaded.

At one point I thought I might even pass out.

Willing myself forward, I soon heard Leandra's plaintive cry. "I see Noli's mark. We go saǧa...ah, right...like you say."

"Good, girl," I called back softly, "but no more talking. People can hear us through the air vents."

When I reached the same turn, I slid into the larger duct and breathed more easily. Now I had room to extend my elbows some; but it was only slightly less claustrophobic and becoming dark. Soon it would be pitch black, the light from the bedlamp fading fast.

I tried not to dwell on it, focusing instead on Sultana's feet; thinking it odd that she was wearing sandals with little heels. Not the best shoes for inching through ductwork. But then what footwear is...tennis shoes? They wouldn't slide well at all, a must for the cramped quarters that we were in.

✻   ✻   ✻   ✻

Light from the bed lamp finally petered out, replaced by a dim glow from an air vent in an occupied room ahead. Inching forward until I reached the vent, I heard a female groan twice followed by a male voice speaking German.

Herr Brockner!

I peered into the vent. He was making love to Nadja, or maybe Kaya, in a room down the hall from mine. It was hard to tell with him on top of her. Both seemed to be enjoying themselves.

Wriggling past on my belly, my skin prickled. I felt like a voyeur, we were that close to them. Again I worried that Wong might return to see which of the girls I'd chosen and take the other two away. Then again, he might not. Didn't I say I'd try them all?

I hoped he believed that I could.

As our four bodies squirmed forward, I tried to keep southeast in my mind, the approximate direction of the second duct we'd entered. But I soon became distracted by cobwebs in my face and metal burrs snagging my clothes and skinning my arms. I hoped the girls were having less trouble. At least, none of them are talking...or worse, panicking.

Light from Herr Brockner's room faded, making it too dark to read my watch, which I couldn't have brought to my face anyway. It was much too tight for that.

Eventually, the physical exertion didn't seem too bad, just rocking my feet and pushing with my fingers. But the tight quarters magnified everything, and I wondered how long I could keep it up. How long the girls could keep it up.

Heel-toe, heel-toe. Slide-push, slide-push.

After what seemed like an eternity in profound darkness but was probably less than ten minutes, Sultana's feet suddenly stopped in front of me.

"What happened?" I asked in a whisper.

"Two ducts," Leandra whispered from a dozen feet away. "Both same size and no wind."

"Light a match and find Noli's mark."

"Oh!...I forgot."

A bright glow lit up the air duct for an instant followed by an acrid smell. The light helped clear my mind. For those brief seconds, I felt less like we were inside a metal coffin.

"*Saǧa.*" Leandra called. "Noli left a Band-Aid *and* an arrow."

Following that, we made several stops. At each one Leandra would strike a match—or two, look for Noli's mark, then move off in a different direction. And with each turn, it became harder and harder to remember which way was southeast.

In one vent, the air in our faces might be quite strong, whipping our hair and rippling our clothes. In another, hardly a breeze, making it hot and sultry.

Heel-toe, heel-toe. Push-pull, push-pull.

My calf muscles ached, as did my arms from dragging my tired body along. Occasionally, one of the girls would cry out when they caught their hair or clothes on a metal burr protruding into the ductwork, or nick a knees or elbow on machine screws.

Fortunately, we passed by no more occupied rooms, one of the few pluses in our tortuous journey as we slid from the wing of guest quarters into the wing of offices.

Heel-toe, heel-toe. Push-pull, push-pull.

I too found my share of metal burrs and machine screws and almost told Leandra to stop and rest. But if she could continue, I could to.

Steeling myself, I pressed on.

Heel-toe, heel-toe. Push-pull, push-pull.

*   *   *   *

Again, we stopped...was it the fifth or sixth time? I was losing track.

I expected a match to strike but it didn't. "What now?" I called out, inching forward until the upper half of my body was on top of Sultana's legs. When she started to whimper, I patted her back to comfort her.

God, what a horrible thing to put a young girl through, I thought. Her parents must be frantic. Carmen's too. How long did Leandra say they'd been inside the mountain? I couldn't remember anymore. My mind wasn't functioning that well.

"No more matches," Leandra whispered back.

"I'll pass you mine," I said, digging for them. "Tell the girls."

After a few Turkish words, Sultana reached back for them, her whimpering stopped.

With another book of matches in hand Leandra continued on, stopping every few minutes to light one and find Noli's mark. By then the euphoria from my three beers had long since worn off and I was totally exhausted. It had been a long day and I was sure it had been for the girls too.

My elbows, back and legs had been nicked so many times I felt like a pin cushion. I could even feel blood trickling down my pant leg.

Striking another match, Leandra called out again. "No Band-aid... only four matches left. What should I do?" There was fear in her voice, her reserve of strength almost gone. We had to get out of there soon.

I retraced the rat maze in my mind, trying to decide which way was southeast. "Go left," I called. "*Sola*...I think."

"Okay," she replied, "*sola*. But the wind is blowing right...saǧa."

"Wait, then," I whispered, going through my mental gymnastics again and deciding south was probably to the right. "Okay, go right then. No wait...try another match. There must be a mark somewhere."

One match flared then another, then..."I see it...a pencil mark. Just a scratch."

"Thank God," I said. "Let's hope it isn't much farther. He must have used up his Band-aids."

"I'm really tired, Dan. Can't we stop and rest?"

We all were tired. Exhausted, really, and dehydrated. We needed water badly.

✳   ✳   ✳   ✳

After a short rest we started again but stopped several times after that. Not for long, though, or our calf muscles would bind up.

Heel-toe, heel-toe. Push-pull, push-pull.

Without water, we couldn't go much farther.

We had to be near the end. Noli had made it out in just over an hour. Of course, he was in better shape than any of us were. I still couldn't look at my watch, the vent was too small. But I guessed we'd been gone for well over an hour...maybe two.

Could Leandra have missed one of Noli's marks? Thus far, she'd found every one, which gave me hope. We had to keep going, despite finding no breeze in one duct or bracing against a twenty-knot gale in another. We couldn't stop now. Not until we could breath fresh, clean air again.

Heel-toe, heel-toe. Push-pull, push-pull.

How often I wished we'd brought some water. But how would we have carried it? Even a candy bar sounded good. At least Noli had one of those.

Again we paused as Leandra decided which way to go; and again I tried to help with familiar advice, "Turn into the wind, Leandra. Choose the larger duct."

A pillar of strength until then, knowing she was following Noli's trail, I could feel Leandra begin to crumble, her voice on the edge of hysteria. "Matches gone...no wind...ducts are same size. I tired, Dan. You come. I can't do this anymore."

"Wait there," I said. "Tell the girls I will squeeze past them."

After several whispered words Leandra said, "Okay, Dan. You come now."

As I shimmied over Sultana, I caught my belt on something and couldn't get it loose. Finally, I pulled it out of my pants and managed to squeeze by her somehow.

Inching past Carmen was more difficult. I nearly didn't make it. Only when she rolled to one side and sucked in her breath was I able to squeeze by her—face-to-face, lips nearly touching, her twin mounds crushed into my chest. She smelled of peppermint from a candy she must have recently eaten. Smart girl, I thought, hoping the others had candy too.

Leandra had already slid into the adjoining air vent. "Which way?" she sobbed.

I couldn't see her, but she sounded desperate, her nerves raw and on edge. A few more minutes and she might come unglued. And if *she* did, the others might too.

We *had* to find an outside vent, but which way?

I searched my pockets for another matchbook, sure I had one. Finding it in a back pocket, I pulled it out.

It was used. Only five matches left.

I struck one and together we searched for Noli's mark but found nothing. When the match burnt my fingers, I lit another.

"What is that?" Leandra cried suddenly, pointing to a smear on the dull metal.

"That must be it," I replied, putting the match against it just as it went out. "You must have rubbed it somehow." I lit another match—

only two left. "See? It looks like...What do you think...that way?" I pointed right.

Suddenly a wind started up in the air duct and the match went out. Was it trying to tell us something? I don't normally believe in omens, but I believed in that one.

"Come on," I said, taking the lead. "We're going this way...into the wind."

I slid forward on my stomach with renewed energy. But moments later, Leandra called for me to slow down.

Waiting for the girls to catch up, I took in a deep breath. It smelled different, fresher, somehow...even cooler.

We had to be getting close.

Moving on, I came to another long tunnel of darkness—a huge one, large enough to crawl through on our hands and knees. But which way?

I struck my next-to-last match in search of Noli's mark, scaring away two huge rats. I was glad the girls hadn't seen them. They might not have wanted to continue.

Still no mark. So I lit the last match. This was it. Now or never.

I never did find Noli's mark. I didn't need to. He saw the second match from outside. "Dan, Dan!" he called in a hoarse whisper. "This way...out here."

Thank god, I thought. Finally!

Now for the last part of my plan and perhaps the most dangerous: Getting off that mountain without being seen and into the Bluebird before we were discovered missing.

Chapter Fifteen

Being first out, I sucked in a huge gulp of sweet mountain air then nearly hugged Noli to death. It felt so good to be outside—out of that underground tomb, that labyrinth of ductwork. What a relief to be able to breathe normally again with no wind in my face, no sharp burrs scratching my arms and legs.

Leandra scrambled out next, hugging Noli as well, followed quickly by Carmen and Sultana. But before they all started babbling, I cautioned them about making noise. That, of course, didn't stop Leandra from kissing Noli—and it wasn't a sweet sisterly kiss either.

A three-quarter moon provided some light but not much. We were in a tiny ravine hidden from the parking lot by low brush and a few spindly trees. We'd have to be careful or we'd stumble and attract attention to ourselves. This was not the time for a sprained ankle.

Quickly explaining who the girls were, I asked Noli if he'd seen any guards.

"One...by tunnel. We go that way." He pointed toward the flat plain where the runway would be, if Simaphong ever built one. "I see boy with goats, but he no see me."

"He works for Simaphong. We need to steer clear of him."

"We go that way, then." This time Noli pointed downhill. "Around parking lot."

Climbing down sounded better than up so I said, "Good. Since you've done this before, you lead the way. But no talking! Tell the girls, Leandra."

Once out of the ravine, I could see the parking lot but not the guard. Reaching behind me, I felt for Leandra's hand. She took it immediately.

Scrambling and sliding but staying quiet, it took us nearly an hour to circumvent the parking lot on the low side and reach the access road, coming out well below the tunnel entrance, close to the spot where Nazif and Hasan should have been waiting for us.

Noli whistled softly. "No shoot...is me, Noli...and, Dan."

Nazif suddenly appeared with my rifle. Seconds later, his brother emerged from the shadows ready to crush our heads in with his huge fists if we'd been guards.

"Ovmek, Allah," Nazif whispered, embracing Leandra warmly. "You found her...brought her out. Is a miracle...a blessing from Allah."

"That, and a brave boy and three brave girls," I added, panting from our long hike.

"We thought you guards..." Hasan muttered, smashing his fists together.

I was glad Noli had whistled. I never would have thought of it.

                *   *   *   *

After a hurried introduction, Nazif embraced the other girls, saying something to each of them in Turkish. Leandra looked elated, although, a bit bedraggled. We all did—torn clothes, muddy shoes, hair uncombed. Sultana still appeared to be in shock. Carmen too. We probably all were, but extremely happy.

"We go now...okay?" Nazif said finally. "Leandra in front seat with me."

"Great," I replied. "I'll ride in back with the other two. Noli, you squeeze in front with Leandra." I knew he wouldn't mind. And when Leandra kissed his cheek, I knew she wouldn't either.

Following Sultana and Carmen into the backseat, I told Hasan to cover our backside in case we were followed. "If we are, back away from use; try to delay them long enough for us to reach the marina and get the Bluebird started."

Hasan nodded his understanding. But when Leandra started to protest, I added, "Don't worry, we won't leave without him."

What I feared most was Wong returning to my room and discovering we'd escaped. If he did, he could call the marina and have the guards there stop us from ever reaching the Bluebird.

I looked at my watch: three o'clock. We'd spent over two hours in the air vents and another hour or more to reach the two brothers. It felt more like four days, and Noli had made it through in just over an hour.

"Hasan good driver," Nazif said with pride, starting the rental car and pulling away. "He watch *arkaya*...'backside', you say.

Leave it to Nazif to lighten things up a bit.

   ✻   ✻   ✻   ✻

The three girls babbled in Turkish halfway down the mountain. Each telling about their ordeal in the air ducts, I guessed. What they'd seen…and didn't see in the pitch black. What they'd endured—leg cramps, hot sweats, tiresome burrs and cobwebs. Pent up emotions, really, and having to remain quiet for so long.

I heard Noli's name mentioned several times.

Holding Leandra to him, he smiled but said little. He was obviously proud of the role he'd played in our escape, and so was I.

"We wait long time," Nazif broke in finally, making another hairpin turn at high speed, as if the devil himself was after us. And in a way he was, or soon would be. "We *çok* worry. But we happy when Noli get out."

I started to tell him why it took so long but decided against it. The less he knew about what went on inside that mountain, the less he'd worry about what had happened to his daughter. She could tell him, in her own time.

Looking back, I saw Hasan trying to keep up but the truck headlights fell farther and farther behind us. At least, no one was following him and that was good. So far, that is.

Once, while careening a little too close to the edge of the road, I cautioned Nazif about driving so fast in the mountains. He slowed for a few miles then gradually increased his speed. I didn't say anymore about it, knowing the anguish he'd gone through, waiting so long to regain his daughter with only his stoic brother to console him.

Besides, I was as anxious to reach the marina as he was.

As we flashed though the second lifeless village, I couldn't help but reflect on what we'd accomplished so far…more than I thought possible. Especially Noli's part.

Reaching forward, I patted his arm. "We were sure glad to see you when we reached that last turn in the ductwork. Did you know that I spotted you briefly while I was outside with Simaphong?

Noli shook his head that he didn't.

"That's how I knew you'd found your way out, and that we could too, eventually. It took a lot of courage to inch your way through that airshaft alone and in the dark, marking the way for us. I doubt I could have done that. I get claustrophobic in small, cramped places like that."

"You do!" Leandra cried. "We *all* do. I thought I would die in there." After a several words in Turkish, Carmen and Sultana nodded in agreement and started babbling again.

"All girls very brave," Nazif interrupted, taking his eyes off the road briefly, only to have to careen left to keep the car on it. He continued talking unfazed. "Noli too. He good boy. Leandra like. I like too."

Leandra blushed then hugged Noli. I was sure he was blushing too. I just couldn't see his face.

Suddenly the car swerved left. Nazif slowed to better control it, then sped up again. Again I said nothing. Our lives were in his hands. We had to trust him, as he'd trusted me to recover his daughter.

✻   ✻   ✻   ✻

Speeding along, indistinct shapes flashed by in misty darkness—a shepherd's hovel, a gnarled olive tree, a third sleeping village, and finally the main highway. Good, I thought with a sigh. Less than thirty minutes to go now. But will Simaphong's thugs be waiting for us at the marina, or did Wong believe me when I said I'd try them all?

I glanced at Carmen and Sultana. They still seemed frightened, sitting so rigidly, eyes straight ahead. Yet color had returned to their faces.

Hoping to put them at ease, I said, "Is okay. We leave Izmir soon...fly away. Find your parents."

Both look bewildered until Leandra translated, then Carmen cried, "Baba...Anne, ah...gone...not in Izmir."

"Their cruiseship left," Leandra said. "They might even think she is dead."

"We'll find them," I said. "Tell her I'm a pilot and have a plane. And that I will fly all of us to Bodrum so Sultana can be with her family. Carmen can call her parents from there. I'll even fly her to Athens, if necessary."

When Leandra translated what I'd said, Sultana gave me a half smile and thanked me. But Carmen burst into tears, followed by a flood of Turkish.

"She is frightened, Dan," Leandra said finally. "Afraid her parents left on the cruiseship."

"They no leave!" Nazif blurted out. "They wait for her." He spoke as if it would be impossible for Turkish parents to do otherwise. And maybe it would. Greeks too. In fact, parents the world over.

As Leandra reassured Carmen in Turkish that we would find her parents, Nazif approached the first traffic circle. It wouldn't be long now. Looking back, I couldn't see the truck and worried that Hasan might still be on the mountain.

Suddenly, Nazif swerved to avoid hitting a wooden cart filled with metal milk jugs. The cart was pulled by a mule and guided by a white-haired man wearing a dark suit coat, light colored pants and a faded green beret. The local milkman, I guessed.

That's when I first realized it was becoming light. It was four o'clock. The sun would soon be up, warming that part of the world. I relished the thought after so many hours inside a mountain. It's easy to take sunshine for granted until you lose it for a while. Same with freedom, when you're stuck in a stinking root cellar.

Just thinking about Captain Tokolu made me boil with revenge.

Carmen still looked grief-stricken. I didn't know what to say to her. I wanted to return both girls to their parents, but first I had to get them away from Izmir. Even Bodrum wasn't far enough. We'd learned that the hard way.

At once, an idea came to me. I asked Leandra to ask Carmen if she knew her grandparent's phone number. The people her family had visited before her abduction.

Again more Turkish, then Leandra shook her head. "Only that they live in Hatay, just south of the city."

"Tell her we'll call them from Bodrum. If her parents are in Athens, I'll fly her there. We can't take the time to find them now. As soon as Simaphong finds out that we are gone, he'll send his goons to the marina. They might even be there now."

"What then?" Nazif asked, clearing the traffic circle.

"I'm not sure...Plan B, I guess."

         ✻   ✻   ✻   ✻

Instead of pulling into the marina, Nazif parked a block away in an alley behind Mahoud's tour office. Nazif had arranged to meet Hasan there if they became separated.

Ten minutes later the clanking truck arrived. It belonged to a friend of Mahoud's and was on its last legs, like so many cars I'd seen in Turkey. Hasan said the truck died twice, once in the middle of the traffic circle.

"I am glad you got it going again," I said. "Can we leave both vehicles here?"

"*Evet,*" Nazif replied. "Mahoud will return car and truck. I call from Bodrum."

"Good. Hasan, get my rifle. You and I will see if there are guards at the marina."

"I no need rifle," he replied. "I hit good with this." Hasan raised his balled fist.

"I'm sure you could, but I may need it. Nazif, you and Noli keep the girls on the other side of the ferry terminal until I whistle."

Noli quickly stood by Leandra, his arm over her shoulders. She smiled and snuggled closer. Carmen and Sultana stood with Nazif. They still looked confused, even afraid.

I could hardly blame them. They'd been through a lot in the past few days. "Stay together and be quiet," I cautioned as they left.

Nazif said something to the girls in Turkish, hopefully, what was about to happen.

Clutching the rifle, I approached the marina cautiously and saw two guards. The old man who tied up the Bluebird the previous day was asleep on the same bench Noli and I had sat on while watching the dancing bear. A much younger and much bigger guard was smoking a cigarette with one foot resting on a piling near the plane.

Scampering into a debris littered alley between the marina office and the ferry lobby, I hid between two trashcans, the younger guard just thirty steps away. Hasan followed.

"I'll get his attention," I whispered "You—" I lowered my arm in a chopping motion.

Hasan grinned as if it would be a pleasure.

The guard was gazing out to sea, probably hearing and seeing nothing. Steeling myself I laid the rifle behind a trashcan and stood, took several uneven steps toward him and slumped down against the ferry building, coughing as if a drunken derelict, which wasn't difficult in my present condition.

I'd spent most of the day inside a mountain fortress with a maniacal crime lord followed by two hours in a rat maze trying to escape from him, then hiked through weeds and thistles for an hour, raced down a mountain with a madman, and was now trying to entice a brutish-looking guard, probably with a gun, to notice me.

And for this I gave up a cushy airline job?

The guard started toward me, drawing a pistol from a shoulder holster. I shut my eyes, dropped my head and prayed he wouldn't shoot first and ask questions later.

He yelled something I didn't understand but kept coming. I pretended to be asleep or unconscious, but I could feel his presence, even hear his breathing. The suspense was maddening.

"*Kalkmak!*" he growled when he reached me. Body odor and tobacco smoke clung to him like a second skin as he prodded me with his grimy boot.

Knowing I had to turn him around, I stood, tottering for a second then lean against him.

That's all it took.

"Thunk!" The noise was sickening, like a cantaloupe dropped on pavement.

The guard slumped to one knee, started to rise, then fell to the ground. I hoped he wasn't dead, but neither of us took the time to find out. "Come on," I said, picking up the rifle, "let's get the other one."

Hasan was right, all he needed was his fist.

*   * *   * *   * *

The old man struggled to sit up, disoriented by deep sleep. Hasan hit him with another hammer blow. The old man slumped, dazed and immobile, then passed out.

I immediately whistled for the others, then unlocked the plane and scrambled into the cockpit. Moments later, I had the right engine started and was cranking up the left.

With the others on board and buckled into their seats, Noli cast off the mooring lines, then jumped aboard, secured the entry door and scrambled into the copilot's seat.

"Everyone strapped in," he said breathlessly, buckling himself up as well.

Just then, two pair of automobile lights turned into the marina. I could see the younger guard trying to stand. I doubted the older one would for hours. Maybe never.

"Duck everyone!" I yelled behind me. "Simaphong goons are here."

I taxied away from the pier before the left engine had fully stabilized. Over the engine roar I heard pistol shots but I was too busy weaving around yachts to care.

Clear of the marina, I slammed the throttles forward. I'd thought of flying to Karsiyaka and calling Carmen's grandparents; but with Simaphong's thugs that close, they'd see us land and come after us.

At sixty-five knots, I pulled back the yoke. The Bluebird plowed out of the water, leaving a wake, I'm sure. Familiar G forces pressed me into my seat. I looked over at Noli and gave him an "okay" sign. His grin was even wider than usual.

Rising from earthly evils, I felt cleansed somehow, rid of vice and corruption, of brutish behavior—even of Turkey. We were above it now, free and clean. It couldn't hurt us anymore. It's hard to describe the feeling unless you've been in a similar situation. As if my body—and my mind, had somehow been transported a little closer to heaven.

Unfortunately, we'd soon have to land and it would start all over again.

Chapter Sixteen

At three thousand feet I leveled off and headed south, then waved at Nazif to come forward. Leandra followed right behind, holding him around the waist. Neither seemed to want to be separated from each other for even a moment. I couldn't blame them. Not after what they'd been through.

"Any ideas on where to land?" I asked, shrugging my shoulders. "Gümbet Cove? The isolated cove? We could even fly to Athens, although, I'm not sure that's smart. We need to get Sultana home. Besides, I've been awake for a long time. We all have. I need to sleep. Ask Carmen if she knows of a way to get her grandparent's phone number."

Leandra did the asking.

Returning, she said Carmen's aunt was watching their house and two cats in Athens and would know her grandparent's phone number.

"Good," Nazif said. "You land Gümbet. We take Sultana home, call about Carmen, find parents, then sleep. Fly Athens tomorrow. Bodrum *çok* bad! You no land there."

"Sounds good to me. What about Leandra?"

"I stay with *Baba*," she said immediately, still holding him around the waist, a stretch for a girl her size.

"*Evet,*" Nazif grunted. "We get Simaphong later…Captain Tokolu, too."

The way he said it made me think he had a plan but he didn't elaborate. The sleeping part sounded especially good. I was really tired.

I was also convinced that Simaphong didn't have men searching the countryside for fair maidens; but men like Tokolu knew that he would pay good money for them so they did the searching for him…and kidnapping. First Carmen, then Sultana.

In Leandra's case, Tokolu might have heard that the Kesfin Brothers had engineered my escape from the root cellar—probably through

Ahmet's loose tongue—and sent men to trash Nazif's boat factory. Kidnapping Leandra might have been an afterthought...a bonus. Noli too. But Simaphong didn't want him, so he was released. Which made me wonder if he would have released Leandra, if I'd asked him too. Of course, that would have blown my cover story.

Oh, well, it's over and done with...too late to worry about that now.

     ✳   ✳   ✳   ✳

Taxiing up to the pier in Gümbet Bay, I shut down the engines and climbed from my seat. Hasan look worried, probably about the kidnapping...would his girls be next?

I suggested he take his family out on his boat for a few days, until things settled down. "Regina too," I added. "They will be safer there."

The giant shook his head. "I no run from *pislik* like Tokolu," he snarled.

I don't know what the word meant but the way he said it, it didn't sound good. "Okay, but watch out for him," I replied, almost adding, *"and Ahmet."*

His younger brother needed to be watched too.

"I watch," the frowning giant repeated. Balling his mallet-size fist, he smashed it into his other hand. "Someday, I get Tokolu good."

"I agree, but let's do it together. Remember, I have a score to settle with him too."

He nodded grimly, but I wasn't sure he'd wait, especially after witnessing how easily he'd dispatched the two guards at the marina.

     ✳   ✳   ✳   ✳

Nazif and I returned Sultana to her parents, and what a treat that was. She just lived a block from the marina and despite it being six in the morning, after kisses and hugs and many thanks, they insisted we all toast to their good fortune with *raki*...several times.

Hasan, Noli, Leandra and Carmen went straight to Hasan's house, so they weren't involved in the merriment.

Sultana's parents knew Nazif vaguely, but they had no idea who I was or that anyone was even looking for their daughter. The mother, bless her heart, couldn't stop hugging Sultana and her father couldn't stop grinning.

After the initial excitement and hurried explanations of what had happened to her—so bizarre it was still hard for me to believe—they invited us to eat with them. But three drinks and little sleep had caught up with us both, so Nazif and I said our goodbyes and hurried back to Hasan's house to see if he'd reached anyone in Athens or Izmir yet.

He hadn't. No one had answered in Athens and the Izmir telephone operator had been unable to come up with the grandparent's phone number without a street address.

Carmen was asleep on the living room couch already, which didn't surprise me. The poor girl must have been exhausted after all she'd been through. I never did find out what happened to her, or the others, inside the mountain, except that they hadn't been raped.

Which figures. The whole idea was to train them to serve wealthy clients and sell them intact, which would account for why Wong was so upset about giving me three virgins.

Leaving Carmen on the couch, Nazif and I returned to his house, where Noli and Leandra had gone an hour earlier. It felt good to be "home" again. But as tired as I was, I slept uneasily on my cot in the patio, worried about finding Carmen's parents and wondering what Simaphong might do next. Would he guess that we'd return to Bodrum?

Why would he? He knew nothing of Nazif and his family—unless he contacted Captain Tokolu.

In which case he knew everything!

*　　　*　　　*　　　*

I awoke about noon, surprised to find Nazif already drinking coffee in the kitchen. He hadn't slept well either and wanted to leave for Athens right away. Dark circles ringed his eyes. His wispy hair, already thin, flew in all directions as he spoke, his heavy brows twitching as usual when he started pacing the floor.

Noli and Leandra joined us on our second cup. After we ate, we all walked over to Hasan's house. Carmen was still asleep, as was Hasan and Regina; and Phidaleia was having trouble keeping her two girls quiet. Before he'd gone to bed, Hasan had insisted the girls stay inside today for obvious reason, although, not totally supported by Phidaleia. When we arrived she decided to leave them with us and go to the market alone, muttering something about having a houseful to feed again.

"Always complain, that woman," Nazif said after she left, making a magpie motion with his hand. Then, looking at our sleeping beauty on the couch, he sighed. "I *çok* worry about how we find parents."

Why not call Athens again?" I replied, pouring myself another cup of coffee. After yesterday, I couldn't seem to get enough liquids in me.

"I do...already," he said, meaning earlier that morning. "No one there. It hard to call Greece from here, sometime."

I chuckled, thinking it was probably hard to call *anywhere* from here, or vice versa. "Do you think we should fly to Athens without calling first?"

"What else can we do? Carmen's aunt come to house sometime...to feed cats."

Just then Carman awoke. She seemed startled at seeing us. Then a soft smile crept across her winsome face as she remembered. "We go now...find *Baba e Anne?*"

I nodded, knowing we didn't have a choice. "But eat first," I said, picking up the spoon next to my cup...before Phidaleia returns. It's easier that way."

*   *   *   *

Back in Nazif's house, four of us packed a few things, Noli and I in zipper bags, Leandra and Nazif in battered suitcases.

Returning in his truck, we found Phidaleia back from the market harping at Hasan in the living room. The children were playing in the patio and Regina and Carmen were having coffee in the kitchen. The way I understood the argument, Hasan had decided to take his family fishing with him and was anxious to leave, but his wife wasn't, holding her nose as if the smell of the boat would do her and their children bodily harm.

Regina had no part in the argument, although, I assumed she'd be going too; and Carmen still appeared to be in shock. With no make-up she wasn't as pretty as before.

During a pause in the argument, I tried to convince Phidaleia that it would be dangerous to remain at home until Captain Tokolu and his crew had been captured and turned over to the police.

Or killed, I thought. The way Hasan and Nazif felt about what he'd done, nothing short of death was likely to satisfy them; and I was inclined to agree. To hell with Western justice, he hadn't practiced it on us. Why should we practice it on him?

"You men *akilsiz!*" Phidaleia spat out in disgust. "We safe here. Children safe. Regina safe. We stay!"

They finally compromised. They would spend the night on his boat, and the next day they would meet us at the secluded cove, the safest place to hide the Bluebird until Tokolu was in jail...or until Noli and I left Turkey forever.

"If not that day, the following," I added to Hasan with caution, not knowing how all this might play out.

*   *   *   *

Boarding the Bluebird in Gümbet Cove, I called out, *"Allahaismarladik,"* to Regina and Hasan who saw us off. That's "goodbye" in Turkish, said by the one who is leaving.

Regina looked sad, even had a pout. I suppose she could have come with us; but there didn't seem much point to it, unless there was something developing between us; which I didn't think there was...or could be.

Of course, as I've said before, when it comes to women, I'm in the dark most of the time.

"Güle güle," she replied with half smile, the response by the one who is remaining.

In a way I felt sorry for her. She didn't have much of a life in Bodrum, especially with Ahmet to contend with. And living with in-laws couldn't be much fun.

Maybe I should fly *her* somewhere, I mused, taxiing away from the pier. She said she loved to travel.

Maybe I will next time, if there *is* a next time.

*   *   *   *

The metropolitan area of Athens is huge, over three million people, according to my guidebook. Stretching for miles in a tangle of highways and byways, it's an intimidating place to fly over.

Carmen said she lived in a southern suburb, between the new airport, still under construction, and Hellinikon, the old airport on the coast. Receiving a clearance to land on the east side of Hellinikon—the west side reserved for Olympia Airlines—we passed over the site of the new airport. A sprawling complex of runways, taxiways and departure gates, according to my guidebook, it was currently the largest construction project in Europe.

The main terminal looked immense and expected to handle fifteen million passengers a year—and that was only Phase One. When finished, it would be one of the finest airports in the world, and it couldn't come soon enough for me.

On my approach I had to dodge an exiting business jet the tower had forgotten to mention, only to find myself jammed between two jumbos, probably crammed with tourists.

My landing was fair—no hard bumps, but enough to clench a few teeth. Taxiing toward the terminal I hoped for a quick visit with Carmen's aunt then return to the isolated cove—today, if possible.

My only concern; I'd just identified the Bluebird to Hellinikon Tower and wondered if Simaphong might find me through friends or business associates in Athens because of it.

Eventually he'd find me. I knew that. It would be impossible to hide from him forever. Unless, of course, Noli and I left the area completely, letting the Kesfin Brothers deal with Simaphong and Tokolu alone. But I couldn't do that. I had to help them rid Turkey of both. But how, with Simaphong hidden inside a nearly impregnable fortress, and Tokolu hiding where...on his boat?

There must be a way.

*   *   *   *

At ten in the morning the lines through customs seemed endless and our wait for a taxi amidst a crush of people took forever. Carmen did managed to get a quick call through to her aunt, telling her that she was safe, back in Greece and on her way home. Her aunt was thrilled, of course, and would call Izmir right away and tell Carmen's parents; who'd left the cruise and moved to a hotel near the American Embassy because the grandparents had such a small apartment.

In a cab, Carmen told us, through Leandra, that her father had called her aunt twice. First, to tell her about the kidnapping. Then, what had happened next: the halfhearted effort of the Izmir police to locate Carmen, his frantic search of Kulture Park talking to people who might have witnessed the kidnapping, and the long nights spent waiting and praying. A tense time for everyone.

Carmen also expressed concern over her mother, who she explained, again through Leandra, was recovering from a stroke. She'd only gone on the cruise because she wouldn't have to do much if she didn't feel up to it, and hoped the sea air would do her some good.

"When I taken..." Carmen continued haltingly. "Tashi say, *Anne çalgin!*...ah—act crazy. *Baba*, too...him not well either..." Pausing, she clutched her hands to her chest.

"You mean he had a heart attack?" I asked.

"*Evet*...in hotel. He have *hastabakici*—ah, nurse...help him now."

"Tell her everything will be all right, Leandra. They can come home now. It's all over."

As she did, I started to say something to Nazif, but he said it first. "Izmir Police do nothing. Simaphong too *önemi*...ah—important."

"And wealthy," I added. "We'll have to take care of him ourselves."

His half smile told me that he agreed but he said no more. I hoped he had something up his sleeve besides crashing though Simaphong's vault doors, guns a blazing.

✻   ✻   ✻   ✻

From my guidebook I learned that the U.S. had a consulate in Izmir because a major NATO headquarters was still there, with many Americans assigned to it. In addition, our consulate helped stranded Greeks, or those in trouble, since Turkey and Greece had broken diplomatic relations in the seventies over Cyprus. Whether the Greeks tried to take the island for themselves, as Turkey claimed, was still in dispute. In any case Turkey invaded the eastern part, where most Turkish Cypriots live, and still had forces there.

Fortunately, our cab driver knew the area where Carmen lived. Approaching her neighborhood the worried teen guided him in Greek, a language as familiar to her as Turkish, except that no one but him understood her.

The Uzul home was a tidy brick townhouse in an up-scale neighborhood. Since Carmen's aunt knew we were coming, I wasn't surprised to see her on the front steps when the cab pulled up to the curb and stopped. I guessed she'd been looking out the front window, although she seemed confused as we approached, even distraught, her dark eyes glaring first at Nazif then at me.

Having Noli and Leandra walking behind us seemed to confuse her even more. But that didn't keep her from hugging Carmen and twirl her around until both nearly fell over.

Only after much kissing and jabbering did the comely women in her late thirties turned toward us—guardedly, I thought—and thanked us for bringing Carmen home. But she didn't extend her hand in welcome or invite us in. Strange behavior, I thought, toward people who'd risked their lives returning her niece, unless she didn't know that.

I wasn't sure how much Carmen had told her aunt on the hurried call from the airport. Probably little, she only had a few minutes.

Carmen introduced her aunt as *Tashi*—a nickname from early years, then more formally as Natasha. After introducing Leandra, Carmen paused, her eyes sparkling. It was obvious she was excited about being home, even if her parents weren't there, but she'd momentarily forgotten our names and looked to her captive-in-arms for help.

Leandra first introduced her father, who smiled and greeted her aunt in Turkish. Then Noli, who did the same in Portuguese, which required a bit of explaining. After my introduction the aunt greeted us all in Turkish, then in paced English, thanking us again for returning her niece, but with little feeling, as if afraid of us.

Carmen seemed confused by her aunt's reticence to embrace us whole-heartedly for all we'd done. I was surprised too, remembering how warmly Noli and I had been greeted by Alexis' family. Returning Carmen—an only child—literally from the grave, should have been a big deal and called for a celebration. But to Tashi it wasn't.

Something was wrong.

Turning to her, her face flushed with embarrassment, Carmen said something harsh in Greek. Berating her, I suppose, for not being more friendly and inviting us in.

The attractive women in a modest print dress, her dark hair pulled back in a bun, looked stunned and quickly dissolved into tears, causing Carmen to guide her inside to a chair in the entryway. If she hadn't, Tasha would have fallen down, her aunt was that distraught. I suppose from all that had happened to her niece—the waiting, the anguish—then meeting all of us, such a diverse group. It would be upsetting to anyone.

But that wasn't it at all.

According to Leandra, who interpreted, it went like this: Natasha thought we were returning Carmen after receiving ransom money from her father in Izmir. It seems she hadn't been able to reach him since talking to Carmen at the airport, although she did reach the grandparents who were much relieved that Carmen was safe and unharmed.

A bit confusing, I know, and not the kind of reception I expected; and that anticipated another concern. What if Carmen's parents thought the same thing when they heard the news, only in reverse? That we were extorting money from them for the return of their daughter in Athens.

We'd have to be careful how they were told, and by whom.

*　　　*　　　*　　　*

It took all of us to convince Natasha—a widow, we learned, with a son in college—that we were who we said we were and nothing more. At least, I hoped we did. In three languages, it's hard to tell. Natasha was fluent in Turkish and Greek but not English. Leandra was fluent in Turkish and English but not Greek. Noli and I and Nazif were...well, you get the idea.

It was a tangle for a while; but through it all, I got the distinct impression that Natasha still wasn't keen on having us stay there without an okay from Carmen's parents. And rightly so, perhaps. After all, it was *their* house, not hers, and I didn't want to stay there anyway. The longer we waited to seek revenge on Bai Simaphong and Captain Tokolu, the longer Noli and I would have to remain in that brutish, God-forsaken part of the world. A place I'd never return to but was unlikely to forget.

With Natasha in partial control of herself but still in the front entry, I suggested she call Izmir again and straightened things out. I almost said I'd fly Carmen's parents home, myself, but didn't. The mere thought of landing in Izmir Bay set me on edge.

Waiting for her reply I wondered what Simaphong was up to—besides looking for me; and if he knew I was in Athens? He must know that three girls are missing and guessed I would fly them home—for a reward, if he still believed I was a mercenary pilot. If he put two and two together, he'd probably search for me in Bodrum *and* in Athens.

In either place, two and two could count me dead, as far as I was concerned.

*　　　*　　　*　　　*

Natasha finally did call, but the Uzuls were not at the hotel or at the grandparent's apartment, and that *really* upset her. First Carmen is missing, then Carmen's parents.

"I...ah, try...later," Natasha said haltingly as she hung up, then continued to rage in Turkish about how worried she was. How worried the whole family was, including her nineteen-year-old son. There was more, Leandra interpreted as best she could, but some of it got lost, I'm sure.

I sympathized with Natasha but left the consoling to Nazif, who appeared taken with her soft smile and trim figure, and understood her perfectly. So well, that during a third and successful call, lasting nearly thirty minutes, he stayed right with her, feeding her information when she needed it and comforting her when she broke into tears.

The result was a gracious invitation from Carmen's father to spend the night, even suggesting where we might all sleep. Following that, Natasha, Carmen and Leandra prepared lunch for us: fish sandwiches made with cod found in the freezer, along with chips and dill pickles, plus a Greek salad studded with sardines, green peppers, black olives and freshly made croutons and sprinkled with light vinaigrette.

It hit the spot for me, especially with steaming hot coffee. Carmen and Leandra seemed to get along well, neither showing any obvious signs of their ordeal, although I suspected they might later. We all might.

Our meal was informal, despite eating in the dining room at a table that could easily have sat ten. Through French doors, I could see an orderly garden filled with flowers and lined with trimmed hedges. Being early June, it was ablaze with blooms. And when I complimented Carmen on it, she told us it was her mother's passion until recently.

"Now man come...not same anymore."

Sadness tinged her deep brown eyes over her mother's recent stroke and her father's failed heart. Were both brought on by Carmen's ordeal...and was it really over?

I could only hope that it was.

*   *   *   *

Throughout the meal, our conversation was bright and animated with everyone speaking in a favored language. I only caught some of it and could tell by Noli's blank expression that he understood even less. But that didn't keep him from talking to Leandra in broken English as often as he could attract her attention away from the others.

Until then we'd heard little of the girl's underground nightmare, only imagined horrors. Too shy to tell us much, Carmen admitting that she'd spent several afternoons, "learning about men," which she said directly to me.

Her aunt didn't press for details, as if a subject not discussed with strangers, no matter how bizarre. Which might have been true, but I suspected by Carmen's sly glances at Noli, it had more to do with him being there than anything else. I just hoped she didn't develop a crush on him, as Leandra appeared to have; knowing it would make it even harder for him to return to the "real world" someday with me.

Leandra, on the other hand, had less trouble telling about her ordeal—her abduction with Noli, being taken to an old house in Izmir and held overnight. The penthouse spa where she was washed, primped, even slapped a few times, then "inspected" by Wong. Probed might be a better word.

Then the drive into the mountains, the vault doors, the maze of hallways, the eerie, underground facility, meeting the other girls, then being brought to me by Wong and slapped again...remaining feisty to the end.

Through the telling, I could see the burden of her capture lifting from her narrow shoulders like a therapeutic catharsis; but I felt sorry for Noli, having to hear it all. I knew he was tired. We all were. But he also looked down, not his usual upbeat self.

Concerned, I mouthed to him, "Are you all right?"

He just nodded and grinned, then looked at Leandra, as if his happiness lay there.

*   *   *   *

After lunch we adjourned to the living room, a spacious room with a vaulted ceiling and tall windows facing the garden, bright noonday sun streaming in. The furniture was comfortable and in good taste, as if selected and arranged by an interior designer. Baby spots were embedded in the ceiling, and I guessed more were recessed behind cove molding that ringed the room. A nice touch for nighttime entertaining.

Carmen's parents appeared to be well off, which would account for Natasha's fear of ransom—a price they probably would have paid, if given the chance. But ransom had never been an option, never part of Simaphong's sinister plan. And if I hadn't been lucky, and Noli less brave, their darling daughter would have disappeared from their lives forever, to begin a more odious one as a nanny in Europe or a love-slave in an oil-rich country in the Middle East. Or even servicing Simaphong's wealthy clients inside his underground stronghold, which I still wasn't sure Natasha believed existed, despite being described in detail by Leandra. I hardly believed it myself, and I'd spent a night there.

Each time I'd mention it or something that happened there, Natasha would sigh in disbelief. To which Nazif would add comforting words and pat her hand, which seemed to help regain her poise and precise smile. A nice lady, but a bit too prissy for my taste.

✻   ✻   ✻   ✻

I awoke the next morning stiff from sleeping so hard. Nazif was snoring softly in a bed next to me. Noli was still asleep on a floor pad, as sunlight brightened the guestroom window facing the street. Refreshing myself in the bathroom, I retraced my steps to the kitchen in the same grungy clothes I'd worn for three days and poured myself a cup of coffee, remembering to dilute it with cream, this time. Greek coffee is just as strong as Turkish coffee.

Natasha suddenly appeared from a pantry, wearing a flowered housedress and holding a sack of flour. Her hair was loose around her shoulders, more feminine than yesterday and less prissy.

"Good...morning," she said, as if not sure I'd understand or she'd said it correctly.

She seemed more relaxed, less anxious, but still nervous. Speaking Greek, then switching to Turkish, she stopped and laughed, realizing I didn't understand either.

She had a beautiful smile, although probably not quite herself yet, not with so many strangers in the house. And it wasn't even her house.

By the way, I never did see the cats. They probably didn't care for strangers either.

"*Günaydin*," I said in Turkish, adding, "Or should I say, *Kaleemera?*" "Good morning" was one of the few phrases I knew in Turkish *and* Greek. Alexis had tried to teach me a few Greek words, but I'd forgotten most of them already.

Suppressed memory, I suppose, forgetting things that brought back grim realities.

Natasha smiled again. "You—ah...sleep good?" She pantomimed her words by laying her head on her hands.

"*Evet, çok iyi,*" I replied with enthusiasm, remembering words I'd learned from Nazif. Only then did I notice the tall, handsome youth sitting in the living room; so engrossed in a Greek newspaper, he hadn't reacted to either of us.

Following my eyes, Natasha seemed surprised as well, as if she didn't know he was there either. "Oh!...My...ah, son...Jon," she stammered. "I tell him good news."

After a flurry of Greek, Jon hugged his mother, a huge smile splitting his square-cut face. But when introduced to me, his smile faded. Fearing, perhaps, that I was a bad guy as his mother had.

Fortunately, Carmen arrived seconds later; and after a long hug, explained who I was and what I had done.

Only then did Jon extend his hand and thank me, adding, "We so happy...see Carmen...again. We worry..." He looked at his mother for help.

"We all worry," she said, hugging her niece. "Carmen *Baba y Anne*...happy now. Come home tonight...You wait. Okay?"

I said I would, knowing Hasan would come to the secluded cove a second day; even a third, if we didn't return. Besides, missing the family reunion would be discourteous, to say the least, and I was looking forward to it. I only wished I'd brought more girls out. Filled Hasan's truck with them. But then, I'd have to fly them home as well. To Algeria? To England? Eastern Europe? Had I really met girls from all those places?

Carmen then explained in Greek what had happened to her, but I could tell by his shocked expression that Jon was having trouble believing it. I heard Kulture Park mentioned and her description of the drive *up* the mountain involved much hand waving. The rest of what she told him, I assumed included the underground fortress, the many girls, the spas, our escape through a maze of air vents, followed by a race *down* the mountain, the guards at the marina, flying off to Bodrum in a hail of bullets, then on to Athens the next day.

It was no wonder that Jon was having trouble believing it all. If he did, he probably also believed in the tooth fairy and the Easter Bunny.

*　　　　*　　　　*　　　　*

Over coffee, I learned that Jon had grown up with Carmen and now attended Athens University. Their fathers were brothers and also business partners, first in Izmir then Athens, until Jon's father died of a heart attack two years earlier. I never did find out why they'd come to Athens, but guessed it was for business reasons rather than political ones.

Jon warmed further when I told him I flew a seaplane.

"Really? What kind? Where is it?" His English improved as words came to him.

I suspected he wanted a ride in it, but I didn't encourage him. Instead, I described it but said nothing of its location. It wasn't that I thought Jon might tell someone, who might know Bai Simaphong or a business associate; I was just being cautious…paranoid, if the truth be known. My biggest concern was sending Simaphong and Tokolu to jail, then vacating this part of the world…hopefully forever.

As Jon and Carmen continued talking, my mind wandered. Where would Noli and I go when we left here, back to Homestead and see Mackey? Luscious Mackey, the gourmet cook. It was certainly tempting and fun too. Also seeing Buster again…and Turk, the orchid king.

I chuckled. Along the way we could stop at Terceira, Noli's home island. We could hide from Simaphong indefinitely out there. I wonder if he has men looking for us in Athens, closing in on us right now.

No way! That's crazy. I must *really* be getting paranoid. Not even the CIA could find us that fast.

Or could they?

*   *   *   *

Halfway through my third cup of coffee, and what Natasha called *teeropeetàkia*—a triangle-shaped pastry filled with tangy feta cheese—Leandra and Noli joined us; making it look as if they'd slept together, which they hadn't. Leandra had bunked in with Carmen, leaving the master bedroom for her aunt.

During introductions, Jon's dark smoldering eyes never left Leandra's angelic face. And while she ate a bowl of Mueslix, I noticed her eyes fell on him more often than on Noli; which didn't bode well with the Portuguese youth, as envy creased his sunshine face.

Again the talk was lively and in three languages. The part I understood was mostly about Izmir—what teens did there to entertain themselves, what they wore—but very little about our escape.

The discussion became even more animated when Nazif joined us. After his introduction to Jon, he told of *his* part in our nail-biting adventure: tailing Simaphong to the top of the mountain, the long wait, our daring dash to freedom. The way he told it—hands waving, eyebrows bristling—you'd thought he'd done it alone, including the part at the marina.

He later explained how he'd found Noli in his boat factory, my midnight rescue from the root cellar, the flights we'd taken, places we'd seen;

then about taking me to a bistro, where Simaphong's men frequented. He hardly mentioned Mahoud, or his brothers.

Both Jon and Natasha seemed impressed, at least the way Nazif told it, filled with excitement and wonder. Watching Tashi—what Nazif had started calling her, it was obvious they were attracted to each other. And since both had lost a spouse, they apparently needed someone.

They always spoke Turkish when addressing each other; and later, I learned from Nazif that the lovely widow had been recently yearning to return to Turkey. With her husband gone, she missed her sister who lived in Kuşadusi, and her brother who was ported there in the Turkish Navy. But she worried about Carmen's mother—and now her father, and felt she couldn't leave until they found someone they could trust to care for them.

After breakfast, Natasha suggested we spend the day in Athens. "And tonight we celebrate…with Carmen's *baba y anne*."

It sounded good to me. I wasn't ready to attack Simaphong's fortress yet. I needed time to regenerate, to make plans, to control my compulsion to hit hard and without thought; which I would have done five years ago. This time, I was determined to move more cautiously. And I knew I could control my impatience best, if I remained active but did something I didn't have to think about much.

Sightseeing was perfect—mindless wandering among crowds, where I wouldn't worry about being seen by a rotund Thai man with a sick grin, or a Cossack giant with baggy pants and a gleaming sword.

      *   *   *   *

Rather than take a cab, Carmen suggested we catch a bus a few blocks from her house, which would take us to Sìntagma Square, the center of town. I agreed—less easily to be identified than in a cab—but at the last minute, her aunt had some reservations about leaving. "Maybe *baba telefon*," she said to Carmen, "Is best I stay…young people, you go."

Nazif quickly volunteered to remain as well, which brought a smile to Tasha's engaging face. Something was definitely going on between those two.

Jon quickly staked his claim on Leandra by standing next to her, leaving Noli looking confused and Carmen with a grin, making me wonder what kind of an afternoon it would be.

Teenagers. Oh, well, it was all part of growing up.

Seeing Noli's hurt expression, Carmen took his arm. "You like Athens...Noli. We go now. Okay?" Her coy smile said more than her words.

"Sure," he replied, drawing her closer. *"Istiyorum şu?"*

He'd learned a little Turkish too.

✻   ✻   ✻   ✻

Our bus ride was a collage of blurred images. Streets filled with whitewashed houses—many side-by-side—in cramped neighborhoods separated by business centers bustling with activity. My mind became saturated with the sights, sounds and spicy smells of one of the world's most famous and ancient cities.

This being Sunday, the streets were crowded with people—some shopping, some chatting in sidewalk cafés, some strolling along broad avenues. Bouncing along in the bus, I decided that Athens felt more European than Izmir, although Greek men looked similar to Turkish men—same ruddy skin, same heavy beards or mustaches. Yet Greece was known for its democratic ideals, rejecting the autocratic rule of the East—Russian Tsars, Tartar Warlords, and despots like Bai Simaphong.

I cringed just thinking about him and vowed not to for the rest of the day.

Gazing at shoppers milling about in a crowded bazaar, I was also struck by how similarly Turkish and Greek men dressed—old men, that is, in dark suit pants and mismatched coats, white dress shirts with no ties, soft berets and fingering worry beads behind their backs. Or when sitting, often smoking, they would flip through the thirty-three beads, one bead at a time, until they reached the end then start over.

Older Greek women, on the other hand, didn't dress like older Turkish women, except for a shawl wrapped around their wizened faces. Turkish women wore flowered dresses with mismatched pantaloons overlaid with colorful vests, sweaters or other wraps.

For the most part, older Greek women were indistinguishable from Western women, as were young people who wore jeans, T-shirts and sneakers. Common attire everywhere.

It seems such a shame that Greeks and Turks dislike each other so much; but then so do the Palestinians and the Jews, the North Irish Catholics and the Brits.

Hatred never ends, does it? And it's universal.

✻   ✻   ✻   ✻

According to my guidebook, Sìntagma Square, or Constitution Square, where the bus unloaded us, was originally the Royal Garden of the King. The palace, across Amalias Boulevard, was now home to the Greek Parliament. And fronting that, the Monument of the Unknown Soldier; where ceremonial guards dressed in white skirts and leggings, their dark tunics cinched with black belts and wearing soft red caps, marched stiffly back and forth, much to the delight of camera-laden tourists.

I could have spent the afternoon watching the elite guard perform their solemn ritual with high-stepping precision and exaggerated arm swings. But I stifled a chuckle when I noticed their red leather shoes with black pompoms, guessing they were teased about them. Also, what they wore under their thigh-high skirts, like Scottish kilt-wearers were.

Sìntagma Square is surrounded by office buildings on all four sides, many with trendy sidewalk cafes or fashionable department stores on the first floor, which fascinated the four teenagers. I felt like a chaperon on a field trip, but I enjoyed their company, their unbounding enthusiasm and their raucous laughter.

I also enjoyed watching Jon and Noli vie for Leandra. She, in turn, acted uninterested in both and spent as much time with Carmen as with them. It was all quite amusing and kept the girl's minds distracted from the trauma of Disko Hit.

*   *   *   *

The Parthenon, although magnificent and steeped in history was a bit of a let down —just another partially reconstructed ruin; until Jon explained that there were no straight lines in the surrounding colonnade, called the *peristyle*. Instead, the colonnade, consisting of seventeen columns on two sides and eight on the ends, had been imperceptibly curved to meet, theoretically, at a distant vanishing point; and the columns bowed to do the same vertically, as well as diminish in thickness as they approached the center of each side.

"See...columns lean," Jon explained, motioning with his hands for emphasis, "and space between get *meekrotero*, ah—*küçük*...I mean, smaller." Thinking in one language and speaking in two others is confusing even for a professional linguist.

He laughed at himself for the mix up, his teeth flashing in the warm Mediterranean sun. He was quite handsome, an attribute not over-loooked by Leandra, and I'm sure envied by Noli. In addition, Jon was two years older than him and attended the University, a definite plus. On the other hand, Noli was also attractive, in an awkward sort of way, came from an exotic Atlantic island, *and* was learning to fly a seaplane. How big was that?

Tearing my eyes away from the marble colonnades honoring Goddess Athena, I gazed across the city at another hill, barely visible in the summer haze which blanketed the busy city like gauze dipped in contaminated water.

"Likavittòs," Jon said with pride. "Big park. Bigger than Central Park in New York." He raised his hand to emphasize the size. I was impressed and would have like to spend some time there. But we only had a day; not nearly long enough to see a world-class city like this. *Three* days wouldn't have been enough. It certainly wasn't in Lisbon or Madrid.

Leaving the Acropolis, Jon pointed out a large seat amphitheater, built in 161 A.D. by a wealthy Roman as a memorial to his wife. In recent years, it had become even more famous, he said, by the concerts held there. "You know Yani?" he asked, as if I should. "He play there. I see him. *Eene meghaloprepes! È Magnifico!* Magnificent!"

Whoever Yani was, I figured he had to be great to warrant being called "magnificent" in three languages.

*　　　　*　　　　*　　　　*

We returned to Sìntagma Square by way of the *Plaka*. A lively section of Athens on the north slope of the Acropolis, crammed with one-story houses; dating back to the time when the Greeks successfully overthrew the Ottoman Turks, ending two thousand years of occupation. So crowded with people, the streets were impassable by car. And on nearly every corner there was a tiny square, ringed with sidewalk cafes and taverns. I was tempted to stop for a beer and probably would have if Nazif had come along. But I didn't mention it to my youthful companions, who'd lost little of their zeal despite our long walk.

Passing a vine-covered pergola, we saw three young people about Jon's age playing traditional Greek music for coins. We lingered for a while, emptied our pockets into their basket, then walked on, stopping at a sidewalk café down the street for a cold drink. I almost ordered coffee but didn't—my need to dilute it and then sweeten it made it hardly worthwhile. Instead, we all had Cokes with no ice—the way *all* Europeans drink them.

Sipping my drink, my four charges jabbering about little that I could understand, I felt ten years older. But I also sensed that we were being watched.

Saying nothing, I looked around but saw no one who looked out of place—only me, with my fair skin and light brown hair. When the feeling persisted, I decided it was my paranoia kicking in again.

I tried to resist looking at each person in the café but couldn't.

Someone was watching us, I was sure of it. But who? The tall man smoking a cigarette? No, too well dressed. The man on the corner by the magazine rack? Maybe…he keeps glancing our way. But is he looking at the girls or at me?

Finishing my drink, I suggested we move on. The kids immediately jumped up. The man at the magazine rack remained for a moment then walked the other way. I'd have to find someone else to worry about, or quit worrying at all.

       *   *   *   *

Our return to Carmen's home on the bus was uneventful, except that Jon seemed to have won Leandra's heart over completely, leaving Carmen to Noli. I sat alone, which suited me fine. I had a few ideas concerning our attack on Disko Hit that needed mulling over. Not a way to break in but to sneak in…through the air ducts.

But what would we do then?

Nothing came to me; and except for my paranoia at the sidewalk café, I was proud of myself for not seeing stalking killers at every turn. Only one man gave me pause.

He'd been following us from the time we left the *Plaka* to the time we reached the bus stop at Sìntagma Square; but that could be just a coincidence, many lines must meet at that bus terminal. The sidewalk was jammed with passengers when we arrived there.

Still, I was concerned. I doubt I would have noticed had the man not climbed on to our bus. That was just too much of a coincidence.

Again, I said nothing to the others; but I did think about getting off before our stop, just in case. By the time we arrived, however, I was so deep in thought, working out how to strike Disko Hit, I completely forgot about the man. I didn't even look back to see if he remained on the bus.

It was only later that I even remembered him, at all. And by then, it was too late to worry about.

If Simaphong's men showed up at Carmen's house, I decided, I'd deal with it them with Nazif, my strong right arm. I'd miss him when Noli and I left Turkey…Hasan and Regina too—especially, Regina.

Maybe we should hang around Bodrum for a while? Forget about returning to Terceira and Homestead.

Chapter Seventeen

Carmen's parents arrived about nine that evening. A tearful reunion with much hugging and kissing ensued followed by handshakes, half smiles and guarded appreciation, first in Turkish then in English.

I was disappointed. I expected a much warmer welcome after all we'd been through to save their daughter from an evil despot. Unless they thought we expected a reward, which we didn't. Nothing was ever said about one, so it didn't make any sense. After all, it was *his* idea that we remain in Athens until they arrived so they could thank us properly.

So why didn't they…with toasts, good cheer and Greek ouzo?

Maybe they're just tired, I rationalized. Exhausted, really. They've been through a lot lately and both are hurting. Him with a heart attack, her with a stroke. Or maybe they're just shy and this is awkward for them—a natural reaction to a tense situation.

Both parent stood close to their daughter, patting her arm and stroking her hair; and Carmen was beaming from ear-to-ear. Her ordeal was finally over.

When we settled in the living room, the first rush of questions answered, I asked Carmen's father, a small nervous man in his mid-forties and seldom without a cigarette, if he'd talked to the Izmir police, after he knew that Carmen was here.

He spoke quite good English, although his wife spoke little. She looked as if she should be in bed, her skin ashen and slack. This whole business had obviously put a huge strain on both of them.

"Ah…well, yes," he started, "I told them that she was safe now…in Athens."

He seemed nervous—almost afraid, surprising for a successful man who ran an olive oil factory. Natasha had told us that earlier.

I then asked what the police had said, wishing I had a brandy—something to settle *my* nerves. We'd been offered nothing and his actions were getting to me, as if he expected us to leave soon. This whole situation was becoming surreal.

"Well, they, ah—" Pausing, his eyes darted to his wife's then back to me. It was obvious something was wrong. "At first, they congratulated us and wished us well—God Speed...Allah's will, that sort of thing. You know the Turks."

"No, I don't know the Turks," I replied stiffly. "Noli and I have only been in Turkey for—" I had to pause to think. "Less than two weeks, although, it seems like two years after all we've been through."

"I am sure it has," Mister Uzul replied, equally stiffly, a curling smile twisting his upper lip. "And how is it that you came to *be* in Izmir, Mister Sylvester?"

For a moment he reminded me of a Goya painting I'd seen in the Prado in Madrid, a Spanish inquisition scene; only I was the one on trial. Looking at Noli, then at Nazif, I wondered how much I should tell him. It was obvious he still mistrusted me, probably Nazif too.

"The short of it is this," I began crisply. "Noli and I were flying a client from Chios to Kos when we saw a fishing boat in trouble..."

Skipping the gruesome details, I ended with, "...then we raced down the mountain, overpowered the guards at the marina and flew back to Bodrum. The next day we flew here. All-in-all, a harrowing experience... for your daughter, and for us."

"I agree, if what you say is true...although, some of it sounds self-inflicted. I mean, really, helping distressed fishermen? Beating up marina guards? I hardly see where—"

"It's God's truth, *Mister* Uzul," I interrupted bitterly, "every damn word of it. Why do I get the feeling that you think we were involved in the abduction of your daughter, somehow? That happened before Noli and I even arrived in Bodrum...several days, as I recall."

Mister Uzul cleared his throat nervously and glanced at his wife, who immediately began staring at her hands in her lap. "Yes...well...I suppose it is because—" He paused again, the silence was ominous.

"*Vallahi, Baba!*" Carmen suddenly exploded, followed so fast by a string of Turkish invectives I could only catch a few. Expressing her disbelief, I suspected, of the way her father was acting toward people who'd risked their lives to rescue her from an underground cesspool of crime and corruption.

She spoke with great emotion, hands waving, very dramatic, as only a teenage girl—an only child, at that—could speak in a fit of pique. "If-

if…not for them," she stammered finally in English, waving her hand at us. "I-I would be—"

Tears overwhelmed her before she could finish. Leaping from the couch, she left the room, followed by her mother who shouted what sounded like a threat to her husband.

"I am sorry," he quickly said, his head bowed. "We are, as you can see, upset by all this. Pleased, but upset. This is difficult for me…for us. I-I…that is, Nese and I appreciate what you have done for us…for Carmen. It's just that—" Pausing, he took a deep breath and looked straight at me. "It is what the Izmir police said about you before we left, Mister Sylvester."

Again he paused.

Thinking it was my angry stare that caused it, I looked away. "What *did* they say, Mister Uzul?" I asked, with syrupy sarcasm.

"They have issued a warrant for your arrest," he replied, "for murdering a guard at the marina and for beating up an older man. The one who looks after the boats and does odd jobs."

"My God!" I gasped, stunned by the revelation. "Anything else?"

"Yes. An important business man in Izmir—Bai Simaphong, I believe they said, an import-export dealer—has filed charges against you for assaulting him and his man servant in his penthouse apartment in the Büyük Hotel. They have a description of you. Quite good, I'd say, now that I've seen you."

"Damn!" I exploded, not knowing how to respond.

I looked at Nazif, who shrugged his massive shoulders. "Simaphong *değersiz yara!*…a worthless scab. He buy Carmen and my Leandra from Captain Tokolu. He buy many girls. Train them…sell them to Arabs!"

"Tell him about cornering the fish market…and boat building," I added in disgust. "He needs to hear our side too."

With a broad smile, Nazif said simply, "I tell…but in Turkish. Is easier."

For the next five minutes, Carmen's father listened without interruption as Nazif explained Simaphong's many and nefarious enterprises. Also his penchant for pretty girls; and how depraved men like Vedat Tokolu kidnapped them in hopes the notorious crime lord would buy them for his harem or train them as mistresses for wealthy men abroad.

At least, I hoped that was what Nazif told him, not embellishing it so much it became even more unbelievable. Then, before the olive oil merchant could respond, Leandra began *her* gruesome tale.

By then our host was wringing his hands in anguish, insisting he'd heard none of this and was just relieved to have Carmen back home.

When introduced to me earlier, he'd only asked if she'd been abused. Giving me the impression that his primary interest centered on whether she would still be a suitable bride, more than anything else. This time, he heard everything, and I was glad his wife wasn't there. She would have had another stroke if she'd heard it all.

It was pretty gruesome. Leandra even told us a few things she'd forgotten...or had repressed. And when she finished, Mister Uzul sat quietly, deep in thought.

Finally, he looked up at me with tears in his eyes. "I'm sorry, Mister Sylvester, I have misjudged you terribly and owe you my profoundest apology. Based on what the Izmir police told us, I never...well—"

He broke off and looked away, wiping his eyes with a handkerchief.

"I understand," I replied. "And call me Dan. 'Mister' makes me uncomfortable...like I'm in trouble or something. And I guess I am, but call me Dan, anyway."

"I am sorry...ah—Dan. I am Cemil. My wife is Nese. Please accept our sincerest regrets for the way we have treated you. We were not brought up that way. Strangers have always been welcome in the Uzul home."

"But not suspected murderers," I added to lighten things up and ease his pain.

"No, never...but enough of that. Tell me what you plan to do and if there is any way I can help. I am as anxious to see this despicable man and his evil empire destroyed as you are; and I am not without contacts in Izmir, even some influence. My parents have lived there all their lives and, well—"

He paused to collect his thoughts and then looked up. "I'm sorry. I seem to have lost my manners, so much has happened. Please, may I offer you some brandy?" Rising quickly, he said, "I have a special bottle—very old and unopened, for special occasions like this. Will you join me?"

I looked at Nazif, who returned my smile. "This *is* special occasion," he said mischievously. "We *both* have our daughters back!"

Leandra grinned broadly and patted his arm.

      *   *   *   *

The rest of the evening went rather well, I thought, considering how awkwardly it had begun. Carmen and her mother returned when our conversation became less heated. By then, I was sure Carmen had told her mother more of the details of her capture and dramatic escape because Nese looked far less frightened, although still pale.

Over brandy, I described the underground facility again, stressing how formidable it was and how difficult our escape had been, including Noli's part. But I couldn't help thinking how much more difficult it would be to get *into*—past the guards and the two vault doors.

A formidable task, indeed.

Neither parent asked for more details of what their daughter had gone through, and Carmen added nothing. But I now felt that they, at least, believed there *was* a crime lord named Bai Simaphong, who had an underground headquarters, and that showed some progress. Although, no one had the slightest idea of what to do about it, or if there was anything that we *could* do about it.

Unless we could flushed Simaphong and his gang out of his command post, a thought which had begun to swirl around in my tired brain lately.

But how…and then what?

    *   *   *   *

The next morning I suggested that Cemil Uzul call the Izmir Police, for what it was worth, and tell them what he now thought to be the truth. I knew it wouldn't stop them from looking for me or reduce the charges against me, but I hoped it might plant some doubt in their mind. Unless, of course, they'd been haplessly corrupted by Simaphong. In which case, they'd just thank Uzul politely and hang up.

Cemil agreed, telling the police that I was his houseguest and he feared nothing; nor did his daughter, who I'd safely returned the day prior.

Leandra interpreted for me as Cemil spoke. We were sitting in the living room having a second cup of coffee after a breakfast of soft boiled eggs, thinly sliced prosciutto, toast and marmalade, black olives and of course, feta cheese. A meal fixed by Tashi and Carmen, by the way, not by Nese, who was too ill to eat and remained in her bedroom.

"He didn't believe me!" Cemil gasped when he hung up. "He thought you were forcing me to say that with a gun pointed to my head. Asked me about it twice. He did finally agree to check on Captain Tokolu, however, who I said had kidnapped other girls."

"I suppose it doesn't matter," I replied with a sigh. "The big guard is dead and the older one got hit pretty hard."

I didn't admit to hitting either, nor did I implicate Hasan, for which Nazif later thanked me. I'd be leaving Turkey soon, even with a warrant on my head. Hasan wouldn't; he had a wife and family to take care of. He just didn't know his own strength.

                    *   *   *   *

The minivan cab we ordered arrived an hour later. Just prior, Jon had dropped by to say good-bye. During the confusion of loading, I saw Tashi give Nazif a big hug and a kiss on his cheek. Leandra received an even better one. As I passed by her bedroom on the way to get my zipper bag, I saw her in a tight embrace with Jon.

I felt sorry for Noli. But he was young, he'd find someone else.

Before leaving I told Cemil that Noli and I would return, if we could, on our way home.

Where *is* home?" he asked, less nervous than he'd been the day before. He'd been through a lot. We all had.

For a moment I had to think. Atlanta? Hardly, not any more. North Carolina, where my dad lived? I didn't know anyone there, except him. Certainly not Nags Head. "I'm not sure," I finally said. "In the Bluebird, I guess. Wherever my plane is, that's home."

"How about you, Noli?" he then asked.

"Wherever Dan is," he said with a huge smile.

And I was elated.

Chapter Eighteen

I landed near the isolated cove just after mid-day. Waving at us from Hasan's boat inside the cove was Phidaleia, the two children, and Regina. I guessed that Hasan and Ahmet were asleep below deck, having fished most of the night.

After anchoring the Bluebird behind two house-size boulders, we boarded the boat. According to Regina, it was the second night they'd spent there, and she had begun to worry. I apologized and explained why it had taken so long.

Moments later, Hasan came on deck and gave us a sleepy smile. Nazif told him everything had worked out fine, and that he would return the boat to Gümbet Cove so Hasan and Ahmet could continue sleeping. His hulking brother thanked him and went below.

As Nazif guided his brother's badly chipped boat out of the sheltered cove, I glanced back at the Bluebird to again assure myself that it was safely moored and couldn't be seen from the sea. I then sat with the others in the stern and listened to Leandra tell of our adventure in Athens. I heard Jon's name mentioned twice, followed by an impish smile, and Tashi was coupled with Leandra's father several times. I was sure she thought something was going on between them and so did I.

Nazif heard none of this from the tiller, of course, intent on maneuvering the boat past two small Turkish islands and then Kos, as close to Turkey as Chios had been.

I was a little surprised that Regina and Phidaleia didn't ask about the charges leveled against me, unless the news hadn't reach Bodrum yet; and thankfully, Leandra skipped that part. It was also possible they didn't know because they'd been on the Aegean for two days.

When Leandra finished, I asked Regina if there had been any problems with Captain Tokolu.

She blanched. I knew she was terrified of him, so was Phidaleia. "Ah, well...not him," she stumbled, "but someone else."

Phidaleia suddenly became distracted when her two girls shouted at her to look at a large fish that was following the boat...and to settle the argument about who'd seen it first. Two days on that smelly craft had taken its toll on everyone.

Before saying anything else, Regina cast a furtive glance at the open hatch which led to the sleeping room below. She seemed anxious, afraid of something...or someone.

Had Ahmet been bothering her again? Instead of him, she needed someone who could make her life normal again, and I did too. I hardly knew what normal was anymore, since I'd quit flying for Continental.

With another glance at the hatch opening, she confirmed it was Ahmet. "He insists I marry him...says, it is his right. In Koran it says, if widow has no children, brother of dead husband must marry her and give her one.

Suddenly, she burst into tears and leaned against me. "Oh, Dan, I don't know what to do."

"Why would he expect that now?" I asked, stunned by the disturbing news as I patted her shaking back.

I knew Ahmet liked Regina. He'd made that clear several times. Also, his snide remarks about how horny she must be without a husband or words to that effect.

Once, I saw him pat her behind. It was after dinner. He'd been drinking. She brushed him off with word and gesture, making it obvious she wasn't interested and didn't appreciate his unwarranted attention.

Sobbing against my shoulder, Regina stammered, "M-my two years of mourning...they are over now."

I took her into my arms to comfort her, wondering what I could do or say to make things better, but a disturbing thought came to me. Maybe she's hoping I'll marry her; rescue her from her tormentor as I had Leandra from hers.

Dan Sylvester, knight in shining armor!

The thought was appalling and I pushed her away. More brusquely than I should have, perhaps. Instant hurt scored Regina's face, misting her deep brown eyes.

She was really quite attractive, her inner beauty glowing like a soft flame. Was I becoming attracted to her as a moth is to a flame, yet trying to avoid being burn by it as I'd been before?

Without thinking I kissed her, realizing immediately that was the worse thing I could have done at that moment.

The lovely schoolteacher melted into my arms, her lips parting, her ample breasts pressed against my chest. Phidaleia had just taken the children to the bow to watch Leandra and Noli feed a flurry of seabirds, squawking noisily overhead, and didn't see the kiss. But as fate would have it, Ahmet chose that exact moment to stumble up the ladder from below.

"*Vallah! Bu ne?*" he shouted, shaking his fist at me.

I stood quickly, causing Regina to fall into a heap on the deck. "It's not what you think!" I said, hoping to avert a nasty fight over a woman I felt more like a brother to than a lover. The way Ahmet *should* have felt, instead of lusting after her like a jungle animal.

Standing poised, waiting for his next move, I wondered how long he'd felt that way toward Regina, even before her husband died? I was sure it's all sex—raw and demeaning.

Ahmet didn't have an ounce of compassion in his whole body. He'd proven that several times—his insolence, his biting sarcasm. His need to be paid for every good deed he performed, whether he did it or not. His whole life seemed to rotate around himself, and the misery he brought to others by drinking, gambling and whoring.

"What then?" he bellowed, raising his chest like a bandy rooster to impress barnyard hens. Growing up on a farm, I'd seen them strutting about many time. "Just a friendly kiss?"

"*Du...du!*" Phidaleia screamed from the bow after hearing Ahmet's angry words above the chattering seagulls, the rumble of the engine, and the water slapping against the hull.

"*Sakim kadin!*" Ahmet exploded, before she could say anymore.

Drawing a serrated fishing knife from a sheath hanging from his belt, he took a step closer, holding it up so the sun would reflect off the blade into my eyes. He appeared to be nearing a breaking point, clenched fist, menacing dark eyes, face contorted with rage.

Instinctively, I jerked my head to one side but held my ground.

He did it again, blinding me.

"Knock it off!" I challenged, tiring of his childishness, my heart beating like a trip hammer, my head throbbing in unison. "No need to get all riled. Regina and I were only—"

"Only what, *katil?*" he screamed, his bushy eyebrows shading his eyes completely.

I said nothing, not understanding the word.

As if taking my silence as a sign of weakness, he lunged at me.

I stepped aside easily, his knife missing me by several inches. I sensed he really didn't intend to cause me bodily harm, not having the balls for it, just wanted to scare me.

Which he was doing, his dark eyes riveted on me, his grin intimidating.

This was all for Regina, of course. To make her think he was man enough to be her husband. He'd made it clear from the start that he resented my intrusion into the family. Seeing us kiss must have pricked his inflated ego and forced him over the edge.

Regina looked up at me but remained at my feet. "Why he call you, *katil*, Dan? Murderer. What did you do?"

My expression went blank. How did Ahmet know that? Unless...

Patting her head, I said nothing, keeping my focus on her brother-in-law. If I could just calm him down some, maybe I could explain things and get him on our side.

I began circling the deck with him, like boys do who really don't want to fight but think they're expected to...or need to for their own vanity.

Seeing our silent dance from the helm, Nazif yelled at Ahmet to put the knife away or he'd take it from him, or words to that effect.

Undeterred, Ahmet pressed forward, blinding me with sunlight again. It was a tense moment. One that could have ended in tragedy but didn't.

Hasan suddenly appeared from the hatch opening, took two steps and hoisted Ahmet off the deck with a bear hug from behind. *"Damla biçak!"* he grunted, squeezing his brother until he couldn't breathe.

The knife dropped to the deck and skidded toward me. I picked it up. "Thanks, Hasan, this was getting out of hand. Let him down. He'll be all right. We need to talk."

Hasan did what I said, then replaced Nazif at the helm.

For the next hour, until we reached Gümbet Cove, Nazif and I, interrupted occasionally by Phidaleia, talked to Ahmet. I first explained about the guards at the marina, how I regretted the one had been hit so hard but not saying who did it. Ahmet assumed that I had and I didn't tell him otherwise. Nazif didn't correct me, either. Although, by then, I was sure he knew the truth. Noli probably also knew but said nothing. The rest of our talk centered on Ahmet and Regina, most of which was in Turkish, except for this sharp exchange.

"It my right!" Ahmet raged, shaking his fist at his older brother.

Nazif shook his head. "Not done anymore. Besides, Regina no love you."

To which Ahmet returned vehemently. "It not matter. Koran say, I take…she obey!"

The problem never was settled, but it was obvious that Regina wanted no part of Ahmet. I didn't blame her. Once she was pregnant, he'd dump her like a drown rat and find a younger wife—or mistress. He might not even wait *that* long. He acted like he had several already. Although, his boasting had a shallow ring to it—like most of what he said.

*   *   *   *

We pulled into Gümbet Cove about four that afternoon. In the two days they'd been waiting for us, Hasan and Ahmet had caught a ton of fish. So I volunteered to fly Nazif to Denizli once more so he could sell them; and at the same time, appease Ahmet somehow; make things better between us so he wouldn't rat on me to the Bodrum police.

"*Iyi,*" Nazif replied with an appreciative grin. "We go tomorrow—early…before fish die."

Climbing over the rail to help the women off the boat, I wondered if Bodrum even had a police force. When Nazif followed, I asked him. By then the women and children were out of earshot, and Hasan and Ahmet had gone below to get their gear.

"*Evet, ama küçük*…but small," he replied with a grin, as if knowing why I'd asked. "Bodrum small…but many tourists." He waved his hands to show how seasonal visiters enlarged the population.

I nodded, noting a second sleek yacht moored in Gümbet Cove. I was glad we'd left the Bluebird far from prying eyes. But I did want to stop in Chios once more to refuel, use the last of Alexis' line of credit. I was sure she'd want me to.

Turning to Nazif, I asked how early in the morning we'd have to leave. Just then, his brothers caught up with us. They others had gone ahead.

Pausing to add up the various times on his fingers, he said, "*Beê.*"

"Five?" I gasped, wishing Ahmet hadn't heard and aghast at the early hour.

"*Evet.* Get up four…eat on boat. Two hours to plane…one hour to Denizli. Oh…and Leandra come too. I no leave her here again."

"Okay…" I replied with reservation. I wasn't concerend about Leandra coming along, just hoping I'd get enough sleep. Turning to Hasan, I asked if that was all right with him.

He nodded. "I stay on boat. Fix nets. Phidaleia bring food…for all of us."

Ahmet said nothing, a black frown warping his chubby face.

In a way I felt sorry for him; but I also wished he'd move to some other city, *anywhere* to get him out of my hair—and Regina's.

Catching up with her before she reached Hasan's house, I asked Regina if she was all right now.

She nodded that she was and thanked me, adding with a frown, "But I afraid to stay here alone. Afraid Ahmet—"

"Come with us then," I said quickly, "But you'll have to be ready early." As soon as I said it, a thought came to me: she could even spend the night at Nazif's house, so we didn't have to wake up Hasan's entire family when we came by to pick her up.

But would she take it the wrong way and think I was coming on to her?

Tentatively, I asked, adding quickly, "You know…sleep with Leandra. I'm sure she wouldn't mind. She and Noli are going with us too."

Regina looked startled and studied my face…searching for hidden meanings, I suppose. But there weren't any—not this time, just a practical suggestion. She didn't want to be left with Ahmet, and I didn't want him to know where we were going.

Nothing sinister, just common sense. Well…maybe a little wishful thinking. After all she was pretty, even with a Roman nose.

Regina's long pause made me realized I'd put her in an awkward position. If she slept at Nazif's house, it might appear that we were lovers and that would make Ahmet even more irate. Mad enough, perhaps, to tell the police where I was or where I'd be tomorrow. Yet if she didn't come over, Ahmet might abuse her, and Hasan wouldn't be there to stop him.

Regina finally said she'd come over later. "After Ahmet go out. He is very angry. He will get drunk tonight and feel bad tomorrow."

With a wave and a nervous laugh, she entered Hasan's house and closed the door.

*   *   *   *

It didn't even take Regina that long. She came over during dinner with an ugly bruise on her cheek. "Ahmet hit me!" she cried, tears flowing. "I no live there anymore."

Nazif swore loudly in Turkish then held her until she stopped whimpering. "Is good you come," he said for my benefit as much as hers. "Ahmet no good. You go with us tomorrow."

Good, that settled that, I thought, but would Ahmet tell the police?

After dinner Nazif called his friend in Denizli to ask that he meet us like before. After a pause, I heard Nazif repeat *Neveêhir* twice, then, *"Evet, çok restoran, çok tourist."*

When he hung up, Nazif said it was too soon to sell fish in Denizli. "Neveêhir in Cappadocia is better. My friend will arrange…for his usual fee."

"Where is that?" I asked. "How far?"

He said eight hundred kilometers by car, about five hundred miles, but less by plane. A man would meet us at Göl Sife, a lake near Kirêehir, eighty kilometers from Nevêehir.

"Why not land at an airport? Doesn't Nevêehir have one?"

"Evet…a good one. But better we land on lake. Many small towns, he say…on road to Nevêehir…many *restorans*. We sell *çok balik*. Okay?"

I smiled at his cleverness. Besides, landing on a lake would be more private and much less conspicuous. "How big is the lake?"

"Seven kilometers, he say. Is big enough?"

"Plenty…that's four miles, if it's clear of stumps and weeds." It would also ease my mind about Ahmet, not knowing where we were.

Nazif seemed to sense my concern. "Don't worry, Ahmet no tell." Nazif raised his fist like a prizefighter. "He know I kill him, if he does."

"If Hasan doesn't do it first," I muttered softly.

"You have fuel?" Nazif asked, his mind clearer than mine, less encumbered with worry. Of course, he wasn't charged with murder as I was.

"Plenty, for five hundred miles. We'll refuel at Chios Airport on the way back."

"Okay, but we leave at *dort*, not *beş*…get up *üç!*"

"At three?" I gasped.

"Evet. Üç."

Not being a morning person, rising at three, an ungodly hour, was unsettling. But the more I thought about it, the more I liked the idea. Ahmet not only wouldn't know *where* we were going, he wouldn't know *when*.

My greatest concern, that he blabbed to his bar buddies about me while drinking tonight. One might be sober enough to call the police in hopes of a reward. After all, we had to return to Bodrum, eventually.

✻   ✻   ✻   ✻

When Regina finished eating her chicken and rice, she praised Leandra twice, once in Turkish then in English. The pretty teenager beamed with pride from the unexpected compliment. Although Leandra did all the cooking for herself and her father, and was quite good at it, Nazif just took it all for granted. As if women—even teenage girls—had a proclivity for cooking, like an inherent gift or something.

After dinner Regina offered to wash dishes and hinted that I might dry them. I agreed, although I doubted that few men she knew would have. Turkish men smoke after dinner, often with water pipes, and drink coffee or *raki*. I'd seen restaurants with water pipes that patrons could use…rent, I suppose.

But then this was Turkey.

"You like Cappadocia," she said, handing me a rinsed dish. "Much Christian history there."

"Really? I don't know anything about it," I replied, drying the plate and hoping the trip wouldn't lead to more awkwardness between us, or more unpleasantness with Ahmet. I could still feel his seething hatred as I circled with him on the boat. But I could also still feel Regina's passion during our interrupted kiss.

It stirred me more that it should have, more than I wanted it too.

"Cappadocia is in your Bible," Regina explained further. "Christians lived in caves there and painted pictures on walls. Then Byzantines come. They didn't like pictures and destroyed them…mark them." She made a slashing motion with a fork she had in her hand.

"The Iconoclasts," I said, remembering something I'd learned in college years ago.

"I-con-o-clasts," Regina repeated, a smile splitting her classic Romanesque face as she handed me a dripping cup. "Funny name, I-con-o-clasts."

"What happened to Christians?" Noli asked from the kitchen table. It surprised me. I'd forgotten he was there, assuming he was with Leandra. Although, since Athens they hadn't been as lovey-dovey as before. Since her Greek Adonis had entered the picture.

"They live underground—build big cities."

"Cappadocia, *çok kireç taşi,*" Nazif added. He'd just returned from having a cigarette in the patio, a concession to a household of non-smokers.

When it was obvious by my blank expression that I didn't understand, he looked at Leandra for help. She'd also returned from somewhere and joined the conversation.

"Caves are built in soft limestone," she said. "But there is also much lava there, which caps tall pillars—stiff pillars." Pausing to blush, she added softly, "...erotic pillars."

I was beginning to get the picture—pillars of limestone covered with hard porous rock. I'd say, erotic. "Should be interesting," I commented, trying to visualize it.

"Interesting" turned out to be a gross understatement, a bit like describing the Grand Canyon as a ditch.

Chapter Nineteen

Noli and I slept for a few hours on the patio that night, but again I didn't sleep well, obsessed with the idea that Ahmet might rat on me. I also wondered if Regina—the lovely lady with the flashing smile and curvaceous figure—was also having trouble sleeping.

I knew she liked me, maybe even more than that, and I liked her. But what could I offer her? Certainly not a home, that was the Bluebird. Not an unpleasant concept to me but not the kind of life a woman yearns for.

Besides, I could never live in Turkey, not with a warrant on my head. But what if I was exonerated and cleared of all charges? Would I stay then...fly for Alex Margoles, maybe, or some other wealthy Greek? How would that suit Regina?

Not very well. The Margoles family would never accept her—not a Turk, even a comely schoolteacher with a bright smile.

And what about Noli? What would become of him, or should I even worry about him? He's a big boy now. He can take care of himself. Or can he?

Perhaps a more pertinent question: Do I want him to?

*   *   *   *

Later, I managed nearly two hours of sleep on Hasan's boat. Regina and Noli did too, while Leandra and her father mended nets. The police weren't there when we left, which wasn't surprising. I doubt if Ahmet even came home last night...too drunk to find it, probably.

As Hasan guided the boat into the sheltered cove, we finished the last of our sandwiches and coffee, prepared by Phidaleia the night before. She hadn't come with us, taking the children to a friend's house, instead. Hasan had indicated with a shrug that she was still upset about having to spend two days on his boat, waiting for our return from Athens. Nazif and I were probably not on her most-favored list either, if we ever were.

By the time Hasan had maneuvered the stern of his boat next to the Bluebird and Nazif had secured it with two ropes, the sun was just beginning a new day, the eastern sky brushed with soft gold, as if Midas has touched it himself.

I was anxious to get started, wanting to stay one step ahead of the police.

With everyone helping, loading the plane went quickly. Most of the fish were still alive, but they didn't stay that way long, not after dumping them on the ice that Hasan had brought for the bottom of each cooler. Enough to last several hours, he said, before reminding us that he would return to the cove at sunset to pick us up.

"But remember," I cautioned, "if we spend the night in Chios, we won't return until tomorrow…say about noon. Okay?"

The big man just nodded and waved goodbye, as if it didn't matter. Hasan was hard to provoke, but if you did—watch out. As he'd demonstrated several times, he was outrageously strong, dragging me from the root cellar, killing a guard with one blow, and lifting Ahmet, a two-hundred pound man, as if he were a little boy.

After starting the engines, I feathered the props several times to warm up the oil and check the manifold pressure. Each time the engines roared, the pressure reduced as it should. But I noticed a slight catch—a waver in the left engine. I tried it several times but didn't hear it again, something to keep an eye on; have a mechanic on Chios check for me.

One more thing to worry about.

*   *   *   *

Our destination path took us over Denizli.

At five thousand feet, I marveled again at the rugged terrain as we followed the Menderes River slogging its way through a wide valley, green with vegetation at this time of year. The Menderes, from which our word *meander* is derived because of the way it snakes and turns back on itself, reminded me of the lower Mississippi.

At the head of the valley, passing Afyon—Turkish for opium, Nazif offered from the cockpit entry—I took a more easterly heading.

Noli did, that is. He was flying while I was looking out the window with a map, checking towns and lakes as we flew by. At that altitude map reading is easy, as long as there aren't too many towns and lakes, which there soon were—a half dozen of each on our left, and several more on our right.

Shortly after that we flew out of the mountains into a broad flat plain centered by the oddest lake I'd ever seen—clear, shallow water covering crystalline sand, or perhaps salt. I wasn't sure. At least thirty miles across, it was shaped like a human hand with one finger pointing north. And even stranger, it had a soft pinkish cast, shimmering in the morning sun like a sheets of corrugated aluminum.

Nazif called it, *Tuz Gölü*, salt lake.

"See people? They stand in water…up to here." He touched his ankle. "Ankara, Turkish capital, not far—that way." He motioned toward the lake's north-pointing finger.

"It's amazing," I said, looking at a half dozen flea specks wading a mile from shore. "Like our Great Salt Lake, only smaller."

"It drying up," he said with a shrug, as if nothing would be done to save it.

Checking my guidebook, I noted the lake was the second largest in Turkey and that the population of Ankara was over two million, second only to Istanbul.

A dozen miles beyond Tuz Gölü, we flew over Kizil River, dammed up to form a long snake-like lake. Here the terrain changed again, more like the Badlands of South Dakota, a place where no one should have to live. Yet, according to my map, this was Cappadocia, ancient home of perse-cuted Christians in the center of Asia Minor, land of Tatars and Mongols; and now, the heart of a fiercely independent Moslem nation.

An astonishing sight, the entire valley was strewn with limestone spires, some, one hundred feet high and capped with dark lava. Sentinels to an all-powerful, single God.

From the air it looked as if we'd discovered another planet—stark and lifeless. Yet Christians flourished here for hundreds of years, beginning in 200 A.D., despite scorching sand and searing heat, soil littered with rocks, and marauding bands of raiders happy with their plethora of gods.

I thought of the Roman Christians and what they'd endured at about that same time. Living here made life in Italy seem like a walk in the park. All the Christian *there* had to worry about were the lions.

*   *   *   *

Just beyond Kirşehir, I spotted the lake where I was to land. It appeared a bit narrow, decidedly barren and surrounded by seared earth littered with rocks. If Turkey could only export them, it would be a fabulously wealthy country by now.

Descending, I checked the lake for stumps and pleasure boats. Finding none, I lowered the flaps ten percent and lined up for my descent.

It was ten o'clock, the time we'd said we'd be there.

"Did your friend tell you which end of the lake he would meet us?" I yelled at Nazif, strapped into the first seat on the right. Leandra was behind him and Regina was across the aisle.

Before Nazif could answer, I saw someone waving at us from the lakeshore.

"That must be him," I yelled, "near that pick-up truck."

"I see," Nazif said excitedly, waving back.

Knowing the man couldn't see Nazif waving at him, I waggled the wings. The man continued waving as if he didn't understand my signal.

My landing was good. It should have been. A mild breeze rippled the water, making it easy to judge the distance above it. I taxied toward a stubby pier where the man now stood. He was still waving, as if we hadn't seen him yet. If I'd had a horn I would have blown it.

To make things easier, I taxied onto the shore. It looked dry enough, parched from scant rain, and firm enough to hold the plane until we off-loaded the fish.

With another pair of hands, the unloading went even faster, although we all smelled of fish when we finished. Noli and Leandra wrestled the ice chests to the truck, one filled with anchovies, the other sardines. They also agreed to stay with the plane when I expressed concern about leaving it there unguarded.

Nazif agreed as well, which surprised me, as protective as he'd been toward Leandra since her rescue. "We may be gone several hours," I cautioned, beginning to have second doubts about leaving them, wondering how they would entertain themselves for that long.

Since our return from Greece, Leandra's ardor toward Noli had dissipated some. But you know, out-of-sight, out-of-mind. It could return at anytime; although lately, they'd been acting more like siblings than good friends.

"We okay," Noli replied. "We watch Bluebird good."

Leandra nodded. "We will be fine...nothing will bad happen, way out here." She waved her arm at the desolation surrounding the lake.

There wasn't a house or road for miles and plenty of sandwiches and pop in the two coolers we'd brought. They'd find something to do—take a walk, take a nap. I just hoped they wouldn't do anything more intimate than that.

✳   ✳   ✳   ✳

Driving away from the lake on a dirt road barely distinguishable from the crusty hardpan alongside it, our first stop was Kirşehir fifteen miles away, a bustling town of thirty thousand with several main streets and two good-size restaurants.

Nazif said thousand of tourists came there every year, foreign *and* Turkish, to visit ancient Christian cities dug twenty meters or more underground, the equivalent of ten floors. Some, according to my guidebook, housed over two thousand believers.

I was anxious to see them; anything to keep my mind off what awaited us in Izmir.

After selling a third of the fish to two restaurants, our driver headed toward Hacibektas. According to Regina, the city was named for the man who first brought the many Turkic tribes into a coherent nation. A cleric, he espoused some pretty radical ideas for that time. For example, the three most important activities in life are, working for a living, helping those in need, and preparing for the future by studying science.

Pretty heady stuff for the thirteenth century.

He also thought woman should pray with men, learn with men, and vote with men; unheard of until after World War One when Kemal Attaturk came to power and decreed that women no longer had to wear the much hated black chador and veil.

"He also says," Regina added with a grin, "that a woman is dangerous when she is far from man but loving when she is not.'"

With Regina sitting on my lap in a crowded truck, driving through a barren, moon-like landscape, I understood perfectly what Haci Bektas meant: God placed Adam and Eve in the Garden to become soulmates and expected all living creatures to do the same.

The trick was finding the right one. A constant battle for me, and having Regina's warm body bouncing along with mine didn't make it any easier.

When I didn't comment, she further explained that, despite Haci Bektas' call to "Love Ones Neighbor," he formed the Janissary, a ruthless band of soldiers who scoured the countryside for *infidels* while he encouraged the growth of Islam through preaching and prayer. "In Ottoman Time, Janissary *çok fena,* killed many people," she added with a frown.

Feeling goose bumps ripple up her arm, I pulled her closer. She willingly sank into my chest. Too willingly, I feared.

If the driver didn't stop soon, I'd be in a heap of trouble.

*   *   *   *

Fortunately, he did; but not at a restaurant, at the Haci Bektas Museum and burial site.

"Come," Regina said with her most fetching smile, while scrambling off my lap, "I show you while Nazif sells his smelly fish." To emphasize her point she held her nose.

By then, I was used to the smell. I hardly noticed it at all anymore.

Inside the museum, we saw rooms filled with artifacts, clothing, cooking utensils, paintings on clay tablets, and much more. It was all fascinating. I'd always thought the Koran forbade painting—even sculpture. Anything representing the human form, I'd learned in college, was considered idolatry.

Which was true, our guide said in near perfect English, "But Haci Bektas believed that art and science were the same and should be continued always."

The more I heard about their revered leader, the more I appreciated his startling philosophy, especially in those times, and in a Moslem nation. Too bad they'd chosen to disregard so much of it; especially the part about treating women as equals.

Seated in a room with a group of tourists, a second guide told us about the Whirling Dervishes who performed there years ago, one of many dervish sects in Islam. In a film, we saw six men enter a circular room, wearing black, ankle-length capes and cone-shaped, camelhair hats. Waiting for them were two musicians—one with a long reed instrument, the other with a pair of squat drums. Next to them was a man with the Koran in his lap. All three were dressed in flowing white gowns and camelhair hats.

When the six men were seated, the reed player began a high-pitched melody, which sounded Chinese, accompanied by a slow steady beat on the drums. When the reader began chanting from the Koran, each dancer arose one at a time and cast off his cape, revealing a dazzling white, ankle-length skirt—full and magnificent, and a richly embroidered waistcoat.

The tempo quickened.

After bowing to the reader, each dancer in turn raised his arms—left palm up as a receiver of gifts, right palm down as a giver of gifts—and began to rotate on his right foot.

How they kept their balance was a mystery because the dance continued for a long time, until each man collapsed in a hovel. An incredible display of balance and dexterity in a grueling performance.

The guide explained what the dance meant as we followed him through a garden toward the tomb of Haci Bektas. "The black cape represents Death, which the dancers cast off, revealing the white skirt of Life. They twirl until they enter a trance and become one with Allah. It is very inspirational but also dangerous. So dangerous, the dance is banned, except in Konya once a year. That is why we only saw a film, not the real thing."

When I looked puzzled, he explained. "The men fall occasionally, hurting themselves or the musicians. Others have past out, gone into a coma, even had epileptic fits."

I thanked him, in awe of the skill—and faith—of the remarkable men in flowing white skirts, and dazzled by the forward-looking ideas of Haci Bektas. If more people would ascribe to them—Moslems and Christians alike, our world would be a better place.

*   *   *   *

In Nevşehir, a city built in the shadow of a magnificent castle, the driver again let Regina and me off while Nazif sold fish. This time we took a cab a few miles south to Kaymakli, site of one of several underground cities built by early Christians.

Now a museum, we paid to go inside. Across a courtyard, we slithered through a low tunnel just wide enough for one person. At the end of the tunnel, inside a room carved out of a mountain, stood an enormous round stone, ten feet high and three feet thick, with a hole in the middle. It looked like a huge grinding wheel, but it wasn't. Regina explained.

"They rolled it in front of the tunnel when enemy soldiers came."

"It must have taken many men to do that," I said. "What if they didn't have time?"

"Two men can do it easily; but if they didn't have time, they did this…" Laughing, she raised her hand above her head, as if she had a club then brought it down quickly.

"I get the picture. Only one person can crawl through the tunnel at a time so each is easily dispatched. But why is there a hole in the middle of the stone?"

"Sometimes they use two stones, one on each end of the tunnel."

"So the hole is to look at the enemy?"

"No...the hole is to shoot them with arrows."

This time she didn't laugh.

Taking my hand, she guided me through one room and into the next, both lit by a bare bulb hanging from six-foot ceilings. I had to crouch to keep from scraping my head.

"People must have been shorter in those days."

"They were, and they only had candles." Again Regina held her nose. "That is why it smells smoky in here."

From there, she led me through a maze of rooms, each carved out of soft limestone, then down a rickety ladder to a lower level and more rooms. Most were for sleeping with carved out niches for beds, but a few had fireplaces vented straight up to the outside.

After fifteen minutes, I'd had about enough. The air ducts of Disko Hit suddenly flashed through my mind and my skin began to crawl.

I also began to sweat.

"When a family had a new baby," Regina continued, oblivious of my fear of being trapped inside a closed-in place, "they just dug another room...and more beds."

"Incredible," I mumbled, following her down a set of carved-out stairs to a third level underground. I began to feel light-headed and slowed my breathing to fight off the growing nausea. It only helped a little.

"This is a Disco," she said with a chuckle, leading me into a dimly lit room filled with tables and chairs, even a bandstand. "They play music here on weekend...and dance."

"Christians surely didn't build this," I said with sarcasm.

"No, Turks did."

Suddenly, Regina spun around like a child—or a woman in love, acting as if we were on a mountaintop or in a field of wild flowers. Yet we weren't. We were thirty feet underground in a darken hovel only fit for rats.

Fighting back the nausea, a stab of guilt ripped through me. She looked so happy, like a teen queen at her first prom. It wasn't right leading her on like this. We'd have to talk, but what could I say?

That I'd be leaving soon, flying away from all this? Where would I tell her that I'm going? More importantly, why *am* I going?

"Because you're wanted for murder," I said to myself as we climbed up to the second floor, then the first—first cave, really. There weren't any floors, just passageways and rooms, one on top of another. "Besides that, you don't love her...not yet, anyway."

Crawling back through that same entry tunnel, a terrifying realization came to me: What if I was convicted of murder? I could spend the rest of my life in a Turkish prison.

The thought increased my phobia. I'm sure my face blanched, I could feel it.

Exiting the tunnel, I must have looked sick because Regina asked me if I was all right. "*Evet*," I replied weakly, relishing the sunlight. "But happy to be out of there. I get queasy in cramped places, especially when I can't see outside."

"I'm so sorry," she said, patting my cheek. "I didn't know. We didn't have to go down that far."

Taking her hand, I kissed it. Another dumb move. "That's all right...I wanted to. I'm all right...now."

Still holding hands, we walked out to the street and found the same cab we'd arrived in. Looking at my watch, I was surprised. We'd been underground less than an hour.

It felt like a half a day.

         *   *   *   *

By the time we returned to Nevşehir, Nazif had sold the remaining fish. I was glad. I was ready to leave now and return to Izmir. I'd just faced my worst fear—being buried alive—and survived. Now if I could just figure out a way to attack Disko Hit and survive.

But first, Regina had one more thing to show me.

Just out of town our driver stopped at a small chapel carved into the side of a thirty-foot crag of limestone. Faded frescos of Christ, the Virgin Mary and Saint John adorned the ceilings and walls. What devotion, I thought as I studied them carefully. For seven centuries, against incredible odds, Christians had kept their faith here, surrounded by Moslems who called them *infidels* and tried to destroy them.

Climbing back into the truck, I shook my head in amazement. Suddenly, my problems seemed far less important.

         *   *   *   *

In Hacibektas we stopped at a caravansary, one of many way-stations built during the Ottoman era for travelers, each about a day's walk apart, like the Spanish missions of California. The dining room was large but spartan, strictly Moslem, with polished tile floors, softly pointed arches and thick clay walls.

"*Nefis*...delicious," Nazif cried after biting into his fish filet.

After handling fish all day, even smelling like one, it surprised me that he'd ordered cod. The driver did too. Regina and I had *döner kebab*, thinly sliced lamb on a bed of rice topped with sour cream sauce. I could see the savory meat roasting behind a counter on a vertical spit, which allowed the juices to seep back into the meat instead of onto the charcoal.

The aroma was delightful, my favorite Turkish meal. And one of my last, I thought, if the Izmir police catch me. But how could we attack Disko Hit without first entering Izmir?

On the drive back to Kirşehir, I was again drawn to the incredible landscape. Phallic spires, hardened by a merciless sun, mushroomed out of scarred outcroppings. Farther on, a terrace of caves carved into a steep hillside, residences for locals with conventional doors and windows, one even had a television antenna.

A crazy thought came to me: How a colony of explorers might live on the moon.

Following my gaze, her arm about my neck, Regina sighed. "People are not supposed to live in caves anymore, but some still do and the police say nothing."

"With no heat or plumbing?" I asked, pushing her forward so I could see a little better—and breath a little easier.

"*Evet*, but it is cool in summer." She laughed at her joke, which was no doubt true.

Regina was such a joy, always cheerful, always smiling, and so well packaged. I had to say something soon about us as a couple, but what?

In the distance, row after row of folded limestone ridges, glistening white in the stifling heat, sand blown into perfect alignment, like a modern artist might dream up to mystify viewers. Nearby, three stone pillars, silent sentries watching over an ancient landscape, once seething with violence and intolerance, now seething with tourists from around the world.

A remarkable place, one I was unlikely to ever forget.

     *   *   *   *

Noli and Leandra were happy to see us, waving as we bumped down the dirt path which led to the lake. Noli was also hungry, quickly devouring the sliced lamb I'd brought on a paper plate. Leandra only picked at hers, said she wasn't hungry and would eat it later.

I guessed they'd had a spat.

With a hearty farewell to our driver—now a few *lire* richer, we climbed aboard the Bluebird and I fired up the engines. Everything sounded good; so when Noli had secured the entry door and was strapped into his seat, I taxied into the lake and feathered the left prop. It worked perfectly this time, not a hitch or a squeak, which happens in a plane as old as the Bluebird. Same thing with people—a hitch or a squeak, once in a while.

After takeoff, I leveled off at five thousand feet then glanced down for a last look at Cappadocia. A place of courage, inspiration and faith in the midst of the most formidable landscape I'd ever seen. A place steeped in Christian history, kept alive for tourists by a nation of Moslems.

I doubt we'd do the same for them in the States.

*   *   *   *

Noli put his hands on the wheel, as if wanting to fly. I nodded then asked over the intercom how he and Leandra had faired while we were away.

"Okay," he replied stiffly. "We talk...we sleep in plane...we talk more. She like Jon but like me too. I happy."

That was simple enough, I thought, wishing it was that simple with Regina and me. And maybe it was. A kiss and some handholding hardly constituted a romance, or did it?

Maybe, it depended on what Regina thought about it...and hoped for.

Moments later, Noli pointed off the right wing. Two American F-16s were flying formation with us—trying to, that is. The Mach-two fighter can barely fly under two hundred knots without stalling.

They only stayed with us for a brief moment, waved, then flew off. On a hunch, I called them on channel nineteen, an inter-plane frequency.

"Roger, Bluebird, we're out of Adana," one of them replied to my query. "Are you a yank?"

"Roger, Air Force, just visiting here."

"What kind of plane is that?"

"A Grumman Mallard."

"It's a beaut, a real classic."

"Thanks. See you guys around."

"Roger, Bluebird. We're out-oh-here."

Watching them peel away, I thought of the olden days, on the Silk Road to China, when merchants on camels passed each other going to markets. Only instead of camels loaded with silk and spices, we'd carried fish and they carried air-to-air missiles.

     ✳   ✳   ✳   ✳

Our flight to Chios took almost three hours and was uneventful. I had *some* reservations flying over Izmir, wondering if the Turkish Air Force would be looking for a blue and white seaplane. But the only plane I saw was a Boeing 737 approaching Izmir Airport.

Landing on Chios, I was relieved to still find a credit balance on Alexis' account and arranged to have the Bluebird refueled one more time. They apparently hadn't been informed that she'd died, and I didn't tell them. It probably wouldn't have mattered as the fuel had already been paid for anyway.

We then took a cab to the Kyna Hotel, which I'd seen near the harbor on our previous trip, and secured a room for Regina and Leandra, and one for Nazif. Noli and I would stay with Alexis' family. I knew we'd be welcome, even without telling them we were coming, and planned to return the Crucifix and St Christopher Medal. Also explain how useful they'd been opening the air vents in Disko Hit.

The hotel prices weren't bad and included breakfast. A brochure on the front desk explained that the hotel was built in 1917 as a villa for John Livinos. When I asked who he was, the hotel clerk said a wealthy landowner. With a glint in his eye, he suggested I look at the dining room ceiling. There, I saw several portraits of Mrs. Livinos, a real beauty. But what a strange place to be immortalized, I thought.

     ✳   ✳   ✳   ✳

It was nearly ten when the cab pulled up in front of the old farm house. Fortunately, Alexis' parents were still up; and after a warm greeting, they were delighted to receive their daughter's religious keepsakes and surprised by how we'd used them to escape.

Again I didn't mention Alexis' brutal rape, remembering her dying wish to spare them the gruesome details. I did, however, apologize for not giving them the medals sooner, but I doubt they even heard me, still caught up in their grief.

Brother Michael was also there, looking as scholarly as before, and his lovely wife, the former actress, her dark molding eyes heavy with tears. She was trying hard not to cry but not succeeding too well.

While we talked, Alexis' mother served a full-bodied red wine from the Geromilos Farms in Peloponnisos. Noli tried some also. Called Dimitra, the Goddess of Agriculture, according to Michael, his further comment stunned me. That vineyard had been tended by the same family for three hundred years, not possible in the United States. We were too young a nation for that kind of longevity. Besides, it's unlikely that, that many generations would remain in one occupation, no matter what it was.

I'd only learned to enjoy the grape in Portugal, and I particularly liked this one, dry and fruity with a hint of vanilla. At least, that's what it tasted like to me. It's hard to describe the subtle flavor of a good wine. It's best to just try it and decide for yourself.

As I suspected, Noli and I were invited to spend the night; but the next morning Alexis's mother returned the Crucifix to me, and the Saint Christopher's Medal to Noli.

"Keep with blessing," she said, struggling with her English. "You wear…think Alexis…*moo omorfus moro.*"

I told her I would always remember *her beautiful baby*, a remarkable woman who I missed a lot. Just thinking of Alexis steeled my resolve to avenge her death, but putting Simaphong and Tokolu in prison would be a difficult task…as well as dangerous.

                    *   *   *   *

After our goodbyes, Noli and I returned to the Kyra Hotel. The others had already eaten and were ready to leave.

On the way to the airport, the chatter was lively and mostly about Bodrum, at least I heard that name several times. Everyone seemed to be in good spirits, but I wasn't sure I was ready to return there yet. In a way I was, to rid the world of two vicious people, but in another way I wanted to leave Turkey right then, never to return.

Regina seemed to sense my indecision and asked me what I would do in Bodrum. I told her that I honestly didn't know, and that was the truth.

I *didn't* know, not for sure, anyway. I knew we had to strike back at Simaphong and Tokolu for all they'd done, but I had no plan and wasn't sure we even could. I also knew that, if we weren't successful—if either survived to live another day, I'd probably end up in a Turkish prison and the kidnappings would continue.

In fact, we all might end up in a Turkish prison, but we had to do something...and soon. Time was running out.

Chapter Twenty

The Bluebird was fully fueled and ready to go when we arrived at the airport, and thirty minutes later we were at the end of the runway.

Running up the engines, I feathered the props. Again, everything sounded normal.

"Roger, Tower," Noli responded to the call. I'd been letting him take radio calls lately to give him some practice. "We cleared for takeoff. Have good day."

Said like a professional pilot, I thought, smiling at his tag line.

After takeoff I glanced over at the Turkish coast, so close in distance, yet so far in so many respects. Greece seemed so much more modern and certainly more European. Turkey was still quite Asian and obviously proud of it. But there was more.

Greece had ample resources and milder weather. Life was good there; a Christian nation noted for its democratic ideals and tradition of inquiry. Home of Socrates, Plato, and Aristotle, the basis for Western justice and equality. Turkey, just a few miles away, was a Moslem nation with few resources, struggling with a democracy less than one hundred years old, in a fledgling free-market tottering on the edge of collapse. A place where men like Bai Simaphong could flourish, yet teenagers received long prison terms for minor offenses. Where women, honored in the Koran, had few rights other than to serve men.

Quite a difference, I thought, banking south. And if that weren't enough, in ancient times, Western Turkey from Troy to Ephesus was owned by Greece. Could there be any more reason for two countries to distrust each other?

*　　　　*　　　　*　　　　*

I landed just north of the sheltered cove near Myndos and taxied toward it, skirting several house-size boulders along the way. But rounding the last two, which hid the cove from the sea, I was stunned by what I saw and immediately called Nazif forward.

Tied to Hasan's boat was another fishing boat, the same one Alexis and I had been lured into with an SOS sign painted on the deck. And facing us with a rifle and a menacing grin was Captain Tokolu, himself.

He waved at us to come aboard. Not a greeting, a demand backed by force of arms. Two of his crew stood by his side with pistols, a third at the helm.

I was tempted to turn tail and run, but I knew I couldn't. Hasan had obviously been killed or taken below in chains, nothing else could hold him. I half expected to see Ahmet at the helm of Hasan's boat but didn't, guessing he'd told the Captain that we'd come there eventually. It was doubtful Tokolu would have found Hasan's boat without Ahmet's help.

"What we do?" Nazif cried from the cockpit entry. "Where Hasan?"

"Probably tied up below...maybe with Ahmet."

I stopped the Bluebird well short of the two boats then realized we were still within rifle range. A few bullets into the spinning props would be disastrous.

Turning to Noli, I asked if he could shoot a man in cold blood. I knew he could shoot. I'd seen him do it in the Azores.

"Him?" he replied, pointing at the Captain. "...is easy. How I do it?"

"Through the trapdoor in the nose of the plane."

Without turning, I yelled at Nazif to get my rifle, adding, "...and a clip of bullets," never taking my eyes off Tokolu's rifle. If he raised it, I'd have to turn tail and run. "It's in the cupboard next to the lifeboat," I yelled as he rushed to the rear of the plane.

"Stow your control wheel," I then said to Noli, "and climb into the nose. Hurry, it's our only chance. I'll line you up, but it may be difficult with the plane bobbing in the water."

"*Sim, facil,*" he replied, reverting to Portuguese in his excitement, "*Donde...o pieto? A cabeça?*"

"English," I growled as Noli pushed aside his rudder pedals then removed the panel behind them.

"*Desculpe!*" he apologized. "Where I shoot him...leg or chest? You want him dead?"

"Just wound him...enough to knock him down. We're in enough trouble already."

"Is easy," Noli said, slipping through the narrow passage. "I shoot other men too?"

"Not unless they do. Disarming the Captain might be enough."

Nazif returned with the rifle and bullets and handed them to Noli through the opening. By then, Tokolu had stepped forward and knelt down, resting his rifle on the bulkhead.

I felt so helpless, like a treed raccoon, but there was nothing I could. I thought about shutting down the engines, but I had to keep them running to steer the plane…and to make a hasty retreat if a hail of bullets began raining on us.

Suddenly, and without warning, I saw his rifle recoil but couldn't hear the sound. Twelve hundred horsepower makes a lot of noise.

The bullet must have flown overhead—a warning shot, perhaps. The next one would be dead on, either through the front windshield or into an engine.

The Captain stood and waved at us to come aboard.

"Hurry, Noli!" I yelled through the opening in front on his seat. "He just gave us a warning shot, or else he missed."

"Sim, muito pronto. Vire à esquerda."

"English, Noli," I screamed in frustration.

"Sorry…turn left."

I eased the Bluebird left, remembering the trapdoor Noli was shooting through was quite small.

CRACK!

Noli's bullet creased the Captain's ribcage.

Spinning around, he dropped the rifle and fell to one knee, grabbing his side. The other men stared in disbelief at what they'd just seen.

The Captain yelled something and waved his hand at us menacingly.

One of his men raised his pistol toward us but Noli fired first, clipping the man's arm near the wrist. The gun flew into the air then dropped harmlessly into teal blue water.

The man grabbed his bleeding wound and fell to one knee.

The second man, frozen with uncertainty, looked at the Bluebird as if were a mythological sea monster spitting fire. And maybe it was—a serpent bird with a forked tongue.

With a shrug, the man tossed his pistol overboard. And when the Captain didn't make a move toward the rifle lying just a few feet behind him, I yelled, "Enough, Noli! They look ready to surrender. Good job, but keep the rifle pointed at them."

Noli replied with two clicks on his intercom button like I'd taught him. The previous owner had installed it when he added the trapdoor, which he'd used for a similar purpose.

I turned to Nazif. "Inflate the lifeboat, then tie it to the plane and paddle over to Tokolu's boat. But be careful, he's sneaky and might try something."

"*Evet,*" he replied quickly. "I find Hasan. He—" With a grimace, he squeezed his neck with both hands.

"Fine," I said, taxiing closer, "but grab the Captain's rifle…and watch the man at the helm. He might have a gun too. Have *him* free Hasan instead of you doing it."

✻   ✻   ✻   ✻

Nazif boarded Tokolu's boat easily from the liferaft. Barking something, he picked up the rifle and pointed it at the Captain. The unhurt crewman immediately hurried below with a frightened look on his face. Only then did I shut down the engines, but readied the plane for a quick departure.

Moments later, Hasan emerged from below, shielding his eyes from the noonday sun. No telling how long he'd been down there, probably all night. At least, all that morning.

Ahmet did not appear with him.

Nazif waved at the helmsman to come out. The man stepped forward slowly then dropped into a policeman's crouch, revealing a hidden pistol.

Nazif shot him in the shoulder. But at that same instant, Noli fired and hit him in the thigh. Blood oozed from both places as the man reeled, took two half steps backwards, and fell—first to his knees then on his face.

"We got him!" Noli yelled over the intercom. "We got him…*bom!*"

"You sure did," I called back. "Now come out and pull the lifeboat back to the plane." Standing, I told Regina to grab the first-aid kit. "There are wounded men on board. Although, Hasan looks okay from here."

At first Regina and Leandra didn't move, both had frozen expressions on their faces.

"Let's go, girls," I yelled as Noli scampered past me to open the entry door, "it's time to become nurses. The first-aid kit is in the latrine,

Regina. There are rags in the cabinet next to it, Leandra. The Captain and two of his men are wounded; the third might be dead. I'm not sure."

Regina finally responded, with Leandra right behind her. They were comical in their efforts to find the items I'd asked for, both crowding into the narrow space at the same time. One thing I'd learned about Turkish women; they are obedient, almost to an extreme, to male authority. Except for those like Phidaleia, of course.

        ✻   ✻   ✻   ✻

With the lifeboat returned, Noli helped them into it, held it close for me, then jumped in himself, leaving the entry door ajar.

Once on board the fishing boat, Noli secured the Bluebird to it, while Regina tended the Captain and Leandra bound up the other man's arm.

The third man was dead. After Hasan mumbled a prayer in Turkish, I helped him toss the body overboard. It took no longer than it had for Alexis, only she hadn't even received a token prayer.

As it turned out, neither the Captain nor his mate were seriously hurt, their wounds only superficial. The mate probably wouldn't be using one arm for a while and the Captain might have trouble breathing at times, but no bones were broken.

Nazif and Hasan wanted to trash the Captain's boat—sink it right there in the cove then take him to the police, but I cautioned otherwise. "Remember, it will be our word against theirs. And who do you think they'll believe, with you killing one and wounding two others, and me with a murder charge on my head?"

"I shoot them too!" Noli corrected, spitting in the Captain's face. "For what he do to Señora Alexis."

"*Evet!* He must pay!" Nazif demanded, smashing one fist into another. His giant brother scowling his agreement with a vigorous nod.

It was a real problem, one the Captain couldn't understand, since he knew so little English. I remembered that from before. I could still feel his spittle running down my cheek after he yelled, "A-mer-i-can!" at me after raping Alexis.

"I suppose Hasan could press charges for hijacking his boat and false imprisonment, but without witnesses he won't have much of a case."

"Regina…Leandra…could say," Hasan stammered, his frown deepening.

"Hayir!" Nazif exploded. "I no want them…ah, ah—"

"Involved?" I offered.

"Evet, involved...in any way."

I could hardly blame him, not after what Leandra had been through. Regina too, for that matter, with Ahmet. Besides, a woman's word meant little in Turkey. I'd learned that already. And in court, it would probably mean even less. I knew that Nazif wanted to avenge Leandra's abduction, but proving Captain Tokolu had anything to do with it would be a formidable task with no witnesses.

As I wrestled with these weighty issues, Nazif began a tirade in Turkish at Captain Tokolu, now sitting with his back against a bulkhead near the starboard scupper, wet with draining sea water and smelling strongly of fish. Regina was gingerly dabbing his side with antiseptic. Each time, he'd winced, causing her to smile as if she enjoyed inflicting pain on him.

Nazif continued unabated for several minutes then Tokolu shouted something that turned Regina's face ashen. Then, wincing badly, he even moved to hit her, but Nazif raised the rifle and the Captain withdrew his fist.

Undeterred, Nazif kept after him about something until Regina finished and moved away. By then, Hasan and Noli had tied up the other two crewmen and dragged them below, using the same stout cord that had held Hasan in check for so long.

After a long pause, the Captain again responded, this time with defeat in his voice, nodding as if agreeing to some kind of offer. Although, the way Nazif was shaking his fist and stomping the deck, it sounded more like an ultimatum.

I knew Nazif was anxious to get back to doing what he did best— build boats. He still hadn't repaired his damaged factory, and he now had two more orders. Maybe more, after our trip to Cappadocia. I'd forgotten to ask.

With the tirade over, Hasan herded the Captain below and tied him up, then locked the hatchway door with a key he found in the helm. He then scrambled over the side of the boat and into his. I was sure he was pleased to be back there. It was where he belonged.

Noli agreed to stand guard over the crew with the Captain's rifle while Nazif drove the Captain's boat back to Gümbet Bay. Leandra said she would help.

Moving closer to Noli, she seemed to be looking at him differently now—with singular pride. A look that said, "*I may have misjudged you,*

Noli, even overlooked a few things. Things I might not have found in my Greek Adonis."

✳   ✳   ✳   ✳

With the Captain and his crew subdued and Noli on guard, Nazif grinned as he entered the helm. He was obviously pleased with himself but didn't divulge what the Captain had agreed to, although it appeared to be related to the boat, somehow.

Maybe Nazif owned it now? But what would he do with it? Give it to Ahmet for his treachery? Hardly, although I knew Ahmet wanted a boat and coveted Hasan's. Maybe if he had one of his own, he'd be more satisfied and quit drinking...even leave Regina alone.

An off-the-wall idea that was unlikely to happen, but it could.

Thus far, neither brother had said anything about Ahmet or why he wasn't there, but I was sure they would. He must have ratted on us. But why? To get back at me, puting his family in danger? Hardly. Maybe he hadn't thought it through that well. Maybe he was drunk when he did it.

Either way, it was treachery in its most venal form. Hasan could easily have been shot. If it hadn't been for Noli and Nazif, we might *all* be dead; no telling what would have happened to Regina and Leandra. To say nothing of the Bluebird.

Goosebumps arose on my skin just thinking about it. Then, another thought hit me, a less distressing thought. With Captain Tokolu and his crew in custody, there was no reason to keep the Bluebird hidden anymore. So before Nazif started the boat, I told him I would fly it back to Bodrum and meet them there.

He agreed, but as I moved to disembark in the lifeboat, Regina asked if she could come too. Seeing no reason not to, I nodded and invited her to sit in the copilot's seat.

Moments later, as we strapped in, I couldn't help but notice the deep depression between her breasts formed by the shoulder harness.

That's quite a women, I mused. I wonder what she's thinking and what she expects from me. Maybe nothing or maybe everything, even a walk down the center aisle of a church. Or would it be a mosque? Except they don't have center aisles—or any aisles, just a large open space for men to kneel on prayers rugs—facing east, of course.

It was a real dilemma. One I'd been struggling with for days, knowing I was being lured into a dangerous but alluring web. One I wasn't sure I was ready for yet.

Chapter Twenty One

Regina and I arrived in Gümbet Cove early in the afternoon. We didn't talk much in the plane—the flight only lasting twenty minutes—so when she invited me to visit Saint Peter's Castle in the center of Bodrum Bay, I could hardly refuse.

According to my guidebook, the castle was built by the Knights of Rhodes in the Fifteen Century. In part, from marble salvaged from King Mausolos' tomb nearby, one of the Seven Wonders of the ancient world but destroyed by an earthquake. Little remained of the tomb but according to my guidebook it was huge, built on a pedestal requiring twenty-four stairs to enter and surrounded by a colonnade of thirty-six marble columns, nearly as large as the Parthenon in Athens, which was built about one hundred years earlier.

Unlike King Mausolos' tomb, the fairytale castle, rough hewn and grayish brown, was fully intact and magnificently preserved, with ramparts around its perimeter marked by heraldic crests of the fifty knights who once lived there. Two towers anchored the ancient citadel: the English and the Italian, the two nationalities of knights who lived there until the conquest of Rhodes in 1523 by Sultan Süleyman.

In the Italian Tower, I was stunned to see the name of a guard and the year he'd served there carved on a wall: Joseppe Giotto—1492. The year Columbus first sailed to the Western Hemisphere.

In the interior courtyard, peacocks pecked between flowerbeds nurtured by water from one of fourteen cisterns inside the castle. A formidable fortress indeed, and according to a brochure I picked up, the finest example of Crusader Architecture in the Orient, which struck me as odd. I never thought of Turkey as the Orient, until Regina reminded me that Asia began in Istanbul.

So much for what I remembered in Geography 101.

Descending into the Underwater Museum, formerly the Knight's Chapel, Regina led me through rooms filled with artifacts taken from the Aegean Sea—clay amphorae, used to carry wine and olive oil before oaken barrels were invented, colorful Islamic glassware, sun-baked earthenware lamps, highly glazed cachets for sealing envelopes, marvelous ancient weapons, and most surprising, a fully-restored, twenty-seven ton cargo ship lifted from the sea bottom just off the north coast of Turkey.

With Regina adding what she knew, we investigated the magnificent sailing vessel for nearly an hour. An incredible experience, leaving me with a better understanding of what ancient mariners had gone through to reach foreign markets. In the case of this ship, a one thousand mile trip from Syria to the Black Sea. A formidable journey then, but hardly a trip at all now. Even in the slow flying Mallard, it would only have taken three hours, as the crow flies. Or should I say, Bluebird?

Thinking of the Bluebird, and leaving Turkey, brought me back to reality. What should I say to this lovely creature hugging my arm like we were a couple and chatting happily about all we'd just seen?

"I love it here," she said excitedly. "I like the glassware best. I wish they made glass like that now."

"Haven't you seen this place before?" I admired her enthusiasm and nearly had to drag her back to the courtyard or she would have stayed even longer.

"Many times, but—" Pausing, she looked at me, her dark brown eyes sparkling in the sun, a coy smile creeping into her satin-smooth face, "is different now…with you."

Those eyes, that face, this was a woman in love. "Ah, Regina…we need to talk. Is there somewhere we could get a sandwich and a cup of coffee?"

"*Evet*," she replied with her usual vibrancy, steering me toward the walkway beside the castle and lined with vendors selling souvenirs and curios to tourists. "A special place…very romantic."

I knew what she was thinking—what she was probably expecting, and was sorry I'd brought it up. I felt like I'd been caught in quicksand, going under for the last time. What could I say to this lovely lady that wouldn't destroy her glorious smile, her inner beauty, inherent in every sexy woman?

Beyond the castle, we walked along the quay for several blocks, admiring the many sailing yachts, elaborate and small, filling the marina. On board some, well-dressed matrons dripping in jewels sipped cocktails. Other yachts boasted women in skimpy bikinis drinking beer, they're only jewelry in their belly button. In crowded sidewalk cafes, locals and tourists alike sat drinking, eating and talking. And with every face, I feared recognition. Someone who knew I'd been charged with murder.

I began looking for wanted posters, thinking the police might have plastered them all over that sleepy town. I saw none, but that didn't assuage my growing paranoia.

I had to get away from here—from Turkey; but I had this delightful creature on my arm who obviously wanted me to stay...even expected me to propose, someday, if that was even done in Turkey.

I'd probably have to ask permission first...starting with Nazif, I suppose.

Besides that, I still had unfinished business to attend to. Important business, which had to come before anything else. In addition to ridding society of Bai Simaphong, I had to protect Regina from Ahmet...get him out of her life forever.

As it turned out, the problem with Ahmet came up first.

> *   *   *   *

He was hunched over the bar in the Han Hotel; the romantic spot Regina lead me to, intending that we eat in the restaurant ajacent to the bar. According to her, the Han was once a Crusader waystation; and later, a caravansary complete with sleeping rooms on a balconied second floor overlooking a courtyard where horses had been stalled. Now the courtyard was an open-air restaurant with wooden tables and benches placed around a stand of broadleaf palms trees.

When our eyes met, Ahmet's mouth flew open, as if he'd seen a ghost. And perhaps he had, with us returning so quickly and unharmed. He looked away, then back, as if to reassure himself that it was really me.

I waved, not thinking of the consequences. After all, he *was* part of the family, so what else would I do?

Regina hadn't seen him yet, more intent on selecting the best table for an intimate tête-à-tête.

It wasn't until we were seated that Ahmet approached with a glass of *raki* in his hand, although, swagger would describe it better. I was sure he'd deny everything, pretend innocence; and I didn't know for sure that he wasn't.

Regina paled and grabbed my arm. "Why is *he* here?" she hissed under her breath.

"How was Cappadocia?" Ahmet asked before I could reply. He looked at Regina more than me. And why not? Under a light sweater, she was wearing tight jeans and a skimpy top. Both emphasized her shapely figure. An outfit, I suspected, she thought to impress me with; but regrettably, until then, I'd hardly noticed.

She turned away from his salacious gaze, obviously uncomfortable, and didn't reply.

I felt sorry for her, knowing this wasn't what she had in mind when she brought me here; and hoping, as I did, it wouldn't turn into another fight. It appeared to be an upscale restaurant, although few were eating in mid-afternoon. Just two other couples and a few men at the bar. None of them were paying the slightest attention to us, which was good.

"An interesting trip," I replied with a smile, despite my churning stomach, "and Nazif sold all of your fish." I looked hard into his dark eyes, hoping to see a glimmer of fear. Fear that he'd been caught ratting on us, but I saw nothing.

"*Fevkalâda!*" he cried, downing half his drink. He didn't act drunk, but he soon would be if he continued at that rate. "Any plane trouble?" he added cautiously.

A strange question, I thought. Had he tried to sabotage the Bluebird and failed. More treachery?

A waiter suddenly appeared with menus and remained standing by the table to take our order. Neither of us asked Ahmet to sit with us. With him there, I wasn't hungry, so I just ordered a beer. Regina asked for *çay* and Ahmet ordered another *raki*.

"Only when we returned from Athens," I said, trying to remain civil to a man I wanted to beat to a pulp but doubted I could. He looked as strong as his brothers.

"What trouble?" Ahmet now ignored Regina, totally focusing on me.

"Captain Tokolu met us with his crew…all armed. Hasan was tied below deck."

"*Vallah!*" Ahmet gasped, downing the rest of his *raki*. "That bad…very bad. What you do?"

"Your brother shot him with *my* rifle, his mate too…in self defense, of course." I left out Noli's part. I didn't want him to become involved.

Ahmet quickly rattled off a string of Turkish—swear words by the sound of them, then asked where his brothers were. He looked worried. Probably about what his brothers would do to him, especially if he'd pulled a Judas on them for a few pieces of silver.

I looked at my watch. It had been nearly three hours since we'd returned. "Home, I'd guess. They left when we did, Nazif in Tokolu's boat, with Leandra and Noli, Hasan in his own boat."

"*Fevkalâde!* Everyone safe," Ahmet shouted, raising his empty glass. "We toast!"

Right on cue the waiter appeared with our drinks. Taking his, Ahmet raised it aloft. I didn't bother, feeling no joy that day. Regina looked bummed. No shapely beauty now.

"What matter?" Ahmet asked, loosing his smile. "You alive. You no hurt. Nazif capture Tokolu...has his boat. We drink." He raised his glass, but again he drank alone.

"The question is," I said with clenched teeth. "Who told Captain Tokolu that Hasan would meet us in that cove?"

"Dan, please," Regina intervened, her hand on my arm. "Not here... not now."

Ignoring her, I pressed on. "Only *you* knew that we'd be there!"

"*Ovmek, Allah*...I swear! I tell no one." Ahmet raised his hand in a pledge. He sounded so convincing I almost believed him. "I drink some last night," he continued. "And, well...maybe I—"

"Got drunk?" I finished for him.

"*Evet*...but I no tell. Why I tell? They my brothers."

Again I wondered if he was telling the truth. "Whether you did or not, Ahmet, I suggest you find them. And best you are sober when you do. You need to be at your finest to talk your way out of this one."

Throwing a ten spot on the table, I stood, my beer untouched. "Come on, Regina. The stench in here suddenly got foul. I'm having trouble breathing...maybe some other time."

"*Evet, Dan,*" she said as a child might, head down, chest fallen, hurrying to keep up, her romantic moment crushed by Ahmet's idiocy.

We'd talk another day...when I was more up to it.

✳   ✳   ✳   ✳

On the patio after dinner—prepared by an exuberant Phidaleia, happy to have her husband back—Regina told Nazif what Ahmet had said at the Han Hotel then excused herself and went to bed. Noli and Leandra then followed Nazif and I back to his house. Lagged behind, might better describe how they walked. I was sure they'd stopped for a kiss or two, but I didn't turn around to see or ask about it later.

Nazif seemed totally absorbed with Ahmet and what he'd done. His brother never did show up, which didn't surprise Nazif. "He know...he tell. Ahmet afraid now. Hide somewhere. But we find..."

He didn't finish, his anger was too intense.

Later, seated within his enclosed patio in fading light, while Leandra and Noli took a romantic walk along the harbor—for more kissing, I guessed—I asked Nazif about his harsh words with Captain Tokolu and what they'd agreed to.

"I say, leave Bodrum and I no tell police." Nazif waved his hand dramatically.

The night was stifling—muggy and hot, not a breath of fresh air. But storm clouds swirled overhead, a promise of cooling rain.

"Is he married? Does he have a family?"

"His wife die, his family—" He flipped his hands up. "All gone."

"They died too?" I asked in amazement.

Nazif laughed. "They marry, move away. No like Bodrum. Too-too...How you say, *kalabalik?*"

"You mean, crowded?"

"*Evet, çok kalabalik.*"

"Where do they live?"

"Daughter in Denizli, son in Konya...where Dervish dance." He made a twirling motion with his hands. "I say, go live with *filha*...go live with *filho*...no fish anymore. He say, okay. He old man...*yetmiş, yedi.*"

"Seventy-seven?" I repeated to make sure I was correct.

"*Evet, yetmiş, yedi.*"

"What will you do with his boat?"

"I give Ahmet, if he stop *içecek!*" Nazif made a drinking motion with his hand. "And stop *tâciz* Regina!" This time he feigned a slap at himself. Without hand gestures, it would be harder to understand him. With them, he did quite well. "Ahmet good man, but he weak to...ah-ah..."

"Temptation?" I offered.

"*Evet,* temptation...need strong woman like Phidaleia."

"Tell him to stop gambling too," I suggested.

"*Evet.* I do. No more gambling."

"Would he stay in Bodrum?" I was beginning to understand Nazif's logic, steering his errant brother toward good with rewards rather than punishment; but I felt uneasy about letting Tokolu off the hook after what he'd done to Alexis. On the other hand, how would we prosecute him without witnesses; also, without implicating ourselves over what we'd done to him? Maybe Nazif was right. Maybe his way *was* better...certainly much simpler.

"Never! Ahmet must go!" Nazif became so agitated he stood and began pacing.

I asked where, although, I hardly cared. Having him leave was enough to satisfy me, maybe Regina too.

"No matter," Nazif riled. "Marmaris, Fethiye, Antalya, he choose. Find strong wife, settle down, have babies."

Nazif finally sat down, his soliloquy over, his decision made, as if ready to re-order his life again and get things back to normal. But before that could happen, we had one other problem to settle. I almost said something about Simaphong, but instead I waited.

It didn't take long. After lighting his well-worn Meerschaum, shaped like a dragon's head, he bent over close and asked if I had any ideas about capturing Simaphong. The way he asked, made me feel as if he thought the walls had ears.

People had been passing by the open gate as we talked. A few even looked in and waved. It was probably those who *didn't* wave that worried him.

"I'm not sure," I replied, glad he hadn't asked about Regina and me. That would come later, at her prompting. "We can't very well attack his underground fortress, unless we get the people out first, and that would be difficult, unless.... My mind drifted off, thinking of other ways.

"I get them out!" Nazif said abruptly.

"How?"

"How you say, *gözyaşi gaz*" He pointed to his eye then acted as if he were crying.

"Tear gas!" I gasped. "You have? You get?" We'd been talking so long I was beginning to speak in short sentences like he did.

"*Evet*, tear *gaz*. I get plenty. We throw in air vent. Everyone come out."

"Brilliant," I cried, remembering how we'd had almost constant air in our faces as we slithered through the ventilation shafts. It would suck gas throughout the entire underground complex. But would it be enough to force everyone out? And how would we get tear gas into the vent opening in the first place?

Fortunately, Nazif had that figured out too. He would do it, through the vent we used for our escape. And Hasan would protect him from harm with the rifle that Nazif had claimed from Captain Tokolu. The spoils of war, as it were.

"And what will *I* be doing?" I asked suspiciously, wondering if I was involved at all.

A gleam caught Nazif's dark eyes. By then the sun had set, only lingering rays of light penetrated the muggy air through darkening clouds. "You fly over *kale*, ah—fortress. Noli shoot men like he shoot Captain— boom, boom!"

"How will we know one from another?"

"Leandra know. She tell Noli. He shoot them all."

I shook my head, amazed at his audacity. The first part sounded great, the second part had serious flaws. But at least it gave me something to think about, a way to put Simaphong out of business for good. But would it work?

It had to. It was the only chance we'd have…the only *plan* we had.

Chapter Twenty Two

The next day, the four us of walked to the boat factory and surveyed the damage, which turned out to be not as bad as we thought—scattered tools, overturned boxes of varnish, papers from the office scattered about. We could clean it up in half a day. Repairing the damaged boats would take a bit longer.

Nazif said nothing more about Captain Tokolu or his crew, other than they all would be leaving Bodrum soon. Very soon!

By noon we had the room in good working order and took time out for lunch. I knew Nazif was anxious to finish the two damaged boats and start work on his new orders. Especially, the one for the restaurant owner in Denizli, so I was surprised when he left for a couple of hours and didn't eat with us.

Returning, he looked pleased with himself but said nothing, and I didn't ask, wondering if he might have had it out with Ahmet.

If not then, he would soon, I thought, applying the varnish to the keel of one of the row boats while he repaired the damage. It would be impossible for him to keep something like that bottled up inside him for long. He'd tell me eventually, when he was ready.

For the remainder of the afternoon, Nazif and I caulked hammer marks then covered them with two coats of varnish. Noli helped Leandra in the officer, although I doubt he helped much. They seemed besotted with each other again, Jon Uzul a dimming memory.

All in all it was a good day. One more coat of varnish on one boat and a few more caulks on the other and the damage would be invisible. Then all he had to do was finish the side rails and seats, install oarlocks, apply two more coats of lacquer and he'd be finished, everything back to normal again.

Yet a shroud of fear over what was to come pervaded everything we said and did, especially around Leandra. Nazif didn't want her to know about what we planned to do, afraid she'd worry. He would tell her later...or I would flying to Disko Hit.

I did tell Noli, however, that we'd be flying over overhead with Leandra; but I didn't tell him what Nazif expected him to do. There was no way I'd ask Noli do that. I'd leave that part to someone else...the police, maybe.

Not surprising, Noli was eager to be involved and asked if Leandra knew.

"Not yet, so don't say anything. Her father wlll tell her later...or I will."

He solemnly muttered that he wouldn't, but I wondered if he would anyway.

*   *   *   *

That night in his patio, Nazif and I spoke of his plan again. I told him it wasn't realistic to have Noli shooting men from the Bluebird. "It's too much to ask of a boy that young, even if he could. Hell, he'd carry the guilt for the rest of his life. It just isn't right. There has to be a better way."

When Nazif agreed, I reminded him what Carmen's father had said: the influence he had in Izmir. "Maybe he could get the Izmir police to raid Disko Hit, after you flush everyone out with tear gas."

Nazif scratched his stubble beard, his bushy brows twitching, as he pondered that thought. "Maybe...if—" Pausing, his mind drifted off.

We were drinking çay, strong and black, from tiny glasses on equally tiny saucers. I was beginning to enjoy tea that way, especially in the evenings.

It had rained heavily that afternoon, clearing out the humidity. The air was crisp, the sky clear. Sirius, the brightest star in the sky, and Venus, the brightest planet, had just penetrated the dimming light.

Noli and Leandra were watching television in the living room. Their relationship continued, slightly less intense but still very friendly. Perhaps, learning to enjoy each other as people rather than as lust-starved teenagers with raging hormones.

From all outward appearance, they were "in love", whatever that meant at their age. I could see it in their smiles and hear it in their voices. Lately, they were seldom apart, him mooning over her pretty face and trim figure, her deferring to him and following his advice.

On the other hand, my situation with Regina hadn't changed. I still hadn't spoken to her about our future together—or lack thereof. She moved back to Hasan's house the night we returned with Captain Tokolu and his crew, and nothing more had been said about our run-in with Ahmet at the Han Restaurant.

After lighting yet another Meerschaum—a magnificent ram's head, this time—Nazif finally told me what he'd learned from Ahmet: that he admitted telling the Captain when and where we would meet Hasan and had received one hundred Turkish *lire* for it.

With eyes cast down, his broad shoulders slumped in shame, Nazif continued. "I tell him to leave Bodrum...no want him in family anymore. He say he sorry...need *lire* for *kagits...kumar.* How you say?" He acted as if dealing a deck of cards.

"To play poker...for a gambling debt?"

"*Evet*...gambling debt. He say he leave...but want Tokolu's boat. I say maybe, if he stop drinking...stay away from Regina. I say, sleep in Hasan's boat, not in little house anymore. He say he will."

"Do you think Ahmet will keep his word?"

The heavy-set man with bristling eyebrows gave me a shrug. "If Allah's will."

Seconds later, he brightened, as if thinking of something else. "*Vallah,*" he cried suddenly. "Tomorrow, I call Tashi. *She* tell Carmen's *baba* to call Izmir police."

"Sounds good to me, but shouldn't we decide a few things first? When can you get the tear gas?"

"Tomorrow...I get tomorrow."

"Could you get a few pipe bombs too? They might be better than a rifle."

"*Bu ne*...pipe bomb?"

I looked in the Turkish-English dictionary Regina had given me. "*Buro*" was Turkish for pipe and "*bomba*", easy enough, was bomb. Saying the two together, I raised my arms over my head like an explosion, crying, "Boom!" for effect.

Nazif smiled his understanding. "*Evet, buro bomba! Büyük bomba!* I get. How many you want?"

I raised three fingers, then added a fourth, not having any idea how I might use them. I just wanted more firepower, something to throw out of the plane in case things turned nasty.

Mostly, I didn't want Noli shooting people. Winging a man on the ground was one thing, firing from the air was another. It would be dangerous. Innocent people could be killed, young girls from Simaphong's harem, for example. Pipe bombs, I rationalized, could be dropped on the narrow mountain road, if Simaphong tried to escape. Although, dropping them accurately from out the window of a plane might prove difficult.

All it would take was one, though, to block the road enough to slow them down until the police could catch them. All pretty dicey, of course, not having any idea whether the Izmir police would cooperate, or if they were in the hire of Simaphong already.

Whatever happened, I didn't want to be around to explain my part in it, or my part in the guard's death at the marina. Nor did I want to implicate Hasan or Noli.

When this was over, Noli and I needed to be winging our way out of The Aegean for good. Hopefully west, with things settled with Regina, the curvaceous beauty with a big smile and luscious body.

✣   ✣   ✣   ✣

That problem came to a head early the next evening when I stopped by Hasan's house. Just as Phidaleia invited me for dinner, Regina asked if I'd take her back to the Han Restaurant. With so many other things on my mind, I hesitated, knowing she'd want to discuss our future—whether I'd stay or leave—and I wasn't sure I was ready to make that decision yet.

There were too many things up in the air right now, like our attack on Disko Hit. Would it be successful, ending the threat of Simaphong forever, or would our sorry butts be rotting in a Turkish jail for trying?

I was also concerned about Noli. Whether he was becoming too serious with Leandra. Serious enough to not want to leave. I could hardly leave without him, or could I?

Both were tough calls; but ones I'd have to make soon, so I agreed to take Regina to dinner.

We arrived at the Han by cab about eight. The courtyard dining room was teeming with people. A group of boisterous young men were seated on three long tables, pushed end-to-end. Turkish naval officer, our waiter said, after an arduous NATO training exercise in the Aegean.

The men had coaxed several single women to join them, and for the rest of the evening they ate, drank and sang lively songs. For the most part, other patrons ignored them, until the toasts began. First to their Captain, Regina explained, then to the President of Turkey, followed by the Commander of NATO, and so on. As each man finished a toast, whether serious or comical, he'd tossed his dinner plate into a huge rock fireplace, each plate duly recorded by a waiter and added to their bill.

It was all quite harmless and loads of fun, each toss receiving a hearty round of applause from other patrons.

Prior to that, Regina and I talked about everything but what I expected we'd talk about. A history major in college, she told me that Asia Minor, present-day Turkey, had been inhabited for over 10,000 years; the first civilized culture being Hittites in the Second Millennium. Starting near the Black Sea, Hittites warriors had moved south to Syria where they met the Egyptian Army under Ramses II. The battle of Kadesh, she said, was one of the bloodiest in the ancient world. Although, neither side won, it stopped the southward migration of Hittites and established the border between Asia Minor and Egypt.

"Many Hittite ruins are close to Izmir," Regina added with a half smile. "…if you stay I will show them to you."

She paused, feeling me out, I suppose, testing the waters. Would I stay or not?

I nodded but said nothing. I know I should have, but I just couldn't. Not yet.

"Maybe it is too soon to decide," she said finally. "I know much bad has happened to you here, and it may not be over yet."

"Much good has happened too," I added quickly, taking her hand.

Her smile turned radiant, but she couldn't maintain eye contact and blushed like a teenager. *"Evet?"* she coaxed, as if hoping for more.

"Of course, I met you."

"You say so, but—" Pausing, she sighed then looked up. "Will you stay?"

I hesitated for just a second then shook my head. "I'm sorry, Regina, it isn't you, believe me. It's me. You are a wonderful woman—intelligent, vivacious, fun to be with, but I have nothing to offer you, no job, no house. The Bluebird is my life now. I'm not even sure I can give you children."

I then told her about my first marriage—five years with no kids, the reason my ex divorced me. And how she'd had one within a year of her second marriage. "That's why Noli is with me. He is the son I never had, but you deserve one of your own—and daughters. You'd make a wonderful mother."

Taking a breath, I paused. "You're right about Turkey, though. I've seen a lot of pain here, but a lot of good has come from my visit. I now know how warm and loving Turkish people can be. People like you and

Nazif, even Hasan in his own quiet way. You need to find a good Turkish man, a man who will love you and provide for you. Either that or move away, live somewhere else for a while. Meet new people, new men."

"But where?" she cried, clinging to my hand. "I know no another place. I went to college in Izmir, came here to teach, met Selim, then he drown in bad storm."

Tears filled her doe brown eyes, but she forced them back. "Then you come, and for the first time I think I can fall in love again. If you go away, I am all alone again."

Suddenly an idea came to me: Carmen's mother—and maybe her father too, needed help because Tashi didn't want to care for them anymore. "Would you be willing to move away from here, if I helped you get started?"

"Where?" Regina replied, wiping her tear-stained eyes.

"The mother of the girl that I flew home to Athens is an invalid and needs help. Her father too, perhaps. He just had a heart attack. They are Turkish, but he owns an olive oil plant and is quite successful—*çok lira,* live in a pretty house with a flower garden. You could live with them and help them...maybe even become a private tutor."

"Will you be there too...in Athens?"

"For a little while...until you get settled."

"Maybe you stay longer, *evet*?" She gave me an inviting smile.

"Maybe...it depends on who I fly for next."

Regina smiled broadly. She seemed pleased, and I'd put off the inevitable for another day. At least, it gave her something to think about while I thought about other things. Namely, how to aid Nazif and Hasan attack Disko Hit without being caught.

Later, at Hasan's door, Regina turned and kissed me, holding me so close I could feel her heart thumping against my chest. "You like?" she asked, pulling away but keeping her hips pressed to mine. "If you stay, you can have more...all you want."

It was a tempting offer—too tempting. If we'd had a place to be alone, I might have taken her up on the offer right then. "I'd like more," I mumbled, returning her kiss. "But—"

"Maybe in Athens," she said, brushing her lips to mine.

Then she went inside.

It took more than the walk to Nazif's house to stem my passion that night. I lay on my cot in the patio for nearly an hour before drifting off to sleep.

Maybe I'd rushed my thinking about Regina. Maybe in Athens things *would* be different, less worries, more warm lips and more softness.

It certainly would be an exciting and historical place to live.

✻   ✻   ✻   ✻

Nazif called Tashi the next morning. At first, their conversation was sprinkled with boisterous laughter then Nazif got down to serious business.

Our plan was to have Carmen's father convince the Izmir police that Simaphong was indeed a crime lord. And that, if they were at Disko Hit at dawn in four days—time for Nazif to secure the pipe bombs—they could see for themselves.

It would be a tough sell, not telling them anymore than that; but Cemil Uzul could do it, he was the perfect type. A man who wouldn't take no for an answer. He'd proven that already, bugging the Izmir police for days after his daughter's capture until finally hearing from us. In the process, he'd even had a mild heart attack.

I'd call that tenacity. The police would *have* to believe him.

When Tashi agreed to pass along our plan to her brother-in-law, Nazif then told her my idea of having Regina work for the Uzuls—helping Nese...even tutoring some. He said she became very excited about having Regina come there, making it possible for her to return to Turkey. She would tell Cemil right away and knew he would be happy too.

"Her only worry," Nazif added, "is Izmir police. Will they help?"

"I worry about them too," I replied, pausing as an idea came to me. "You know...if I fly Regina to Athens...you could fly there too...and see Tashi."

He grinned broadly. "She ask me to come. But I say, 'When Simaphong *ölü*'." He sliced one finger across his neck—the universal sign for death.

I could only hope that if that happened the police did it, not one of us. In any event, Nazif had set the ball rolling. Now it was up to Carmen's father to keep it rolling.

Chapter Twenty Three

Tashi phoned Sunday afternoon to say that Cemil Uzul would call the Izmir police Monday morning, and that he was pleased to know that someone was interested in tending his wife. Despite his recent heart attack, he didn't feel that he needed tending, having recently returned to work part time.

The next evening, Nazif came home with four pipe bombs. They hadn't taken as long to find as he thought. Said he bought them from a friend of a friend.

Some friend, I thought, but didn't press him on details.

Since we had two days to spare, I suggested we fly a load of fish to Chios.

Nazif agreed and with typical cunning, told Hasan to encourage other fishermen to cast their lot with us. We'd load up the Bluebird early the next morning. Noli would help, this time, and Leandra would stay with Phidaleia and Regina, with a promise not to go anywhere, even to the boat factory. Nazif still feared for her safety when he was gone.

Besides the fish, there were two other reasons for going to Chios. Nazif wanted to show Simon Margoles the sketches he'd made of a motor launch he thought might please him. And I wanted to top off the fuel in the Bluebird and have a mechanic check it over. Whether our attack on Disko Hit was successful or not, I wanted to head back to the Azores with Noli just as soon as Regina was settled and the Bluebird was ready, then on to the States to see my dad.

I'd had enough of Asia Minor and hankered for a twelveounce rib eye…even a Big Mac sounded good.

✳   ✳   ✳   ✳

In Chios, after helping Nazif load fish into a rented van, Noli went with him while I had the plane refueled and checked over. I was glad I did. The mechanic found an oil leak in the right fuel pump, which he fixed with a gasket he shaped from a pressed sheet of cork, replacing the oil that had been lost. When he finished, he checked the propeller oil along with the other fluids then suggested I run both engines, with him in the copilot's seat.

I agreed, then took him for a ride around his tranquil island.

It was an apple bright day, clear and forty, and the mechanic acted like a kid with a new bike. He'd only been in a plane a few times and never a seaplane. To add to his excitement I landed on the Aegean, taxied for a few minutes on the water to let him experience the washboard, then tookoff again.

Returning to the airport, he thanked me three times, and I was sure he shaved the price of the maintenance. It had taken him three hours and he only charged me half what they charged in the Azores.

Of course, there, a millionaire had paid for it. On Chios, repairs came out of *my* pocket, gas too. Alexis' account had been abruptly closed, tied up in litigation, they said.

I don't think the mechanic even charged me for fuel. If he did, it wasn't much.

When Nazif and Noli returned from the cannery, Nazif looked pleased. And rightly so. He'd just sold three hundred pounds of fish and had an order for a twenty-four foot motor launch.

Since it was only two in the afternoon, I asked him if he wanted to fly to Denizli to see the man who'd ordered a boat from him and show him his sketches. "I want to fly over Disko Hit and see if I can spot the air vent we escaped from, in case I have to drop a pipe bomb into it."

He looked at me quizzically then smiled and nodded. I could see he was excited about our pending attack on the mountain stronghold and wondered why I wasn't. After all, *he* had the dangerous job, planting tear gas without being caught. All I had to do was fly overhead and help if I could. Which reminded me: we should have CB radios, so I could tell them what I was seeing from above. Who was escaping—or worse, who was coming after them.

Just thinking about it made me feel uneasy. A premonition, I suppose, that Noli and I might be in danger too. But how? It's unlikely that Simaphong would have guns that could shoot down a plane. Or could he...left over from the Cold War?

Swinging into my seat, I waited for Noli to lock the entry door and climb into his.

Our biggest problem: If a police informer told Simaphong about our attack, giving him time to prepare for it. But how would he prepare, if he doesn't know what we plan to do? Nazif didn't tell Cemil Uzul that. Unless…

My God! What if Simaphong had a mercenary pilot standing by?

Damn! Why didn't I think of that before.

My stomach roiled with anxiety as one terrifying scenario after another flashed through my mind—each worst than the last. Not only could Simaphong hire a pilot to attack us, he could attack us in a plane, himself; or have the Turkish Air Force do it, after convincing them that I was a killer on the loose…that I'd killed before and would do it again.

Suddenly, the two F-16 fighters we'd seen on the flight from Cappadocia flashed through my mind. What if they came after us? There was no way I could out-maneuver an F-16. Not in a seaplane. I wouldn't last two minutes in a dogfight with them.

"Closed and locked!" Noli announced from the copilot's seat, sounding as if he didn't have a care in the world. "Where we go…Bodrum?"

I didn't even see him enter the cockpit, my thoughts—and fears, so deep.

Clearing my mind, I told him Disko Hit, then cranked up the left engine, checking the gauges carefully. Everything was in the green. I felt some comfort knowing the Bluebird was in good shape, better than my churning stomach. "I want to see if we can find the air vent we crawled through when we escaped from the underground fortress."

"Is easy," he said with more confidence than I had, a mark of youth and exuberance. "I do like you say…leave branches." He crossed his arms on his chest.

"Good, boy," I replied, starting the right engine. "But spotting it from the air may be tougher than you think."

✻   ✻   ✻   ✻

After takeoff I circled Chios once for altitude then headed east. Even at three thousand feet the ancient fortress at Çesme looked impressive. My guidebook said it was started in the fourteenth century. It was hard to imagine anything that old and still be so well preserved, a fortress that could withstanding months of siege from sea *or* land.

Could Disko Hit withstand a siege that long? I hoped not.

Nearby, a quaint fishing village basked in the sun, except nothing about Turkey seemed quaint anymore. Everything had been soured by two men, Vedat Tokolu and Bai Simaphong.

I'd learned a lot about Turkey since we arrived so ingloriously, but there was so much more I could learn. So much I could *see* if I stayed...and wasn't thrown into prison. But seeing more of Turkey was a remote concept to me right then. My only thought: seeking revenge on a smooth talking crime lord who traded young women for gold, then leave this hellish place forever.

Coming out of my reverie, I realized the Bluebird had climbed one-hundred feet, as if wanting more distance between itself and Izmir, as I did.

The bay shimmered pale blue in the hot afternoon sun. A ferry was crossing toward Konak Square, leaving a small wake. Near the marina, stood a sixty-foot, stone clock tower decorated with cupolas, columns and spires.

Seeing the marina, reminded me of how easily Hasan had dispatched that guard. A quick stroke to the head was all it took...his life over.

I wondered if he had a wife and family. Probably...most men did at that age. But I doubt he was a regular guard like the old man. More likely he was hired by Simaphong to watch the Bluebird...a plane I knew he wanted. I could see the greed—and envy, in his thin, arching brows and deeply slanted eyes.

✳   ✳   ✳   ✳

Flying over Izmir at three thousand feet, Kulture Park looked huge, nearly a third of the business district, and crossed by walkways bordered with palms and pepper trees. And beyond Izmir, at the foot of the mountains, lay Bornova, its cement plants belching clouds of smog-laden smoke.

Passing over low foothills, the population thinned and six eyes began searching for Disko Hit.

Nazif peered over my shoulder from the cockpit entry. "Look!" he shouted, pointing below. "BP station where I wait...where you see me."

"Yes...and just beyond is the road we took into the mountains."

Banking toward it, I could see the road twist and turn though the first and second villages, then snake along a narrow rock ledge, faced with a sheer drop-off on one side, then around a granite outcropping and along a straight stretch to the last hovel of dun colored huts, stopping about two miles away.

This time Noli shouted. "I see parque de automòveis. Over there, Dan, see?"

"Good job, Noli. It looks smaller from the air, doesn't it? Hardly bigger than a postage stamp. Can you spot the air vent, or should I fly lower?"

"Fly lower," he said, his face pressed against the cockpit glass.

Nazif looked out from the first passenger seat just behind him.

Dropping to one thousand feet, the pitch of the engines hardly changed. A guard stood at the tunnel entry; someone with him was smoking a cigarette. Only the guard appeared to have a gun, in a holster strapped to his waist.

The two men looked up. One pointed.

I hoped the guard hadn't been told about my plane. If not, he might just think I was a private pilot cruising around overhead…on a weekday ride.

I crisscrossed the hill behind the tunnel several times and almost gave up, then Noli shouted. "I see! I see!" pointing to his right.

I banked the plane so I could see as well.

"Down there, Dan, see branches?"

They weren't as clear as I'd hoped. I never would have found them without Noli, just two branches across a cement culvert. "That's it?" I called, not using the intercom. "Are you sure?"

"Sim…I sure. No one touch."

"I see too," Nazif yelled, pointing frantically. He got so excited about everything I had to laugh.

Nearby, I spotted a better marker, an olive tree, in line with the end of the parking lot about three hundred yards from the tunnel entrance. I had no idea why I thought it might be important to be able to locate the vent from the air. I just wanted to know that I could.

                *   *   *   *

The flight to Denizli was uneventful but worthwhile. Nazif received assurance from the wealthy restaurant owner that he would buy a boat from him, if he could finish it by the end of the year.

Just before takeoff I glanced back at Nazif, his bushy eyebrows twitching as he pondered his two boat orders, probably trying to decide how many more workers he'd have to hire.

Smiling at his good fortune, I reminded him to buckle up.

About six that evening, I taxied into Gümbet Cove, half-expecting to be met by the local police. I knew it wouldn't be long before they tracked me down, but I hoped it wouldn't be before our attack on Disko Hit.

I was sure they would drop all charges against me, when they find out what was going inside Disko Hit...unless the police were on Simaphong's pay roll. In that case, we were in big trouble. They'd round up the lot of us, toss us into jail, and throw away the key.

A lump came to my throat and my breathing became labored.

Easy, Dan. Remember, Nazif and Hasan have the hard part. All you and Noli have to do is fly around and watch the fun.

*   *   *   *

That night everyone ate at Hasan's house. A celebration for the huge fish sale and the two boat orders. But also, I felt, a show of comradery among the four men involved in what we planned to do. Well—three men and a boy. Four people who would attack the lion in his den, and hopefully bring an end to the mayhem ruining people's lives so needlessly.

By then, I'd convinced Nazif that since Noli would have no active part in our plan, Leandra would be safer with Phidaleia and Regina than in the Bluebird, and he agreed. Because of that, the women only knew that we planned to dethrone Simaphong soon, but not how. Nor did Ahmet, who was also there. Consequently, nothing was said about the time or location of the attack.

We weren't taking any chances, this time.

During dinner, Ahmet was quite personable. He could be when not drinking, which we kept to a minimum. Just wine and only one toast, by Nazif, to better days for all of us.

Raki was definitely out for Ahmet. I'd seen how it turned him into a pompous ass who abused women to inflate the sorry image he had of himself. However, one comment he made during dinner rankled me. Something about how much fish he would catch on the South Coast when he had his own boat, adding in English, "especially between Marmaris and Antaya."

Said for my benefit, I'm sure, so I'd know that he was leaving Bodrum soon; and with him gone, the door would be open for me to move in on Regina. As if his leaving had anything to do with Regina and I getting together. Which it didn't, nothing at all.

Regina said little during our meal; and later, alone on the front patio, she became even more pensive. Guessing that it was our plan to go after Simaphong, I told her not to worry, that everything would be okay. "Nazif and Hasan will do most of the work…nothing dangerous, though. All Noli and I will do is watch", adding, "And when it's over, we'll meet in Karşiyaka, across the bay from Izmir."

"I suppose…" she said with a frown. "But be careful. We will worry about all of you, until you are safely back here again."

Pausing, Regina looked away.

She seemed unsure of herself and a bit distant, as if there in body but not in mind. She knew we'd called Carmen's father, and that he was working with the Izmir police, but little else. That way, there was less chance for Ahmet to discover anything. Of course, if he did—and told anyone—it would be the last thing he'd do. The only question would be was which of his two brothers would do him in? Both were certainly capable of it.

I just hoped Noli hadn't told Leandra.

With a half smile, Regina finally looked up. "Just do what you have to…men always do. I'm more worried about Athens. Do you really think I should go?"

The question surprised me. I expected her to be more worry about what we planned to do in Izmir. "It's up to you," I sidestepped, knowing what she was really asking. *"Would I stay, find a job and, perhaps, marry her?"*

I couldn't answer that, not until Simaphong was dead or in jail. But what if Alex Margoles offered me a job…or even Carmen's dad? Both had factories and could afford a private pilot. What would I say to Regina then?

Maybe it was time to quit flying. To get a steady job and settle down somewhere, with a white picket fence, a mortgage, three kids and an adoring wife. After all, I wasn't getting any younger and Regina was a fine woman—smart, attractive and with a lush body. Not so attractive that men would covet her—gorgeous women can be a pain sometimes— yet attractive enough to keep the fires of passion burning for a long time.

But if I didn't fly, what would I do and where would I do it—in Athens? Chios? Bodrum? The weather is good in *all* those places, and the cost of living isn't bad either. Maybe I should give *that* some thought…reconsider my options.

And give up flying? No way. I might as well give up breathing.

❊   ❊   ❊   ❊

"Dan?" Regina said, waving her hand across my eyes. "Are you there? I ask if you think Carmen's mother will like me. I worry about that too."

"Oh...sorry 'bout that. Yes. I'm sure of it. Mister Uzul was delighted with the idea. Carmen's aunt too. I think she likes Nazif, and I'm sure that he likes her. She wants to move back to Turkey, where she's from. Maybe they *all* will. I doubt you'll spend the rest of your life over there...a year, maybe, a chance to get away, meet new people."

"I would like that...if-if—"

"Yeah, I know, if I'm there. And I will be...for a while. How long, will depend on...well, if I find a flying job. They don't grow on trees, you know." For some reason I didn't want to tell her that I already had a nibble with a cannery owner on Chios.

"Grow on trees? *Anlamiyorum*...ah, I don't understand."

"It's an American expression, meaning flying jobs are hard to find; jobs that pay a living wage. You know, above the cost of flying and maintaining the plane. I haven't made any money for a month, and I don't have much left...enough to get back to the States, but not enough to live on for very long."

"Maybe you fly in Greece," Regina said with her biggest smile.

"Maybe...it depends on several good things coming together at once," adding under my breath, "*But don't depend on it. A lot of bad thinks can happen too...and already have.*"

"We have a lot to think about then, don't we?"

With that, she said goodnight with the warmest kiss yet. A kiss that promised everything. All I had to do was ask.

✻   ✻   ✻   ✻

The next morning Nazif called Tashi in Athens: The police would send a few men to Disko Hit early Thursday morning, but don't expect too much. They already knew about the girls in Simaphong's underground fortress. They'd had several reports of that. But they didn't have enough evidence or firepower to warrant an all out attack on the nearly impregnable facility.

"We have *çok* firepower," Nazif added.

Walking to a cupboard, he pulled out a canvas bag filled with four tear gas canisters and four pipe bombs. My stomach flipped. Saying it and doing it were two different things. A bully says things, a hero does them. Which was I?

Our plan would start in Karşiyaka, where we would fly that afternoon, Wednesday. From there Nazif and Hasan would take the ferry to Izmir and spend the night with Mahoud, who would find them a vehicle. Noli and I would remain on the Bluebird.

Early Thursday morning, well before daylight, they would drive to the last village, just short of the underground fortress. After hiding the vehicle, they would hike around the parking lot with the tear gas and find the air vent, hopefully without being seen by a guard or the goatherd. Both a distinct possibility.

At daybreak, when they saw the Bluebird overhead, they'd roll four canisters into the vent then race back to their vehicle and wait, which I knew would be hard to do. But I didn't want them driving down the narrow mountain road just as the police were driving up. For one thing, the police might stop and detain them, delaying the police's arrival at Disko Hit. Secondly, they could physically run into the police, injuring someone and delaying their arrival even longer.

Carmen's father had only told the police that, if they were in the parking lot at dawn, roughly six o'clock, they'd find all the evidence they needed to convict Simaphong, including the captive girls. Later, when there was less traffic, Nazif and Hasan would drive down the mountain…slowly, I hoped. After returning the vehicle, they would take the ferry back to Karşiyaka where Noli and I would be waiting.

If all went according to plan, that is.

A big *if* in my book. I didn't trust Simaphong at all. He didn't get were he was by being dumb. Besides, he was ruthless. I'd seen that already.

All Noli and I had to do was fly around the mountain in case Simaphong made a break for it, either by car or on foot. I was sure he'd have an alternate escape route, maybe two. That was another reason I wanted Nazif and Hasan to hang around, so they could help catch him, if necessary. Hopefully, without incriminating themselves.

Our plan was sound, but only if Nazif and Hasan could reach the air vent without detection and the canisters worked. *And*, if the police hadn't already told Simaphong, or worse, brought in reinforcements— the Turkish Air Force, the United States Air Force, even a mercenary pilot, all to help capture a wanted murderer.

At this point, all we could do was hope. If we didn't stop Simaphong, at least we'd put Vedat Tokolu out of business. According to Nazif, he'd already moved to his son's house in Konya, much to everyone's relief. It wasn't the revenge I'd hoped for, for all he'd done to Alexis; but it was probably the best I could get in this part of the world.

After all, she *was* just a woman...and a Greek woman at that.

        ❄   ❄   ❄   ❄

Several hours later, I tookoff from Gümbet Cove. The air was heavy. Dark clouds swirled ominously in the north. It looked like rain, even thunderstorms. Two more things to worry about—lightening strikes and slippery mountain roads.

The farther north we flew the darker the clouds became. I thought about calling someone and ask about the weather, but what was the point? We couldn't postpone anything. We'd just have to work around the weather somehow.

Passing Samos, it looked as if a huge cumulonimbus cloud was straddling Izmir Bay. Lightening bolts zigzagged eerily in all directions. I banked toward Chios, hoping the giant storm would drift farther east. Even then, I'd have to taxi on the water for a few miles. There was no way I'd fly close to *that* monster.

I leveled off at five thousand feet. Noli looked tense and stared straight ahead. "I never see so much, *relâmpago*." He made quick downward motions with his hands to indicate the many lightening strikes.

"We call it *lightening*, and it's especially dangerous to a plane."

I circled Chios once then did it again. "It looks like it's drifing east a little," I said with some relief. "Or maybe it's just that I want it to."

"I think it is," was Noli's only comment.

Circling the comma-shaped island a third time—an island that held less fascination for me now that Alexis was gone—I headed east and dropped to three thousand. My thought was to descend toward the dark morass until I couldn't fly any farther then land and taxi the rest of the way.

It would be touch-and-go making Karsiyaka in the air, and I didn't want to press my luck. We weren't in any hurry. None of us had much to do for twelve hours anyway, except eat and sleep.

At one thousand I decided to return to Chios and try again in twenty minutes. Better to err on the long side than the short. But as I turned, climbing to four thousand, we became engulfed in a perilously dark cloud.

The sun suddenly blinked out, as if someone had flipped off a light switch.

As I turned on the landing lights, pea-size hail began beating down on the plane. Then, without warning, a lightning bolt filled the cockpit with blinding white light.

An instant later, thunder buffeted us so hard the plane bounced like a ball batted by a playful cat. Only this wasn't play, this was real...deadly real.

Despite our shoulder straps, Noli and I were hurled hard to the right, then left. My head struck the side of the plane with such force a stab of excruciating pain shot down my neck and into my back.

Blood began trickling down my cheek. I forced my eyes open so I wouldn't pass out. It didn't help and I began swirling into oblivion.

I blinked my eyes twice to stop the swirling and clear my vision. The altimeter was spinning wildly as the plane hurtled toward the sea. I blinked again to make sure. This time I saw *two* altimeters, *both* spinning wildly.

Fighting to remain conscious, I felt the control wheel slam back against my chest.

Noli had started a pull out, but had he started soon enough?

Grabbing the wheel, I yanked back with him. The Bluebird groaned, every rivet screaming, *"Stop this...I'm at my breaking point!"*

The engines howled in protest—banshee-like, wild and untamed. Outside, bright flashes of light exploded like roman candles on the Fourth of July.

Death loomed everywhere. The world had suddenly gone mad.

Straining against the control wheel, I heard a popping sound. Was it a rivet? Was a wing coming off?

No...it was the radio!

Quickly, I turned it off before it exploded from built-up static electricity.

As the Bluebird strained to level off, the lightning stopped as suddenly as it had started. Was it over? Were we safe?

At once, the starboard engine sputtered and died.

The plane jerked left. "Damn! Now what?" I yelled as the Bluebird fell through two thousand feet. Without thought, I jammed my foot into the left rudder pedal.

The plane swerved right but continued plummeting toward the sea. Straining to hold the wheel full back, the nose slowly lifted...inch by inch.

At one thousand feet and level, I tried restarting the right engine. It coughed once, sputtered then caught.

We'd be all right. We were still flying.

Easing the plane back toward Chios, I felt resistance on the control wheel.

"Now what?" I muttered.

I looked over at Noli. He still had an iron-fisted grip on it. "Good job," I yelled. "You saved our fannies back there. I was out of it for a few seconds. Let's climb to six thousand and head back toward Chios. We'll try again in a few minutes."

Noli nodded but didn't smile, as if still in shock. I looked back at Nazif and Hasan. Both looked shaken but okay. I gave them a "thumbs up" sign.

Nazif barely smiled. Hasan stared straight ahead. Both would have a marvelous tale to tell their grandchildren someday. How they were at death's door and Noli—or a higher power—saved them. Thank, God, Noli hadn't panicked. Like a born pilot, he'd acted instinctively, without waiting for me to tell him what to do.

I was proud of him. Reaching over, I patted his arm. Only then did he smile, my reassurance that he was okay again, a seventeen-year-old kid on a grand adventure.

And I was too, still just a kid at heart...a thirty-four-year-old kid.

   *   *   *   *

Twenty minutes later, I landed a mile short of Karşiyaka and taxied to the wharf. By then the swirling storm had rolled past Izmir and was pelting the mountains to the east with much needed rain. Nazif and Hasan would have to be careful. Mountain roads would be slippery, even treacherous, now. One missed turn and they could careen off the narrow asphalt pavement and plunge to their deaths in a canyon below—just one more thing to worry about.

After the two brothers boarded the ferry, Noli and I found a restaurant featuring American food. We both ordered a tossed salad, a twelve-ounce T-bone, medium rare, and French fries. It was the best meal I'd had in ages. They even played American music from the seventies—Jimi Hendrix, Janis Joplin, Credence, all of them.

Noli and I spent nearly two hours there, talking about everything and nothing, then returned to the Bluebird and talked some more.

What Noli thought of Turkey so far—a scary place but interesting. Nazif and Hasan—he liked them, trusted them. Ahmet? Strange. How about Leandra? Pretty and nice, but maybe too...Noli wasn't sure, still finding it difficult to express himself about personal matters.

I suspected the word he wanted was *independent*. Leandra was definitely independent, also a bit spoiled. But I doubted that Noli knew what
independent meant, or why he wasn't comfortable with her because of it.

About leaving Turkey? He was as ready as I was.

Then we slept. I didn't dream, but awoke several times with a start.
Fortunately, the soft slapping sound of water against the hull lulled me
back to sleep each time.

Maybe living in the Bluebird wouldn't be so bad. The latrine was a bit
crowded, but the bed seats were comfortable.

In what seemed like only minutes later, I awoke to the incessant
buzzing of my travel alarm. I hardly needed it. The raspy calls of
seabirds looking for breakfast filled the cabin.

It was five o'clock. One hour before the attack in Disko Hit.

Chapter Twenty Four

"I wonder if Nazif and Hasan have made it to the air vent by now," I asked idly, pouring the last of the coffee from the thermos into two mugs, adding ruefully, "hopefully, without being seen?"

Noli drank his coffee black as I did. "We go now…look around some. Okay?"

He was anxious and so was I. "As soon as we finish our coffee. Are there any sandwiches left in the cooler? We may not have time to eat until later."

From the back of the plane, Noli yelled, "Muitos…five, six. Leandra make."

I was glad Nazif had agreed that Leandra should remain in Bodrum. He almost didn't, fearing she'd be kidnapped again. I convinced him otherwise, saying, "She'll be safer here than with you or me," thinking, *"And one less distraction for Noli."*

    *   *   *   *

At five-thirty I fired up the right engine. It roared back its welcome response quickly. I was worried the engines might balk because of the lightening strikes.

I waved at Noli to cast off the mooring lines and lock the entry door. When he had, I tried the left engine.

It coughed twice, sputtered and died. "Come on, sweetheart," I coaxed, "not today. Please, not today."

I tried again. This time it belched. A bit unseemly for a female, I mused, trying it a third time. A jet of white smoke shot from the engine, obscuring the windshield for a moment, then it coughed and started.

Within seconds both engines were roaring sweet music in tandem.

With Noli strapped into the copilot's seat, I checked the instruments and fine-tuned the props. Everything looked and sounded good, including the radios. I worried about them too. Nazif hadn't been able to locate a CB radio, so we'd just make-do without one. We wouldn't need one after we left Turkey…if we left. And we wouldn't need *anything*, if we ended up in jail…except maybe a saw to cut our way out.

The thought sickened me as I eased the plane forward.

Well away from the wharf and facing west, I ran up the engines and checked each prop, running from feather to full, listening for a hitch, a subtle variation in the engines during transition from high revs to low.

Everything sounded okay.

Readying the props for takeoff, I checked for boats. Seeing none, I pushed the throttles forward. At sixty-five knots, I pulled back the yolk.

The Bluebird instantly transformed from a boat to a bird; and at one thousand feet, with the landing gear stowed, I turned east and climbed to three thousand.

Amber sunlight was beginning to glow just below the eastern horizon. Only a few scudsy clouds remained, remnants of yesterday's storm. "At least, the weather is good," I said to break the tension.

Noli nodded but didn't respond. Scared out of his wits, I guessed…as I was.

Again I wondered about Nazif and Hasan, if they'd made it to air vent without detection, and if four canisters of tear gas would be enough…*and* would even ignite?

They looked homemade.

God, I hope no one tipped off Simaphong, I thought. My greatest fear: that he'd vanished into the night, Cossack, Orientals, harem and all.

My second greatest fear: that he would remain and use his harem as hostages.

          *   *   *   *

We flew over the clock tower in Konak Square at five forty-five. Few people were up at that hour—street sweepers with hand brooms, delivery-men with aging carts, soldiers guarding VIP apartments. Soon, the third largest city in Turkey would be bustling with jay-walking pedestrians and crazed motorists, all headed for work.

Moments later, I spotted the BP station and the mountain road leading to Disko Hit. Following it to the last village as I had before, I checked my watch. Five fifty-five and no police cars were in sight, on the mountain road or anywhere.

I looked down at the parking lot. Only half dozen cars were in it.

Where *was* everyone? Had they all left…vanished in the night?

Then I remembered, most workers were bussed there and stayed for a month. But what about Simaphong? Was he here, inside his mountain fortress, or in his palacial penthouse suite? And what of the police? Weren't they coming?

Would *anyone* be here to help Nazif and Hasan?

Descending to one thousand feet, I eased the Bluebird into a twenty degree bank to the right and made a slow, three-hundred and sixty degree turn to kill four minutes. The suspense was killing me.

"See anything?" I yelled at Noli, holding the turn while descending five hundred more feet.

"I see guard with rifle. I see *seis automòveis. Nao* Nazif…*nao* Hasan."

Noli was nervous. He'd switched to Portuguese. I was nervous too. At least, Simaphong didn't have an army of assassins waiting for us. No other airplanes either, but where were the police? And where were the Kesfin brothers? Had a guard found them sneaking around and dragged them inside the mountain already?

I chucked. It would take more than *one* guard to do that. Four maybe, but even then they'd put up one hell of a fight.

Rolling out, I looked down. The guard was watching us, but I couldn't pick out the air vent, only the lone olive tree.

Suddenly Noli shouted and pointing to the left out my window. "I see! I see!…near olive tree."

Quickly, I banked left—too quickly. The coolers in back slammed against a bulkhead. I should have tied them down. Ignoring them, I looked down. Two figures, nearly covered with foliage, were huddled next to a chunk of concrete—the air vent opening.

They'd made it.

At that moment a puff of white smoke arose for their position—a small ravine in the side of the mountain. A gash, nothing more.

A second puff followed, then a third.

They were igniting the tear gas. The contrast of white smoke against dun-colored hills was striking.

"You think this work?" Noli asked, his voice mixed with optimism and fear.

"God, I hope so, but where are the police? It won't do any good to drive everyone out of the mountain, if no one is there to round them up."

Staying close, I banked toward the parking lot. A second guard suddenly appeared. Both were looking toward the white smoke, but neither seemed able to determine the source from were they were standing.

The guard with the rifle looked agitated, pointing at the Bluebird then at the smoke. "He must think that *we* started a fire," I said, "as a prank maybe. Let's hope so. Nazif and Hasan will have a better chance of getting away if no one is looking for them."

I eased the plane away from the guards, fearing the one with the rifle might shoot at us. Both were shouting and shaking their fists. One was even stomping his feet, like a kid with a temper tantrum. Frustrated, I suppose, because he couldn't do anything.

Leveling out, I saw one guard turn and run inside the tunnel, probably to tell someone or get help. I swung the plane back toward the mountain road.

"See any police cars, Noli?"

"Sim! *Um...não, dois!*" He pointed toward the last village.

I spotted them also—two cars. They'd come, but without enough firepower. They would need six or seven cruisers, at least. Simaphong had dozens of men and many would be armed. Besides that, they'll need a paddy wagon to haul them away, if they intend to.

Maybe they didn't. Maybe they just came up for a look-see.

"At least they're here," I said. "I hope they block the road so no one can escape—especially, Simaphong, if he's in there."

A chill ran through me. If Simaphong had a tip from the police that we were coming, he might have left already, his whole sorry gang. But if he knew that, why would the guards still be posted?

"To protect his fortress," I answered myself, "...his computers, his women, his entire slimy operation."

I turned east in time to see Nazif and Hasan scrambling away from the air vent and into another draw, then into a third. They were staying low so they couldn't be seen as they skirted the parking lot on the low side before heading back to toward the village.

They'd done their job; now, hopefully, the police would do theirs.

Remaining at five hundred feet, I had to bank sharply to remain over the parking lot. The two coolers slammed into the entry door...another irritant.

Leveling out, I told Noli to go back and tie them down.

He was back in less than two minutes. He didn't want to miss anything.

By then two more guards had joined the first, who pointed at the white smoke dissipating into the air, then at the Bluebird. He apparently still thought we'd caused it.

Two guards immediately raced toward the vent, glancing occasionally at the blue and white seaplane circling overhead, its two-roaring turbos inhibiting their speech.

Looking toward the mountain road, I saw Nazif and Hasan. They were well below the parking lot now, scrambling toward the village, dodging between scrub brush and large rocks. That was the last time I saw them, and I doubted the police had seen them either.

Satisfied they'd make it back safely, I again banked toward the parking lot. Six policemen in dark blue uniforms were piling out of two cruisers with their pistols raised. A scattering of people had begun to emerge from the tunnel, many holding handkerchiefs to their faces.

First ten, then twenty, then fifty or more, including a dozen women in flimsy nightgowns.

For a moment the tunnel entrance became clogged as people tumbled out, clustering in threes and fours. The most distinctive from five hundred feet, a man and a woman wearing brocaded gowns standing apart from the others.

Wong Fung and Lai Ling, which meant Simaphong was probably inside the mountain too. Our plan had worked and the Kesfin Brothers had gotten away.

I couldn't keep from smiling at our cleverness. And right on cue, two more police cars arrived.

Two men in each bolted out, also with pistols raised.

Confusion reigned as they herded the girls into two cruisers and began cuffing the twenty to thirty men. They would need a truck or van for that bunch of thugs.

Continuing to circle, I saw two policemen strip the guards of their weapons then search everyone else. One policeman remained in his cruiser.

Calling for back up, I hoped.

In the melee, four men in dark business suits casually walked toward one of the parked cars. Noli could see then better than I could. "Can you tell if one of them is Simaphong?" I asked, forgetting he'd never seen the crime lord.

Noli shrugged his shoulders as I climbed to one thousand feet—a safer altitude in mountainous terrain.

Even with four police car, the road was only partially blocked, a serious error on the part of the police.

The car with the four suited men suddenly sped across the parking lot.

The policeman seated in the patrol car eased forward to block their escape but the driver swerved around him, stopped long enough to snatch the gowned Orientals, then raced down the mountain road, a cloud of dust billowing behind.

Descending, I flew after them.

At five hundred feet, I told Noli to take the controls. "I'm going to throw a couple of pipe bombs in front of them to block the road if I can, but watch that mountain on the right. Don't get too close to it."

Noli gripped his yoke and grinned. My anxiety, and his, had suddenly disappeared.

Finally, we were doing something…in the Bluebird, where we both belonged. A glorious feeling.

Reaching behind my seat I pulled out two pipe bombs and opened my side window. "More to the right," I yelled, "and down a little."

Seconds later. "Good…that's low enough. Now hold her steady."

The escaping car had reached the first village. I'd have to wait.

There was a stretch of straight road just beyond. Maybe I could stop them there.

After that it would be too difficult, too many sharp curves as the road descended.

I glanced at Noli. Sweat was beading on his temples and forehead, his hands tightly clamped on the control wheel.

I pulled back the throttles until the stall warning horn came on then threw out both bombs, hoping at least one would hit the road.

I was lucky…both did, about ten feet apart and a half mile beyond the village.

I immediately took the plane, added power and climbed to one thousand feet, then yanked it into a tight turn so we could see what happened.

The coolers broke their hurried bonds but the pipe bombs did their job.

The escaping car might have avoided one crater but not both. The front left wheel caught the second one and flipped the car over, skidding on its roof. A shower of sparks rained on the road for several breath-dispelling moments then the car turned upright again.

Fortunately, the car didn't burst into flames and stayed on the road. The people inside had one hell of a ride, but soon would be carted off to jail.

After that, who cared what happened to them?

    *   *   *   *

A patrol car arrived at the crash site and two policemen began hauling people from the car, cuffing each one then shoving them to the ground. All seemed to be intact, but the road was blocked. Nazif and Hasan would have to wait before they could leave.

Which was all right, as that was our plan.

Over the parking lot again, a nagging thought kept after me. I hadn't seen Simaphong or his giant bodyguard and wondered if there was another escaped route. Or maybe Simaphong hadn't spent the night in his underground fortress after all.

Below, everything appeared to be under control, but I saw no one resembling the corpulent crime lord or his pantalooned guard. "It doesn't look like Simaphong is down there," I said to Noli over the intercom. "Or in that escaping car either."

"We go now?" he replied, his excitement dimming with mine. "Big show over."

"Sim, we go now."

"Where?"

"Back to Karşiyaka and wait for Nazif and Hasan."

"We have big steak again?"

"I guess we could. We have some time to kill."

"What about Simaphong?"

"I never saw him or his bodyguard. You can't miss that one, he's about six foot six, wears baggy pants and carries a sword—a gleaming saber. But inside that mountain the police will find enough evidence to put Simaphong away for a long time…if they can catch him. He may be long gone by now."

"I hope not. He bad man, do bad things to Carmen and Leandra."

"Are you okay?" I asked, banking toward Izmir. "You sound a bit down."

Below, I saw two more police cruisers and a truck twisting up the mountain.

Thank God, here comes the cavalry. I felt like the Lone Ranger, slipping away unknown and unheralded. At least we weren't on our way to jail. Not yet, anyway.

Noli looked away and said nothing. I asked if he was worried about something. "You shouldn't be. It's all over. The police will find Simaphong, eventually, now that they have the evidence on him. Even if he's flown to another country."

The slim youth nodded. "I no worry about him. I worry about us. What we do now...leave Turkey?"

"Do you want to?"

"Sometimes yes...sometimes no."

"Is it Leandra?"

Noli nodded.

"What happened between you two? First you acted like friends...then, well...things got more serious. Now what?"

"We friends again."

"Would you like to be more than that?"

"Maybe...but she like Jon too."

"Your Greek competition. Well, that a woman for you. You never know what they want. One day it's roses and apple pie, the next it's thistles and sour lemons."

Noli frown like I was speaking nonsense, and maybe I was. What did I know about females? Not much, based on my track record. "When it comes to women," I said, approaching Izmir, "it's best to just take one day at a time. Enjoy them when you can and try to avoid them the rest of the time."

*   *   *   *

Attaturk Boulevard looked crowded from the air, a gently curved line stretching from one side of Izmir Bay to the other and bordered by a wide, intricately patterned sidewalk. Iridescent under a bright Aegean sun, the bay shifted from dark teal to pale aqua with streaks of turquoise arcing through it.

Beautiful, I thought, too bad it's polluted. Nazif had told me that. But then a lot of things look more beautiful than they really are. People too, sometimes. Yet, others, like Alexis and Regina, are beautiful inside and out.

It would be tough leaving here. We wouldn't forget them soon... Leandra either.

But life goes on, crossed with many triumphs and tragedies, ups and downs. And today was definitely an upper.

I felt good over what we'd accomplished, yet sad at what might have been. Simaphong was still at large, a menace to society. We'd have to be careful and watch our step, until we were many miles from here.

Heading west and climbing to five thousand feet, I asked Noli if he wanted to fly some more.

You can guess his answer. "Sure...where we go?"

His smile had erased his uneasiness, his concern over Leandra and their future together. If they had one, which I doubted. Regina and I either. "Head for Chios, where there aren't any—"

"DAMN!" I bellowed, jerking the Bluebird hard left and fearing the worst. "What the hell was that?"

A white blur streaked passed us, coming within a few feet of the right wing tip.

Noli cringed away from his window, his head nearly in my lap. "I don't know...I no see."

"Look!" I pointed ahead and to our right. "A plane! Damn fool nearly rammed us! Came out of nowhere. Wish I'd gotten his tail number."

Noli sat upright. "*Meu Deo*, he come close."

It sounded more like a prayer than a statement of fact.

Wrestling the Bluebird level and regaining the altitude lost, I caught sight of the plane briefly but couldn't make out what kind it was.

An ominous thought suddenly came to me. "Can you still see it, Noli? Does it have a low wing and T-tail?" I held the Bluebird level, fearing the plane might return, yet wondering what it could do to us...to the Bluebird.

"Sim...and one engine."

"Just as I thought. It's Simaphong, that fat bastard. He must have known we were coming and planned to meet us over Disko Hit. Probably has his Cossack giant with him.

"Sorry, you pompous prick," I said, shaking my fist at the plane. "But you're ten minutes too late. The police have arrived and your empire is gone."

"Look!" Noli yelled. "He come again." He pointed to the right, out his window.

This time I saw the plane clearly—a four-passenger Piper Arrow. A sweet little bird with retractable gear, but hardly a match for the Bluebird.

I banked away, and on a hunch tuned the HF radio to Channel Nineteen, the inter-plane frequency. "Simaphong…this is Dan Sylvester. What the hell are you trying to prove? It's too late. The Izmir police have already raided your command post and are dismantling it piece by piece."

"Thanks to you…you traitor!" he screamed. "I should have snuffed you when I had the chance. I could of, you know, several times."

"Too bad, scum ball. How can you live with yourself, selling dope to addicts, arms to mercenaries and diddling girls in between? You're a sick man, Simaphong. Real sick."

"And you're a knight in shining armor that's going to stop me, I suppose. Ha! You make me laugh. I'll snap you like a twig, you meddlesome twerp. But I'm going to play with you first, like a cat does a mouse, just to see what you're made of. See what kind of pilot you *really* are."

The Piper started a climb, probably for another pass. But why? What could he accomplish, except to harass me? Make a suicidal attack and destroy both of us? Hardly. He has too much to lose for that. Shoot at us in the air? Maybe, but he'd never hit us unless someone with him has a—

"DAMN, a rifle!"

I yanked back hard on the yoke. Positive Gs immediately slammed Noli and me into our seats as the Bluebird climbed. "Hang on," I yelled, "this might get a little rough."

Passing the Piper, the climb indicator pegged at 1,000 feet per minute.

Seconds later, I leveled out at eight thousand feet. The piper at six.

"So you want to play, do you?" Simaphong sneered over the radio. "That's good. I need the practice. I thought you might run like a scared rabbit."

"I don't know why," I called back. "There's nothing you can do to me in that tin lizzy." Switching to interphone, I told Noli to get the rifle and climb into the nose. "Be ready to shoot if he fires on us."

Noli smiled and stowed his control wheel.

"Don't worry about that, Sylvester; I'll come up with something. I always do…and it won't be long either. Very soon, I'll have a little surprise for you, something that will *really* test your mettle."

While he spoke, Noli slithered into the nose with my rifle. I could feel cold air swirling around my feet when he opened the trapdoor.

"Pronto, Dan…ah—I mean, ready," he yelled, giving me two clicks on his mike button so I'd know he was listening on intercom as well.

By then we'd flown past Karşiyaka, so I turned back toward Izmir, ready for anything Simaphong might have in mind but no knowing what. I didn't want Noli shooting at him unless we were in imminent danger. I was in enough trouble already, without adding assault with a deadly weapon to my growing list of charges.

"You know you're finished, Simaphong," I called. "The Izmir police have rounded up your whole gang, including your teenage harem."

"So I heard," he replied with no hint of remorse, as he also turned back toward Izmir. He did sound nervous, though, his voice thin and crackley, making me wonder how much flying experience he'd had. Probably not much and that was to my advantage.

"And it was all your doing, I understand. Pretty ingenious the way you escaped. Too bad. We would have made a good team. We think ahead of the rest, innovating and daring."

He was beginning to sound like he was stalling...but for what, or whom?

All I could do was wait.

"Maybe so, Simaphong, except I'm no pervert. I prefer women my own age. Women who *want* to be with me, not who are forced to be with me."

"That's so American...so naïve. Old fashioned, really. You people don't even know what life's pleasures are all about...how our maker intended them to be. Thai men have enjoyed young women for centuries, but it hardly matters now...not to you, anyway. You won't live long enough to find out. Look over your left shoulder, traitor! We have company."

At that moment, I heard a sharp ping behind me, followed by a hissing sound.

Glancing back into the cabin, I saw a bullet hole in the second window on the right and a gash in the seat beside it.

Someone in another plane had a rifle and wasn't afraid to use it.

Fortunately, the Bluebird wasn't pressurized so nothing happened. Just another source of cold air—a tiny source. Simaphong probably didn't know that and was hoping I'd have to land. But I didn't.

Simaphong rattled off a string of words I couldn't understand. Probably Thai, but they sounded like gibberish to me.

Moments later, the second plane came abreast of the Bluebird on the right, only slightly higher and a few yards forward. I recognized the plane immediately—a nine-passenger Cessna Caravan, a single turbo which could fly as fast and high as the Bluebird.

We were in big trouble now.

Banking sharply to the right, under the Caravan, I dropped two thousand feet, yelling, "Hang on, Noli. We've got *two* planes after us now."

"I do, Dan, I do," Noli called back.

The Caravan followed me like a shadow. I couldn't shake him, even during a climbing, 360-degree turn.

Heading east at eight thousand feet, I started fishtailing so he wouldn't have a clear shot at me. I couldn't see him but I knew he was behind me.

I could feel him.

By then, I'd lost sight of the Piper and guessed it was below me. I was surprised when moments later Simaphong pulled alongside. His Cossack giant was in the copilot's seat, making me wondered if he could fly too...or worse, had a rifle.

"Nice try, Sylvester, but it didn't work. So what next?" The crime lord's voice was silky and taunting now. He obviously enjoyed this, but where was the Caravan?

I wished I had someone to watch below and behind the plane. Without Noli, I was blind on one side.

Again I heard clipped words spoken in a foreign language followed by a mumbled response.

At once the Piper banked sharply to the left and cut across my flight path, missing the Bluebird by inches.

Crunch!

The Bluebird bucked and veered left. The horizontal stabilizer had been hit, probably by the Caravan's wing tip.

Only by adding right rudder was I able to compensate, but just barely.

"What do you think of that, Sylvester?" Simaphong taunted. "Evened up the odds a bit, haven't I? Care for another aerial sandwich?" He chuckled at his lame joke then spouted off another stream of foreign words.

The other pilot responded with two clicks.

What next? I thought, dropping a thousand feet and turning hard right, doing all I could to complicate their attack. "Hold on tight, Noli, this might get dicey."

"What happen? I feel big bump." His voice rose in fear. I felt sorry for him and almost told him to climb back into his seat. It was cold down there, and I knew he couldn't hear what was said on Channel Nineteen, only on intercom.

"They hit us, but we're okay." Thinking, *at least I hope we are.* "Hold on to something, though, in case they do it again."

Rolling out, I was again headed east toward Karşiyaka. Glancing left, I saw the Caravan turning toward us. On our right, the Arrow was doing the same. Another crosswise sandwich, but this time I'd have a little surprise for them.

Both planes were angling to reach the Bluebird at the same moment, so I kept my airspeed constant and my heading steady to accommodate them. Remembering what I'd done just before we arrived at Chios—and said I'd never do again—I waited until they were within seconds of hitting us, then yanked both throttles back to the stops, passed the detent and into the Beta range.

The thrust-reversers engaged immediately, drastically slowing our forward motion. A little like crashing into a brick wall only with no noise or violent shudder, only rapid deceleration.

My body slammed against the shoulder harness as bile filled my mouth. I felt like we were on a runaway elevator with a broken cable. "Hang on, Noli!" I cried, the Bluebird falling from the sky like a six ton rock.

My only thought: Would the wings stay on, flexed as much as they were in the electrical storm?

The altimeter unwound like a spinning top, yet my eyes remained fixed on the airspeed, now below one hundred knots. The stall warning horn began a shrill, high-pitched squeal, the warning light blinking incessantly.

We fell three thousand feet in less than fifteen seconds, then another thousand before I could lower the nose to avert a flat spin.

Pulling out at two thousand feet, I looked up. The Arrow and the Caravan had crossed and clipped each other's wings. The Caravan was in a spin from which it would never recover.

For a moment, I felt sorry for the pilot until I remembered who'd hired him and why. "Serves him right," I muttered. "He knew the risks."

"Damn you, Sylvester," Simaphong screamed as he turned his plane toward Izmir, weaving dangerously, struggling to keep it in the air. "I'll get you for this. You haven't seen the last of me. I'll dog you to the ends of the earth. You'll never feel safe again, you son-of a bitch!"

The Piper went into a shallow dive. I doubted he would make it to the airport, but he might try landing in the bay where one of several fishing boats I'd seen could easily rescue him before his plane sank.

Then he *would* dog me for the rest of my life. He certainly had the resources; and I doubted he'd ever go to jail, despite the evidence the police would have on him, to say nothing of the young girls.

Money speaks when justice is on the line.

Turning east also, I climbed to six thousand and headed toward the crippled plane, wobbling awkwardly as it descended. I kept pressure on the left rudder and followed.

"Are you all right, Noli?" I asked, fast closing on the disabled Piper.

"I hit my—oooh—arm. But is okay...I think."

"Good. I want you to shoot at the plane in front of us. Can you see it yet?"

"I look...Oh, *Vallah!*" he cursed in Turkish, followed by a similar Portuguese swear word. "My arm...it hurts *mau.* Maybe I break it."

"Try holding it tight with your other hand."

Seconds later. "I do...that better. Now...maybe...Okay...I see plane. *Vire ã esquerda.*"

"Left, Noli?" I asked, easing the plane that way. We were less than fifty yards behind the Piper and slightly above it.

"*Um pouco mais...*Okay, right there!"

CRACK! CRACK! Two shots rang out.

The first must have missed but the second went into a left side window. I could see the hole. I doubt if it hit anything, but it probably scared the hell out of Simaphong. With his mike button still open, I could hear him rattle off a string of Thai invectives, each louder than the last.

Before he could change heading, Noli shot again. This time, right though the left cockpit window.

The Piper veered right and descended to two thousand feet. Closing, I could see Simaphong slumped against the yoke. "You son-of-a-bitch," he gasped, barely able to raise his head, his voice strained and weak, as the Piper descended more rapidly—too rapidly.

"You've ruined me. My empire...my grand plan...it's over...all gone...forever."

"I wonder who's flying his plane," I muttered to no one as I followed him down. Then on Channel Nineteen, "It's like you said, Simaphong, we think ahead of the rest. Only, this time, I thought farther ahead than you did."

He coughed as if dying. Then suddenly, at about one hundred feet, the Piper leveled and skidded into the bay. Someone was still flying...even made a tolerable landing.

Simaphong or the Cossack?

Climbing back to two thousand feet, I told Noli to return to his seat. The party was over. Simaphong was nearly dead and the Caravan had gone in head first and never surfaced.

I circled, as two fishing boats closed on the Piper. They'll have to hurry, I thought. It won't remain afloat for long.

Noli climbed out of the nose and scrambled into his seat, holding his arm tightly to his chest.

"Are you okay?" I asked, easing the Bluebird down to a thousand feet for better viewing. One boat had just reached the Piper. The Cossack was partially out of the plane, pointing toward his master.

Noli nodded, his eyes closed. It was obvious he was in pain.

Below us, the Cossack lifted Simaphong's limp body from the plane and lowered him into the fishing boat, where someone covered him with a blanket. The Cossack then climbed aboard and pressed his ear to Simaphong's chest, listening for a heartbeat.

Seconds later, the plane sank without a trace.

Making another tight orbit, I saw the Cossack shake his head. If the crime lord was still alive, it would be a miracle; and for Noli's sake, I hoped he was alive. One less burden to carry the rest of his life.

"They got Simaphong off the plane," I said, rolling out and climbing, "His bodyguard too."

Noli nodded but didn't look down. With his head laid back and eyes closed, he looked pale and very tired.

"You did good," I said, patting his hand. "I'm proud of you."

Heading west, I glanced down once more. Someone had pulled the blanket over Simaphong's face.

"Let's go get that steak you wanted," I said to Noli, his eyes still closed. "And maybe a beer."

"Bom," he replied weakly, a soft smile creeping across ruddy his face.

Chapter Twenty Five

Landing in the bay near Karşiyaka, I taxied to the wharf and secured the plane. Noli said he was all right, that his arm was better, but I insisted he have it checked by a doctor.

"You might have a hairline fracture. In any case, you should have it wrapped up good. It will feel better and heal faster."

I hailed a cab and told the driver to take us to the nearest hospital. I was surprised that he understood where we wanted to go, although, seeing Noli grimacing and holding his arm tightly to his chest might have given him a clue. When we stopped in front of a low brick building a few minutes later, I found out why he understood me so easily.

A sign on the building read, *Hospital*, the same word as in English.

I asked the driver to wait, if he had no other fares. He nodded that he would and picked up a Turkish newspaper from the seat next to him and started reading it.

Inside, I realized it was more of a clinic than a hospital, but it would do. After filling out a form and having Noli's arm X-rayed, we waited for a doctor.

As it turned out, Noli's arm wasn't broken, only badly bruised. A nurse wrapped it in an Ace bandage, gave him a supply of aspirin and charged me one hundred *lire*.

I would have paid ten times that amount.

Back in the same cab, I suggested we save the steak dinner until later. "You look tired. Maybe you should take a nap."

I looked at my watch: only eight o'clock, four hours until lunchtime. So much had happened that morning it felt like eight in the evening and time for supper.

✳   ✳   ✳   ✳

While Noli napped, I examined the right elevator. It was bent but fly-able, if I held extra left rudder. I'd straighten it out in Bodrum with a rubber mallet I'd seen in Nazif's factory. The rest of the horizontal stabilizer looked fine.

After that, I waited at the ferry terminal for Nazif and Hasan to arrive, which they did in about an hour. "Where Simaphong?" Nazif asked after hugging me.

I felt like his long lost brother...another brother. "Dead. Noli is asleep in the Bluebird. He got knocked about some and is all wrapped up, but he'll be all right."

"Noli good boy," Nazif said with a nod. "Is good he okay. You blow up Simaphong on road? We hear *bombas*." He raised his hand violently to simulate an explosion.

"Not then...later, in his plane. It sank in the bay. But your *bombas* worked well. I threw out two while Noli flew the plane."

"Is good. Simaphong bad man," Hasan said with a wry smile.

"After you fly away," Nazif continued, "we see other plane." He made a motion as if the plane had circled them, or maybe the parking lot.

"That was Simaphong looking for me. He found me over Izmir Bay. We had a little run in and he crashed...Noli shot him. A second plane crashed too."

"Sound like big trouble for you. Is good you made it here. I worry."

"We were worried too...about you guys. We saw you running away from the air vent then we lost you."

"*Gaz bomba* work good," Nazif said before launching into his narrative, most of which I'd seen from the air, ending with..."We stay on mountain long time...until police leave."

We talked and napped until Noli awoke...about noon, then had our steak dinner, toasting each other and our good fortune with a beer. Noli's arm was still sore but better. He now had feeling in it. Before, he said it felt like his arm was asleep.

He was lucky he didn't lose it.

✳   ✳   ✳   ✳

We landed in Gümbet Cove about two that afternoon and walked to Hasan's house, knowing everyone would be anxious to hear what happened. They were, and delighted to see us alive and well and hear our exploits, each ooh-ing and ahh-ing at our bravery.

Leandra and Regina interrupted constantly for more details. "How did you shoot him down?"

"Noli did it, with my rifle from the nose of the Bluebird."

"Did Simaphong shoot back?"

"No, but another pilot did, in another plane."

"How many were there?"

It went on and on then Nazif and Hasan started on their part, although, as usually, Hasan said little.

Not surprising, the adventure became more heroic with the telling. And the next day, when it had spread around Gümbet Bay and into Bodrum, it was out of control. Friends came by for two days to verify it and hear it told again.

In the meantime I straightened the right elevator as best I could. It wasn't pretty but good enough to fly to Athens where I'd have it straightened properly.

✳   ✳   ✳   ✳

Friday, we were all invited to the Han Restaurant for a special appreciation dinner and several speeches. The mayor, after much bluster and thanks for ridding the town of Captain Tokolu and his kidnapping crew, said that charges against me had been dropped. According to Regina, who translated for me, the mayor said the marina guard that died had been an employee of Simaphong's and was wanted for murder, himself.

The President of Bodrum Yacht Club then presented a check to the Kesfin Family for five hundred *lire*, contributions from its jet-set members.

Finally, a representative from Bayazit Tours offered us all a five-day cruise along the Turkish Rivera, the South Coast. "We make many exciting stops," he intoned in stilted English, as if talking to a group of tourists, "the lighthouse of Knidos, ancient Rodas, Baths of Cleopatra, and a magnificent view of the finest villas in all of Turkey."

He made it sound so inviting we could hardly refuse.

Of course, the news of the raid on Disko Hit and the return of the captive girls made the local newspaper. A few of the girls had not wanted to return to their homes but most did—happily, with great joy in their hearts. I could see it in their smiling faces as they were released to their parents. Sixteen of them, ranging in age from fourteen to eighteen, all on front-page photos tacked to a bulletin board behind the head table where we all sat. Also tacked up there were photos of scantily clad spa workers in Simaphong's Izmir penthouse.

Seeing them all, my mind drifted back to the girls I'd seen—and been offered, in both places. It was quite a scandal. One that would keep mouths flapping for a long time. I just hoped it wouldn't happen again. That the police would *keep* it from happening again.

Leandra and Sultana were also honored that night, and I was sorry that Carmen couldn't have been there too. And in the middle of it all, loving every minute, was Nazif, telling our story to anyone who would listen.

Noli and I contributed little—not out of modesty, only because so few spoke English—but we reveled in the adulation and the many offers of *raki* we received.

I was glad Ahmet wasn't there, having already left in Tokolu's boat for parts unknown, according to Nazif.

*   *   *   *

The next day I had a beastly headache and was ready to leave Turkey for good. Regina and I had talked little more about it. But that afternoon, we strolled along the marina, hand-in hand, admiring the many yachts moored there and talking of many things. The bottom line was this: I wasn't ready to settle down and she was. Because of this, we decided to skip the cruise and head for Athens. By then, she'd accepted the position with the Uzul family; and I told her that I would stay in Athens until the Bluebird was repaired but didn't promise anything after that.

Two days later, after securing a battered steamer truck filled with Regina's clothes and keepsakes into the Bluebird, the rest of the family handed out parting gifts: a kiss from Phidaleia for me and Noli and a basket of food for Regina, "In case...ah...new boss no feed you good." A hug from Nazif, along with the rubber mallet I'd used to straighten the elevator, "In case you need again." And a box of iced scrimp and an even bigger hug from Hasan.

I thanked them all, surprised that so many others had gathered to watch. Not to see us off, I was told, to see the Bluebird. The dock attendant said that hundreds had come by all week long after hearing of our exploits. "If I charge...I be rich," he added with a silly grin.

Goodbyes are always hard for me and this one was particularly difficult. Nazif and Hasan were like brothers now, and I was sure they felt the same way. Even cranky Phidaleia cried. Leandra did too, drawing

Noli off to one side and planting a loving kiss on him before telling him to return someday.

After saying he would, they kissed again.

"Need some help there, Noli?" I finally asked to break them up.

Noli and Hasan then carried the last of our suitcases abroad, while Regina chose a seat and I cinched down the ice cooler filled with shrimp. I didn't want anything crashing about as it had before.

Noli then closed and locked the entry door and scrambled into the copilot's seat.

With a final wave from the cockpit, I fired up the engines, checked the instruments, then taxied away from the marina and took off. Just for the hell of it, I flew back over Gümbet Bay, waggled the wings then headed west.

✳   ✳   ✳   ✳

Hellinikon Airport was just as crowded as before.

After clearing customs, we loaded a cab with our suitcases—the steamer trunk on top—and were driven to the Uzul home. There, we were greeted by an excited Tashi, who explained as we unloaded the cab that Cemil Uzul was at his olive oil factory but would be home soon. "Didn't Nazif come?" she then asked, disappointment lining her pretty face.

"Not this time," I said. "He is up to his ears in boat orders, but he'd love to have you visit him in Bodrum and promised to make it worth your while if you did."

"That's it?" she asked, stepping aside so we could enter the house.

"Oh...one more thing," I said with a tease. "He will call you tonight at eight. He has something important he wants to ask you."

"Really? What?" Suddenly Tashi looked as radiant as a teenager.

"I don't know. You'll just have to wait and see."

That night at dinner, Cemil Uzul beamed when I told him about the raid on Disko Hit. "What about Simaphong. Is he dead?"

I glanced at Noli, wondering if he felt any guilt over what he'd done. When he didn't even look up from his soup, I nodded that the crime lord was but said no more.

The quicker Noli forgot about *that* day, the better he would be.

✳   ✳   ✳   ✳

For the next few days Regina tended Nese Uzul night and day. She needed considerably more help than before, although Cemil seemed to be doing quite well and expressed delight with Regina several times, hoping she'd stay as long as necessary.

Tashi came by twice, first to announce her engagement to Nazif. The second time to tell us that she was going to visit him in Bodrum. Everyone expressed delight with that as well.

Regina and I spoke some about me staying. I knew she wanted me too. She'd made that pretty obvious. I just wasn't ready for marriage and all that it details, and was getting antsy about leaving. Noli was too. I could tell by the way he paced the floor, as if he couldn't sit still. By then, he'd removed the ace bandage. Said he didn't need it anymore, although I noticed that he favored that arm some.

A week later, the mechanic called to say the Bluebird was ready. And that night after dinner, I told Regina that we would leave the next day and fly to the Azores to visit what was left of Noli's family. I'm sure for her that sounded like the end of the world, and in a way it was. But it was all I could think of to say, knowing in my heart I'd never marry her and live in Greece, or Turkey.

What time?" she asked plaintively.

"No hurry, but before noon."

      *   *   *   *

Tashi insisted on driving us to the airport. I told her not to bother, that we could take a cab, but she wouldn't hear of it. I suspected that Regina had asked her to, hoping one last ride...one last kiss, might change my mind.

Inside the terminal, Regina and I walked hand-in-hand to the business aircraft loading ramp. Noli followed behind carrying our two hanging bags. The rest of our clothes were still in the Bluebird. Tashi had said her goodbyes at the curb and would wait in a No Parking Zone. Typical of Greek irreverence toward traffic rules of any kind.

Noli said goodbye to Regina and was rewarded with a kiss on the cheek. I knew he liked her, as I did, and smiled as he walked down the ramp with our bags.

Turning to Regina I kissed her warmly then told her I would miss her.

As always, she melted into my arms. "And I'll miss you...more than you'll ever know,"she said, keeping her warm body pressed to mine, her soft lips only inches away. Thank you so much for all you have done. You have given us our lives back."

"I'm glad I was there...that I could help," I muttered, not wanting to release her but knowing I must or else I never would.

"Will you return...someday?" She looked at me briefly, then her eyes cast down.

"Do you want me to?"

She didn't have to answer; her beaming smile told me everything.

"Then I will. Turkey is a remarkable place and you are a remarkable woman."

With that, I turned and left.

The End

About the Author

Colonel Mann is a retired Air Force navigator with two unforgettable flights in a Grumman Mallard. This is his third *Dan Sylvester Adventure*. He lives in St. Paul, MN with his wife, Gerry, and is working on *The Locket,* an epic novel set in Cambodia during the holocaust of the seventies.

0-595-27877-9